ALSO BY SERESSIA GLASS

Shadow Blade
Shadow Chase

Available from Pocket Juno Books

SERESSIA GLASS

SHADOW FALL

SHADOWCHASERS BOOK THREE

POCKET BOOKS

New York   London   Toronto   Sydney

Pocket Books
A Division of Simon & Schuster, Inc.
1230 Avenue of the Americas
New York, NY 10020

This book is a work of fiction. Names, characters, places, and incidents either are products of the author's imagination or are used fictitiously. Any resemblance to actual events or locales or persons, living or dead, is entirely coincidental.

First Juno Books/Pocket Books paperback edition August 2011

JUNO BOOKS and colophon are trademarks of Wildside Press LLC used under license by Simon & Schuster, Inc., the publisher of this work.

POCKET and colophon are registered trademarks of Simon & Schuster, Inc.

For information about special discounts for bulk purchases, please contact Simon & Schuster Special Sales at 1-866-506-1949 or business@simonandschuster.com.

The Simon & Schuster Speakers Bureau can bring authors to your live event. For more information or to book an event contact the Simon & Schuster Speakers Bureau at 1-866-248-3049 or visit our website at www.simonspeakers.com.

Cover illustration by Craig White

Manufactured in the United States of America

10 9 8 7 6 5 4 3 2 1

ISBN 978-1-5011-0027-7

To the readers, the dreamers, and the secret believers.
Thanks so much for the encouragement
and the inspiration.

To editors Paula Guran and Jennifer Heddle,
and my agent, Jenny Bent.
All of you are appreciated more than you know.

Acknowledgments

I've learned quite a bit during the course of researching the Egyptian and archaeological background for this series. I want to especially thank the Michael C. Carlos Museum at Emory University in Atlanta; the American Research Center in Egypt; the Cairo Museum; Petrie Museum of Egyptian Archaeology, University College London; and Theirry Benderitter and Jon Hirst of Osirisnet.

Any mistakes in this book are solely my own.

SHADOW
FALL

Chapter 1

Kira drew her Lightblade, but didn't bother calling its power. She didn't need it, not against this opponent. "If you think you can take me," she taunted, "come and get me."

Her adversary crouched low. "I will take you, Kira Solomon," he assured her. "Soon enough."

They circled one other, each looking for the other's weak spot, an opening to rush into and seize advantage. The world fell away as Kira focused all her attention on defeating her antagonist. Adrenaline surged through her, pushing her senses to full alert. Muscles hummed with the anticipation of action, of fight, of victory.

He rushed forward, a dark blur, ducking beneath her instinctive swing. A shoulder to her sternum sent her crashing to the floor. With her free hand, Kira grabbed him and pulled him down, shoving her feet into his stomach to send him catapulting over her. She spun to cover him, but he rolled out of reach. He scrambled to his feet, hands up in a defensive position.

She grinned and straightened, sheathing her Lightblade. He cocked an eyebrow. "Sure you don't want to keep your tiny knife in hand?"

"Since you have your little blade sheathed, I wouldn't want you to accuse me of having you at a disadvantage," Kira said, making a great show of un-buckling her dagger's leather rig and sliding it off her thigh.

His lips thinned. "There is nothing 'little' about my dagger. Or me, as well you know."

She knew, all right. If she forgot—she'd had a lot on her mind of late—Khefar was there to remind her. He had refreshed her memory almost every night since they had returned from London, and she had yet to become accustomed to being intimate with another human being after living so long apart.

"Why, Khefar," she said in mock wide-eyed inno-cence, "I didn't realize you were a size queen."

"A *size queen*?" He frowned. "I don't know what that means."

"Right. Never mind." It was easy to forget that Khefar wasn't your regular modern extreme fighter, but rather a four-thousand-year-old, near-immortal Nubian warrior. It wasn't as if he ran around in a breechcloth carrying a bow and quiver of arrows. Kira smiled as an image sprang unbidden to her mind. Too bad they'd had other things occupying their time around Halloween. Khefar in period dress at a costume party would be a sight to—

"Hey!" She landed flat on her back on the mat. Khefar sat atop her, hands on her shoulders, knees pressing her arms down to the padded exercise floor to keep her immobilized. The black tank shirt and baggy gray sweatpants he wore only served to emphasize his wiry, lanky physique. His biceps were cut, tightened by the force he exerted to keep her still, his dark, dark mahogany satin skin so very touchable.

"You got careless, Kira," he admonished her. "I saw the exact moment your thoughts wandered."

She relaxed for a moment, smiled up at him. "Would you like to know why my thoughts wandered? What I was thinking about?"

His gaze flickered, only a moment, but it was enough. She swung her legs up, wrapping her thighs about his neck before dragging him down. With his knees still on her shoulders, it had to be a painful position—his back arched, knees over-flexed. He didn't move.

"Hey," Kira complained, "you're not even trying to get away."

"Why should I?" he said, his voice strained. "I'm enjoying myself immensely right now."

"Ahem." A discreet cough came from the vicinity of the room's entrance.

Kira looked up. Anansi stood in the doorway of their exercise room, a bemused smile on his face. At first glance he looked as he always did: an older black man of indeterminate age with more salt than pepper to his thick, wavy hair. But now his usual dark suit looked more custom-made than off the rack and lived-in, and he wore a diamond-studded cravat instead of a tie. "If I may interrupt for a moment?"

Heat suffused Kira's cheeks as she let Khefar go. He rolled away and stood with supple grace and then extended a hand to help her to her feet. "What do you want, old man?" he demanded, glaring at the demigod. "And why are you dressed like that? The gala's not until later tonight."

"Easy, Medjay," the trickster said, holding up

his hands. "I'll let you return to your foreplay soon enough. I simply wanted to say thank you for the invitation to the gala, but I won't be attending. I've come to say good-bye."

"Good-bye?" Kira echoed, refusing to react to the demigod's barb. Sure, most—okay, all—of her workouts with Khefar usually ended with them horizontal on the mats or the weight bench, but still . . . "What do you mean, good-bye?"

"Your domestic bliss has inspired me," Anansi told them. "I've decided to pay a visit to my lovely wife, Aso."

"You're still married?" Kira blurted out, surprised. She knew the folktales sometimes made mention of the spider god's wife, but considering how much time Anansi spent away from wherever he considered home, she'd assumed the more domestic tales to be myth instead of fact.

"Is Mrs. Anansi going to let you in?" Khefar wondered. "Didn't it take a while for her to welcome you back last time?"

"Really, children, there's no need to be unkind," the spider god chided. He spread his arms. "Though it has been some time since I've seen her, it's true what they say: absence makes the heart grow fonder. My Aso is a wonderful lady, a terrific cook, nimble of mind, and you should see the size of her—" Anansi cleared his throat. "Anyway, I have many new tales to tell. She always gives me a most enthusiastic welcome, thanks to those."

"How long will you be gone?" Kira wondered, feeling strangely sad. She wondered which she'd miss most, the demigod's stories or his cooking.

"Time is an immeasurable thing where I'm going," he answered. "Which is a nice way of saying that my father is many things, but a timekeeper isn't one of them."

He lifted a fedora from his head that had been bare a moment ago, and then sketched a deep bow, the hat sweeping through the air. "If you need me, of course, you know how to call me. Otherwise, feel free to drop me an email."

"Email?" Kira echoed.

Khefar cocked his head. "Inventor of the World Wide Web, remember?"

"Oh right. Of course you have email. Did you invent computer viruses, spam, and those Nigerian prince money-laundering scams too?"

The old man grinned. "What is it the Americans say? I plead the Fifth—I refuse to answer on the grounds I may incriminate myself. I would remind you, Shadowchaser, that I am a trickster. Still, I'm hardly the only one. Many a cunning demigod lives on, thanks to pranks and hoaxes on the Internet. You should see what Loki comes up with, and don't get me started on what Coyote has done."

Kira could imagine well enough to give her a headache. She rubbed her forehead. "I so didn't need to know that."

"You should know better than to ask Anansi questions like that," Khefar told her. "You're never going to like the answers."

Khefar crossed to the spider god, grasped his forearm. "Safe journeys, Anansi."

Anansi clapped the Medjay on the back. "Of

course. You two take care of yourselves. I'll be back before you know it."

"Or when Mrs. Anansi kicks you out."

"Bite your tongue, Medjay," the demigod said. A surprisingly solemn look—as if he wanted to tell them something particularly profound—drew down his features, but his expression softened as he spoke. "Look after each other and try not to destroy the city while I'm gone."

Kira folded her arms. "Gee, Grandpa, you never let us have any fun."

"Not you too." Anansi sighed, lifted his eyes heavenward. "I think I'm actually going to enjoy my time away from you two ungrateful wretches. I'll see you when I see you."

He reached out a hand. A door appeared in the middle of the exercise room, made of a rich goldenbrown wood. As Anansi turned the knob, Khefar stepped up behind her and dropped a hand over Kira's eyes, his other arm encircling her waist.

"Hey!"

"Believe me, you don't want to look through that door."

She made a halfhearted effort to free herself. "Why not? Isn't that the way he got Wynne and Zoo from London to Cairo?"

"No, not through *that* door. It's not the door we used either. That's a god's door. The one time I looked through a door like that, I was dead for two days."

"Oh." She froze. "I suddenly find myself a lot less curious about Anansi's method of travel. Is he gone?"

"Yes."

"Then, do you think you could let me see and move again?"

His hand dropped from her eyes to her shoulder, but tightened his grip on her waist. "I could, but I'm enjoying holding you like this."

She reached up, cupping the back of his neck with her hand. "I'm enjoying it too. Otherwise, I'd have thrown you to the mat by now."

His breath was warm against her cheek. "You can throw me down now, if you like."

Without a word, she bent low at the waist, flipping him over her shoulder. "I like," she said with a grin, leaning over him.

He dug his hands into her braids. Her eyes slid shut as she reveled in the tactile experience, no less potent than the first time he'd touched her.

When he spoke, his voice acquired a rough rumble. "I'm thinking it's time for the second part of our workout."

"I like that part even better." She bent to kiss him.

Despite more than three weeks of intimacy, Kira still felt the initial shock of being skin to skin with another person, a surge of fear that she'd made a mistake in touching him. Then he would hold her, kiss her, move deep inside her, and her heart would race for an entirely different reason.

She kept her eyes open, focusing on Khefar's face, drinking in his expression, running her hands over his body. With him, she could forget the world and its troubles, could forget she was different, could even forget she lived on borrowed time. With him, she could share an extraordinary pleasure that made her feel blissfully normal.

• • •

A while later, Khefar pulled her to her feet. "Not too much longer before we have to head out to the gala," he said, a little unsteady on his feet. Fighting, training, and lovemaking—they both went at it with all the same level of intensity. "We need to get showered and dressed."

"Will you do the lotion thing for me?" she asked, stretching to loosen her muscles again. Having Khefar rub her specially made shea butter lotion into her skin was pure heaven.

He watched her move, pleasure lighting his dark eyes. "I'm not sure which part you like better, the sex or the after-shower lotion rub."

"You're good at both, and I'm greedy. Do I have to choose?"

"No. Especially since that rubdown usually leads to other things."

"Yeah." She headed for the door. "Like a good, deep sleep."

"Keep it up and you'll be rubbing yourself." He paused. "Wait. That didn't come out right."

He tried to explain further, but Kira was laughing too loud to hear him.

Chapter 2

The Balm of Gilead, head of the Gilead Commission and the current living embodiment of Light, pushed back from her desk with a sigh. She straightened slowly, working the kinks from her back. Sleep had never been a close companion, even before she became head of the organization dedicated to opposing Shadow in all its forms.

The job of leading the organization of Shadow-chasers, Light Adepts, field agents, and support personnel that policed the preternatural community was never an easy one. Not a thousand years ago when she'd first been elevated to take the mantle and honorific of Balm. Not now, when she'd been forced to replace the entire senior staff of Gilead London, send a renegade Shadowchaser to Refinement, and attempt to dissuade her recalcitrant daughter from an inevitable path. Of those, only the third continued to be cause for concern.

"Kira," she murmured to herself, "what am I going to do with you?"

It was a question she'd frequently asked herself of late. Balm couldn't afford to look back or second-guess herself. If she did, she'd never get any work done, and there was always work to do. With Kira however, she always wondered if she'd done the right thing, if she'd fulfilled the promise she'd made to Ana so long ago, to ensure that her daughter would always walk in the Light.

Balm had done her best to prepare Kira for each stage of her life. She'd taken Kira out of fosterage and placed her with a carefully screened, loving family once Balm was certain the young girl wouldn't display any Shadow tendencies. Immediately bringing Kira to Santa Costa once she'd discovered that Kira's adopted family hadn't made her welfare a priority. Then channeling the understandable rage and despair into the one role guaranteed to ensure Kira's survival: that of a Shadowchaser.

Balm stepped back from the hand-carved wood desk, and then strolled over to a beveled window set into the stone outer wall. A half-moon hung over the sea, its light barely illuminating the restless water below. She could hear the wind howling outside through the thickness of the glass. A storm was coming to Santa Costa.

The symbolism wasn't lost on her. The tempest mirrored the changes she would soon have to weather, perhaps as soon as a few days. Circumstances pulled Kira in multiple directions, even more now than at any other time since her birth.

Balm had tried to stem the tide by beginning to train Kira in all the processes needed to run Gilead's sprawling divisons and managing the Commission with the idea of Kira someday heading the organization. Diplomacy and restraint, however, weren't Kira's strong suit. With that necessary component absent from Kira's nature, Balm had had little choice but to put Kira through Shadowchaser training.

And Kira had excelled. Balm allowed herself a self-congratulatory smile. Kira was one of those rare individuals the Commission coveted: inherently powerful, intelligent, tough, and even stubborn. Though there were Commissioners who handled each aspect of a Chaser's training—physical, mental, or magical—Balm had personally overseen Kira's development.

The head of Gilead showed no favoritism, and her foster daughter's training had been no different. A Shadowchaser's training was rigorous out of necessity, a forewarning of what they would be required to face in the field. Despite careful screening, some candidates failed or were killed even before they reached the Crucible, the rigorous final performance examination before candidates claimed their Lightblades. Kira had passed every standard Chaser test. She had also passed extra ones Balm had devised. She had survived the Crucible, completing the trial faster than any Chaser to date. Kira Solomon was the best and the brightest the Gilead Commission had to offer, and Balm would make sure that she remained that way.

Balm crossed back to her desk. A small cedar chest sat atop the blotter, a foot wide and about the same deep, weathered with age and constant use. It contained her most private and precious possessions: memories. In a few hours the chest would be on its way to Kira, and Balm could only hope that her daughter would be able to survive the consequences of opening her own personal Pandora's box.

A soft knock announced Lysander's arrival. Her

assistant entered, his slight, androgynous features golden in the lamplight. He carried her ceremonial robe, woven of Light magic and gossamer material. The robe was actually older than she was, a hooded affair worn by the Balms of Gilead since time began. "My lady, it is time."

"A moment longer." Her fingers skimmed the edges of the chest. Times like this, she felt every one of her years. Felt the selfish regret of the choice she had made, anger at the choice that had peeled away her right to live her life for herself instead of living it for the good of everyone else.

She picked up a bundle of letters, bound with a magical cord woven of her own hair, and placed them into the chest before pressing the lid into place. Kira would have to use her magic to open the chest, more magic to untie the cord and read the letters. Balm could only hope her message got to Kira before the memories did.

Lysander hung the pale robe on a jutting stone nodule as Balm approached the interior grotto planted centuries ago on the north side of her office. "Shall I deliver the chest while you are away?"

Balm stared at the indoor garden, the wild vines, overgrown trees, and assorted plants. The verdant display helped to soothe her sublimated soul, a soul that needed growing things, loamy soil, and bright sunshine. "No. I will need to add one more item to it when I return."

"As you wish, my lady."

Lysander helped her disrobe, kneeling to remove her soft leather slippers before helping her settle the pale blue material onto her shoulders. It could barely be called fabric—it seemed spun from light itself, shimmering with every movement she made and breath she took.

Lysander reached for the silver chain about her neck to unfasten it, but Balm wrapped her hand around the locket it supported. "No, I would leave it."

"Mistress, you requested the pendant be placed in the chest you are sending to Kira," he reminded her in gentle tones. Lysander was never harsh, except for when she needed him to be, when he shared her bed.

"So it shall," Balm replied, unpinning her hair, then arranging it about her shoulders. "First, I would have her know of this, if she's able to read the pendant."

"Of course, Mistress."

Her robes shimmered with the emerald sheen of growing things as she touched a dark green tendril. The vines slithered in acknowledgment. At her silent request the verdant strands parted to reveal a thick arched door of golden-red wood so old the tree it had come from was now extinct. Reinforced with heavy bands of black iron, the door bore the symbol of a moon, perfectly split between Light and Shadow with a wide band of apparent emptiness between them.

Balm called up the power that had been conferred on her when she assumed the leadership of Gilead. Wrapped in softly glowing blue light, she placed her right palm over the Light half of the moon. A sliver of elemental magic edged the entry as the portal formed on the other side.

Lysander pulled the heavy door open with one hand. Everything and nothing swirled on the other side, a fog that shimmered and shifted color and shape.

Balm could feel the buildup of pressure as two other portals were opened into this area outside of time and space, a place that neither Light nor Shadow controlled. At the half-moon, when neither Light nor Shadow dominated, each aspect could, and most times would, come together to parley.

Balm paused at the portal's edge. This was the part she dreaded the most, and it had nothing to do with the freezing temperature of the swirling fog. No, the miasma served as purification as well as transportation, cleansing her mind, body, and soul and enabling her to assume the mantle of the embodiment of Light before meeting her sisters. Each time she made the journey she felt as if she lost a piece of herself in the process, another bit of detritus that had made up the person she was before she became Balm. Not that she could remember much about what her life had been like before. She hadn't seen many summers before the Commission chose her to be the Vessel of Light, and she'd been Balm for many lifetimes now.

In keeping with the law of Universal Balance, she gained as well as lost. One benefit was acquisition of the knowledge of those who had gone before her, those who had also been given the name Balm, the women—and a few men—who had accepted the privilege and responsibility of an office far greater than any human position before or since.

She had asked others to sacrifice in the name of Light. Some she had ordered to lay down their lives, and parts more precious. This was but one of many sacrifices she herself had made over the centuries, one of many more she'd still have to make.

"Wait for me," she murmured to her assistant before stepping into the breach. Her body seized up as if she'd gone from boiling lava to a pool of arctic water. The vortex worked like a sieve, painfully separating the physical from the spiritual, filtering out everything but that which made her the Lady of Light. Finally, just before it became too much to bear, she broke through.

The "world" was gray, formless, and void. No up or down, no north or south. Balm couldn't even call it a world; to do so would imply that she actually was somewhere. This was nowhere and everywhere, the All and the Nothing overlapping.

A darker shade of gray heralded the arrival of Solis, the Lady of Between. Solis always arrived second—whether Balm arrived first or last—as if to prevent Light and Shadow from being alone together.

Solis reached up to push back the heavy gray cowl, revealing features identical to Balm's, but older. "Greetings, Balm of Gilead, Lady of Light."

Balm pushed her own Light-infused hood back from her face. "Greetings to you, Solis, Lady of Between."

She had no sooner given her greeting than a dark fissure appeared in the swirling gray, and Myshael, the Lady of Shadows, stepped through. Composed of Chaos as she was, Myshael moved with the frenetic energy of a child in the throes of a sugar rush, darting about in a multidimensional game of tag.

"Greetings, sisters," she said as she pushed back her inky black hood, her features constantly changing from child to crone and everything in between. "Now that the welcome is over, shall we get this party started?"

There was nothing party-like about these conferences, no matter who called them. That Myshael had been the one to request this meeting made it even less so in Balm's opinion. "Why did you call this meeting, Lady of Shadows?"

"You know why. Kira Solomon."

Balm had suspected as much. The knowledge still didn't sit well with her. "What about Kira?"

"You have both had Kira in your company, and I have not," the Lady of Shadows complained. "I have had as much a hand in her creation and development as either of you. I will have my time with her."

Balm kept her expression as neutral as she could, but it took immense effort. She knew something like this was bound to happen sooner or later, ever since Kira's path became difficult to see. Balm's time of training and forging Kira had come to an end.

"Tell me, sister, exactly how do you expect to meet with Kira? She will not willingly go to Shadow, and you cannot force her."

"To borrow an old line, I have my ways."

"Which are?"

"Come on, Balm of Gilead," Myshael chided in a little girl's voice. "You aren't the only one who can play things close to the vest. I will keep my ways to myself. You will know soon enough."

Balm's voice remained impassive with effort as she turned to Solis. "Are you going to act as an intercessor for Myshael, and attempt to bring Kira Between again?"

Solis gave Balm a look of reproach. "You, of all people, know that Kira will do as she wills. If Kira wants to meet our Sister of Shadows, you cannot stop her. Balance must be maintained."

Balm swallowed her frustration. She'd worked hard and long to shelter Ana's daughter, muting the darker aspects of Kira's nature. She would not turn Kira over to Shadow without a fight.

"Balance," Balm said, turning her gaze to Solis. "That's all it's about with you, isn't it?"

"That is what is," Solis replied, "no matter how the pendulum swings."

"And now the pendulum swings to me," Myshael announced, her voice smug.

"What do you intend to do?"

The Lady of Shadows cocked her head. "I will continue that which has already begun," she said, as if Balm should have known the answer already. "Kira Solomon is a seeker of truth, one who desires empirical evidence as well as faith. I simply will stand as the Shaitan did before his public relations firm did him a disservice. Let us see if her faith remains unbroken after she finds the truth she has sought so long. Let us see if she turns away from you and instead turns to me."

"Kira is opposed to Shadow," Balm stated, her voice ringing with certainty. "She will resist you."

Myshael stood before her, her features now a mirror image of Balm's. She placed a hand on Balm's shoulder. "Then, I will do as you have done, sister, and make her an offer she cannot refuse."

Balm batted Myshael's hand away. As the embodiment of Light, having even a touch of Shadow was too much. "Threatening her life will not make her agreeable to you," Balm cautioned, though she secretly dared Myshael to try. "It will have the opposite effect."

"I don't want your Shadowchaser dead, Balm of

Gilead. She is much more valuable alive, full of all the power she possesses."

The words were the ones Balm wanted to hear, but she didn't like Myshael's tone. She cared even less for her eager expression.

Solis moved between the two women. "Universal Balance must be maintained."

"I know the Law, dear sister," Balm retorted. "I do not need you to remind me."

"Do you agree?"

"My agreement is not required." Balm prepared to leave. "Kira Solomon has Free Will. Despite how we may scheme and plan and prepare, Kira will walk the path of her choosing."

"You are so sure of your power?"

"No. I am sure of Kira."

And with that, Balm was done. Without a word further, she felt for the tendril of Light that anchored her to her true self, and allowed it to wrench her back into space and time and corporeal form.

The return journey was even more painful. Light simply did not like being contained; forcing that essence into a fragile mortal shell was excruciating.

Balm spilled out of the vortex and back into the grotto, gasping as her lungs began working again. Lysander was there to catch her, guiding her to a small smooth boulder that functioned as a natural stool before shutting the portal door. Balm dug her hands into the undergrowth, letting the cool herbaceous life force bring her back to herself.

"Mistress?"

Balm opened eyes she didn't realize she'd closed.

Lysander knelt before her, a cup of tea ready. She accepted his assistance, allowing him to bend her forward and press the rim of the cup to her mouth. Together they managed to pour a couple of drops between her lips. Its healing properties seeped into her, easing the shock of returning to the physical plane. "Thank you, Lysander. How long has it been?"

"Only a few hours, Mistress." He leaned over her, his silver eyes concerned. "Your journey seemed more difficult this time."

That he noticed was enough for Balm to rouse her energy, take the cup from him. He was her most trusted assistant, but she couldn't be weak, even in front of him. "The journey is always difficult, whether it is the first time or the four thousandth."

"Of course. What else can I do for you, Mistress?"

He always asked, and she always said nothing—but not today. "Bring the chest to me," she requested, not trusting her ability to stand. "Be sure to put the gloves on first."

He quickly crossed the room to her desk as she sipped more of the restorative tea, or at least made the attempt. Her fingers shook so badly that more spilled down her chin than down her throat. Soaking into her skin worked as well, although somewhat more slowly.

Lysander was back, settling the chest onto her lap before setting the teacup and saucer aside. Balm attempted to pry the lid off, but he had to help her. She did manage to take off the pendant, inelegantly pulling the silver chain over her head, snagging a few strands of hair in the process. She'd worried the locket wouldn't survive the trip beyond, but it had come through.

She dropped the locket into the chest, wrestled the lid back atop the box. She pressed her palms flat against the sides, creating a simple magical lock that would require Kira's touch ability to open.

The task done, Balm looked up into Lysander's worried face. "Take this to Kira."

"Mistress, surely you need me now more than Kira needs this?" Lysander protested. "Perhaps in a few hours—"

"She needs it now!" Balm pressed the chest into Lysander's hands. "It is imperative that Kira receives this as soon as possible. Don't delay."

Lysander accepted the chest, rose to his feet. "Then, I won't take the plane."

His form shimmered into Light, brightened, and slowly disappeared.

Balm settled back into the greenery, finally allowing herself to grimace with pain. Lysander was right, the journey back hurt more than usual. She'd have to recuperate longer this time. She could only hope that she'd given Kira all the tools she needed.

Though it had been more than a thousand years, enough instinct of her former life remained. The former dryad dug her fingers and toes beneath the plants, deep into the rich soil, needing the cool green energy to restore her. Sighing in relief, she closed her eyes, and rested.

Chapter 3

"I don't know about this."

Kira stood in front of her bathroom mirror, staring down at the array of mineral makeup pots on the brown granite countertop. Usually she didn't have more than a passing acquaintance with makeup, but tonight was a special event.

"You're going to be fine," Khefar assured her, his voice wafting to her from the bedroom.

"Fine? I'm in a flippin' dress!" The good mood she'd been in earlier after their workout was gone, replaced by a strong case of nerves. She tossed the makeup brush onto the counter. The other guests at the gala would have to be content with seeing her in eyeliner and lip gloss. It was bad enough that she had on something the salesclerk had assured her was a dress, but seemed more like a shiny, gold-colored silk slip, even with the three-quarter-length sleeves of its matching shrug.

"It's a very nice dress," Khefar said from the doorway, a black tie dangling loosely in his hand. His gaze traveled slowly over her, head to toe, then back again. "It compliments your coloring and shape beautifully. It is as the clerk promised."

"I don't have anywhere to hide my Lightblade," she told him, trying to neither complain nor blush at the compliment he'd given her. Khefar may have been over four thousand years old, but he was still a man. She knew that for a fact. And if she forgot, he had several inventive ways to remind her.

She watched Khefar sling the tie around his neck. The tuxedo-style shirt matched the color of her dress. His onyx cuff links glinted in the overhead light as he worked the tie into a bow. He looked like one of the many upwardly mobile men going to a premier gala and fund-raiser. His hair, a swath of braids down the middle with the sides of his head shaved, gave his debonair air a dangerous slant.

Adding to the edgy look was the leather rigging strapped across his shirt, a side holster capable of holding a gun and his blade, the fabled Dagger of Kheferatum. He turned slightly, allowing her to view the gilded hilt of the mystical blade imbued by the god Atum with the power to create and destroy. She had once wielded the blade, briefly, in order to save Khefar from a Shadow Adept named Marit.

She still coveted the blade's power, especially in the dark of night when the stain of Shadow that lived inside her whispered dangerous temptations.

"You said you would be fine with carrying your Lightblade in your purse," the Nubian said, smoothing the tie into place.

"I don't own a purse, I have bags," Kira said. "Besides, it will take too long to draw it in an emergency."

She brushed past him to return to the bedroom. Here, Khefar's presence in her life was more pronounced—a proliferation of black clothing taking up half of the closet; a statuette of Isis on the dresser next to her icon of Ma'at; less drawer space. Even Anansi had a spot in her home, a partitioned alcove on the main level in which the demigod had installed what looked like a very luxurious string hammock.

After their adventures in London and Cairo, neither she nor Khefar had questioned that they would continue the intimacies they'd begun. They hadn't questioned the details of their affair at all. It was an assumptive relationship, and worked well as long as they ignored the Sword of Damocles hanging over their heads: time.

Time. There didn't seem to be enough of it of late. No time to grieve her mentor and handler, Bernie Comstock. No time to deal with the inheritance he'd left her—the antique shop in London, several mementos of his life, a few precious Egyptian artifacts. No time to come to grips with the fact that her erstwhile foster mother, the Balm of Gilead, had known Kira's birth mother and been responsible for placing her with the Solomon family. Precious little time to come to grips with the fact she now had a healthy dose of Shadow inside her, to understand what it would do to her magic, her ability to wield her Lightblade, and her duty as a Shadowchaser.

"Do you want to try the thigh rigging?" He wiggled his eyebrows. "I'd be more than happy to help you with it."

"I'm sure you would." She gave him a quelling stare in the mirror. "But if I wear it on the outside of my thigh, it'll show through the skirt. And if I wear it on the inside of my thigh, I won't be able to walk."

She gathered her braids into one hand, and then

reached for a rhinestone hairclip atop her dresser with the other. "I should have rented a tux like you did."

Khefar watched her arrange her hair. "You chose the dress," he reminded her. "I believe your words were, 'I'm going to dress like a girl for a change, dammit.' Or something to that effect."

"And what's wrong with that?" she demanded, suddenly feeling the need for an argument. It wasn't as if she had a case of the nerves or anything. Why would she be nervous? Because it was the first time they were going out on a dress-up date? Other than saving one another's lives and souls, she'd known him for three months, been sharing her bed with him for most of that time, and this was their first date.

"Nothing's wrong with you dressing 'like a girl,' as far as I'm concerned. I'm enjoying the show, though I find it hard to forget that you are, indeed, all girl, no matter what you are or aren't wearing."

"Thanks," she said, instantly mollified.

"I feel the need to point out that I'm more than willing to be a decoy in order to buy you time to pull your blade out of your purse," he continued, his voice dry. "I might even be able to hold my own for a whole minute before I die."

Kira rolled her eyes. "Sorry if I bruised your ego, Mr. Ultimate Warrior."

"My ego isn't bruised. I know my skills and so do you. I've been patrolling with you every night since we've been back."

"So what are you trying to say? That you're more capable than me in a fight?" Back to combative, gods help her.

"What I'm trying to say is it's okay for you to forgo being a Shadowchaser for a few hours of hobnobbing. The city won't go to hell that soon."

It was an intriguing idea. Atlanta hadn't imploded during her trip to London. The southeast division of the Gilead Commission had a good group of investigators and security personnel, despite the people skills of its section chief, Estrella Sanchez. It was worth remembering that most of the city's human and passing-as-human dignitaries would be at the same event she and Khefar were attending: a private fund-raiser at the pre-opening night of "Journey Through the Underworld," an interactive multimedia production based on the Egyptian Book of the Dead.

Of course, Kira and Khefar knew the collection of prayers and spells was commonly called the Book of Going Forth by Day, but since the papyri containing the spells were traditionally found buried with the dead, the colloquial name had stuck. It would be one of many things they'd have to grin and bear during the course of the exhibit.

"I tried not being a Shadowchaser before," she muttered to herself, reaching for a necklace made of lapis beads and adorned with gold lotus leaves. It had been one of the pieces in Bernie's collection, a replica of a Middle Kingdom necklace. "Fat lot of good that did me."

Khefar stepped behind her, pushing her braids over her left shoulder with a gentle stroke of his hand. "You were alone and powerless then," he said softly, taking the necklace from her. He fastened it about her neck, his calloused fingers brushing over her skin. "You are neither now."

She shivered as his fingers glided across her neck. This elemental sensation—this simple human contact of flesh against flesh—was still new, still precious. Khefar could touch her, and she him, without triggering her extrasense. There was no danger of reading his life's history in every vivid detail; no danger of downloading every thought and emotion from this particular heartbeat all the way back to birth; no danger of draining his life force and leaving him in a coma; nothing to fear, only the exquisite sensations of the heat of his skin, the rough pads of his fingers, the press of his body against hers.

"Kira."

She met his gaze in the mirror. A hard expression, the warrior's expression, softened as she watched. His dark eyes had seen civilizations rise and fall, during four thousand years of caring and fighting, trying and failing, living and dying, believing and doubting. He was an extraordinary fighter in every sense of the word, with an extraordinary burden. An extraordinary man who'd appeared at the exact moment she needed someone like him. If only she could keep him. With him at her back, standing by her side, she could handle whatever and whomever the universe put in her way.

She reached up, brushing his hand with hers. The world and all its troubles receded slightly. For a moment, she didn't think about the dreams that haunted her sleep. She didn't think about quitting the bed every night after Khefar fell asleep, driven away from his comfort by her dreams. She didn't think about the secrets Balm had kept from her about her parentage. She would think about all of that later, but for now, she didn't have to think about anything at all.

Khefar tangled his fingers with hers, squeezed. "You look as if you should be reclining on cushions as you sail down the Nile."

His voice, rough and low, rumbled over her skin, causing her to shiver with awareness. She quickly wet her lips. "If I didn't know any better, I'd say you were trying to distract me with compliments."

He retrieved her black elbow-length gloves from the dresser, his gaze playful as he handed them to her. "Did it work, or should I step it up?"

"I can't imagine what you could do to step it up," she said, tugging on the gloves. "And we don't have time for anything that requires being naked."

"What about this?"

He pulled a small black box out of the dresser drawer he'd claimed upon their return from Europe. The box looked like a smaller version of the archive cases she used to transport artifacts back and forth, a discreet gunmetal gray. That let her know that the contents were very important and, coming from Khefar, very old.

She lifted the lid. Nestled inside the display form was a gold arm cuff, delicately carved and inlaid with blue and red enamel. With a start, she recognized some of the design elements indicative of Meroitic culture.

"Wow, it looks like a fine example of craftwork from the Kushite kingdom, or Meroë." She looked up at Khefar. "Is it authentic?"

"It belonged to Kandake Amanirenas."

The box wobbled in her hands. "*The* Kandake Amanirenas, warrior-queen of Meroë, who led an army against the Romans in Egypt?"

He nodded. "She gifted it to me as thanks for saving her son."

Kira's mouth dropped open. "By the Light. You saved Akinidad's life. There's got to be a story there and you're so going to tell me all about it. I can't believe you'd keep a story like that from me. Actually, you've kept almost all your stories from me."

"Kira—"

"No talking. Looking now." She lifted the box to eye level so that she could examine every intricate detail of the arm cuff without touching it. If he'd gotten it from Kandake Amanirenas, that meant the bracelet was more than two thousand years old. What would she learn if she did touch it?

"It's beautiful, a fantastic use of the glass to mimic rubies and sapphires. Pure gold, with an intricate geometric pattern around both edges. The hinge work is amazing. It's simply a stunning work of art." She handed it back to him.

He pushed it back at her. "It's yours."

"What? No. No." She held her hands up, panic coiling in her stomach. "I couldn't accept something like this. It's precious, it's priceless. Kandake Amanirenas owned this! It belongs in a museum, not my jewelry box! Why in the world would you give me something like this?"

He took her gloved hand, pressed the box into her palm. "It belongs to someone who will truly appreciate what it is, and what it means. I think Amanirenas would be pleased to know you have her bracelet. In fact, I know it."

Kira bit her lip, gazing down at the cuff with pure

unadulterated longing. It was an unbelievably beautiful piece, and she wanted it, wanted it badly. She wanted to settle it on her bare wrist, wait for the impressions to bombard her. How much of a glimpse would she have of Amanirenas's life? Would she uncover something that would enable her to be the first to decipher Meroitic writing? She could write an article, no, a whole book, on the ruler. She could publish in archaeological journals, and speak at symposiums. Maybe even get the opportunity to lead a dig.

She looked at Khefar. The Nubian had carried the bracelet with him for more than two millennia. Would she be able to learn more about his life if she touched the bracelet? Touching his dagger had shown her Khefar's life as a warrior over the last four thousand years. She knew he carried a fetish bag that contained mementos of the devastating loss of his family, the event that had set him on a four-thousand-year-old path to redemption. She'd accidentally touched that small leather pouch, and experienced the death of his wife and children, his grief, his rage. Experienced his revenge.

So why give the bracelet to her? Surely, he'd had plenty of opportunity to present it to someone else over the centuries. Why would he give this to her? Why now?

Maybe there wasn't a deeper meaning other than he wanted her to have it because she'd have the highest appreciation of it. If so, that was more than reason enough to satisfy her.

She wrapped her gloved fingers about the bracelet, pulled it free of the box. "It would be appropriate to wear it to the gala tonight, but I'm afraid to let it out of the house," she said, holding it close to her chest. "I'll take good care of it."

"I know you will," he said with a smile. "I have faith in you. Now, we should probably get going or we'll miss the tour of the exhibit."

Chapter 4

Kira directed Khefar into downtown, onto Marietta Street and then down Andrew Young International Boulevard to the Georgia World Congress Center. The center was part of a sprawling sports and entertainment complex that also encompassed an arena and Centennial Olympic Park. Though it was mainly used for conventions and trade shows, the center had three buildings that could handle anything from a movie showing to graduations to special exhibits expected to attract thousands of people. Kira knew the organizers of the underworld exhibit were hoping to break attendance records with their show. Given the public response to other shows and the always popular subject of ancient Egypt, Kira thought they stood a good chance of doing just that.

Khefar found a place to park his black Charger on a lower level close to the main entrance of Building A, and then helped Kira out of the car. She looped the strap of her beaded purse diagonally across her chest, like she would her messenger bag. Purses had never been a part of her daily wardrobe; she usually needed easy access to more things at any given time than the largest purse could hold. Even before college, it was easier to tuck the things she needed into pockets or a backpack, which could hold much more than tissues and a tube of lipstick.

They made their way down and across the International Plaza to the main doors. The arena dominated the view on the east side of the deck while the dome took up much of the west, with the main entrance to the center across the street directly in front of them. A little ways away, above the hum of traffic, they could hear crowds at Centennial Olympic Park. This time of year part of the main field held an ice-skating rink. Kira had yet to go, but then, her jobs kept her schedule full.

Khefar stopped short. "That's not subtle."

The main entrance to Building A was emblazoned with banners heralding JOURNEY THROUGH THE UNDERWORLD: AN INTERACTIVE TOUR OF THE EGYPTIAN BOOK OF THE DEAD.

"That's a lot of words to fit on a small banner," Kira said. "Besides, you've got the Great Pyramid, the Great Sphinx, Rameses the Great. Since when has Egypt been small scale about anything?"

"True, but I'm not talking about the banners." Khefar pointed. It was hard to miss the two giant statues of Anubis that flanked the main entrance. Black and gold and two stories high, the statues advertised the Book of the Dead exhibit in no uncertain terms.

Kira settled her black velvet wrap about her shoulders, made sure the beaded strap of her purse was secure across her chest. "I should warn you now, if you don't like the outside, you're probably not going to like the inside all that much either."

"The exhibit?" Khefar frowned. "Why wouldn't I?"

"Well . . ." She hesitated. "Maybe we should say it's more of a show than an exhibit. I worked on the displays for the artifacts and reproductions section, but a production company handled the interactive Journey Through the Underworld exhibit."

They crossed the plaza and headed up the steps to the doors. "Meaning it's meant to entertain, not educate."

"I think the term they're using is *edutainment*. I haven't been through it yet so I don't know how closely it resembles Ani's Book of Going Forth by Day, but maybe it's a good thing that it doesn't."

The Book of the Dead exhibit was being staged on the first level of the A Building at the Georgia World Congress Center, not far from the Georgia Aquarium. It was a massive undertaking, so massive that the exhibit took up the entire level. The whole floor had been decorated in the theme, with scenes from the funerary text printed on banners hanging from the rafters along the main walkway.

Guests were thick on the floor by the time Kira and Khefar made their way to the lower level. People gathered in knots around high-top tables draped with gold and black fabric, or clustered near the portable open bars. She recognized several members of Atlanta's thriving music community and other local celebrities. Kira chatted with a few of her colleagues and used Khefar to run interference with people who she knew tended to become a little too grab-happy when they were deep in their cups.

"How are you going to manage this?" Khefar wondered as Kira shook hands with yet another colleague. "Alcohol to dull the senses?"

"No, I don't do alcohol. Besides, I'm not going to do anything to blunt my extrasense."

"Why not? Are you expecting any trouble?"

"There are a lot of people here, people who have no problem hugging and shaking hands and even kissing one another on the cheek as a way of being polite."

"Oh. This is going to be difficult for you, isn't it?"

She nodded. "The gloves and shrug will help, but I'm shielding so hard right now that any psychic within a mile is going to think they ran into a brick wall."

Concern filled his eyes. "How long before you reach critical mass?"

"I should be able to make it through the meet and greet without needing to run out of here screaming," she answered. "The tour shouldn't be a problem. I think the whole event shouldn't be more than three hours, four tops."

"So you won't be able to detect any Shadow trouble?"

"No. Gilead's got sweepers and Special Response Teams on standby. Sanchez herself will be here, since Gilead, under the auspices of its umbrella company, Light International, made a sizable donation to the arts and culture program this benefit showing is for. Like you said, it'll be all right to forgo being a Shadowchaser for one night."

"And I, for one, think it's a good idea for you to relax every now and again."

Kira turned, and then broke into a smile as she recognized the speaker and his companion. "Bale, Rinna. I didn't know you would be here tonight!"

"As if I could miss an opportunity to see you in

your nonlethal element," Bale said, humor sparkling in his amazing clear eyes. "Or your nonlethal clothes."

She allowed the air kiss. "I may be wearing a dress, but I can still kick ass. Hi, Rinna."

The dark-haired beauty in a ruby-colored sheath gave her a warm nod. They both knew not to touch her. "You'd think Bale would remember that a soft exterior can cover an interior of steel," Rinna said with a smile. "But it's fun reminding him."

Kira grinned at the couple. It was hard not to, considering how striking they were. She could even call their human forms beautiful, perfect examples of their Turkish homeland. Bale stood six foot three, dark hair carelessly sweeping to his shoulders and framing his unusual color-changing eyes. The thin moustache and goatee only enhanced his *Prince of Persia* air. Moreover, Kira could admit to herself, he looked damned good in a tuxedo. That she knew he was as dangerous as he was debonair only added to Bale's mystique.

Rinna was an excellent partner for him. Model gorgeous, she stood a few inches shorter than Bale, her wavy auburn hair falling to her waist. Together they exuded understated power, the kind that attracted and encouraged people, and they worked it to their advantage.

A soft cough refocused her attention. She gestured to Khefar. "Bale, Rinna, this is Khefar, also known as Kevin Lambert. Bale is head of a banaranjan clan here in Atlanta," she explained. "But he works with everyone in the preternatural community to help them get acclimated to the city and find homes and jobs that suit their particular talents. His information network is nearly as vast as Demoz's is."

"But much more altruistic," Bale interjected.

Khefar shook their hands. "Banaranjans were a force to be reckoned with during the time of the Ottoman Empire. Your reputation as fierce fighters is well known and well earned."

"Thank you," Bale said, with a sharp inclination of his head. "The reputation of the eternal warrior who dies to fight another day is also well-known. We heard of how you helped Kira back in October. How long do you plan to stay in our fair city?"

"As long as necessary."

Suppressing the urge to roll her eyes in exasperation, Kira watched the two men do the testosterone display that males do no matter their species. She caught Rinna's gaze, and the other woman lifted her gaze skyward for both of them.

"So . . . what brings you out tonight?" Kira asked, deciding not to comment on the display.

"Money," Bale answered. "With so many generous donors here tonight, I figured it would behoove me to approach the hybrids among them to donate to our own community outreach programs."

"How many hybrids are here tonight?" Khefar asked. His tone sounded idle, but Kira knew he was considering potential threats as he stepped back, settling his hand at the small of her back.

"There are hybrids everywhere," Rinna answered, "in plain sight, from bartenders to guests."

"Like I said, I doubt we'll have any trouble tonight," Kira said. "If anything, people will be sizing each other up in different ways, the same way humans do."

"But tonight is all about pharaohs and fund-raising.

And with that, we'll get to our business so you can get to yours."

The banaranjans left. Khefar's hand tightened at her back. "Were you involved with him?"

She frowned at him. "Why would you ask me a question like that?"

"A man doesn't look at a woman the way that man looked at you unless he wanted to see you naked or already has."

Kira dropped a hand to her hip. "First of all, did you happen to see the woman he's with? Second, you have no reason to be jealous. Third, did you see the woman he's with?"

"You're as hot as she is," Khefar told her, making the declaration in his no-nonsense tone. "Does that mean that you used to have a thing with him?"

Khefar was jealous. No outright denial, no letting the subject go. Maybe giving her the bracelet was his way of staking a claim. The thought was as disturbing as it was flattering. "How much do you know about banaranjans?"

"I know the clans were partly responsible for the Ottoman Empire stretching as far as it did. They are fierce fighters, matched only by Vlad Dracul in ruthlessness."

She pursed her lips as she considered his words. "Did you fight with them, or against them?"

It took him a moment to admit, "I was among those who were alongside Sultan Mehmed II as he rode victorious into Constantinople."

Of course he had been present at the fall of Constantinople. "I've seen a couple of depictions of that historic moment, painted by a Frenchman named Constant." She folded her arms. "I suppose next you're going to tell me that you convinced the artist to paint you in."

"I met him when I was in Morocco, having left America after the States' War." Khefar shrugged. "He wanted a vivid representation of that day. I gave it to him."

She gaped at him. "When I ask for details you brush me off, saying you can't remember! What am I going to have to do to get you to come up off of these stories? Seriously, dude—if you can't tell me, who can you tell?"

"I'm a fighter, not a talker. Besides, we were talking about your close personal relationship with that banaranjan and what you know about them."

"Banaranjans are notoriously clannish and disdainful of any perceived weaknesses," Kira said, "and they consider humans weak. They're also adrenaline junkies and night flyers. They mate on the fly, and by that I mean several dozen stories above street level, ending with a climactic freefall. Anyone who's not banaranjan or has their own wings would have to be suicidal to consider mating with one of them. And if you call me suicidal, I'm going to stab you and watch you bleed all over that pretty tux."

"I don't think you're suicidal," he said, the unspoken word *anymore* hanging in the air between them.

"Bale and I have a close professional relationship. We share a vested interest in the hybrid community coexisting peacefully with the human one. And did you forget the whole touching thing?"

Dark jealousy fled his face, chased off by contrition. "I did forget. I'm sorry. Perhaps next time you could introduce me as if I'm more than some random guy you know."

"How should I introduce you?" she wondered, surprised.

"I'm sure you'll come up with something if you put your mind to it."

"Fine. I'll think of something. In the meantime, do you think you could try to be civil? I have to work with these people."

"Interesting. Most Chasers seemed programmed to work alone, except for their handlers, of course."

"Yeah, well, since I consider myself to have been without a handler for longer than I've had one, I figure learning how to get along with the hybrid community means fewer Shadowlings I have to kill, which in turn means less paperwork I have to deal with at Gilead East."

"Kira? Kira Solomon!"

She turned to see a thin blond-haired man in wire-rimmed glasses approaching her. He was the manager of the edutainment portion of the show, Bruce Hammond. "Be nice," Kira muttered.

"You mean me, or yourself?" Khefar muttered back.

"Both. Follow my lead, okay?" She pasted on a smile. "Mr. Hammond, it's good to see you again." She extended a gloved hand, belatedly turning it from a blocking move to a greeting. Hammond had the limpest handshake she'd ever had the misfortune to experience. Better to suffer through a handshake behind the security of her gloves than the consequences of one misaligned air kiss. "Kevin, this is Bruce Hammond. Mr. Hammond, this is my partner, Kevin Lambert. Mr. Hammond is the production manager for the show and exhibit."

"Pleased to meet you, Mr. Lambert," the manager said, shaking Khefar's hand. "I didn't realize Kira was involved with someone."

"Kira's a firm believer in discretion being the better part of valor," Khefar said, extricating himself from the other man's lifeless grip. He gave Kira a veiled look. "You wouldn't believe the things she keeps close to the vest."

"When she wears a vest, that is," the basso profundo voice of Demoz pronounced as he joined them. Instead of the traditional black tie that Hammond wore, or the spike of gold that Khefar had added to his tux, the rotund club owner was all in black: bowler hat; silk shirt; custom-made, black shadow-striped suit; and black tourmaline studs for cuff links, earrings, and tie pin.

Kira wasn't all that surprised to see Demoz at the fund-raiser. It was a prime information-gathering event featuring the who's who of Atlanta's up-and-comings and already-theres, and the psychic vampire was the premier information broker in the preternatural community, if not the city. What did surprise her was that he'd bought his assistant, Yessara, and it looked very much like they were on a date.

The peace angel was resplendent in a silvery gray slip dress and opal jewelry that accentuated her ethereal beauty. Her normally peaceful demeanor seemed even more blissful. Given the way Yessara had her small hand tucked into the crook of Demoz's massive arm and the addled expression the psychic vampire wore, Kira had a good idea of where the bliss stemmed from.

"Mr. Hammond, I believe you already know Mr. Demoz, one of our city's entertainment moguls," Kira said, making introductions. "And this lovely woman is his assistant, Yessara."

"So many beautiful women in this city," Hammond exclaimed, bending low over Yessara's hand. "I think I need to move here permanently!"

"Beware, Mr. Hammond," Demoz said smoothly. "It would be wise to remember that every rose has its thorns."

Hammond tugged on his tie, suddenly and completely uncomfortable. "Quite right."

Kira decided to rescue the poor man. "Mr. Hammond, there's the mayor. I believe you've already met the professor he's talking to."

"Indeed, indeed. I'll go over and introduce myself. I hope to see you all when the tour begins." He scurried away.

Demoz took a deep breath. "Thank you, Kira, for clearing the desperation from the air. It has an over-ripeness to it that is not to my taste."

"He was simply trying to be nice," Yessara said in her softly rolling voice. "There was no ill intent in his words or actions, my dear."

"He's harmless," Kira added, waving her hand in dismissal. Truthfully, she felt she was able to breathe better with the too-slick manager away chatting up other guests. "It's just his way of working the room."

Demoz made a gallant attempt to erase his irritation, due, no doubt, to Yessara's touch on his arm. A blocked psychic vampire had no defense against a peace angel. "Still, we've already made a sizable donation tonight. There was no need to fawn."

"It's an instinctive reaction," Khefar explained, "especially when in the presence of such beauty as we are."

Demoz looked from Kira to Khefar and back again. Then a smile split the inky blackness of his face. "I'd say dating agrees with you, Kira Solomon."

"I could say the same about you, Demoz," Kira retorted, unable to hide her delight. She had no idea why the psychic vampire and the peace angel had decided to move their relationship from strictly professional to personal, but she was truly glad for them. With Demoz being born of Shadow and Yessara being an agent of Light, their successful relationship could prove that both sides could get along if they tried. "I'm glad you guys decided to step it up a notch. It's about time you allow her to have some influence on you."

"You have no idea the influence she's had on me," Demoz said softly. "And no one 'allows' Yessara to do anything."

The lady in question merely smiled one of her beatific smiles, dark curls shining in the bright lights as she inclined her head. "I am as I am, and I am content," she said in the sweetest of tones. "Do you not agree, Kira Solomon?"

Kira had no idea what Yessara meant, but found herself nodding anyway. "Of course. Congratulations."

"Thank you." The other woman beamed, and despite having her extrasense dialed up to the thickness of a shield, Kira almost smiled in pure puppy-like pleasure. It was a direct effect of being in the presence of a peace angel. From what Kira understood, the Light hybrids were related to guardian angels, but they deflected negative emotions from everyone instead of protecting a specific individual.

Of course, those negative emotions needed to go somewhere after a peace angel had siphoned them off. They could absorb them, of course, but it was so much easier to pass turbulent emotions off to someone used to partaking of them, like a psychic vampire.

Where sanguinarian vampires fed on blood, Demoz's kind fed on emotions, the stronger the better. Usually, Demoz partook from the people who visited his club, an industrial Goth rock complex that catered to Light and Shadow, using a massive slab of clear quartz as a booster. On the very few occasions that Kira had seen him away from the club, the information broker usually wore Herkimer diamonds. The black tourmalines signified he was not only not feeding, but he was blocking outside emotions altogether.

"Are you well, Demoz?" Kira asked. He may have been born of Shadow, but Demoz had done a lot of good in the community. Many truces and agreements had been negotiated inside the neutral territory of his club. Atlanta needed him. Heck, the Universal Balance needed him.

"As well as one can be out of their element, Shadowchaser," he replied. "As Yessara says, I am as I am. What about you? Certainly this isn't your usual environment or attire, though I must say the dress suits you."

"Don't forget the heels," she said, showing off the black stilettos that looked far better than they felt.

"Hard to be comfortable in something like this with all of these touchy-feely people around. I'd much rather be in my steel-toed boots and cargo pants. But as you said, I am as I am. This event was a good excuse to dress up. The money raised tonight will enable a lot of our local museums to make upgrades."

"Then, it's good we have a sizable crowd here tonight," Demoz observed. "Quite a different clientele than those who visit my club."

"Most of the DMZ's regular patrons don't have the two hundred and fifty dollars a ticket in loose change to come to an event like this," Kira pointed out. "Or the altruism."

"You'd be surprised, Kira Solomon, what people would give when there's a benefit to be had."

Kira was about to question him further when Khefar touched her arm. "Looks like we're about to get to the main event," he said, and then pointed.

Hammond tapped on a microphone near the main bar. "Ladies and gentlemen, thank you for opening your hearts—and your wallets—to our exhibition." The audience tittered with polite laughter. "Your generous donations will go directly to your city's local museums and cultural outreach programs, so thank you."

The crowd applauded. "Now, I know most of you came to be seen and to drink the free booze. But if you would care for a little culture with your liquor, I would like to invite you to stick around."

Hammond's voice dropped to a dramatic whisper as he raised his glass high. "So eat, drink, and be merry. For tonight, we journey through the Egyptian underworld!"

Chapter 5

"Naturally the first exhibit hall houses the gift shop," Hammond told the throng gathered around him as he led them through the first room. "No journey through the underworld would be complete without a souvenir to remember it by."

"Of course not," Khefar mumbled. "Gods forbid we forgo a trinket made in China to mark our trip through ancient Egypt."

Kira coughed to smother her laughter. Hammond gamely ignored them, making his way through to the second hall. "The second exhibit hall contains original pieces and reproductions of famous artifacts from this mysterious and magical culture. Some of the artifacts have been loaned from various museums and collections around the world, thanks in large part to the hard work and connections of Kira Solomon."

Kira acknowledged the polite applause with a dip of her head, and then gestured for Hammond to continue. She'd worked her butt off to acquire a cross section of examples of the funerary texts of ancient Egypt, drawing on all of her professional contacts and even calling in a favor here and there. The effort had paid off, and she'd managed to obtain enough for a good representation of the history of funerary texts. Everything from engraved chunks of tomb walls, known as the Pyramid Texts, dating back to the Old Kingdom; to wooden fragments from the Middle Kingdom, Coffin Texts; to photos and remnants of papyri from the New Kingdom and the Saite period, all carefully mounted and secured beneath glass displays. They'd also brought in examples of mummification equipment, burial artifacts such as shabti, shawabti, and ushabti funerary figurines, and canopic jars of exquisite beauty and detail.

Hammond guided his group farther into the cavernous hall. "Aside from these ancient literary relics, you'll also see a replica of the most famous version of the Book of the Dead. Ladies and gentlemen, I present to you the Papyrus of Ani as it would have looked shortly after it was created."

He gestured, and lights slowly grew in brightness along a set of wall panels covered in maroon cloth. The attendees gasped in appreciation as a true-to-size reproduction of Ani's funerary papyrus came into view— all seventy-eight feet of it.

Intrigued, Kira stepped closer to examine the reproductions of Ani and his wife making offerings to the sun god, the Weighing of the Heart ceremony, and ending with the vignette with the goddesses Tawaret and Hathor in their animal forms, watching over Ani's tomb in the western cliffs. She'd seen pictures in books and online, even seen sections of the original papyrus in the British Museum, but never had a chance to see it like this.

The Book of Going Forth by Day as it was meant to be viewed was breathtaking. The replica stretched the length of the wall and looked to be made of actual papyrus, like many of the gilded souvenir papers sold in gift shops around the world. This one, however, hummed with power. It felt benign, though, crafted by an artist gifted to the point of unconsciously imbuing his work with magic.

"As some of you may be aware, we've reproduced every exact detail of the original, which is currently housed at the British Museum," Hammond explained. "Small insets below the book describe some of the texts and illustrations and offer translations of the hieroglyphs. For those who don't know, the Book of the Dead is a collection of spells, organized into 'chapters,' that enable the dead to make their way past traps, riddles, and deadly encounters. The book contains passwords and spells that are supposed to be spoken aloud before you are allowed to pass to the next stage, and other spells that help the deceased move about in the land of the living."

He gestured them forward, stopping before massive golden velvet curtains hanging from the rafters. "There were nearly two hundred spells that could be used in a Book of the Dead, but not every spell went into every book. However, by the time of the Third Intermediate Period some standardization began to occur, including selling ready-made books that simply needed the deceased's name added."

Hammond seemed to realize that he'd entered lecturing mode. He gave a self-deprecating laugh. "You'll have to forgive me—teachers never stop teaching!"

He grabbed the curtain panels. "Besides, I wanted to prepare you for this, our pièce de resistance: the Journey Through the Underworld."

He jerked the curtains open. A sand-colored carpet led to a carved façade that was more theatrical than historically accurate. Four twenty-foot-tall obelisks drenched with hieroglyphs, designed to simulate a limestone façade, flanked a wide entrance with a winged sun disk over the lintel.

"Did you use any particular tomb as a blueprint?" Kira asked.

"We took inspiration from several tombs and papyri so visitors could have a well-rounded idea of what a journey through the underworld is like," Hammond replied, "with a bit of embellishment for dramatic effect."

"Meaning not based in reality all that much," Khefar muttered.

Kira coughed. "Remember, we're supposed to be nice," she whispered. "It's not for us, it's for the audience."

That audience seemed appropriately awed as they shuffled between the pillars into the first room. "The oldest of the funerary texts is called the Amduat, literally That Which Is in the Underworld. It recounts the twelve-hour journey that the pharaoh makes through the underworld in his solar boat. A later incarnation is known as the Book of Gates, and the twelve hours have thus become gates guarded by violent serpents. Of course, we won't make you fine people take half a day to traverse the tomb, though we surely hope we have enough crowds to make it seem as if you've waited twelve hours."

Hammond laughed, though few joined in. Atlanta wasn't a town known for its patience with lines. "Given that, you can consider what we have here, inscribed on the walls and ceilings around us, to be the highlight reel."

He guided them along the decorated corridor. "As you progress through, you can hear and see a translation of the text and images, and can simply pass through or have the full immersive experience of going through the gates correctly and battling Apep, the Serpent of Chaos. The pathway is completely wired with audio and video to further enhance the feeling of making a journey far beneath the earth.

"We have a representation of a sarcophagus in the burial chamber just to the west of the corridor, as well as depictions of the burials of some of the more well-known kings of Egypt. At the end of a most perilous journey—which you can experience in full when the exhibit opens tomorrow—we come to a final test, at least for the purposes of this exhibit: The Hall of Two Truths."

The corridor opened onto a high-ceilinged chamber. This time, when the gathering gasped, Kira gasped with them.

Directly in front of them, a life-sized statue of Osiris sat on a gilded throne, wrapped feet to neck as a mummy. A soft spotlight shone down on the *atef* crown, the gleaming green skin, and the gilded symbols of kingship held crossed in front of him: the crook and the flail. Standing beside the throne, one hand on her husband's shoulder, stood Isis, a gilded throne-crown atop her sleek braided hair. Behind them and to the right stood two ornately carved doors, a discreet exit sign lit above them.

A large pair of golden scales stood in front of Osiris. The jackal-headed god Anubis knelt beside it, one hand placing a large scarab, representing the heart, into the left pan. A white ostrich feather balanced in the right pan, the feather of Truth. The heart scarab had to balance perfectly with Ma'at's feather, which seemed an impossibility.

Thoth, with his impressive ibis beak, stood to the right of the scales, ready to transcribe the outcome of the weighing. If the heart was out of balance with Ma'at's truth, the person's soul was doomed to be fed to Ammit the Devourer, removing that person from existence. Gleaming red eyes shone in the darkness behind Thoth, Ammit waiting her chance to feed.

Kira locked her knees, fighting to stay upright and outwardly calm. The scene was too real, too lifelike. She'd been in this place before when the Fallen had killed her in Demoz's club. When she'd died, she'd gone to the Hall of Justice, stood before Isis and Ma'at, the Divine Tribunal and the forty-two assessor gods, and waited to have her heart weighed.

It was exactly like this.

Fingers wrapped around hers, squeezed hard. She blinked, feeling as if she'd broken through the surface of thickened water, and then glanced at Khefar. He held his jaw clenched so tight she could see the muscles working beneath his skin. *So it's not just me.*

Hammond stepped forward, clapping a hand on the Anubis statue's shoulder. Kira winced. "As you can see, we spared no expense in creating a faithful rendition of the Weighing of the Heart Ceremony from Ani the scribe's Book of the Dead. What do you think?"

Kira managed to find her voice. "I think visitors are going to be awed."

Hammond beamed. "We certainly hope so. To complete the public's experience, visitors will have the opportunity to actively participate in the judging ritual."

Excited murmurs from the audience. The hairs on Kira's neck stood on end. "How will they do that?"

"It's all mechanical," Hammond explained. "Tomorrow we're installing a machine that will dispense scarabs for a dollar each. The scarab will fall into the Anubis statue's hand, and Anubis will drop the scarab into the measuring plate. It will then be weighed against Ma'at's feather before their very eyes."

Hammond held up a low-grade amethyst carved into a scarab shape. He offered it to Kira. "Would you like to do the honors?"

"No." Her gloved hand reached up to touch the tattoo at her throat, the feather of Ma'at etched there. She felt no warming rush, either of warning or reassurance. Perhaps there wasn't any magic in the tableau before her, but in Kira's mind it certainly felt like there should have been.

Hammond smiled. "There's no need to worry, Ms. Solomon. I'm sure your soul isn't in jeopardy."

A ripple of amusement swept through the crowd. Kira refused to be pressured. There was no way she'd commit sacrilege in order to amuse Hammond and this monkey-suited crowd. "Why don't you show us how it's done, Doctor?"

Very carefully, he placed the heart-stone in the center of the measuring pan opposite the feather. The gilded pans began to rise and lower, slowly swinging as it measured the weights. It seemed that everyone held their collective breath, but the scales finally stopped in perfect balance.

The sudden tension eased. "What happens if the heart doesn't balance with the feather?" someone asked.

The director paused dramatically. "On those rare occasions, the Ammit creature will slide forward, jaws gnashing and stage-effect 'steam' issuing from its mouth, and snatch the soul away."

Hammond chuckled. "Of course, that won't really happen. However, we do advise that the young ones bypass this part of the exhibit as it may be too intense for some." He gestured toward the open doors at the end of the panoramic display. "Shall we?"

They followed him out through the doors, spilling back into the open area near the gift shop entrance. "The gift shop will sell trinkets as souvenirs of the experience, including hard-carved gemstone scarabs. We hope that you'll come back and journey through the interactive exhibit as it is meant to be experienced, and therefore gain a better understanding of the beliefs of the ancient Egyptians. Thank you all for your generous time—and donations."

He turned to Kira. "My apologies, Kira. I didn't mean to put you on the spot back there."

Kira waved him off. "No worries, Mr. Hammond," she said. "I suppose I was as surprised as everyone else by the breadth and depth of the display you have there."

He beamed. "It is genius, isn't it?"

Kira couldn't bring herself to agree and settled for "It's certainly impressive. Who designed it?"

"The production company brought in some set designers who've worked on big-budget Hollywood films," Hammond explained. "We gave them the most exciting portions of the Book of Gates, the Amduat, and the Book of the Dead, and they created sections in each of the tomb rooms."

With a total disregard for a logical or accurate progression through the pathway. Then again, the collection of prayers and spells was supposed to protect the dead, not make sense to the living. "I'm sure you'll thrill lots of visitors, Mr. Hammond."

"I certainly hope so." He pulled out a handkerchief, dabbed at his forehead. "If you'll excuse me, I'm being called over for an interview. Every bit of publicity helps. Please, enjoy the rest of your evening."

Khefar sidled up next to her. "You know how I'll enjoy the rest of my evening?"

"Getting the hell out of here?"

"It's as if you read my mind."

Chapter 6

"What was that?" Khefar asked as soon as they reached the car.

"I have no idea," Kira said, pulling off her stilettos and tossing them in the backseat. She wriggled her toes back to life with a sigh. "I worked on acquiring and the display of the artifacts, and I wasn't here when they installed the papyrus of Ani. I didn't have the time or inclination to visit the third hall to see what they were developing. Now I wish I had."

Khefar pulled out of the parking deck, revving the engine more than needed. "It was the way we saw it," he said, his voice clipped. "The Hall of Judgment. The gods, the scales, and Ammit, all there. Exactly the way we saw it."

"I know." Kira shimmied out of her pantyhose, wishing she'd thought to put a pair of sweats in the car. She might freeze her butt off getting into the house, but at least she'd be able to move quickly.

"And you knew nothing about it?"

The tone of his voice stopped her, had her turning to face him. "What are you trying to say? That I decided to re-create the most harrowing and beautiful spiritual experience of my life to become a sideshow amusement for complete strangers? I know you don't know me that well, but you should know me better than that."

"You're right." Khefar sighed in exasperation. "I apologize. It's just that—"

"Ma'at wasn't there," she cut in irritably. "In the version at the Congress Center, Ma'at wasn't personified as she was in our vision. The scale had a baboon figurine atop it, not a statuette of Ma'at."

"And Isis stood behind Osiris, not in front of us near the scales," Khefar added. "It's not the same."

"No, it's a good representation based on the Book of the Dead buried with the scribe Ani." Kira rubbed her arms. "But there was something about it. I can't really explain it, but it was off somehow."

"Shadow?"

"I don't know. Since we were all closed in together, I was shielding at maximum. Once I got over my shock of seeing the Hall of Judgment in 3-D, I got the sense of something sleeping, waiting."

"That doesn't sound good."

"No." She rubbed her arms again, thinking about the dreams she'd been having since Cairo. Dreams of Chaos, of growing Shadow, of making choices that would change everything.

"Are you all right?"

"Yeah. Shielding like that wipes me out."

"Liar."

She glanced at him again. "You didn't even have to think about that, did you?"

He shrugged. "As you say, I don't know you as well as I will, but I am a good observer."

"That you are." She settled back into the seat, her

arms folded across her chest. Being in his car no longer bothered her since she'd tried to read it shortly after they'd returned from overseas. She didn't feel guilty about doing it behind his back either—she had to have some way of learning more about the man she'd let into her home and her bed. Unfortunately all she'd gotten was the impression of miles and miles of asphalt. Boring. "At least now I know why you do it."

"Do what?"

"Look at me when you think I'm not looking."

"I like looking at you. You're good to look at."

She shook her head, not that he could see it. "It's not that kind of look."

"What kind of look do you think it is?"

"The kind that makes you wonder if I'm dangerous. If I've gone over to Shadow. The kind where you're wondering how long it's going to be before you have to pull your dagger against me."

"Oh." He paused. "That look."

"Yeah. That look." She fisted her hands. "I'm not in danger of slipping."

"If you were, would you know?"

"I'd know." She hoped liked hell that she would, if only so she could choose the way she'd be taken out.

"Would you? You've changed, Kira. You can't deny that. We spent nearly three days behind the Veil. You had to channel Light and Shadow to get us out of Set's temple alive. It was hard for you to let that power go. I've got to believe it was just as hard for the power to let you go too."

It was. Channeling both Light and Shadow felt the way being thrown into a blender must feel. She'd felt the power, beautiful, delicious power, and was instantly addicted. She wanted more of it. If she allowed herself, she'd go searching for it, taking it wherever she could get it. Reason enough not to think about it.

"You don't know me well enough to know if I've changed. Maybe I've always been this bitchy."

"I didn't say anything about you being bitchy," he said in his reasonable tone that was beginning to get on her nerves. Maybe she was PMS-ing. "What I am saying is that power affects people. Everyone, no matter who it is. Gods, hybrids, humans—they're either scared of it and try to shut it down, or they crave it and want more of it."

He paused at a stop sign. "You don't seem afraid."

The man was too observant for her peace of mind. Not that she'd had a lot of peace in, like, ever, but still . . . "I can handle it."

"I never said you couldn't," he said, so sincerely it made her wince. "Doesn't mean that I'm not going to be concerned about you. It's the least I can do for someone who's trusting me with their life."

"When you put it like that, you make it hard to be mad at you."

He smiled. "I'm sure you'll find a way."

"And there it is."

He slowed the car, his amusement instantly changing to tension. "Looks like we've got company," he said, nodding to the windshield.

They'd pulled into her neighborhood, a collection of storefronts converted into mixed-use developments on the eastern edge of downtown. She saw the figure, swathed in a light-gray all-weather coat, pacing in front of her home, and recognized him as Balm's assistant.

Something had happened to Balm.

She forced herself to think logically past the sudden tightening in her chest. No, surely she'd know something was wrong with Balm long before anyone showed up to tell her. Section Chief Sanchez had stayed at the gala after Kira and Khefar left, and she wouldn't have done that if something had happened to the commander in chief of the Gilead Commission.

"Is it trouble?"

"Probably, but nothing that requires knives and guns."

Khefar pulled to a stop. "You know him?"

"Yeah. That's Balm's assistant, Lysander. Since I've never seen him without her, and they're both supposed to be back on Santa Costa, he's probably not the bearer of good news."

She retrieved her shoes from the backseat. Reluctantly she shoved her protesting feet back into them before grabbing her Lightblade from the glove compartment and getting out of the car. The biometric scanner mounted on the wall beside the front door read her vitals, raising the garage door in response. Khefar drove through, leaving her in the cold with Balm's assistant.

With his pale hair and fair skin, Lysander looked to be about her age, mid-twenties. She knew he wasn't simply because he'd looked much the same when she'd first seen him more than a decade ago. "Lysander."

"Greetings, Kira Solomon."

"What are you doing here?"

The man gestured to a small crate sitting on her doorstep. "The Balm of Gilead bade me bring this to you."

Kira stared at the box, wondering if it contained what she thought it did, hoped and dreaded it did. Finally. "She didn't tell me you were coming." Figures. "Where is she, anyway?"

"Our Lady of Light remains on Santa Costa," the young man said, his breath steaming in the night. The chill air didn't seem to bother him, which was good, since Kira had no plans to invite him in. Vampires weren't the only creatures one shouldn't invite into their homes. "It was decided but a few hours ago to deliver this to you."

She glanced at the crate again, wary. *A few hours ago* meant Lysander had to already have been somewhere in North America in Balm's Gulfstream, or he'd used alternative methods of travel. Either way, it meant that whatever was in the crate was important enough that it required a special delivery, and that didn't mean UPS.

"What is it?"

"The answers you seek," Lysander said, surprising her. "And hopefully understanding on your part on why your life is as it is, and why Balm is as she is."

"Wow. That's, like, the most you've said to me at one time ever. And you're so nice about it that I don't even mind that you're verbally rapping me on my knuckles."

Lysander gave a graceful incline of his head, adding a ghost of a smile. "I speak when it's important enough."

Balm? Kira called out mentally. *Lysander's here. I've got the box. Why did you send this to me now?*

A wall of silence answered her. Kira tried again, got the same result. She knew Balm was there, but for some reason the head of Gilead wasn't answering. Yet it felt different from being shut out or ignored.

Kira frowned at Lysander. "Balm's not answering me. I can barely sense her. What's going on?"

Lysander's expression closed. "Balm is indisposed at the moment."

"Indisposed?" she echoed as Khefar came out of the garage to join them. "Balm's never indisposed. At least not to me. So I'll ask you again: What's going on?"

Instead of answering, he picked up the crate, held it out to her. "Everything that the Balm of Gilead wants you to know is in here," he said.

"Meaning there are things she doesn't want me to know," Kira shot back.

"Believe me when I say that she went through great pains to get this information to you," Lysander said, reproach in his voice. "There is a pendant in here that is precious to my mistress. For the first time I can remember, my mistress took it off and urged me to bring this to you. If you want answers, you should start there."

Khefar took the crate from Lysander when Kira made no move to reach for it. "Is Balm going to be all right?"

"When have you known her not to be?" Lysander asked. He instantly grew serious again. "My duty here is done. If you will excuse me, I have been apart from my mistress longer than I feel comfortable with." He bowed low. "May the Light shine on you both."

The wind picked up, causing Kira to shiver deep in her lightweight dress coat. As she watched, Lysander's solid image became like static across a television screen.

Her skin prickled as his form elongated, faded, transmuted into crackling energy. The wind blew harder, catching the particles that Lysander had become before sending them spiraling up into the darkness of the night.

Kira looked after him until there was nothing left to see. Even then, she continued staring into the stars and the half-moon. Why wasn't Balm talking to her? Why send the crate now?

"That's one way to travel," Khefar remarked, the crate balanced against his chest. "What's in here?"

"Lysander said answers. The only thing I've been questioning with Balm is who I am, who my parents were. I'm guessing I'll find out when I open it."

"Then, let's go inside," Khefar said. "At the very least, we won't be standing outside, cold and vulnerable."

"True." It took effort to make her feet move, to head inside. Each step, it seemed, took her closer to a cliff's edge, and she felt powerless to stop it. She could simply not open the box, of course. Keep on in ignorant bliss. Yet her whole life, from the moment she realized she was different, that she was an orphan, had been building to this moment, uncovering truth. Now that the moment was at hand, she felt curiously let down and reluctant.

Once inside, she automatically went through the motions of setting the perimeter defenses as Khefar set the chest on her high-top table. Her movements were slow, almost clumsy, and she wondered if she was in some sort of shock. Not hearing from Balm shook her.

She'd always been able to talk mind-to-mind with Balm. She hadn't given it much thought, not even when she'd pestered the head of the Gilead Commission with thousands of *why* questions as a teen. Kira had simply assumed that Balm, as head of Gilead and its Shadow-chaser organization, could talk to whomever she wanted. Balm had more power than she revealed; only a fool would think otherwise.

There had been plenty of times over the years when Kira hadn't wanted to talk mind-to-mind with Balm, and vice versa. But it had never felt this . . . final.

"You're worried," Khefar said, pulling his tie loose.

"Yeah." She kicked her shoes off, curling her toes against the soothing smoothness of the wood floor. "Balm and I have always talked through a mental link or through dream walks, unless one of us was mad at the other. Or she wanted to teach me a lesson."

"Maybe this is another one of her lessons."

"Maybe you're right."

"This has completely thrown you off, hasn't it?"

Kira nodded, staring at the chest, trying to ease the wild thumping of her heart. "Years."

"What?"

"It's been years. I've been pestering Balm for answers since I first met her and realized there was more to her than met the eye. For more than a decade I've been trying to find out who I am and why I have this ability. Balm's left me fumbling in the dark all this time. But now that I've gone to that in-Between place and spoken with Solis, the lady of Between, Balm suddenly wants to share information." Kira shook her head. "Something's not right."

Khefar pulled off his jacket, carefully folded it, and draped it neatly over the back of the couch. The tux would have to go back in the morning. She was glad they wouldn't have to explain seeker demon acid or hybrid bloodstains on the material. "You think Balm has other motives?"

"Balm always has other motives. My problem is trying to figure out what they are."

"Do you need to know the why of Balm's actions right now, when your other long-held questions are so close to being answered?"

"I suppose not." She sighed, ready to get out of the dress and into something more comfortable, like bike leathers. "But I have to tell you, I'm feeling a little bit like Pandora, about to unleash a world of hurt."

Which was why she stood completely across the room from the box, her dress gloves still securely in place. She wouldn't go so far as to say she was afraid. It was just that experience had taught her she had plenty of reason to be cautious.

Yes, she wanted—needed—the truth. But she also wanted to be ready to deal with the fallout of learning that truth.

Kira crossed to the high table, then stared down at the chest, trying to view it as she would any other artifact that had come into her possession. For artifact it was, clearly, decades—perhaps centuries—old, and handcrafted. The lower portion of the chest appeared to be formed from a single piece of wood gone gray with age, the lid from another.

Other than its age, nothing remarkable about the box jumped out at her. Knowing the Balm of Gilead, that meant the box was anything but unremarkable.

Her gloved hand edged along the lid. She could feel a slight thrum through the dense fabric shielding her fingers.

Khafer touched her shoulder. "Do you want to be alone for this?"

She shook her head. "It's magically locked. That means it's going to require using my touch ability and pushing beyond the Veil to open the lid. I don't think I'm ready to receive whatever extra message the box might have in it, so I think I'm going to hold off on opening it. At least for a little while."

"Why?"

"I'm pretty sure it's not going to be fun, no matter what's in there. I think it might be best if I go through everything alone. But I've got to prepare for it. Maybe tomorrow. The gala wiped me out mentally, and my brain could use a rest."

"All right." He kissed her forehead, an unexpected tender gesture. "I'm here if you need me."

Are you? she almost asked, but bit the words back. She had no reason to doubt him. He'd died for her, fought for her, shared his body with her. He'd given her a priceless bracelet and promised to end her life if she slipped into Shadow. He'd suspended his four-thousand-year-old quest for redemption in order to help her. He'd put off joining his slain family in the afterlife in order to stay with her. That was enough, wasn't it? She didn't need more, no matter how much she wanted it.

Khefar had given her everything. She didn't need his heart too.

"Come on." He grabbed her hand, tugging her toward the stairs. "You're exhausted. The box will still be here in the morning. And who knows? Maybe Balm will be more talkative during the night."

Chapter 7

The sky spread cloudless above her, a turquoise bowl cupping the brilliant yellow-white light of the sun. She stood on a slight rise, the beginnings of the desert. To the east lay the Nile valley, a fertile swath of lush, dark-green life split by the river itself. On her left, to the west, stretched a high plateau, the gold-red sands of the desert, dotted with thousands of burial sites. The timeless place, the resting place of those whose souls no longer had use of their physical forms.

Voices swirled on the hot wind, indecipherable. Voices of those long gone, or perhaps waiting their time to return. Kira wrapped her arms about her torso, careful not to touch anything. She had no idea if this was merely a simple dream or a dreamwalk. If it was more than a dream, there was the possibility that millennia of death and life might overload her brain, render her useless.

This was not the Valley of the Kings, she knew. Nor was it Saqqara. This was somewhere else. She walked through a deserted town built of mud bricks, ruins claimed long ago by the desert. With a sinking feeling, Kira realized the desert only claimed what had already been his, a town dedicated to the golden lord, the lord of the desert, the lord of chaos: Set.

She was in Naqada, birthplace of Set.

The desire to excavate filled her, pushed aside her apprehension. She wanted to stay, do an extensive survey, to rework the field evaluation William Flinders Petrie and others had completed, conduct her own excavation.

"Why can't you?" a familiar voice asked.

Bernie Comstock, her former mentor, came to a stop beside her. He was dressed for excavation in his khaki cargo pants, rugged work boots, a madras shirt, and a wide-brimmed hat. Though her own attire was much the same, he managed to give the field dress a dapper air.

"Because I'd first have to secure the permits from the Egyptian military and the Supreme Council of Antiquities and hire the crews needed to launch a dig," she said. She then felt compelled to point out, "Besides, I've got other work to do, and you're dead."

"Yes, but this is a dream, isn't it?" the old man asked, a smile crinkling the corners of his eyes. "We can do whatever we want in dreams."

He gestured at the landscape around them. Sure enough, it bustled with activity, native workmen scurrying about, digging in meter-square sites with trowels for up-close work and picks and shovels for larger earth removal, carrying buckets of detritus to a dump site to be sifted. She could feel the heat, the grit of the sand, the thuds and rapid patter of the workers working and talking. She could smell the sweat of everyone toiling beneath the hot sun and, faintly, the scent of the Red Sea.

She turned back to Bernie, who grinned at her

with all the eagerness of a young boy with his first bike. "You're good, old man."

"Thank you." He gave her a slight bow.

Even though it was a dream born of wishes and longing, Kira gave herself over to the excavation work. Native workers did the actual digging. Students and interns, many of whom looked a lot like her college classmates, sorted through the sifted materials for any fragment of potential archaeological value. Kira picked up a framed screen and began to gently sift the sand in it.

Comstock straightened, surveying the site. An extensive pre-dynastic cemetery lay in the west, one of the largest on record, from the earliest settlements in the region. More burial sites lay upriver of South Town. All told, more than two thousand burial sites had been found for a city that housed perhaps two hundred and fifty people at its peak.

"Why excavate here, Kira?" he asked. "Why not the Valley of the Kings? Or Luxor?"

"Everyone wants to dig in the Valley of the Kings, hoping to be the next Howard Carter," she answered, heading for the temple site. "Saqqara is a close second. As for Naqada, I know there's been extensive work here with plenty of artifacts recovered and catalogued, but layers and layers of sand hide thousands of years of history. People lived and died here, and I'd like to know more about them and their lives."

It was more than that, though. Nubt was Set's town, where he reigned as *Set Nubti*. She wondered what life had been like for the people who lived here, in this outpost between the gold mines of the eastern desert and the cities of Lower Egypt. She knew it had been a thriving area since before there were pharaohs. From the collection of homes in the southern town to the remains of structures around the temple and a structure that some argued was a pyramid, scholars knew Nubt had been a vibrant city with a large necropolis, a living city supporting a larger city of the dead, proud to have Set as its patron god.

She couldn't help wondering what it was like to have the god of chaos at the center of one's life. She'd been programmed from her studies at University College in London that Set was the bad guy. From the story of Isis and Osiris in which Set killed and dismembered Osiris because he coveted the throne—and Isis—to his battle with Horus for the right to rule Egypt, few stories existed that cast Set in a positive light.

One of the few stories that did was the recounting of Ra's journey through the Duat, the Egyptian netherworld. In that story, Set was more of a hero, standing at the front of Ra's solar boat, slaying the snake demon Apep to prevent it from killing Ra. Yet, even in that instance, Set didn't show modesty or humility. He boldly proclaimed that Ra was safe due to him—Set, his mighty arm, his sound aim.

If ever a god was in need of a public relations expert, Set was the one.

There had been pharaohs who had honored the desert god, though. Peribsen from the First Dynasty had, as did the eighteenth-dynasty military genius Thutmose III. Seti I and his descendants bore the god's name. So, Set wasn't all bad.

Memories sifted through her mind as she and

Bernie sifted a quadrant of the dig site. Slipping through a portal and landing on an alternate Giza Plateau, upon which had stood a temple dedicated to the Egyptian god of chaos. Talking to the Lady of Balance, who looked like an older version of Balm, causing her to question herself. Seeing Khefar tortured by a new Shadowling adversary, Marit. Channeling power, gorgeous power, Light and Shadow roiling through her, one hair short of too much. Knowing she could feel it again, if she allowed herself to slip.

"What's weighing so heavily on your mind?" Comstock asked.

Kira realized she still held the screen, but had been standing motionless, lost in thought. "What makes you think anything's wrong?"

"Kira." Comstock's voice brimmed with remonstration. "I'm dead, not senile. More than that, I'm a metaphysical construct that includes part of your psyche. I know when you're out of sorts."

"I never could hide anything from you, could I?"

"No." Comstock smiled. "Most of the time, I pretended not to notice. I didn't want to make you uncomfortable."

"I think I would have appreciated having you to talk to, Bernie," she said, her throat tightening. "I'm sorry I didn't confide in you."

"You can confide in me now." He lifted a trowel of debris onto the screen. "I always find that it's easier to apply myself to thinking things through by digging my hands into my work."

Kira looked down at her hands. Even in her dreams, she wore gloves. "When I get my hands down into my work, I'm either incapacitating or killing someone."

Her mentor reached over, took her hands. "True, if all you consider yourself to be is a Shadowchaser. But you are more than that. Your hands also help to properly identify and catalog hundreds of artifacts. Your hands are tools, not weapons. And there's nothing wrong with that."

"Thank you." She squeezed his hands. "I needed that."

"It's what I'm here for." He gave her an encouraging smile. "Now, why don't you tell me what's bothering you."

"Balm had a crate delivered to me today," she told him. "A driftwood box."

"A jewelry box?"

"No, more like a chest."

"I see. What sort of treasure is in this chest?"

Kira poured debris onto the sifter. A couple of dozen workmen were clearing away several grids while the field assistants documented each layer. The sounds of a dig soothed her, allowed her to think. "It supposedly contains some of the answers I've been looking for. The great mysteries of my life."

"Supposedly?" Comstock echoed. "You don't know for certain?"

"I haven't looked inside yet."

"Seriously?"

She could hear the surprise in Bernie's voice, and understood it. "I want to look, and yet I don't want to look at the same time. I know I'm being chickenshit, but I can't seem to help it."

"You are Kira Solomon." Comstock said sternly. "You take the Apis bull by the horns. You spit into the eye of Set's storm and laugh as the eclipse's Shadow engulfs the world. You walked behind the Veil of reality and sent a Fallen back to Shadow. You, my girl, are not afraid to look into a box."

"You have an amazing talent for putting things into perspective, Professor Comstock," Kira said, chagrined. "I guess it's stupid to be so cowardly."

"You aren't a coward." Comstock leaned forward. "Everything you've done, everything you've lived through, has been about this moment, about finding the truth. You even worship Ma'at, the goddess of truth. You have never once turned away from the truth, no matter how awful the view."

"So?"

"So open the box and acquire the truth," Comstock urged. "What is the worst that could happen?"

Kira didn't want to voice her fear. To speak it aloud, even here in this dreamscape, would be to give it life.

"You need to confront your fear." Comstock examined a piece of rubble. "If you can't do that here, where can you?"

Comstock had a point. She had to examine and acknowledge her fears. Only then could she face them, understand them, and then conquer them.

"Balm told me a bit about my mother," she finally said. "That she was part of a family of lightning spirits in West Africa. That her clan had made a decision to become human. But Balm didn't know anything about my father." She chewed on her lower lip. "What if— what if I find out that he's a Shadowling?"

"What if you do?"

Kira blinked at her mentor. "Well, it changes everything!"

"Why does it have to?" Comstock asked, the epitome of reason. "Why would that knowledge change who you were five minutes previous?"

"Because . . . because . . ." Kira thinned her lips. She didn't even have a half-assed rebuttal. So she'd find some lemons on the family tree. So what? She'd pick herself up as she usually did, make a big batch of lemonade, and go on with her life. She'd continue being the Hand of Ma'at. She'd continue being a Shadowchaser for as long as her Lightblade responded to her touch.

"You're right as usual," she said ruefully. "I'm tired of this hanging over my head. I'm tired of the what-ifs. I'm going to find the truth and then I'm going to deal with it."

Comstock beamed. "That's my girl!"

A shout rose from the workers near the outer wall of the temple. Kira quickly made her way up the rise to the mud brick barrier, Bernie following. Workers and field assistants parted like waves breaking before the bow of a ship as she approached. They huddled close as she knelt on the dry, hot earth.

"It's a *was* scepter," she said, carefully brushing bits of debris away. "One of the best preserved I've seen since the cache found in Tutankhamun's tomb. And it's intact."

She took a brush from one of the workers, then slowly worked to free the staff from its baked tomb. Somehow, here, it had been protected from the Nile's annual flooding, perfectly preserved by the dryness and heat of the western desert. If she thought about how something like this could still be found now, after thorough excavations by Petrie and others, the collection of red and black pottery, the dried bodies and other artifacts that enabled dating of several distinct pre-dynastic Naqada cultures, it was a fleeting thought.

The power staff was beautiful, about five feet long, wood sheathed and banded in gold. Two forked prongs served as the foot of the scepter, with the head of the Set-animal carved as the top. The *was* scepter was often depicted in carvings and tomb paintings in the hands of pharaohs and the gods as a symbol of their power and their ability to keep chaos at bay.

"Amazing," Comstock said, eyes dancing with the joy of discovery. His excitement erased years from his features. "Absolutely stunning. Go on, then."

"Go on and what?"

"It's your dig, so you should be the one to bring it back into the world," Comstock said, nodding with emphasis. "Go ahead, pick up the scepter and bring it to light."

Trembling with excitement, Kira wrapped her gloved hands around the wooden rod. She ran her hands along the length, separating the staff from the hard ground. When she was certain it was free, she straightened, holding the staff at arm's length in front of her.

Warmth sank into her fingers, and she realized that her gloves had vanished. The warmth became a hum that vibrated along the entire length of the power scepter, causing her hands to tingle. Tiny hairs along her arms stood on end as power thrummed through the staff, causing it to glow.

The workers, the excavation site, Comstock— everything fell away. Everything except the ruins of the temple. Stone by stone it rebuilt itself, rising out of the desert to dominate the skyline, reclaiming its former glory. The Temple of Set, with two granite statues of the Typhonic beast-god flanking the entrance, towering replicas of the power scepter gripped in massive hands.

For a moment she wasn't sure where she was. The temple looked the same as it had when she'd slipped through a portal into the alternate-Cairo, when she'd traveled completely behind Logic's Veil and met Solis, Lady of Between. But this wasn't Between. This was her dream. Set could have no power here.

As soon as she thought the god's name, the ground rumbled. The sands shifted in front of her as a massive stele pushed up into the air.

She recognized its image, having seen it on a tablet at the Manchester Museum. Set, wearing the dual crown of Upper and Lower Egypt, a *was* scepter in his left hand, an ankh in his right. To his right stood an altar adorned with lotus blossoms. At the top of the stele hieroglyphs proclaimed: SET OF NEBTI, LORD OF PROVISIONS, GREAT OF STRENGTH, POWERFUL OF ARM.

Set had never lost his good press in his hometown. The proclamations continued on the limestone and granite of the temple walls, colorfully etched and painted glyphs extolling the majesty and grandeur of the lord of the desert for all to read. SET, THE MAJESTIC ONE, SLAYER OF APEP, PROTECTOR OF RA, RULER OF NUBT, LORD OF THE DESERT.

The heavy rumbling of stone moving against stone

assaulted her ears. One of the Set statues moved, the trunk-like snout looming as he looked down at her. Except that it didn't seem like a statue, but something caught between stone and flesh. A voice sounded in her head, more an impression of words than sound. *Welcome, daughter.*

No, no, no. "I am not your daughter!"

Laughter like stone grinding against stone hit her like a percussive blast, almost pushing her to her knees. *You are a child of chaos, born of thunder and lightning. You cling to Ma'at and turn your back on Isfret for nothing. You belong with us.*

"Never!" She gripped the scepter like a fighting staff, prepared to defend herself. "I am the Hand of Ma'at. I am a Shadowchaser. I walk in the Light. Always."

The god's eyes flashed golden. *Think you to destroy me with my own power?*

The power scepter ripped free of her grasp, flew to the statue. The desert floor rose up about her, hot sand trapping her from the waist down. She struggled to move, frantic as the god slowly turned the staff so that the spiked prongs pointed at her.

Kira screamed as the tines embedded in her shoulder—the exact spot where the Fallen's dagger had pierced her months before. Pain erupted as Shadow magic poured into her like an electric current, burning her synapses, scorching her defenses. Her vision blurred, fading into a shimmering curtain of shifting green power as the blue sheen of Light met the swirling yellow of Chaos.

Don't fight, a soothing voice whispered in her head. *Accept your gift, what you are. The pain will subside once you do.*

She'd give anything to make the pain end. Would it be so bad? She already had some Shadow in her. The Lady of Between knew it, and the Lady of Light already suspected. So what was the point of fighting what everyone already believed of her anyway? It took too much energy to fight, and for what? It was power, nothing but power, power that she already had running through her veins, through her genes. If she claimed it, claimed her right, she'd be even better at her job. No, she'd be better *than* her job. She wouldn't have to work within Gilead's rules and restrictions, wouldn't have to worry about dealing with Sanchez's condescension or Balm's reticence. She could handle any Shadow or Fallen problems that crossed her path her own way. She didn't need them. She didn't need anyone.

She wrapped her hand around the staff. *Don't resist. Accept it, and soon it will be all over.*

Don't resist? Ha. Resistance was in her very nature.

Wake up, Kira, she admonished herself, fighting to claw herself free of the sand. *This is only a dream. This is not you. Wake up and walk into the Light!*

Chapter 8

Kira's eyes snapped open, her muscles locked against the need to bolt. Darkness arched above her, pierced by bars of ambient orange light coming through the shutters covering the window. She was in her bedroom. Not the desert, not Egypt.

She scrubbed the back of her hand across her mouth, needing to reassure herself that she could move, that she wasn't still trapped in the valley where dreams were all too real. Feeling Khefar's warm bulk beside her, hearing the deep soothing evenness of his breathing pulled her further from the nightmare and back into reality. Only when she was absolutely certain that she couldn't slide back into the dreamscape did she allow herself to relax completely.

The dream. With the exception of discussing Balm's box and her fears about it with Bernie, it was the same damn dream she'd had the last three nights. She'd also dreamt it twice before since they'd returned from London after their journey to restore the Vessel of Nun to its rightful place on Elephantine Island at Egypt's ancient boundary. The vision grew more vivid each time she experienced it. She felt the heat, the grit of the sand, the sun beating down on them. She had heard the click of tools and the excited, rolling cadence of the workers' voices as they moved and sifted rubble. She had even smelled the sweat as she, the interns, and the diggers excavated squared-off sections of the site.

She'd felt the weight of the *was* scepter, felt the power in it, the terror of the temple appearing. Felt the agony of the power staff digging into her shoulder, pumping Shadow and Chaos into her system.

Every sensation was as real as if she'd been awake, much like her waking dreams. Except that she controlled her waking dreams, or Balm did when Kira dreamspoke with the head of the Gilead Commission. This vision, dreamwalk, psychic interlude—whatever it was—she had no control over. What's more, she knew it was a dream but as much as she fought it, she couldn't escape it, couldn't change the outcome. Couldn't fight pulling the preserved *was* scepter free of the dirt, wrapping her bare hands around the gilded shaft, exulting in the power that had coursed through her. Not once had she thought of her Lightblade, of using the Light magic to protect and defend herself against all that Shadow magic.

Khefar's warm body and deep breathing beside her was a reassurance that she truly was awake and in her bedroom. In the handful of weeks since they'd come back from London, despite her occasional qualms, he'd fit neatly into her life and her home as if he'd always been there. Khefar was immune to her extrasense. She couldn't read him, could touch him without siphoning off his life force. The skin hunger, the need to feel another person's touch, still gripped her, but he was only too willing to sate it by sleeping skin to skin.

It should have been comforting, but now it wasn't.

Could she still allow herself to fall deeply asleep beside him? Not with such dangerous dreams stalking her sleep.

Khefar was right. Kira had changed, was changing. Now she understood what was happening. The dream confirmed what she'd wanted to deny: her powers were changing. More Shadow magic entwined with her own Light ability, and she didn't know what the outcome would be.

She didn't want to take any chances that her blended magic could be harmful to Khefar. Her regular touch ability had sent her sister to the hospital, put her in a coma. A wielding of her powers had caused her to injure one of her dearest friends. She didn't want to think what would happen if Shadow grew stronger inside her.

Slowly she extricated herself from beneath Khefar's arm and slid out of bed. She froze as his breathing changed, waiting tensely for it to deepen back to full sleep. Reassured by the return of his regular breathing pattern, she grabbed the tank top and yoga pants off her nightstand, awkwardly dressing as she headed out the bedroom door and down the stairs. She needed to shake off the dream, needed to think. Needed to rinse the dry-sand residue of the nightmare from her mouth.

In the kitchen, she grabbed the water pitcher from the fridge, and a glass. Kira filled it to the rim and then gulped down most of it. The cool liquid soothed her parched throat, rinsed the sand particles away. Another indicator of the realness of the dreamscape. Somehow Set was influencing her sleep, taking over. But why? What in the world could Set want with her?

She gripped the edge of the countertop to keep herself anchored as she remembered what the god had said to her. Words bounced around her skull, inducing a headache. Set wanted her to join them. Them who? *Welcome, daughter.*

Kira rubbed at her shoulder. She could believe a lot of things but she wouldn't believe she was related to Set. For one thing, the god was purported to be impotent, at least as far as the ancient myths were concerned. Then again, Set did have several wives and a few children associated with him in some stories. During thousands of years of Egyptian history, religion and myths had undergone many changes, not all of which were known, let alone understood.

Did he mean for her to become Shadow? Like hell that was going to happen. She could deal with not being human, but she refused to accept she was destined by kind or kin to become a Shadowling.

"I am not a child of Shadow," she whispered fiercely. "I will never be claimed by Chaos."

She drained the rest of the water. Despite all her protestations of being a loner, she knew she had a decent network of people who cared about her. Yet she didn't think she could talk to any of them about the dreams. Kira could talk to Wynne about Chasing, but not really about the big stuff, the close-to-the-quick things.

She wished Bernie were still around, her mentor who—unbeknownst to her—had known about and quietly aided her Shadowchasing duties. Though she hadn't thought she could confide in him about being a Chaser when he was alive, she could talk to him about a plethora of other things, from her touch ability to artifacts.

Now that he was dead—he lived on, so to speak, through special mementos he'd given her—Kira would have talked to Comstock about this dream. But Bernie had been *in the dream*, excavating Naqada with her. Bernie had all but said her family tree wasn't an issue. And Bernie had been the one to encourage her to pull the *was* scepter free of the sand.

Why would he do that? Surely Bernie—the real, now-dead Bernie—would be alarmed to know that there was Shadowling in her heritage. He'd been killed by a Shadowling, a seeker demon. He'd secretly worked for the Gilead Commission, which was all about fighting Shadow. Why would he encourage her to embrace it?

Her gaze fell on the driftwood chest sitting atop the dining table. Answers lay inside, or rather proof lay within. Truth about her origins. Balm had already shared some—that Kira's mother hailed from a tribe of lightning spirits that had their roots near the Fon of West Africa. Balm didn't know who Kira's father was, but everything seemed to point to him being a hybrid—or, more specifically, a Shadowling, if not one of the Fallen.

Kira pressed her knuckles to her forehead. The idea that her father was one of the heavy hitters of Shadow, one of the beings who'd fought in the First Battle against Order and Light at the beginning of time, made her ache all over. It was difficult to comprehend. Yet she had Comstock telling her it was all right, Balm's silent timing in sending the box, and Set reaching out to her from her own dreams. She didn't want her suspected parentage to be true, but what other truth could there be?

She'd always been painfully aware of how different she was. How nonhuman her abilities were. Yes, there were human-born telepaths who were also psychometrists, able to read impressions of a person by touching their personal objects. Kira knew her ability was different, though—a souped-up-on-steroids version. She could read an object and a person with a single touch, essentially downloading their thoughts, emotions, and memories in the ultimate invasion of privacy. That download drained the person she touched, often with fatal consequences if she read too long or too deeply.

With that sort of devastating talent, keeping apart from others was easy, even if it hurt. Becoming a Shadowchaser was one more way to distance herself from the mundane world, the human world. Even her cover profession as an antiquities specialist had her interacting with objects and cultures from the distant past instead of the here and now. She had to face it, she wasn't part of the living, breathing human world even when she tried to be, as if she'd known on some level that she wasn't supposed to be, genetically couldn't be.

She put the empty glass in the sink, the need to clear her head pressing down on her. Going downstairs to talk to Comstock by way of his pocket watch was out; she didn't think she could handle it if he encouraged her to take a walk on the Shadow side. Balm was incommunicado, and Kira could certainly guess what the Lady of Light would say about Shadow. Wynne and Zoo had needed the night off that Kira's attendance at the fund-raiser provided, and she didn't want to burden her friends with what as yet wasn't a big deal. Wynne would certainly worry, and Wynne already worried enough.

That left Khefar. You were supposed to be able to confide in the person you slept with, right? You couldn't get more intimate than sharing with the person you allowed to see you at your most vulnerable. Even though she trusted Khefar to have her back in a battle, even though they slept together, she couldn't tell him about the dreams.

Khefar had made a solemn vow to call the magic of the Dagger of Kheferatum, a mystical blade with the power to create and destroy, and use it to unmake her soul should she ever slide into Shadow. If she told him that she was sired by a Shadowling and Set wanted her to come to the family reunion, he'd have no choice. His honor would compel him to do what she asked of him, to do whatever it took to make sure she didn't become out of Balance.

"Dammit!" She thumped her fist against the counter. "I just want a little bit of time. Just some time to freaking breathe."

She jerked around and headed for the garage. Taking the bike out for a ride in the late-December air would clear her mind. At the very least, it would make her too cold to think. Clearing her head would do her a world of good, and nothing did that like bending low over her handlebars as she blazed down a straightaway. Maybe some of the local stunt bikers would still be out down near the stadium. Anything would be better than standing in the middle of her great room dreading going back to sleep.

Her house had been a warehouse and car repair shop in its former life, which meant the garage area had plenty of room for Khefar's Charger, her custom Buell, racking that held an assortment of tools and spare parts, and a couple of tall steel storage cabinets. Good thing she kept her bike leathers in the garage. It meant she wouldn't have to go upstairs and risk waking the Nubian.

Yeah, she was trying to sneak out of her own damn house and it irritated her. She rolled on a pair of thick socks before exchanging the yoga pants for black and blue leather racing pants complete with lightweight armor and padding. No matter how quickly she wanted to escape, she'd still play it safe while out on the bike. She didn't expect any seeker demons to attack, but the creatures didn't make a habit of announcing their presence.

She stomped into her boots as quickly as she could. Khefar wasn't a heavy sleeper and she had a feeling he'd eventually sense she wasn't in bed with him. Hopefully she'd be long gone before he woke up and he'd assume she was in her prayer room. She didn't want a babysitter and didn't want Khefar to think that he had to be one.

What was Khefar to her? She'd not really gotten that settled in her mind. Partner? She could accept that, as she could accept Wynne and Zoo getting involved in some of her Chases before they'd been recruited into Gilead. Lover? That skated into squishy emotional territory, a place she most certainly wasn't ready to go, even though he was the only person in the world with whom she could find the comfort of physical intimacy. What was love to a man who had lived thousands of years? Still, he had gifted her with Amanirenas's bracelet, a priceless historical artifact. Even if it wasn't a couple of thousand years old, you didn't give a solid gold arm cuff—one that obviously meant something to him—to someone you'd only known for a handful of months.

Then there were the times when Khefar quietly watched her, when she felt very much as if he were her jailer. Those times were the ones she hated the most, and they seemed to come more frequently of late.

She pulled on the matching jacket and grabbed her gloves. Ready to go—

Damn! She'd left her Lightblade upstairs. If she went up to get it, she ran the risk of waking Khefar. If she left home without it, she ran the risk of being vulnerable to a Shadow attack.

Frustration growled through her. She had no choice. It had been quiet for a while, with a minor skirmish or disagreement here and there to break up the monotony. That only meant a storm was on the way. Shadowlings still wanted the Dagger of Kheferatum. Someone needed to step in and fill the power vacuum that had appeared after she'd sent the Fallen called Enig back to Shadow. Then there was Marit, the Shadow Adept she'd tussled with in Cairo. She was out there somewhere, no doubt still incensed over the hand Kira had sliced off.

Kira shook her head. Yeah, it would be suicidal to leave home without her Lightblade. Whatever the state of her mind, suicidal she was not.

Three nights straight.

Khefar folded his hands behind his head, debating. Three nights in a row. This was not the first time

Kira had awakened, carefully extricated herself from the bed, and gone downstairs until sunrise. For three consecutive nights, he'd feigned sleep, keeping his breathing regular and even as she'd stealthily left the bedroom. These nights weren't isolated: Kira had gotten up early several times since they'd returned from London three weeks ago.

At first, his ego had assumed that Kira simply wasn't used to sharing a bed with anyone or anything, not even a pet, since her touch ability could drain the life out of any living thing. But with Khefar, Kira couldn't siphon off his energy or read his thoughts and emotions. Besides, she'd slept well enough beside him in London and Cairo. So sleeping next to him wasn't the problem.

He sighed, sat up, and flipped on the light on his side of the bed. He knew Kira was troubled. She had enough on her mind—beyond her "day job" as an antiquarian and her duties as a Shadowchaser, she was dealing with her mentor's death and memorial service, inheriting his estate . . . and what she'd learned during their journey behind the Veil. And those were the things she'd talked about.

Unspoken were her thoughts about her foster mother, the Balm of Gilead, also known as the Lady of Light. Kira had discovered that Balm was one of three "sisters" who embodied the order of the universe. Kira had met Solis, the Lady of Balance, the place between Light and Shadow. There was a Lady of Shadow, and Khefar could only hope that Kira never crossed paths with the Dark One. Khefar knew from experience that dealing with any of the ladies was an exercise in frustration, and even fear.

And, despite their mutual knowledge that she had Shadow within her, beyond his pledge to use the dagger to unmake her if she ever succumbed, they had never discussed it. It was the elephant in the room that they both intentionally ignored.

Kira also refused to elaborate on the revelation of her origins. She'd painfully admitted that she wasn't fully human once they'd returned from behind the Veil, but she hadn't spoken of it since. Instead she'd buried it, buried it deep, buried it like she'd buried her emotions, her grief and losses and anger. Perhaps even her heart.

Khefar swung his legs over the side of the bed. Something weighed heavily on Kira, heavily enough to disturb her sleep. He did what he could to ease her burden—partner her on patrols, assist with research, put the seat back down every time—anything to give her one less thing to worry about. And yet, she went to bed exhausted only to rouse from sleep and quit their bed a few hours later.

Something made her leave the bed in the middle of the night. It was time to discover what that something was.

He slipped on a pair of jeans, found a dark green sweater to pull on. Grabbing both their blades, he made his way out of the bedroom, traversing the open walkway over to the metal switchback stairs and down to the dimly lit main level. He'd memorized the layout of the converted warehouse a few weeks ago, though Kira had made some changes. The storeroom in the short hallway past the kitchen had been changed into an exercise room in which they practiced their knife-fighting and hand-to-hand-combat skills. The high-top table had regained its true purpose as a dining table, though books still balanced beside each place setting. More shelves and cabinets had been installed around the perimeter of the great room, to further organize Kira's collection and incorporate the artifacts and treasures her late handler had bequeathed to her. Changes without, neat and orderly. The changes within, Khefar believed, were anything but tidy.

The weathered box still sat where he'd placed it earlier. It didn't appear that Kira had opened it yet. Why not? She'd told him she'd searched for answers her entire life. Now that she had those answers literally at her fingertips, she seemed strangely reluctant to literally pull the lid off.

He heard a thump from the garage and went to investigate, his dagger at the ready. Kira stood near the metal supply cabinets, hurriedly pulling on black and blue bike leathers. Going for a ride and not bothering to tell him. She was running from something. He was determined that it wouldn't be him.

He stepped through the doorway. She spun, helmet raised high over her head, ready to do serious damage. "Easy," he said. "I brought your Lightblade to you. You left it upstairs."

She made no move to take it, staring at him with those now-hazel eyes of hers. When she spoke, her voice had a dark edge to it. "Are you spying on me?"

"Spying would imply that I'm reporting my findings to someone. I'm not."

She faced him fully. "And what are your findings?"

"I don't have any yet."

A faint smile pushed the shadows from her eyes. "Liar."

"All right." He folded his arms across his chest, prepared to argue with her if necessary. "I find that you have bags under your eyes. I find that you've lost weight. And I find your temper frayed."

"My temper was never all that finely woven to begin with."

"True." He waited a moment, but she didn't attempt to correct his observations or offer excuses for them. Instead she reached for the Lightblade.

"Thanks for bringing this down," she said, sounding sheepish and on edge at the same time. Made sense, given the nightmares and the literal Pandora's box in the next room. She had a right to be on edge. "I was about to come back upstairs for it."

"No problem," he said, handing the dagger over. He strapped his dagger on, situating it into the side rigging under his left arm, the hilt across his chest. "Did we get a call?"

"No. Still have the night off."

Unease slithered through him. So it wasn't Gilead's business that had her suited up. If she thought he'd go back to bed and let her head out by herself, she was going to be disappointed. "You want to ride double or should I take my car?"

Irritation drew her eyebrows down. "What if I want to be alone?"

"You can be alone. On the bike. I can follow you in my car."

She put her Lightblade on the shelf, then unzipped and removed her jacket. "You know, this is getting old.

What do you think is going to happen if I go off by myself?"

With everything that had happened to her since he'd known her, he didn't want to take any chances. "Maybe nothing." He stepped farther into the garage. "Maybe something. I don't know, which is why I'd rather go with you."

"Like you're leaving me with any choice." She thrust her arms through the leather straps that allowed her to wear the Lightblade sling style across her chest so that the short racing jacket would cover it. Khefar knew from his brief stint as a motorcycle racer in Europe that the body armor and protective padding in her pants prevented her from strapping the blade to her leg in any usable fashion.

"Hey." He dropped a hand on her shoulder, halting her movements. "If it seems like I'm taking your choices away, I'm sorry. I certainly didn't intend that. I know you can handle yourself and you did fine before I came along. My problem is that I've seen what comes after you, so I'm going to be concerned every time you step out that door. So yeah, I'm either coming with you or I'm coming after you."

Discomfort crossed her features, as if she'd smelled sour milk. She usually reacted that way whenever he expressed any sort of sentiment or care for her. She shrugged his hands away. "I don't need a babysitter. Stop treating me like I'm a toddler clutching at firecrackers."

The woman could try the patience of Job. "Hair of Isis, I'm not trying to nanny you, and I certainly don't want to treat you like a baby. Besides, it's not about you."

"What do you mean it's not about me? This whole conversation is about me!"

Not this time, and he hated admitting it to her. "You wanting to go off by yourself is about you. Me not wanting to let you is about me."

"Huh? What the hell does that even mean?"

He cursed under his breath, took a couple of steps back from her. "It means my concern for you . . . upsets my equilibrium. I could not rest here while you're out there with who knows what lurking. So I'm coming with you or following you for my own damn peace of mind."

A grin split her face, reminding him of a mad scientist or a hungry were-hyena. Neither were good. He scowled at her. "What's that look for?"

Instead of answering, she cupped his face between her palms and planted a big, sloppy kiss on his lips. "Thank you. That makes perfect sense now."

She broke away before he could reciprocate, leaving him feeling decidedly off-balance. A usual occurrence around her. "I'm glad one of us understands what just happened."

"Maybe I'll explain later." She zipped back into her jacket, pulled on her gloves, and handed him her spare helmet. "You man enough to ride behind a woman?"

"Yes." He took the helmet. "And man enough to look cool doing it."

Chapter 9

The temperature had dropped considerably while they'd slept, which suited Kira fine. Nothing like thirty-degree temperatures to bring cold clarity.

With the half-moon high in the sky, she headed for the interstate, Khefar riding pillion. She was glad he didn't have some male ego problem with sitting behind her. If he did, he'd be trying to keep up with her in his Charger instead of having his hands on her waist. As a four-thousand-year-old man, misogyny should have been second nature to him. Apparently he'd managed to learn a thing or two about women over the centuries.

Or maybe he'd learned the right things to say to get his way.

A couple of nights a week, bikers and a few car aficionados gathered in one of the parking lots near Turner Field. While a few of the young men showed off their skills, others gathered to watch, hang out, and occasionally exchange information. Despite the late hour and low temps, a sizable crowd still occupied the parking lot. Guess the police were too busy to bother with loiterers.

The groups of bikers and spectators were a disparate crowd, drawn together by their love of fast machines. One mixed clutch of bikers stood apart from the others, either by their own choice or because the others subconsciously recognized them as different. Other.

Kira eased her bike in among a large pack of other motorcycles while spectators watched as a guy on a red and yellow Ducati did a combo wheelie down the open swath of asphalt. A line of stunt bikers waiting their turn snaked to the left. She stopped the bike, then dropped the kickstand. Khefar hopped off the back as she pulled off her helmet and shook out her braids.

Conversation ebbed. A wave of recognition passed over the hybrids gathered nearby, a ripple of uneasy curiosity. Kira realized she hadn't been out to the gathering since before Bernie's death. Or, more importantly to the hybrids, since she'd brought down the Fallen at Demoz's club.

The arrival of any Chaser would grab the interest of hybrids; Kira showing up demanded even more attention.

Gilead grouped the denizens of Shadow and Light along the same scale. Hybrids were the mixed-blood offspring of humans and the lesser children of Light and Shadow who came through the Veil when the first battle between Light and Shadow nearly ripped existence apart. Most had a human form that enabled them to blend into society undetected.

By association, determination, and dedication, humans could eventually become Adepts, wielders of magic, or Avatars, hosts for the non-corporeal beings known as the Fallen. The Fallen were the offspring of Chaos, as old as the first battle between Light and Shadow when the balance of the universe was at stake.

They got their name from being on the losing end of that first battle: they "fell" through the various dimensions to this plane of existence. The only way they could assume physical form was by taking over willing or corrupted humans as their Avatars. Though they promised the human power and riches in return, humans simply weren't able to contain that much power. Human hosts eventually rejected the Fallen, but lost their lives in the process.

Fallen, as the top of the Shadow food chain, were extremely tough to kill. They also tended to bully the other hybrids in their area, coercing them through threat to join the Fallen's cause. The only problem was, any hybrids who chose to back a losing Fallen also lost their lives when that Fallen was sent back to Shadow. And the only one who could take out a Fallen was a Shadowchaser. Their existence necessitated the Shadowchasers' existence. In head-to-head combat, Chasers lost as many times as they won, if not more. It was part of the reason why Chasers didn't have a long life expectancy, and why they needed to be extra tough.

That Kira had brought down one of the Fallen and lived to tell about it had elevated her status in the hybrid community. It meant that the city had stayed relatively quiet while she'd handled her business in London. That quiet wouldn't last, however. It never did.

"Look what the cat dragged in!"

Kira watched as one of the young men separated himself from the rest of the pack. She recognized D'Aurius Amoye, one of two sons of the matriarch of the Westside were-hyena pack. "Don't you mean dog?"

Were-hyena, who called themselves *bultungin* from

their ancestral home in northeast Nigeria, were matriarchal like their natural counterparts. D'Aurius, whom Kira had seen at various bike events around town, had left the pack early on, though he still kept in contact. He looked to be about nineteen in human years with his close-cropped tight curls fading into the dark chocolate of his skin, though Kira knew were-hyenas aged differently.

"What's up, Chaser?" he asked, after a quick glance at his friends for support. "Ain't seen you around here in a hot minute."

"I know, but I'm here now." She tapped his gloved fist with her own. "How's it been so far tonight?"

"Oh, you know how it goes," he said. Even with the black and red Atlanta Falcons leather jacket covering him, one could see he had the medium build of most male were-hyenas, and an open, kind-hearted nature that would set him at odds with almost every type of were-family. He would have been an omega in his mother's clan, but males were ranked even lower than the lowest female.

"Most of the good riders have already packed up and headed out," he told her. "Are you gonna get out there and show us some stuff? I heard you pulled a rolling stoppie on North Avenue."

"I'm only hanging out tonight," Kira told him. "And you can't believe everything you hear. But if I had done it, you can bet it was epic."

"Sweet." D'Aurius gave Khefar a once-over glance. "You gonna introduce me?"

"Sure." Kira turned to Khefar, standing silently behind her. He seemed even more tense than usual, and she wondered if he wasn't used to riding on the back of a motorcycle. Surely the opportunity had come up once or twice in the last century. "Khefar, D'Aurius Amoye. D'Aurius, Khefar."

"That's all I get?" D'Aurius asked, eyes wide. "You reach back to the motherland and claim a guy for the back of your bike, and all we get is a name? He don't even smell all the way human."

"'He' can speak for himself, *bultungin*," Khefar said, making the word sound like an epithet. The permanent scowl deepened to antagonistic. "Ask me what you want to know, pup, if you dare."

D'Aurius bared his teeth. It was an instinctive move, but instinctive didn't equal smart. "Yo, man, who you calling pup?"

Crap. Khefar had to have spent a couple hundred centuries traveling around Africa during his four millennia. Aside from spending time with Kandake Amanirenas in Meroë, it made sense that he'd journeyed all over the continent and encountered were-hyenas during that time. Apparently, that encounter hadn't been all hearts and flowers. Whatever Khefar did or didn't know about were-hyenas, he had to know that males weren't intimidated by other males.

She'd noticed at least one banaranjan in the cluster of hybrids. Of course they'd be drawn to all the human adrenaline soaking the air. That didn't mean she wanted them drawn to her little group, which was certain to happen if the two men kept up their intimidation attempts.

"Guys. We're in a public place, the hybrids are staring and no doubt hearing everything you're saying. I'd rather not have the police shut down this gathering because two guys who should know better decided to show their asses. Stand the fuck down."

D'Aurius, used to taking orders from women, immediately dropped his gaze. Khefar took a few seconds longer to comply. Kira pushed between them, shoving Khefar back as she grabbed the were-hyena by the elbow. "What the hell, D'Aurius?"

"Escort me away for a private talk," he whispered. "I'm going to resist, at least a little."

Kira, recognizing a face-saving move when she saw one, tightened her grip on the young man's jacket, then spun on her heel, dragging him along behind her.

"Hey, I didn't do nothin'!" D'Aurius exclaimed, sounding every bit the harassed put-upon victim and not the perpetrator.

"That's for me to decide," Kira retorted, conscious of the gaggle of hybrids watching their every move. She led the young hybrid a distance away so that neither the other hybrids nor the humans could hear them over the bikers running stunts.

She let him go as Khefar joined them. "All right, we've got as much privacy as we're bound to get out here. What's with the show?"

D'Aurius straightened his jacket, glancing sidelong at Khefar. "Do you trust him?"

"More than most," Kira said, which was true. After that dominance display with Bale earlier in the evening and now the were-hyena, however, Khefar was almost like a stranger.

They watched a rider blow by them doing a

no-handed wheelie. "Does this have something to do with your clan?" she asked when the noise had died down. Clan business was the only reason D'Aurius would want to talk to her privately. Pack issues weren't shared with anyone and everyone.

"I heard that there's a challenge," D'Aurius said, his features pinched.

"Are you sure? You haven't been mixed up in the pack since you were what? Sixteen?"

"I'm sure."

"Is your mother not healthy? And what about your sisters?"

"Kandake Amoye is healthy—or at least she was the last time I saw her. DeVonne isn't the one making the challenge, and neither is DeRhonda."

That made sense. Dolores Amoye had led her clan for more than thirty years, Kira knew. The matriarch's daughters were both strong and smart, and more than capable of fulfilling their hereditary duty of leading the were-hyenas. They were also completely devoted to their mother. Neither would seek to take Kandake Amoye's place until the kandake was ready to hand over power and move to Great Mother status. "Who's the challenge from, then?"

"Roshonda Biers."

Kira had heard the name before, and searched her memory to put details to name. Roshonda couldn't be much older than D'Aurius. What the young woman lacked in years she made up for in deviousness, though. Still, she was nowhere near experienced enough to head up the Westside were-hyena clan.

"Why are you telling me this, D'Aurius?" she asked. "You know I don't get involved in internal power struggles."

"I know you don't, but this don't feel right."

"How would you know?" Khefar interjected. "You haven't been part of the day-to-day pack activities for a while."

D'Aurius rolled his eyes. "I might not live with the clan anymore, but that doesn't mean I don't know what's going on with my own family."

"Khefar." She held up a hand. With his type of help, she wouldn't be able to get any information out of the young hybrid. She turned back to D'Aurius. "Is your mother seriously entertaining this challenge?"

"She has no choice."

He fell silent as another bike blasted by. "Roshonda's been on the fringe of the clan since her mother died, almost as long as I have. She likes the protection of being associated with the clan without having to do any of the heavy lifting of actually making a meaningful contribution, you know what I'm saying?"

"So why is she suddenly making a power play?"

"That's what I'm trying to tell you. It's out of the blue. She suddenly started making noise about how there needs to be a change, that the clan is limiting itself because Kandake Amoye has grown complacent."

"Complacent? Hardly." Antagonizing a were-hyena matriarch in her prime was a suicidal move. "From what I know of Roshonda, she has a healthy sense of self-preservation. Criticizing the current clan matriarch isn't like her."

"I know. That's why I think she's got some outside help."

That would be trouble. "Who?"

"I don't know, and neither do my sisters. I got a feeling that Roshonda's going to try to pull something. She's never done anything the right way if the wrong way is easier."

"She's still got to work within the traditions," Kira pointed out. "There are enough old-school members of the pack who won't take kindly to Roshonda pulling anything. They should be able to keep her in line."

"Why don't you go?" D'Aurius suggested. "If you go oversee the challenge, that may keep Roshonda from trying anything against my mother."

Kira considered it. She didn't get involved in the day-to-day activities of the hybrids who called Atlanta home. That was good business. Then again, she needed to make sure none of the hybrid communities imploded or caught the attention of mundane law enforcement. That was also good business.

"When is the challenge?"

"Two days from now, in the center courtyard at sunset," D'Aurius said, relief smoothing his features. "So you'll go?"

"It won't hurt to patrol over near that area around sunset," Kira said. "I can stop in and pay a visit to your mother while I'm at it."

"Thank you, Chaser, I appreciate it." He turned to head back to his friends, taking a few steps before pausing. "There's one more thing."

"What?" Kira asked, painfully aware of Khefar's disapproval.

"Have you recommended me yet?"

Damn. She was hoping the hybrid had forgotten. "I thought you'd change your mind."

"Yeah, right. And do what? Boost cars or sell drugs?"

"You could join the human military," she pointed out. "Your kind can pass the human physical. You're not tied to lunar or solar phases for your shape-shifting, so you could fit in anywhere. Take some time to explore the world, experience everything—anything."

"The military is full of changelings in the closet," D'Aurius retorted, waving his hand in dismissal. "And if I could fit in anywhere, why can't I fit in with Gilead?"

He had her there. She could feel Khefar's eyes on her as she tried to come up with a suitable answer.

"You don't think I can handle it, do you?" D'Aurius guessed, his shoulders slumping. "That's why you don't want to recommend me."

"No, that's not it at all," Kira said hastily. "Chaser training is nothing like growing up in a were-hyena clan. It's four years of willingly and unwillingly putting your mind, body, and spirit on the line between Light and Shadow. It makes human boot camp look like preschool. The final exam is called the Crucible for a reason, and claiming your dagger if you make it through training can be even more dangerous. There are easier paths to walk in life, D'Aurius. I really want you to be sure before you step onto this one."

The young were-hyena squared his shoulders, his gaze unwavering on hers. He nodded. "I am sure."

She studied him for a long moment. In all her years on Santa Costa, she had seen plenty of novices who'd looked like him, eager, burning with the conviction of being called to serve the Light. Then there had been those for whom Shadowchasing was the only way to survive, those who danced a fine edge between madness and sanity, like she had.

Most Shadowchasers began their training between sixteen and seventeen years of age. She'd been an anomaly, entering training at twelve. She was still an anomaly, but that didn't mean she'd been the only one.

"All right, D'Aurius."

A grin split the were-hyena's face, giving Kira a good indication of what he'd look like in his alternate form. "Thank you, Chaser Solomon," he said. "You won't regret the faith you placed in me."

"Don't thank me yet," she cautioned. "I'm going to discuss this with the section chief. The final decision is hers."

"If you get me an interview with her, I can prove to her that I'm Shadowchaser material."

Kira suppressed a snort. She'd like to be a fly on the wall, if only to see Sanchez's expression as she dealt with the young changeling. Telling the very human section chief a male were-hyena wanted to become a Shadowchaser would be entertaining enough.

"Like I said, I'll put in a word with the section chief. After that, we'll see what we see."

"Cool. I owe you one!"

D'Aurius ran back to join his friends as the crowds began to disperse. Kira turned to Khefar, her hands raised. "Dude, what the hell?"

"What do you mean?"

"You stepped on my toes. I have to maintain order

in the hybrid community here, which means I need to be able to talk to people. I don't know what that attitude of yours was, but you and it can both stay home next time."

"You need someone to watch your back."

"I need someone who's not going to get in my way while watching my back," she retorted. "I'd rather come out alone than have you antagonizing hybrids for no reason. This city is my responsibility. I have to live with these people. You don't."

There was enough ambient light in the parking lot for her to see his jaw clench. "Sorry I stepped on your toes."

Not even the thinnest thread of remorse lined his voice. Okay, so the encounter with the were-hyena was a big deal for some reason. "Mind telling me what the hell that was about?"

"What?"

"Don't you 'what' me, Khefar." She crowded him, their noses almost touching. "D'Aurius is still young by bultungin and human standards. You, however, are old enough and experienced enough to know better. What's your deal?"

He glanced at the thinning crowd. "Not here. I'll tell you when we get home."

"Fine." She turned and stalked toward the bike. "But if you think I'm going to let it go, you've got another thing coming."

Every mile closer to home ratcheted up the tension in Khefar's gut. The longer he was around Kira, the more opportunities there would be to expose his past.

Thousands of years of action and reaction had happened since he'd ended his mourning and decided to follow through on the charge he'd accepted from Isis. A lot of it had been good, a lot of it had been bad. Some of it had even been tragic. Many things he had forgotten, and still more he wished to hell he could forget.

He didn't blame Kira for getting pissed at him over his standoff with the young were-hyena. He was surprised by his own reaction too. He'd schooled himself to get his job done without the complication of emotions. It was easier that way. But the bultungin had gotten to him in ways he could neither ignore nor forgive. And now he had to tell Kira why.

It was still a few hours till daylight by the time they returned home. Khefar knew Kira should get more rest before heading back to the exhibit at the Congress Center. She had to run by the Carlos Museum as well. He also knew that she wouldn't put off getting answers from him, no matter how tired she was.

She gave him time to take his jacket off before she pounced. "All right, we're here. Talk."

He hesitated. Words weren't easy on the best of days. Dancing across hot coals would be easier than this conversation.

Kira settled one hand on her hip. "Khefar, if you weasel out of telling me this story, so help me, I will kill you and store your body in a deep freezer until I'm good and ready to resurrect you."

"Would you really do that?"

"Would you really want to find out?"

He almost reached for his dagger, which would have been a stupid move. Kira was on edge, and it wouldn't take much to push her over and have her draw her Lightblade against him. As interesting as it would be to see which one of them would win with their lives on the line, Khefar didn't want to do anything to propel Kira further into Shadow, not when she had enough of it surging through her as it was. The only reason he was in her house—and her bed—was because she trusted him. He didn't want to ruin that.

She folded her arms across her chest, her defenses at maximum. "Let me break this down for you. In two days I have to go into the den of the Westside were-hyena clan. It's not the best of neighborhoods on a good day. If there's an outside force stirring things up, it's going to get a helluva lot worse when a Shadow-chaser shows up. If you're going to back me up, I need to know that you're not going to screw things up six ways to Sunday and leave me in a shitstorm because you have a bug up your butt about the bultungin."

"Holy hyperbole," he said, dropping his hands to his sides.

"I'm an archaeologist, not an English major." She made a show of unbuckling her Lightblade, placing it carefully on the kitchen counter. "I think it's pretty obvious that you've encountered the bultungin before."

His sudden humor fled. "I have."

She cut her eyes at him. "And it wasn't all hearts and flowers, I'm assuming?"

"Not a bit." Khefar answered. Ghost images danced behind his eyes, half-formed specters of a time he'd rather forget. "I spent some time in Nigeria, in the northern part of the country. There were a couple of villages there that were completely populated by were-hyenas. May still be, for all that I know. Some say they were hyenas who learned to become human, rather than humans who learned to become hyenas. Regardless, they acted like their natural cousins. I learned the hard way that they're best to be avoided, especially when you are a lone male."

"Did someone try to turn you into a were-hyena?" she asked carefully, as if feeling her way across a minefield. Except that he was the one in danger of being hit by shrapnel, not her.

"A man doesn't have to be turned to give to the gene pool," he said, his voice tight. "Though I'm not sure *give* is the right word to use. If the matriarch considered a male a viable stud, he was captured, kept, and encouraged to . . . perform."

Kira stared at him. "'Encouraged'? You mean against your will?"

He nodded curtly. Funny how he couldn't remember images, but he could remember sounds: the eerie crying laughter-howl of the full pack, the panting breath of the dominant female, men making light of their "sentence" until they realized they had to mate both were-hyena forms, the pleas and cries of captive men pushed beyond their mental and physical limits. "Raped, tortured, they didn't care what it took as long as they got what they wanted. The matriarchs aren't called *lipwereri* for nothing."

"Lipwereri?"

"Man-eater."

"Oh." Horror flowed across her face, then was quickly suppressed. "How did you end up there?"

A safer question. "Isis sent me to retrieve a young

woman. I managed to spirit her away, but I was caught during our escape."

"You mean you sacrificed yourself so she could get out."

He grunted. "You know me that well, huh?"

"You did it for me," she reminded him, her voice soft. "I find it hard to believe that in four thousand years I'm the only one you've truly risked your life for."

No, she wasn't the first, but if he managed to protect Kira and see her through whatever plan Ma'at and Isis had for them, she would be the last.

Kira felt her way toward another question. "So the bultungin captured you, and I can guess that they weren't too happy that you helped the female. How long were you with them?"

His jaw worked. "Three seasons."

"Three quarters of a year?"

"No." He stomped down every bit of emotion. *Tell it and get it done. Satisfy her curiosity and she'll never ask you any of this personal crap again.* "Three years. Once they found out I was a quick healer, I was also used to teach the young ones how to hunt."

She made a sound, something between a curse and a half-caught cry. The Dagger of Kheferatum throbbed in its holster beneath his arm, reacting to Kira's unseen flare of power.

He spread his hands, hoping to end the conversation. "As you can see, I escaped. That's my history with the were-hyenas."

"Dammit, Khefar." Anger and power flared in her eyes. "Three friggin' years? Where the hell was Anansi, and why didn't he help you?"

"Politics from on high. The local god had more power and more clout with the were-hyena than a West African trickster, so Anansi couldn't directly interfere."

"So he helped indirectly?" Anger still thrummed through her voice. "Tell me he did something."

"He is a spider, remember? Escaping took three years. Anansi sent a venomous spider, one that had never been seen in Nigeria before or since. Four young bultungin died and several more fell violently ill. In the panic I made a break for it, got chased, and ended up falling off a cliff and drowning in a river with a spear in my gut."

"Oh." She was silent for a long moment after that, her hands fisted at her sides. Finally, she looked up at him. Neither Light nor Shadow filled her eyes but something human, something just as powerful. "I want to hug you," she said, her voice crumbling. "Is that stupid?"

The tension inside him eased. He held out his arms. "No, it's not stupid."

She pressed against him, throwing her arms around his neck and hanging on as if her life depended on it. He ran his hands up and down her spine. The sound of rustling cloth, the sound of *her*, pushed back those remembered noises, drove them back into the dark and distant past where they belonged.

After a long moment she spoke, her voice warm against his neck. "The Westside were-hyenas haven't had a challenge for leadership in more than twenty years, and this one is from an unexpected and questionable source. Someone has to oversee it."

His hands stilled. "And that someone is you."

"Yes. They don't like Gilead field agents all that much—they think their need to follow regulations makes them weak. A Shadowchaser, especially a female one, should be seen as strong. There isn't anyone else."

"Hey." He stepped back, holding her at arm's length. "Don't apologize for doing your job. Especially not to me. Of course you have to go. And I'm going with you."

She searched his face. He hoped liked hell it projected calm acceptance instead of gut-wrenching anxiety. "You know you don't have to go with me if you think it will be too intense."

He shrugged. "I've been through worse." At the moment, he couldn't think of anything that was worse than being a sexual prisoner and prey of the bultungin, and he didn't want to try. No sense bringing more horrifying memories to the surface.

She reached up to touch him then, her hand hesitating before cupping his cheek. "I know you have. That doesn't mean the time with the bultungin didn't leave a lasting impression. It's okay to take a breather."

"I won't let you go alone. Besides, these are Americanized were-hyenas, right? They must have changed greatly to prosper and blend into American society." He hoped like hell they had.

"I don't know about that," Kira said, concerned. "Atlanta does have a large black population so it's easier to blend in. Also, this particular clan took over a housing project over on the west side. People have a certain perception of places like that, which suits the were-hyenas well. They've been sort of isolated."

He fought rising apprehension. "So this could be good, or this could be all kinds of bad."

She covered his hand, making him realize he'd gripped the hilt of his dagger. "Yeah, but we've got a couple of days before we have to worry about that. Take that time to decide if you really want to go or not. I certainly won't think any less of you if you decide not to. I don't know if I could do it, if I had gone through everything you have."

"You would, because no one else can do your job like you can. It's the same reason why I'm going with you."

She drew back with surprise. "Does that mean you're going to take Balm up on her offer to become a Shadowchaser?"

"No. My job is to protect your back. And no one can do that job like I can."

Her lips curved. "Wynne might have a thing or two to say about that when we meet up with her and Zoo for lunch tomorrow."

"Tomorrow?"

"I mean, later today. Wynne wants the complete rundown of the exhibit. I thought I told you."

"Must have put it out of my mind." Khefar grunted. "I'd rather deal with the were-hyenas."

She stilled, caution filling her eyes. "Why would you say that?"

He shrugged again. "I don't know. No reason."

Stubbornness mixing in with the caution. "You're being evasive."

"I'm being guarded," he clarified. "It's only a feeling. I don't have anything other than my gut to go on."

Kira stepped back from him, wrapping her arms about her abdomen. He wondered if she realized that she made the gesture when something stressed her and she wanted comfort. "What is your gut telling you?" she asked, as if dreading the answer.

He decided to be blunt. "Something's going on with the Marlowes. I don't know if it's the Gilead training they've been through or if it's the work in Egypt finally catching up to them. If Wynne thinks no one is looking, she seems troubled, like she's thinking hard about something. As for Zoo—my dagger reacted to him differently the last time we were all together."

"What?" Kira dropped her hands, her gaze automatically going to the Dagger of Kheferatum tucked beneath his arm. "Are you serious? How did it react to him?"

"Zoo's magic is mostly healing magic, with some defensive spells thrown in. The dagger didn't see him as a threat before. Lately, though, the dagger has been reacting to Zoo as if he's a threat."

Tension blanketed Kira's shoulders. "You think he's dabbling in Shadow magic?"

"I don't know. I do know something's changed, and it hasn't been a good change."

He watched as Kira worked through the news. A lot had happened to Kira and her friends in the last couple of months. He doubted that any of them had had time or opportunity to come to grips with all of it. Hell, if he still carried the scars of his time with the bultungin, he couldn't imagine what was going on in Wynne's or Zoo's mind.

"Okay, I'll find some way to broach the subject with Wynne while we're at lunch tomorrow. Hopefully she'll open up to me."

"And if she doesn't?"

"Then, I guess I have one less person to watch my back. Like that's anything new."

"You're not going to lose me."

A small smile bowed her lips. "Of course."

He could tell that she didn't believe him. Well, he would have to convince her.

"Hey." He wrapped a hand around the back of her neck, pulled her back to him. "You're not going to lose me, Kira Solomon. I told you I'm going to have your back and I meant it."

Her eyes searched his face, looking for conviction. She must have found it, because the smile she gave him this time was truer, and reached her hazel eyes. "So you'll have my back," she said, her voice soft. "What about the rest of me?"

He tightened his hold on her. "I'm sure I can come up with something to satisfy you."

Chapter 10

S o how did the gala go last night?" Wynne asked, sliding into one of the padded wooden chairs of the half-booth in the restaurant most people affectionately called the Garage. She had dyed her hair again, and her wild bob was now jet-black with a green streak at her right temple.

"About what you'd expect," Kira answered, automatically scanning the restaurant that couldn't decide if it wanted to be a pub paying homage to roller derby or a dining establishment that catered to drinkers more than diners. As usual, she had her back against the wall, giving her a good view of the entire floor. Khefar sat beside her, Wynne across, and Zoo next to his wife. It was right after the lunch rush, and the tavern was at less than half capacity, giving them the opportunity to talk business if they wanted to.

Dining out was always a harrowing proposition for Kira, and she had learned to apply a process similar to the clock method used by the blind. She blocked off her quarter of the table, her boundary marked by condiments and tableware. She would leave her gloves on until food and drinks arrived. Once everyone was situated she'd be able to take the gloves off and send a blast of her extrasense to discharge any psychic residue.

It was something Balm had taught her before her first Shadowchaser lesson, and though she had overheard people calling her phobic, using this method enabled her to eat food she didn't have to grow and prepare herself.

"Do you have pictures?" Wynne asked.

Khefar obliged her by pulling out his smartphone. "Here you go."

Wynne grabbed it with a squeal of delight. "Sweet. Hey, Kira actually showed some leg? You go, girl!"

"Yeah, well, I'm back to normal now," Kira said grumpily. She turned to Khefar. "I thought I'd kept my eye on you pretty well. When did you have time to take pictures?"

He shrugged. "We posed for a number of pictures last night. It was easy enough to have one of the photographers take extras. That Mr. Hammond certainly made sure he was in every single shot."

"Is this him?" Wynne turned the screen around.

Kira nodded. "Yes. I'm not sure which one Hammond's more interested in—the exhibit or the attention."

"It was neck and neck last night," Khefar said wryly. "Wynne, give me your email address, and I'll forward these to you."

"Thanks!" She handed back his phone.

"As for the exhibit," Khefar added, "it was about what I expected: an inaccurate hash of ancient custom to delight and titillate the uninformed."

Kira kicked him. He coughed. "Not the part that Kira had a hand in. She put together a great collection of artifacts. And most of them were properly identified."

Kira cut him a look. "I seem to recall, when I asked you for clarification on a couple of items, your response to me was along the lines of 'I've forgotten more than I can remember.' Which, I'm beginning to figure out, is your standard answer for anything you don't want to talk about."

A flash of anger caused his jaw to tighten. "Think that if you like. What I told you is the truth. I've died a few dozen times but that doesn't mean I have intimate knowledge of any of the funerary texts. As a warrior, and a Nubian one at that, I wasn't anywhere near the southern pyramids, so you would know more about the pyramid texts than I do. My first death was in a foreign land after a massacre that I initiated. There was no one left to return me to Egypt, put me in a coffin, or give me a Book of Going Forth by Day. Once the Great Lady Isis brought me back and gave me my charge, I had no need for any of the spells. I did pray at the chapel of my lord who gifted me the dagger, and I saw enough then to know that what Hammond has put together is nothing more than a patchwork for the sole purpose of entertaining people like a Halloween fright house. As for your identifications, when I actually saw the displays I did see some small details I could have been of assistance with after all. My apologies for not realizing this earlier."

Kira stared at Khefar. From the silence, she guessed that Wynne and Zoo were also staring at him, surprised by his outburst. "Wow. That was a whopper of a speech. Obviously the way to get you to open up is to get you mad."

Khefar actually bared his teeth. "I suggest that no one push me further."

Luckily, at that moment, their waiter approached the table. They placed their orders. When the waiter left, Kira rested her elbows on the table. "Okay, since the topic of last night's party is off-limits, how about we get to other business?"

"Sure." Zoo picked up the backpack beside his chair, handed it to Khefar. "Here's the gear you asked for, Kira. I even made a couple of extra assault charms for Khefar."

"How is that possible?" The Nubian lost his perpetual scowl. "I don't have magic."

"You don't need it with these," Zoo said, as excited as only a geek talking about his work could get. "These are tap and throw."

"Tap and throw?" Kira echoed. "Are they safe?"

Zoo looked affronted. "Would I give you anything that's not safe?" He took the pack back from Khefar, reached in, and withdrew what looked like a small brown rubber ball, though a knobby, malformed one.

"You may not have magic, but your dagger does," Zoo said. "So all you have to do is tap the charm with your dagger to charge it, throw it, and *poof!*"

Khefar gingerly took the ball between his thumb and forefinger. "*Poof* as in girly sparkles or *poof* as in gonna need a shop vac to get up all the pieces?"

"Door number two," Zoo said.

"Nice."

Kira glared at both men. "You want some girly sparkles, I'm sure Wynne and I can show you both exactly how serious our girly sparkles can be."

Zoo held up his hands with a laugh. "No, thanks. I already know how deadly you two can be."

Kira felt her smile freeze. Zoo spoke lightheartedly enough and had included his wife in the retort, but Kira could only think of how she'd hit him with a blast of her power a couple of months before, almost killing him in the process. Wynne's expression shut down, became blank, and Kira knew Wynne was remembering that terrifying night as well.

Zoo and Wynne had forgiven her and despite her attempt to ease the Marlowes out of her life, out of danger, they insisted of being in the thick of it with her, going so far as to officially join the Gilead Commission. Still, that did little to assuage the lingering guilt she felt over injuring Zoo and killing other innocents.

An awkward silence welled up like a slow-moving mushroom cloud. Kira searched for something to say to defuse the tension. Khefar provided the opening. "Too bad you didn't give me these yesterday. I could have really given Hammond an entertaining exhibit."

"By the Light," Kira groaned as Wynne and Zoo both laughed. "I'm going to make sure you're banned from going anywhere near the Congress Center. I don't trust you to mind your manners if you were to meet Hammond again."

Khefar handed the assault charm back to Zoo, who returned it to the pouch. "I can be a master of manners, when I need to be. I simply think I would have to be a bit more direct with Hammond, if I wanted to make sure he completely understood my point of view."

The waiter arrived with their meals. Hungry and grateful for the distraction, Kira maneuvered her platter of sweet potato fries, steamed asparagus, and beer-battered tilapia sandwich. She pulled her gloves off and steepled her hands over the plate, her elbows on the table. She figured that to many people it probably looked like she was saying grace over her food. She did, a whispered prayer to Ma'at slipping from her lips.

"Lady of Truth, thank you for another day and another meal. Give me the strength to always seek your face, to see your truth with grace and clarity."

Her prayer of thanks done, Kira then called her extrasense. Some days it was like mentally opening a window between the mundane and the magical, or opening a tap to let water flow. Power poured through, pooling into her hands. She didn't need much—she wanted to cleanse her food, not obliterate it—so she cut the current before power could fill her entire body.

The turquoise shade of the haze of power draping her hands still bothered her, but not as much as it had when the mixed hue first manifested two months back. She was more bothered that she wasn't bothered. She was changing, had been changing since Comstock's death, but stressing over the mix of Light and Shadow in her magic wasn't as important as having the Egyptian god of chaos stalk your dreams.

"Tilapia is best while it's hot," Khefar whispered to her. "Is your food not to your liking?"

"It's fine." Khefar couldn't see the color of her extrasense. Neither could Wynne. If Zoo noticed, he didn't show it, busy as he was with his teriyaki noodle bowl. Kira opened her hands, the pool of power widening. She brought it down like a net, draping the power over her food, tea, and quarter of the table. A subsonic hum vibrated the air before the power dissipated.

As they ate, Zoo ran down the other charms he had

fabricated for Kira. Wynne gave a perfunctory description of the new knives she was working on, but her heart didn't seem to be in it. She seemed distracted.

"Hey, guys," Wynne piped up after they finished their meal. "There's a pool table open in the back there. Why don't you two go on back, and Kira and I will join you in a little bit?"

Here it comes, Kira thought. *The showdown finally happens.*

"We can wait for you to finish," Khefar said, unknowingly coming to Kira's aid.

Zoo shoved back his chair, clapping the Nubian on the shoulder. "That was a subtle attempt to make us leave so they could have some girl talk."

"Not all that subtle," Kira muttered, the sweet potato fries congealing unpleasantly in her stomach. Wynne probably didn't want girl talk, though it would be worse if she did. Kira didn't do girl talk.

"How about this, then?" Wynne asked, pointing toward the pool tables. "Boys, go play pool. I need to talk to Kira alone."

Khefar hesitated. He had an uncanny ability to sense her every change in mood, Kira realized, though it wouldn't take a genius to know she was uncomfortable with the thought of talking to Wynne alone. He must have seen the desperation on her face. She certainly felt desperate.

Khefar began to speak, hopefully to bail her out, when Wynne cut in. "So, Kira, what do you use when you have that not-so-fresh feeling?"

"How about a game of nine ball?" Khefar asked Zoo as he pushed out of his chair faster than he needed to.

"Sounds good to me," Zoo answered. They moved off.

Kira glared after them. "The man didn't move that fast during the seeker demon attack at my house."

"Good thing he does know when to retreat," Wynne observed. "For a moment there, I thought I was going to have to get graphic."

Kira leaned back against the redbrick wall. "I guess you don't really want to reenact a feminine hygiene commercial, do you?"

"No." Levity left Wynne's face as she hunched forward. "I kind of feel silly right now, sitting here with a full belly and a beer in my hand, about to have this conversation with you. Especially considering everything we've been through."

Kira concentrated on pulling her gloves back on, smoothing the dark material over her hands. She had no clue what Wynne wanted to talk about, but was beginning to wish it were about girl stuff. "Considering everything we've been through, nothing seems silly. So what's on your mind?"

"Religion." Wynne spun the brown bottle in her hands. "Well, not religion per se, but faith. Belief in the gods and goddesses."

Whoa. This was deeper than Kira had expected Wynne to go. Of all the conversations they could have had at that moment, Kira wouldn't have bet on religion. "Do you really want to talk about this here?"

"Now's as good a time as any." Wynne took a swig of her beer. "I'm agnostic. Was, anyway. Being in wartime situations, either you find faith or you lose it. I didn't have a lot of faith before I served and by the time we got out, I was all but an atheist. I mean, seeing what people do to each other, it was easier to believe that religion was an excuse people used to explain why they do what they do."

"Religion is different than faith," Kira said. "At least, to me it is. To me, religion is something created by a group of people in an effort to tap into godhood. Because it's created by man, it's inherently fallible. Faith is a personal gift given by the gods, a gift that's even better when you give it back to them."

Wynne bobbed her head. "Okay, I can get with the idea that faith and religion are different. I mean, Zoo doesn't do much organized stuff with other people, but his faith has deepened a lot over the last couple of months. Way back in the beginning of our relationship, I thought he was doing that neo-paganism stuff that most of our customers come into the store for. Then I met the rest of his family, especially the ones still in Romania, and magic and spells and charms and faith seemed a natural part of their lives. They all worship the Great Lady and say all their magic comes from her."

She waved a hand. "Zoo tried to explain his magic to me once, but I told him his beliefs were a private thing and I didn't have to know about it, and I also didn't have a problem with it."

"Wynne, are you saying you *do* have a problem with it?" Kira couldn't believe it. "You run a metaphysical store. You make ritual athames and wands."

Wynne held up her hands. "No, I don't have a problem. I really don't. Most of the customers are harmless—they don't have magic like Zoo and his family do. So it's been okay. But then we got that scrying mirror, and then we met you."

"I don't know if *met* is the right word, considering you weren't supposed to see me," Kira said ruefully. "I was supposed to come in, defuse the magic in the mirror, and get out. Should have known the gig was too easy."

"You didn't know a demon lived in that mirror," Wynne said soothingly, though she stumbled over the word *demon*. "Hell, we didn't know either. It never acted up when Zoo came around. Anyway, that was the beginning. That was when everything changed."

Kira studied her friend, trying to figure out what Wynne's point was. As much as Kira needed and appreciated having the Marlowes at her back, she'd tried to shield them from the true nature of her job as much as possible. It hadn't always been easy but she'd managed. At least, she'd thought she'd managed. "How did everything change?"

"My bubble burst. You fought a demon in my stockroom. You have an amazing type of magic, different from Zoo's, more powerful, I think. And you worship an Egyptian goddess, a goddess who marked you."

Kira's fingers automatically strayed to the base of her throat. Her burgundy cashmere turtleneck concealed the feather tattoo etched there, but Wynne knew the mark couldn't be attributed to a human hand. "I guess it's pretty amazing."

"You guess?" Wynne's eyes widened. "Your goddess talks to you. You pal around with a demigod. And now you're sleeping with a guy who doesn't stay dead when you kill him!"

Unease cut through Kira like an icy wind. She scanned the restaurant again, but the post-lunch diners had thinned out almost completely. Their waiter was shooing away one of the vagrants who liked to enter through the all-glass roll-up door that fronted the eatery and shill for change. Kira tried not to think about the homeless people she had injured the same night she'd wounded Zoo, the night the Fallen had captured her, but it was difficult to excise the guilt that had landed squarely atop her ingested meal.

"Wynne, you're part of Gilead now," she pointed out as reasonably as she could. "You went through their assimilation process."

A flash of humor. "You mean Hell Week."

"Yeah, what Balm euphemistically calls Orientation." The on-boarding process for Gilead agents was nothing like the indoctrination that Shadowchasers and their handlers went through. Kira had heard agent training was something like the specialized regimen that Israeli Special Forces endured, with a metaphysical mad-scientist twist.

Kira knew from her time on Santa Costa that many Gilead agents were recruited from spy agencies and special forces teams around the world, but only half of them made it through the Gilead Commission's rigorous program. "You made it through Gilead training," she pointed out to Wynne. "You were green-lighted by Balm and by Section Chief Sanchez. You've got a good idea of what our fight is all about. Don't you think it's a little too late for a freak-out?"

"We were too busy saving the world. I've had time to think now."

"Have you talked to Zoo about this, whatever 'this' is?"

"No." Wynne stared down at her now-empty beer, her black nails tapping the bottle. "He's been . . . different since the accident."

"Oh." Kira didn't have to ask what accident. "Different how?"

"He's thrown himself into his studies, brushing up on his spellcraft, trying to get stronger. He says he wants to make sure he can protect us no matter what. And he gave me this." She reached inside her faded T-shirt, pulling out a black woven cord. A pendant dangled from the end of it, three stones wrapped with silver wire: obsidian, black tourmaline, and rose quartz.

"He says it's a protection amulet and that I shouldn't take it off except to shower. He says it will protect me." Wynne's face scrunched up. "Do you think it will?"

Protect you from what? Kira wondered. "Makes sense," she said aloud. The stones' natural properties, charged with the skill of someone of Zoo's caliber, were sure to offer some protection. However, the amulet needed the wearer to believe it would work in order to be useful. "There's a lot of stuff out there. It's important to be protected."

"Like you have Ma'at protecting you." Wynne shook her head. "This is crazy."

"How is it crazy?" Kira demanded. "You need to clue me in, 'cause I can't get a read on what you're talking about or why. You knew from the outset that I worship Ma'at. Zoo's told you about his relationship with the Great Lady and you said you were cool with that!"

"I know. But the Great Lady doesn't swing by and whisk him off to weird places. He's not getting breakfast made by West African demigods. A demigod cooks for you, Kira!"

"Keep your voice down, okay?" Kira darted a glance around the bar. Both Khefar and Zoo looked up from their game. She waved to them. Zoo made some sort of joke before they resumed their play.

"You spent a lot of time with Anansi in Cairo. You didn't flip out then."

A petulant look crossed Wynne's face. "I was worried about you then. I didn't really have time to think about the meaning of the Universe or the metaphysical origins of it."

"You don't have to worry about it now. It'll just make your head hurt."

"I know. A soldier can get seriously fucked-up if they start questioning their place. I mean, before, we were helping you fight bad guys. I didn't take the time to think about what those bad guys were. It was fun to be able to be all badass and undercover. But after what happened to you in the club, with that Fallen, and in Cairo, and actually seeing a seeker demon with my own eyes . . . everything's upside down now."

"Geez, Wynne, are you having a crisis of faith? You're not even religious!"

"That's the messed up part in all of this!" Wynne exclaimed. "I haven't been a practicing anything in ages. Zoo's got his goddess but I don't know if he's actually seen her, or even had a conversation with her."

She threw a hand out. "But you—you've had face-to-face talks with Ma'at, and Khefar's done the same thing with Isis. I mean, those names are part of fairy tales to me. And then there's Anansi, the cooking, traveling, joking, licorice-eating spider god who lives in your house." Wynne let out a hysterical laugh. "Do you even realize how crazy this sounds?"

"I know it would sound crazy to Normals," Kira said, not knowing what to say to ease Wynne's confusion. "I can see this is bothering you. You know I never tried to convince you of anything when it comes to faith and religion. I think everyone should find their own way, like Jews, Christians, and Muslims all worship the same god, but in different ways."

"I know, and I appreciate that you didn't try to press anything on me. Zoo hasn't either." Wynne wiped at her eyes carefully to avoid ruining her heavy eyeliner. "My parents were existentialists. I believed that Deity was a concept that people used as an explanation and rationalization for what they wanted to do. Now I know that deities are real, and I've seen one, you've seen several, and you and Khefar and Zoo are all protected by your goddesses. I don't have anyone to protect me."

Kira very carefully placed a gloved hand atop Wynne's bare one. "Oh, Wynne. It's not about protection. It's about that missing piece, the little hole you have that can only be filled by a higher power."

Wynne dipped her head. "I've never thought of it like that before. Maybe because I never thought to associate that incompleteness with a lack of faith."

Kira gave Wynne's hand a squeeze. "I'm no philosopher or anything. I know there are people on Santa Costa who have spent their entire lives trying to understand the mysteries of the Universe. Even those who know about the Great Schism that created Order and

Chaos say they still have a lot to learn. All I can do is tell you what I believe."

Wynne sniffed. "What *do* you believe?"

"I believe that we all embody Balance. We are creative and destructive, givers and takers of life, believers and doubters in ourselves and others. We can believe in something so much that it becomes real to us. Enough believers can generate an incredible power, and give power to what they believe in."

"So you're saying that gods exist because people believe they exist?"

Kira nodded. "Some of them. Some of them existed before in some form or another, and those are the children of Light and Shadow. But as far as whom you should follow, that's personal. All I can tell you is there are different types of people, there are different ways of connecting to Deity. Even if you believe Deity is within."

"Well, obviously there are bunches to choose from. Good grief, is the Flying Spaghetti Monster real? Or Cthulhu? Should I worship Ma'at or Isis or Anansi?"

"Do not, under any circumstances, let Anansi hear you say that. His head can barely fit through the garage door as it is."

"You're cracking jokes on a god, you do realize that, don't you? Can't he kill you with a bolt of lightning or something if you piss him off?"

"Anansi is too good natured for that, and he jokes more than I do," Kira said to ease Wynne's sudden worry. "You have seen how he and Khefar interact, haven't you? He's more like a cool uncle than some being from on high. Don't tell him I said that either."

"Do you think I should talk to him about it? My lack of faith, I mean."

"You don't need my permission or approval, Wynne. But Anansi's as good a listener as he is a storyteller. Unfortunately, he left to spend some time with his wife. I don't know how long he'll be gone."

"He's married?" Wynne's eyes widened again. "What does his wife think of what he does? Where does he live?"

"More of those things that will make your head hurt that I was talking about earlier. You don't want to go there."

"Okay. All right." Wynne sat back with a sigh. "I felt better for getting that off my chest."

"Then, I'm glad I could be a sounding board for you. If you ever want to talk about it, you know where I am."

"Of course you are. We girls have got to stick together."

Kira pulled her hands back. "Of course. Speaking of girls sticking together, how about we challenge the guys to a game of pool? We need to make them pay for that 'girly sparklies' comment."

"You're on!"

Chapter 11

Join us, daughter.

"I am not one of you. I am not a child of Chaos!"

Laughter rumbled like an earthquake. *Is this how you walk in Ma'at?* the dark voice mocked. *Do you walk in truth only when it is easy for you?*

"Ma'at is with me. Ma'at will protect me." She channeled power into her Lightblade, reshaping it into a khopesh. The curved sword extended her reach, gave her added protection against the power staff held by the god.

She raised the blade high, shoving as much power as she could into it. "Ma'at will guide me!" she screamed, swinging the weapon with all her strength.

The blade struck home, but only succeeded in angering the god. *You dare believe you have the strength to defeat me?*

The *was* scepter pierced through shirt and skin and bone, lodging deep in her shoulder below her clavicle. Shock drove away pain for one heartbeat. On the next, agony ripped through her. She screamed. Another scream ripped from her as Set twisted the prongs deeper into her flesh.

A word of power dropped from the god's mouth like a twenty-ton hammer, the pressure of it pushing her body deeper into the dirt. Power slammed into her, the pure brute force of Shadow magic, charged by her unwilling blood sacrifice. Her vision swam, drenched in fluorescent green. Heat engulfed her as her body instinctively struggled against the invasion, fought to combat the Chaos magic threatening to consume her.

Wake up, Kira, a voice urged, sounding far away. *It's a dream. You need to wake up. Now!*

Her eyes snapped open, her brain registering bright light, pain, and the sound of dying prey. It took a moment further to realize the sound same from her. Khefar gripped her wrists, his hold like iron manacles. He glared down at her, eyes wild with fear and fury. Mostly fury.

"Sss . . ." She licked her lips, tried again. "Sorry. Had a bad dream, I guess."

"Bad dream my ass." He continued scowling. "You were fighting and screaming and now you're bleeding."

She looked down at her chest. Sure enough, blood stained the left side of her gray tank top close to her shoulder. Khefar looked worse for wear too, his arms decorated with a scattering of welts and cuts. "Did I fight you?"

"You reached for your Lightblade before I could wake you up. Lucky for me, I managed to disarm you before you struck a fatal blow."

He hauled her out of bed, dragging her across the room and into the bathroom. "Sit," he ordered, pushing her toward the toilet before stooping to open the under-sink cabinet.

She shivered. Must be the cold of the floor seeping into her bare feet. "I'm okay."

"Shut up and sit down!"

She sat, stunned by the heat in his tone. "Hey, I said I was sorry. I didn't realize I was sleep fighting. Must have been a really intense dream."

He threw the first aid kit onto the counter. "Whatever that was, it wasn't a normal bad dream and you damn well know it!"

Before she could reply, he reached out and ripped the front of her tank top apart. She grabbed the front closed, wincing. Ignoring the pain, she glared at him instead. "I'm awake now. You want me to finish that fight? You ruined my favorite top!"

He gave her a dark look. "Like the blood hadn't already done that. You ready to talk about this?"

"Can't we patch me up now, then talk later?" she asked, feeling drained. She had no idea what time it was, but as exhausted as she felt, the idea of going back to sleep and possibly facing the nightmare again was too much to contemplate.

"I've been waiting for 'later' to happen since we came back from London," he said, tearing open an antibiotic gauze pack. "It hasn't come yet."

"I've had a lot to do since we got back," she reminded him. "You know I had to hit the ground running with putting the exhibit together. I didn't know settling Bernie's estate was going to take that long, so I was behind schedule organizing the artifacts for my part of the show."

"There's always going to be something going on, Kira," he admonished her, wiping the gauze over her skin and causing her to flinch. "I'm done with waiting."

She steeled herself to see a wound beneath the

blood, to face a barrage of questions. Neither happened.

"You're not wounded." He threw the bandage into the trash.

"Is it your blood, then?" She didn't see any scratches on him deep enough to cause the amount of blood staining her shirt. Her mouth didn't hurt either, so it hadn't come from biting her lips.

"You have a serious bruise here, above your heart," he said, his voice still angry. "Spreading out from two indentations. It looks like you're healing from being stabbed by a pair of chopsticks."

Or a was *scepter,* she thought. Out loud she said, "I don't know what happened."

She'd seen him scowl before. She'd even seen him angry. The look he gave her then actually made her heart skip a beat, and not in a good way.

"Do not lie to me, Kira Solomon," he said, his voice sharp. "I am not so stupefied by being with you that I've become gullible. You are still my charge and I am still responsible for your soul. Lie to your friends. Lie to yourself if you must. But never lie to me."

At that moment, his words stung more than the ache of her fading wound. She wanted to look away from that implacable glare, but she couldn't. Of everyone in her life, Khefar seemed to be the only one without an ulterior motive. She'd known him the shortest amount of time, but she'd trusted him with far more than she had entrusted to others. With Wynne having a faith crisis, Zoo bulking up on spellcraft and magical protections, and Balm being uncommunicative, the Nubian was the only one she could lean on. If you couldn't depend on the man who'd made a pact to kill you with honor, whom could you trust?

His fingers entangled with hers. "You've been jerked out of sleep for the last four nights that I know of," he told her. "You quit our bed and don't come back. Tell me what's going on."

Damn. Kira should have known that Khefar would notice. He had an uncanny ability to gauge her mood, to turn her dark thoughts around and pull her back.

"I've been having dreams," she confessed. "Not waking dreams, like what I have when I communicate across distances with Balm. Not regular dreams either. In the dreams, I'm excavating near Naqada. Comstock and I uncover a *was* scepter. Then a temple of Set rises from the ground and Set tells me to join him. When I refuse, he stabs me with the scepter and injects me with Chaos magic."

Khefar's expression blanked. No anger, no worry, only emptiness. Her heart stuttered again. She leaned forward to speak but he beat her to it.

"You've been having dreams of Set attacking you with his staff of power." His tone made it seem as if they were discussing their dinner choices. "I guess he's been hitting you here, the same spot the Fallen stabbed you?"

She nodded. The press of his fingers against her skin fluctuated somewhere between pleasure and pain. She whimpered. It was hard to be all badass with him touching her, even if there was nothing sensual about the touch.

His gaze caught hers. "This is real, Kira. This isn't a dream. Isis and Ma'at warned us in a 'dream' about the Vessel of Nun and we ended up with a flooded bed."

"I know." She'd thought about that. But Isis and Ma'at were both awake and aware, not a slumbering god as Set was reputed to be.

Khefar apparently had the same thought. "If Set is able to affect your dreams, and has created a physical manifestation of something that happened in your dream . . . do you think he's awakened?"

"I—I think it's possible." Kira's throat closed up as a sudden shiver of fear coursed through her. She almost gagged before managing to whisper, "I think he wants to regain his place of power, and I think the Lady of Shadows is helping him do it."

Khefar stilled. Kira wondered if her expression matched his: the tightness about the mouth, the widening of the eyes, disturbed, worried, and trying not to show it. She shouldn't tell him anything else. What she'd already shared was enough. The need to share her fears, her burden, strained her control. Khefar would understand. Surely he would.

Unless he took it as a sign that she was losing her grip on sanity and was on a fast track to Shadow.

"Kira?" He knelt before her on the cold stone floor, his hands wrapped around hers. "Talk to me."

"The dream." She licked her lips, staring down at his hands wrapped around hers. She started over. "Comstock was in the dream. We excavated the town of Nubt and we happened to uncover an intact *was* scepter. I was surprised when he told me to pick it up, to lift it out of the earth and bring it to Light. When I did, that's when Set's temple appeared in all its glory. He—Set—welcomed me as his daughter, said that I was born of thunder and lightning and belonged with him.

Each time I refused, he stabbed me with the scepter, and more Chaos magic got injected into me."

She dropped her gaze. "I know it's there, the Shadow magic. Solis knew it was there, when we went behind the Veil in Cairo. She said it always will be, because I'm not human. One thing has changed in the dream: since I got that chest from Balm, the last two nights I've told Comstock that I was afraid to open the box because I didn't want to find out my father was a Shadowling. He acted as if it would be no big deal, that I wouldn't be any different than I was before I knew the truth. Maybe I won't be different because I've already got Light and Shadow swirling inside me, but I don't know that for sure. Ma'at could have removed it, but she didn't. Why not? She had to know that Set was gunning for me."

That was the part that scared her, the part she'd been afraid of voicing. Would Ma'at set her up to be taken by Set? Why?

"You can't really believe that the Lady of Truth would allow such a thing," Khefar said. "That's crazy!"

"Is it? Isis might have good reason to stand against Set, but does Ma'at? 'Truth is neither good nor evil. Truth simply is.' Solis said that, and it makes a lot of sense. Truth is what it is. It's what people do with the truth that's the problem."

"That doesn't mean that Ma'at would serve you up to the god of Chaos like a holiday turkey!"

"I didn't say she would do that," Kira said, finally looking up. Indignation mixed with astonishment on Khefar's face. Yeah, she couldn't believe the words coming out of her mouth either. "But Ma'at is Truth."

"And what does the Lady of Truth say to you?"

"Nothing. No warnings like with the Vessel of Nun. I haven't asked directly about it during my prayers because . . . well, it's only been dreams. I thought they were intensified nightmares, you know, some sort of post-traumatic stress manifestation from our time in the Between-Cairo. Has Isis said anything?"

"No." His face reverted back to its usual grim lines. "No warnings about Set awakening. I would think if she would warn us about anything, it would be the return of the god who killed her husband. Perhaps your dreams are simply that, really vivid dreams."

They both looked down at her bloodied bruise. Neither one of them believed Kira's problem to be simply overactive lucid dreaming. She decided to follow that train of thought anyway. "If they are nothing but dreams, my subconscious is trying to tell me something."

"Which is?" Khefar prompted.

"Either I need to go on a dig, or I need to find out my parentage."

Her hand brushed the feather tattoo at her throat, the mark proclaiming her as the Hand of Ma'at, bestowed by the goddess herself. "If I claim to be Ma'at's devotee, if I am truly to be the Hand of Truth, I have to face the truth, no matter how unsavory it is."

"You're ready to open the box?"

"I don't know if I'm ready," she admitted, "but I think it's time. I've been hounding Balm for clues for years. I can't back down now that I've got them."

Bracing her hands on her knees, she stood. "Would

you mind getting me another tank top? I should at least try to be somewhat presentable when I see my mother for the first time."

Fifteen minutes later, Kira sat on her couch, staring at the chest. The box seemed to be carved out of wood that had turned gray with age and sea spray, rough-hewn as if by a moderately skilled hand. Yet Kira had seen enough ancient artifacts to know the wood had been carved by a loving hand.

Kira breathed in deep and out slowly, pushing the mundane away. The Veil of Reality slid aside. Everything about her danced with the various colors of magic: the orange-red glow of the alarm system enhanced with her own aura, the soft golden-white sheen of antiques scattered about the cavernous room, and the bright blue glow that shrouded the opening to the lower level.

She turned her attention back to the box. With her extrasense fully engaged, she could clearly see the magic surrounding the box. Sigils were etched into the side panels—some sort of ancient cuneiform she hadn't seen before but that hinted at Sumerian—glowing violet neon. That must have been the charm that prevented anyone else from opening the chest. With the kind of people she and Balm had to contend with, a puzzle lock would have been too simple.

Her hands shook as she raised them to open the box. She paused, clenching and unclenching her hands to relieve the sudden pressure filling her, tightening her muscles. *It's not Pandora's box. You can do this. You can handle this.*

After a few more breaths to steady herself, Kira carefully pried open the lid. A bright flash of purple light swamped the room as the sigils extinguished themselves. Not knowing what to expect, she was disappointed when nothing happened, no assault of Balm's thoughts or Lysander's memories, or impressions of whoever had carved the chest. She placed the lid to the right of the chest and took her first look inside her past.

A sheet of handmade paper, folded in half, lay atop an ornately decorated golden box that would have done an Egyptian queen proud. She picked up the forceps she'd snagged from her worktable, carefully grasped the note, then set it on the lint-free cloth she'd spread on the coffee table. If she had to guess, she would say that the note had been written by Balm. Probably some sort of admonition concerning the contents of the box, or a chastisement of how headstrong Kira was.

She pulled on a pair of surgical gloves, telling herself she wasn't wimping out. Making every attempt at preserving everything in the state she'd found it was part of her archaeologist's training. If she treated the act of opening the box and examining what it contained as cataloguing an artifact and not discovering her own past, the trembling that randomly shook her subsided.

The box inside the driftwood chest was covered in gold, carved and intricately inlaid with sparkling jewels. The inner box looked to measure roughly the length and width of a sheet of letter-sized paper. Judging by the outer container, the inner box stood maybe seven inches high. Whatever mementos Balm had of Kira's mother, Balm had obviously considered them more precious than Kira had believed.

Making sure no part of her skin touched the outer box, Kira reached inside and lifted the case out. It wasn't heavy. Not a secret cache of ancient gold coins, then. Nothing else lay beneath the jewel-encrusted box.

Kira stared down at the table, reviewing the items arranged before her. Curiosity screamed at her to open the shimmering box immediately, but she resisted. After all this time, years of not knowing, she would finally know something about her birth mother. She'd finally be able to peek inside her mother's mind, to experience the thoughts and emotions, to discover why her mother had decided to entrust her to Balm instead of her birth family.

Silence pressed in on her, thick with anticipation. Her gaze fell onto the folded note. She tried to reach out to her foster mother, sending a simple *Hello?* along their psychic communication link. *Balm, are you there? What's going on?*

No answer. *I'm opening the box now. Is there nothing you want to say to me?*

Again no response. Kira didn't know whether to feel relieved or upset. Either Balm was incapacitated in some way, involved in extremely high-level Gilead business, or ignoring Kira. There had been times on Santa Costa when Kira had gone days without hearing or seeing anything from the leader of the Gilead Commission. There was nothing new about Balm's lack of communication. Kira had also returned the favor, giving her foster mother the silent treatment for days at a time. And yet . . .

She remembered Lysander's anxious demeanor, his urgent desire to return to Balm quickly. Something was going on. Or the Gilead leader wanted to prevent Kira from pumping Balm's assistant for information.

"I know what you'll say, Balm," she said aloud, needing to break the oppressive quiet. "You'll ask me what is the importance of wanting to experience the knowledge instead of just knowing, why what you told me wasn't enough."

She flexed her hands, gripping the edge of the table. "It's not about what knowing will or won't do, or what I'll do with what I learn. It's about truth. My whole life has been about uncovering truth. I will prove myself worthy of being the Hand of Ma'at. The Hand of Truth. I can do nothing less than pursue and uncover truth, no matter how deep in the shadows it lies."

She picked up the thick sheet of handmade paper, unfolded it. Balm's bold strokes only filled part of the sheet. "I had hoped to be with you for this, but I cannot. I've sent your mother's locket to you. She wore it always, and then gave it to me. I now give it to you. Perhaps you will find what it is you seek. When you are ready, come to me."

Balm hadn't signed it, but she didn't need to. No one else could chastise and infuriate and bestow permission all at once like the eternal head of the Gilead Commission. Kira knew Balm wasn't happy that she hadn't traveled to Santa Costa with her after wrapping up Bernie's affairs in London. Kira had still been reeling from her trip behind the Veil and meeting the other Balm, and finding out that Balm had known her mother all along without telling Kira. Going to Santa Costa before processing all of that would have been a big mistake.

With the surgical gloves still firmly in place, Kira lifted the hinged lid of the inlaid box. A stack of letters lay inside, the edges of some envelopes yellowed with age. Kira recognized Balm's bold scrawl in the letters addressed to Ana Guamayo in a town she'd never heard of in the West African nation of Benin. Other letters were addressed to Serena Balm in flowing script.

Balm knew Kira's mother.

Kira had known that, of course, since Balm had shared the information in one of their dream walks. What she hadn't realized was how well Balm knew her birth mother. Apparently very well, and for years, according to some of the time stamps on the envelopes.

A glittering object caught her eye. A gold locket rested in the bottom of the decorated box. The locket looked almost like a Tibetan prayer box, with filigree on each side of the inch-long box and a tiny hinged lid.

This locket had belonged to her mother. All she had to do was take off the surgical gloves, then cup the pendant in the palm of her hand. She was seconds away from finally knowing her mother. And perhaps the identity of her father.

Before she could change her mind, Kira stripped off the gloves and picked up the pendant.

Chapter 12

Sensations bombarded Kira with gale-force strength, scouring away her sense of self. She grimly held on as her world compressed, turned inside out, and seemed to fold in on itself. This horrible wrenching sensation was unlike anything she'd ever felt before during a reading, a sensation that threatened to strip away her extrasense.

Finally, as blackness danced along the edges of her vision, she pushed through the magical vortex to the other side. She found herself falling upward, arms flailing, landing on damp, rocky black earth.

Was this what Balm had experienced before sending the chest? Kira couldn't imagine the head of the Gilead Commission going anywhere that would cause her to soil her expensive clothing, not to mention leave her psychically vulnerable. Unless this wasn't a rewind of Balm's last moment with the pendant, but something else, somewhere else.

Kira's gaze traveled the room, though *room* was a generous designation. It was more like a chamber carved from basalt, the volcanic rock emitting a subtle sheen of magic. Dank, dark, lit only by a sliver of moonlight and the ambient magic, there was no way that this depressing chamber would be high on anyone's must-see list.

A shadow detached itself from the gloom deeper in the chamber. Kira had an impression of a feminine form, a fall of hair as the magical lighting increased. "Balm?"

As soon as she uttered Balm's name, Kira realized her mistake. The young woman had a passing resemblance to Balm, like a reflection on a shop window as the bus whizzes by. Instead of soft brown eyes that flashed to blue, the stranger's eyes were completely golden yellow with fleeting flashes of black.

Kira's hand immediately dropped to her Lightblade—or rather, where her Lightblade would have been if she'd been in her own dreamwalk. "You're not Balm."

"Took you long enough," the woman said. "What gave it away?"

Kira pushed through the fear, reaching for sarcasm in self-defense. "Balm doesn't look like a petulant teen whose parents took her phone privileges."

"Then you should realize how dangerous and unpredictable a teenaged girl can be," the young woman said, the temperature in the chamber dropping rapidly as she floated closer. "After all, you were barely a teen when you hurt your sister. You were still a teen when you got your handler Nico killed. And you certainly acted like a headstrong teen when you ran off by yourself and ended up killing all those people."

"Shut up!" Yellow tinged Kira's vision. "You don't know what you're talking about!"

"Don't I?" She spun in a circle, a little girl playing. "Am I not Myshael, the Lady of Shadows? Does not the darkness belong to me?"

She spun to a stop in front of Kira, her eyes completely black. "Enig was my child. You do remember him, do you not? You gave him your power twice."

"I never gave him my power," Kira shot back. "He took it from me. He took Nico from me. He took my Lightblade from me."

"He couldn't take what you weren't willing to give," the young girl said in a lilting voice. "You wanted so much to be normal, even as you knew deep in your heart that you are not human and have never been. You wanted to be free of your power, and for what? To be like those sacks of flesh who have no idea of their potential? You needed to learn the error of your thinking. I was happy to teach it to you."

"You?" Kira stumbled back a step. "You sent Enig after me? You interfered in my life?"

"Really, there's no need to sound so shocked," Myshael said, clucking her tongue. "Balm's been interfering in your life since before you were born. But I suspect you'll find that out soon enough."

Kira put her hands to her head, trying to grasp the revelations she'd heard. The Lady of Shadows had blatantly admitted to meddling in Kira's life. Kira knew Balm had attempted to direct her path several times, but to know that the head of Gilead had tried her hand at being a puppet master since before Kira's birth was almost too much.

She stared at the female embodiment of Shadow, the very thing she'd been trained to destroy. She couldn't trust the Lady's word. Heck, she didn't trust Balm most of the time. "Where is Balm? Why isn't she here?"

Myshael smiled, an angelic child if not for the glowing yellow eyes and razor-sharp teeth that nearly split her face in half. "The Lady of Light can't help you now. She's doing all she can to help herself."

Anger and fear grappled in Kira's belly. "What the hell did you do to Balm?"

"Do not lay Balm's actions at my feet. I merely capitalized on the situation that presented itself. How's your wound, by the way?"

Kira's hand drifted to her shoulder. "How do you know about that?"

Myshael changed form again, back to a teenager. "Set is my child. And so are you."

Horror iced Kira's back. "You are not my mother. My mother's name is Ana."

The young woman's eyes burned citrine. "Is a mother one who incubates or one who educates and shapes? I did not carry you in my womb, Kira Solomon, but make no mistake—I definitely had a hand in creating you."

The chamber's chill air pressed down on Kira, seeping into her bones. "What do you want?"

"Isn't it obvious? I want joint custody."

"What are you talking about?"

"Balm has had her time with you. Now I will have mine. Some of the best Lightchasers are former Shadowchasers."

"Lightchasers? You have Lightchasers?"

Myshael gave a long-suffering sigh. "Balm's curriculum has been woefully half-assed, I see. Tell me, Kira Solomon: what is Universal Balance?"

"I'm not playing your game."

"I do enjoy games, especially when people are my playthings," Myshael replied. "But in this, I expect an answer. Or is Gilead's vaunted Shadowchaser training unable to live up to its own hype?"

Kira folded her arms. "Balance drives the Universe. Matter and antimatter. Good and evil. Action and reaction. Love and hate."

"Good answer. Now, if the concept of Universal Balance is the foundation of existence, how can there be Shadowchasers without Lightchasers?"

Kira parted her lips to make a pithy retort, but no words came. Of course there were Lightchasers. It was so obvious, she felt foolish for not realizing it earlier, like during her training.

"What do Lightchasers chase?"

Myshael smiled. "Whatever I tell them to. Enig went after the Dagger of Kheferatum, and Marit convinced a Shadowchaser to steal the Vessel of Nun."

"Yeah." Kira sighed in mock sympathy. "That didn't work out too well for them, did it?"

Myshael's smile vanished, replaced with a terrible expression that kicked up a pang of fear in Kira's chest. "Since you've managed to beat both of them, Set decided he would have his chance, though he slumbers still. And after I talked to Balm and Solis, I decided I would try my hand at bringing my recalcitrant daughter into the fold."

Her mood shifted again, this time to eagerness. "So are you going to join the family? Set would like you to, and I know Marit really wants to see you again."

"No." Kira shuddered. "Not only no, but hell no. You and all your little minions are not my family. I belong to Ma'at, not Set. I'm not switching teams, not going to become a Lightchaser, and I'm sure as hell not going to take orders from you."

Childlike laughter pealed through the chamber as Myshael clapped her hands. "Oh, you do have the strength of will of your family. Then again, perhaps it is sheer bravado. Or blind stupidity. Regardless, you will follow the path to its inevitable end, and you will come to heel."

"You may have laid the path." Kira's voice seethed with anger and determination. "You and your sisters have definitely thrown obstacles onto it. But I choose whether or not I step onto it. I choose whether or not to sit down or keep moving forward. Do you understand what I'm telling you? Whatever machinations you and all the other gods have, you cannot trump Free Will. I will always have a choice, and that choice will be mine alone. Not yours, not Solis's, not Balm's. Mine."

The Lady of Shadows rose into the air, her body suffused with the glowing yellow of Shadow magic. An invisible wind lifted her dark hair, swirling the long strands about her head. She floated to a stop before Kira. Kira stood immobile as Myshael pressed her index finger to Kira's shoulder. Pain buckled her knees, but Myshael continued to prod her, her eyes glowing with her power.

With her free hand she cupped Kira's cheek and leaned close. "You are a child of Chaos, my dearest one," she whispered against Kira's ear as she dug her fingers deeper into Kira's shoulder. "That is why Set calls out to you in your dreams. You have already acted in my name and you will again, for it is your nature."

Kira grit her teeth, fighting the pain that radiated from her shoulder. "Get. The hell. Out of my head!"

Myshael drew back. The immediate absence of pain had Kira gasping as she dropped to her hands and knees. "What makes you think we're in your head?" Myshael asked.

"What?"

"Enjoy your trip down memory lane, my child. I'll see you soon."

The Lady of Shadows vanished.

At once the swirling nothingness returned, assaulting Kira's senses. She tried to swim through it, tried to regain control of the vision, tried not to allow the meeting with the Lady of Shadows to throw her completely off-kilter.

She landed in the middle of a fight. Rather, she landed in the consciousness of a person fighting. The opponent glowed with the bright yellow of Shadow magic, a male Shadowling six and a half feet tall and all sinewy muscle.

The Shadowling threw a bolt of bright yellow light. She lifted her blade, blocking the blast. Her blade? No, not her dagger, but the pale blue glow denoted the weapon as a Lightblade.

Realization shook her to her core. She was in the body of another Shadowchaser. Her mother.

The Shadowling had a knife as well, a curving kukri suffused with a phosphorescent yellow glow. He was a Lightchaser.

The fight was quick, brutal, damaging to both sides. A blast of Shadow magic hit her mother directly on the forehead, sending her reeling. The world tilted as she fell. A dark, hulking shape loomed over her. A hand reached down, wrapped around her neck. The Shadowling squeezed, and the world went black . . .

She jerked up screaming. She should have been dead. Why wasn't she dead?

Clothes torn, body bruised and aching. She tried to stand, but pain blossomed in her midsection instead. *Gods, no.*

The Shadowling was still there, on his back, her Lightblade protruding from his chest. At least she'd killed him before he—before he—

Shrieking, she pulled her blade from the still carcass. Raising it high, she plunged it, again and again and again, into the Shadowling's body. Screaming until her voice gave out, she stabbed him until her arms shook with the effort, until she couldn't raise the dagger further. She fell onto her back as a cold rain began to fall, throat sore, body hurting, soul bruised. Staring up at the rain, she gathered her mental energy, sent out one call. *Balm!*

The scene shifted. Now she was on a boat. Brilliant sapphire sky arched overhead, but she didn't care. She was too busy being sick over the side as the ship steamed toward the familiar rocky coast, the stone citadel that stood in sharp relief against the sky. Not the way she expected to return to Santa Costa, but she was glad to be home, glad to be returning to Balm.

The boat glided to a stop at the dock. A woman waited at the end of the pier, beautiful, forever young. Balm, the head of the Gilead Commission, the one person she could always count on.

Balm ran to the boat as she disembarked, caught her as she stumbled. "Ana, are you all right?"

She leaned into Balm's warm embrace and immediately felt better. She'd missed the sun-drenched smell of Balm's hair. "Serena," she whispered, "I've gotten myself into a spot of trouble."

Balm reached out a hand, gently placed it on Ana's protruding belly. "You should have come home earlier," Balm said, her voice thick with emotion. "You shouldn't have left in the first place!"

"You needed Chasers out in the world," she reminded Balm. "It was selfish to stay here as long as I did, when I was needed out there."

Balm pulled her close. "You were needed here too," she whispered. She drew back, gathering herself into the picture of serene command. "But you are here now, and that is all that matters. Everything will be all right."

The scene reset again. She sat in a canvas pavilion overlooking the sea, a teacup before her. Balm sat beside her, their hands loosely tangled together.

Ana turned to Balm. "I made a mistake, didn't I?" she asked, tears streaking down her face. "I shouldn't bring this child into the world."

"She's your daughter, Ana," Balm said, caressing the other woman's face. "It doesn't matter who her father is, she's your daughter. Because of that, she has the best possible chance there is."

Ana caressed her belly. Fatigue dragged at her. She'd spent hours every day since her arrival bathing her womb in Light magic, boosted by Balm and the innate power of Santa Costa. She'd given everything she could, everything to ensure that her daughter would have the best chance possible. "Nurture over nature. That's what we have to hope for."

"That's what we believe." Balm squeezed the other woman's hand. "She will have your nature, Ana. Your sweet and loving heart will belong to her. She will be your daughter."

"*Our* daughter," Ana corrected. "I'll give birth to her, but you will raise her."

Panic swept across Balm's features. "Ana, please, don't talk like that. You're going to make it through—"

"Promise me. Promise me that you'll raise our daughter."

Balm lifted their entwined hands, pressed her lips against their knuckles. "Of course I will."

Ana sighed in relief. "Thank you. It gives me peace to know that Kira is in such good hands."

Another shift. She screamed as pain ripped through her. Bearing down, pressure increasing, grunting with the effort, holding on to Serena's hand with all her might, she pushed her daughter out into the Light, the world.

Balm lifted the baby, placed her onto Ana's chest. Kira/Ana felt the weight of the baby on her heart, herself brand-new. "She's beautiful," she heard herself say.

"She's perfect," Balm said, tears in her eyes.

"Sweet little Kira," her mother whispered. "Grow up brave and strong. Have faith in yourself, in your heart, and you'll never go wrong."

Soft blue light filled her vision. One last breath and she reached out, joined the Light.

"Kira. Kira, can you hear me?"

She slowly blinked the blue light away. Khefar leaned over her, his expression pinched with worry. "Am I on the floor?"

Her voice sounded strange, far away. Not surprising considering how many years of history she'd just witnessed.

"Yeah," Khefar told her, his voice like gravel. "You had the pendant in your hand. All of a sudden you stiffened and fell flat to the floor. That was about ten minutes ago, and I've been trying to rouse you ever since."

"I traveled a long way." The locket slipped from her fingers and to the carpet. "And thus ends my role as Pandora, unleashing the evils of the harshest form of truth to wreak havoc upon my world."

Khefar took her hands. "You're ice cold. I think you're in shock."

"No." She shook her head slowly. "What I am is so far beyond shock. I don't think there's a word for what I am right now."

Khefar helped her roll to a sitting position, then he grabbed an afghan from the back of the couch to wrap around her. "Was it bad?"

"Yeah." She couldn't say anything else. She willed her muscles to move. Slowly they complied, her knees up drawing against her chest. She propped her elbows atop her knees, then covered her face with her hands. "I need to talk to Bernie."

"I am here now." Khefar sat beside her, rubbing her back. "I don't think you're ready for another vision right now anyway."

"You're right." Her muscles obeyed her only with effort. Her body, brain, and magic all felt sluggish. She'd crash hard once the horror faded enough.

"What did you see?"

She didn't answer immediately. "Ana, my mother was a hybrid."

"I know. You told me that in Cairo. It makes sense, considering your touch ability."

She gave him a slow nod. "Balm was pretty tight with my mother. I mean, really tight, as in Sappho tight. I didn't know that. Ana was a Shadowchaser too. I didn't know that either. Have you ever come across Lightchasers?"

His hand paused. "I'm assuming that's the opposite of a Shadowchaser, someone who goes after those aligned with the Light."

"Or whatever Myshael, the Lady of Shadows, wants them to." She pushed her hair back from her face, a feat made more difficult by her trembling hands. "My father was one apparently, and a Shadowling to boot. He attacked my mother. She killed him, but not before he impregnated her. With me."

She huffed. The trembling rolled up her arms to the rest of her body. "That explains why I'll never be able to get rid of the taint of Shadow. It's half of my genetic makeup."

"Hair of Isis," Khefar breathed. "You saw this?"

"Seeing it would have been bad enough." She drew the afghan closer about her, but the chill wouldn't go away. "Remember, I have the perspective of the person whose object I touch. It was my mother's locket."

"Gods, Kira." He dragged her into his lap. "I'm sorry."

"I wanted to know. Now I do." She didn't lean into him, didn't take the comfort he offered. If she did, the numbness holding the anguish back would surely break, and she'd drown in the flood.

"I saw her."

"Saw who? Your mother?"

"No. The Lady of Shadows, Myshael."

"Gods, Kira, don't say her name!" Khefar gripped her shoulders. "You'll call her to you!"

"Too late for that. She was the first thing I saw when I touched the locket. Apparently Balm wore it all the time, even to her meetings with her sisters."

"What do they do in these meetings?" Khefar demanded. "Scheme and plan against us poor mortals?"

"Something like that, if the Lady of Shadows is to be believed. She said that since Balm has had her time with me, it's now her turn."

"What does she want?"

"For me to join the family." Kira huffed again. "I said no, that I wasn't of Shadow and would never join her. All she did was laugh."

A stirring of anger. Oh yeah, anger would work. "She laughed at me, because she knew what I would find out. She knew I'd discover that dear old Dad was a Shadowling who hunted Shadowchasers. Because she sent that Shadowling after my mother."

Khefar's fingers dug into her shoulders. "I'm sorry, Kira."

"Me too. I should have found a way to kill that bitch when I had the chance."

"Which one?"

"Good point." She moved away from him. "The Sisters seem to have a habit of meddling in people's lives. I wouldn't put it past them to have deliberately schemed to create a hybrid of hybrids in order to see which one of them would win. I have no idea what Solis's stake is in this, but I can guess what the ladies of Light and Shadow want. Well, I have no intention of being their pawn, no matter what game they're playing."

"That's a relief." He climbed to his feet.

She watched him, tension gathering in her shoulders. He stood between her and her Lightblade. "What are you going to do?" she asked.

"What do you mean?"

"I'm never going to get rid of the Shadow magic inside me," she reminded him, staring at his back. "It's part of me now. Actually, it's always been a part of me. My mother and Balm were hoping to keep it suppressed. I am of the Light and I am of Shadow. Your mission is to fight Shadow. So I'll ask you again: what are you going to do?"

She could see the muscles of his shoulders bunch, his fingers curl, but he kept his back to her. "My mission has never been to fight Shadow. My mission is to do as my Lady Isis bids, and protect my charges. That hasn't changed."

"But your promise—"

He turned to face her. "You are still you, still the Kira Solomon you were when you went to bed, before you found this out. Are you telling me that the Hand of Truth is unable to bear the burden that the goddess saw fit to give her?"

"That wouldn't make for an interesting story, now, would it?" She climbed to her feet. "The 'Labors of Hercules' wouldn't be nearly as exciting or memorable if it were called the 'Cakewalk of Hercules.'"

"Exactly."

She scrubbed her hands over her face. "Still haven't

heard from Balm. I guess that's not a bad thing right now. She'll contact me when she's good and ready, and I need time to figure out what I'm going to say to her. Tomorrow's the were-hyena challenge, and I need to do some groundwork before we head out there."

"You need rest."

She nodded. "I know. One good thing about going through a vision like that is I'm too tired to do anything other than sleep a dreamless sleep. Tomorrow's soon enough to lose my mind."

She let him lead her back upstairs, let him undress her. Let the warmth of his chest seep into her back as he pulled her close against him, spooning her protectively. Let herself revel in the contact, all the while knowing that moments like this were numbered.

Chapter 13

"Last time: are you sure about this?"

"You've asked me that every five minutes since we left the house," Khefar said, his hands wrapped around the steering wheel. "And since I willingly dressed head to toe in leather like some BDSM version of Shaft, I think it's safe to say that I'm sure about this."

"You look badass," Kira said, managing to keep a straight face with effort. Good to know his sense of humor was still intact. "The were-hyenas will appreciate that."

"I *am* badass," Khefar corrected her. "And if any of the were-hyenas want proof, I'll be more than happy to provide it to them."

The sun had already dropped below the horizon by the time they made their way to the challenge. The Westside were-hyena pack lived in a housing project on the southwest side of downtown Atlanta. It was the perfect cover for the matriarchal hybrids originally from Africa. Ghettos and projects were largely ignored by polite society. No one questioned the lack of adult males, since most assumed there wouldn't be any around in the first place.

A chain-link fence marked the entrance to the complex's main parking lot, near the red and orange brick edifice that housed mailboxes. A few cars took up the allotted spaces, no model close to new. A handful of girls in fur-lined hoodies leaned against one of the cars, bobbing their heads as a hip-hop beat vibrated the windows. Their laughter faded as Khefar backed the Charger into an available parking spot away from the other vehicles. Two of the girls ran off before Kira and Khefar could exit the car.

"They know we're here," he said, tension tightening his voice.

"Good, since we weren't trying to be sneaky about it." She made her way around to the trunk, Khefar joining her.

"How heavily armed do we want to be?" he asked, popping the trunk. "The bultungin appreciate a show of force."

"I want you armed to the teeth."

"Excellent." He lifted a sawed-off shotgun from the compartment.

"Not that. We want them to recognize that we can hold our own, not think that we're looking for trouble."

"But you are looking for trouble." He put the shotgun back.

"I'm looking to prevent trouble," she clarified, strapping another dagger to her left thigh. Like Khefar, she'd donned all leather, soft enough to move in but thick enough that she wouldn't need extra layers. It protected against the cold and most shape-shifting hybrids looking for a fight.

"We'll see how that works. I wouldn't put much past the bultungin." He took out a wide black scabbard instead. He pulled the blade free, exposing the hooked shape of a khopesh. Instead of the classic bronze, the two-foot sickle-like sword had the sheen of finely crafted Toledo steel.

"Talk about working with what you know," Kira said.

"Nothing wrong with being old-school."

"True enough. Do you have those assault charms that Zoo gave you the other day?"

His grimace was clear in the streetlights. "I much prefer my blade and bullets. I'll leave the magical to you."

"True old-school to the end." She grinned as she pulled off her gloves. "Close the trunk and I'll secure the car."

He did. She pressed her palms against the trunk. As she did with her bike, she willed her extrasense to spill out of her hands. Her magic swirled blue and yellow as it flowed across the glossy dark metal, a protective shield better than any alarm system. Anyone who tried to open the car would receive a very nasty physical and psychic shock.

She straightened, trying not to obsess over the encroaching amount of Shadow magic in her extrasense. On the bright side, it meant Light and Shadow both would trigger the car's defense. "Done."

"Good," Khefar said, his voice thin. "We've got company."

Dark shapes loped out of the shadows between the buildings, eyes glowing orange. Hyenas were as creepy as nature shows made them seem, chittering excitedly as they cautiously darted about. The lowing calls the were-hyenas made sounded close to the cries for reinforcements their natural cousins made before attacking a pride of lions to take their kill.

Kira squared her shoulders as she faced them, her power still coating her hands. "I am Kira Solomon, Shadowchaser," she announced. "I received word that there is a leadership challenge tonight. We are here to observe."

More eerie giggling as the clan feinted and darted. "They want to surround us," Khefar murmured tightly.

"Standard operating procedure, no matter the species," Kira reminded him. "Still, your car's charged enough to stop a bull elephant in its tracks. We can hold our own if we have to. But it won't come to that."

"You're sure?"

"I'm sure." She pushed back Logic's Veil a hair more, allowing more of her power to pool into her fingertips. Wind blew at her face and hair, a current of magic that would give any sensitive reason to pause. Since their return to Atlanta, she'd been practicing throwing bolts of power. The power drain that resulted from the raw burst of magic meant that she'd use it only in an emergency or on a group attack, which in her world amounted to the same thing.

An older woman stepped from the shadows, a brightly colored caftan covering her black turtleneck and denims. She wore her hair in a short natural style, a wide multicolored band wrapped around her hair, pushing it back from her forehead. Around her neck hung a double-row necklace of cowrie shells from which dangled a smooth bolt of dark wood that resembled a female hyena's false penis. Kira knew from her research that only ranking females were allowed to wear the symbol.

"Greetings, Grandmother," Kira said, inclining her head slightly as a sign of respect. Any further and the bultungin would think Kira had placed herself lower in rank. As if.

"Shadowchaser Solomon," the older woman said. "We are surprised by your presence here. Outsiders do not come to our contests."

"There's a first time for everything, Grandmother," Kira said respectfully. "It's my duty as a Shadowchaser to be an ambassador of sorts to the preternatural community."

"An ambassador?" The elder's gaze flicked to Khefar. "Then you have brought our kandake a token of your esteem?"

Crap. Diplomatic fail. "My apologies, Grandmother," she said. "Khefar is my partner, not a gift."

Khefar jerked in surprise. Kira slashed her hand at him. "Don't say anything, for the love of Ma'at and Isis."

"Partner?" The elder echoed. "You don't mean that you, Chaser Solomon, think of this one as equal to you?"

Kira suppressed a sigh. "Yes, elder, I do. He helps me with my investigations. I am not bultungin. Your traditions are not my traditions."

"Ah, he works for you. Then, there is no issue with me taking him."

"Does she mean what I think she means?" Khefar whispered, his hand dropping to the Dagger of Kheferatum. The dagger responded with a surge of power. Even without touching it, Kira could feel its need to fight, its craving to draw blood.

"Yeah. I'll handle it. You work on calming that

blade down. We don't need this to get any more ugly than it needs to."

She looked at the gathered were-hyenas milling about, though she doubted there was anything random about their movements. More likely, it was a subtle attempt to keep Kira from getting an accurate count. "I'm going to say this with all due respect, Grandmother: you touch him, you die."

The older woman put her hand on her hip, surprised and affronted. "Excuse me?"

"I mean this for all the bultungin," Kira said, keeping her tone easy, though she meant every word that she spoke. "Khefar is mine, and I will not share him. You will not take him. You will not touch him. You won't even look at him funny. If you do, you die."

The elder cut her eyes at the were-hyenas milling about. "We are bultungin. We do as we please."

"That is your right," Kira said, nodding for emphasis. She bared her teeth. "Just as I have the right to kill you if you harm one hair on his head."

"You can't kill all of us."

"That's true . . . for the time being. You can run faster than I can, so it would take me a while to hunt all of you down." She kept her hands loose at her sides, calling attention to her weapons while simultaneously showing that she wasn't relying on them. "Tell me something, elder."

"Tell you what?" The older woman's voice flattened with anger.

"I simply wonder if the challenge is over, and you have become kandake? I thought there was another who challenged Kandake Amoye for leadership of the clan."

The elder's lips thinned. "There is. The challenge has not been fought yet."

"Then are you not speaking out of turn?" Kira asked, knowing she treaded on thin ice. She couldn't tell which way the elder's loyalties swung, and didn't want to rile the woman further. No one was taking Khefar from her if she could help it, and she certainly could. "I thought that you advise, the kandake decides."

The elder drew back as the high-pitched agitation increased among the clan. Khefar tensed. Kira forced herself to remain outwardly relaxed. She couldn't show weaknesses to a people barely this side of wild. She did not intend to become prey, but she didn't want to create a diplomatic incident and turn an entire breed of hybrid against her either.

The feather-mark at her throat twinged once, a reminder of her role as the Hand of Truth. "Grandmother, I have to wonder if you are deliberately delaying me from seeing the kandake," she said on sudden inspiration. "As the Hand of Ma'at, I have unencumbered passage."

"The Egyptian gods do not hold sway with us, young Shadowchaser," the matriarch replied, heat creeping into her voice. Some of the hyenas tittered in response.

"Perhaps not. But truth is universal, isn't it?" Kira unzipped her jacket enough to expose the mark of Ma'at's feather at her throat. "The light of Truth burns brightest in darkness, whether that darkness is a place or a soul. I'll ask again. Are you delaying my meeting with Kandake Amoye?"

Kira locked gazes with the were-hyena, refusing

to back down. The other bultungin stilled, waiting for direction from the more dominant female. Finally the elder threw out a hand. "Let them pass."

Most clan members faded into the darkness, save for the two largest, who acted as escorts. Kira glanced quickly at Khefar, who gave her a brief smile. "My hero," he whispered.

"Knock it off," she muttered even as she warmed inside. Good to know that Khefar seemed to be a study of composure. Of course, they hadn't gone completely into the hyena's den yet.

The clan guards led them along a hard-packed path of Georgia red clay to a square of apartment buildings stacked five stories high. A door stood open to one of the ground-floor units in the center of the block. With her hand on her Lightblade and her senses on full alert, Kira followed the elder inside.

Comfortable furniture filled the living-dining combination room. Several young were-hyena, in human and animal form, lounged on the taupe-colored sectional, watching a reality television show. They barely looked up as the older woman escorted Kira and Khefar through the serviceable kitchen and out the back door.

Kira had wondered how the bultungin indulged their changeling nature. She'd assumed that some of the reported sightings of coyotes in the Atlanta area could have been attributed to were-hyena being care-less with their shape-shifting. Seeing the courtyard gave her an understanding of how they managed their dual natures.

The central courtyard was huge, far larger than

it had seemed from the outside view of the buildings. The rectangular area sported a towering oak tree that had to be more than a hundred years old, with massive spreading branches covering almost all of the open area, making it impossible for Google Earth or any other satellite system to catch a view of the clan's after-dark work. The bultungin, some in their hyena form, some in human form, crowded the balconies overlooking the courtyard and thronged the grassy area surrounding the large tree, women, children, some teens, and a few men here and there.

"How very circle of life," Khefar murmured.

"Dude, seriously?" Kira shook her head. If joking helped him keep his mind off his memories, he could joke all he wanted.

Under the tree itself sat what could only be called a throne, a wide chair hewn from rustic wood and draped with animal hides. Two young women in black leather jackets and pants stood on either side of it, wearing smaller versions of the necklace the elder wore. They must have been the matriarch's daughters, DeVonne and DeRhonda.

The leader of the Westside Were-hyenas sat in the chair. Delores Amoye looked every bit the African queen she was, draped in an orange-and-gold traditional robe and headdress well suited to her proud chin and sculpted cheeks. Her cowrie-and-wood necklace sported a large false phallus that hung down between her breasts as befitting her rank as the alpha female.

Kira nodded. "Kandake Amoye."

The bultungin leader nodded to the same degree. "Shadowchaser Solomon," she said, her voice thick with a southern flavor. "We weren't expecting you, but you are welcome."

A commotion had some of the bultungin scattering, yipping their eerie call. A young woman, her hair in red and black synthetic braids hanging past her shoulders, pushed through the crowd. She wore an ankle-length dashiki that seemed ill suited to her style and demeanor. The look of irritation that crossed the clan leader's face clearly identified the brash young woman to Kira.

"What the hell is this?" she demanded, stopping in front of the throne.

The kandake didn't acknowledge the young woman, at least not directly. "We met before, Shadow-chaser, but this is the first time that you've visited our clan. Unfortunately *somebody* decided out of the blue that they wanted to challenge me for leadership, and the rules say I have to answer that challenge, no matter how re-damn-diculous it is."

"I understand that, Kandake Amoye," Kira answered, swallowing a smile. Now was not the time to show her amusement. "That's why I'm here, to observe the challenge." She didn't look at the agitated young woman beside the kandake. "Am I correct in assuming that this is the one who thinks to challenge you?"

"Who asked the Chaser to come here?" the young woman, who must be Roshonda, demanded. "We don't need outsiders interfering in our lives."

"That goes to show how you ain't ready to lead anything," the kandake retorted. "The Shadowchaser will stay."

"I don't want her here." Something dicey shifted behind the were-hyena's eyes.

The kandake's lips curled into a snarl. "Child, until you beat me and achieve some rank, it doesn't matter what you want."

Roshonda folded her arms, thrusting out her lower lip. "She shouldn't be here."

"Why not?" Kira asked. "What are you afraid of?"

"I sure as hell ain't afraid of you," the young were-hyena spat, jerking her head to punctuate her words. "I could rip you to shreds without even breaking a sweat."

Khefar stepped in front of Kira, his hand on his dagger. "Try it," he said, his voice overflowing with vengeful eagerness. "Please."

Roshonda tossed her hair. "If she needs a man to protect her, she obviously ain't worth my time."

Oh, no she didn't . . . Kira put a hand on Khefar's shoulder and moved forward to confront the clueless bultungin. "Bitch, please. Because you ain't worth *my* time, you'd fight him instead of me. Oh, and I'm staying." Kira settled her hands on her hips. "Unless you want to try and make me leave?"

The were-hyena cocked her head, as if listening to a disembodied voice. Kira had kept a shade of her magic about her as they'd entered the apartment to act as a buffer and a defensive shield. She tapped into it, allowing her magic to open her third eye and push aside Logic's Veil.

An aura of Shadow magic draped the young were-hyena.

"She's under the influence of outside magic," Kira announced. "Someone is manipulating her."

Roshonda screeched, a high-pitched yowl that grated along Kira's nerves like sliding along asphalt after falling off a motorcycle. The young bultungin's features rippled and ran as she stripped off her robe, then leapt toward Kira, shifting midair. Kira drew her blade, heard Khefar do the same to his khopesh.

A dark blur whizzed past them. Roshonda slammed to the ground. Kandake Amoye stood between them, her right hand partially formed into a claw. "You do not come up in my house, attack my guests, and disrespect me. Your fight is with me, young one. Don't show your ass."

The young were-hyena rose unsteadily to her feet, shaking off the blow. She bared her teeth, her head lowered. There was nothing submissive about her posture, however. She had no choice but to fight or be forever banned from the clan.

"Roshonda, you voluntarily distanced yourself from the clan after your mother died," the kandake said, removing her elaborate headdress and handing it to one of her daughters. "You turned your back on us and refused to accept all the benefits that being part of the clan can offer you. And now you think to come back and attempt to show me up in my own house?"

The bultungin's eyes glowed with her power. Several of the were-hyenas chittered in response. "I can be compassionate and show you mercy because you have not learned all that you would have had you chosen to stay with us. Stand down, and you will be welcomed back into the clan as the lowest-ranking female. You can learn what you need to learn about what it takes to be a true bultungin. If you do not retract your challenge, the lesson you'll learn tonight will not be as easy."

Kira thought the kandake was being excessively

lenient with the young were-hyena, but kept her opinion to herself. If it was up to her, Roshonda would never be allowed anywhere near the clan again.

The hyena bared her teeth again, then spoke, her voice twisted and rolling in her throat. "Shove your mercy. You are past your prime and your time. It is time for you and yours to go."

DeVonne, the elder sister, stepped forward, her features twisted in a snarl. "Let me fight her, kandake. I will show her what it means to be lipwereri!"

Kandake Amoye held up a hand. Silence fell, instant, total, strangely unsettling. The absolute otherness of those gathered around the great tree was easy to see and completely unnerving.

"Your education has been severely lacking, pup." The matriarch's voice rang with reproach as she stripped off her robes, revealing a body at the peak physical condition of an alpha were-hyena in her prime. "You will learn that to your sorrow. Defeat me, if you think you can."

The kandake shifted form quickly and seamlessly, a testament to the depth of her power. Kira could still see the Shadow magic gripping the young female. She almost felt sorry for the challenger, but Roshonda had accepted help from a Shadowling; she'd have to pay the price for that.

The challenger circled the matriarch. Kira didn't know much about were-hyenas or their wild cousins, but it didn't look like a fair fight to her. The matriarch easily outweighed the younger hyena by twenty pounds, all of which seemed to be pure muscle. The alpha female was also taller and broader in the shoulder. Kira couldn't believe that the younger bultun-gin had willingly agreed to challenge the older, more experienced matriarch.

The challenger darted in, powerful jaws opened in a snarl. Kira didn't see the alpha female move, but she did see the young female go flying, skidding across the grass and landing hard against the tree. The smaller hyena climbed to her feet, shaking her snub-nosed head. The alpha female simply stood in the center of the clearing to the right of the great tree, waiting for the challenger to charge again.

Charge she did, barreling into the larger female like a stampeding buffalo. The two combatants rolled, snapping and growling, their breaths steaming the cold night air. Kira heard the distinct crunch of break-ing bone, followed by a howl of pain. The two females broke apart, the smaller one limping, right front paw dangling. She bared her teeth, then growled, a sound of sheer bravado. The larger one stood tall, ears pricked forward, tail up, the picture of confidence.

With the detrimental injury, the outcome of the fight was easy to call. Each time Roshonda launched herself at the kandake, the matriarch raked deep gouges into the younger hyena's hide before tossing her aside. Soon enough the challenger was a bloody mess, while the matriarch only bore one scratch down her left foreleg. Defeated, the young were-hyena rolled over onto her back, exposing her soft vulnerable underbelly and throat. The alpha female stood over her, clearly showing her status as victor to the rest of the bultungin.

Power rolled off the matriarch as she quickly shifted back to her human form, the necklace around her neck. Every female in the clan wore one, Kira now noticed, causing her to wonder if the bultungin's power lay in the shell and wood, or if the necklaces simply were an outward statement of wealth and power. It was information she'd have to pass on to Gilead for the Commission database.

With every bultungin in the courtyard paying obeisance, the eldest daughter immediately stepped forward with the matriarch's clothing. The kandake waved her off. Clothed in nothing but power, the alpha female was an awe-inspiring sight. "Roshonda Biers. You are evicted from this bultungin family. No one will come to your aid. No one will share their den or their kill with you. The clan no longer knows you."

The kandake turned her back on Roshonda, a final insult, and then took the robe from her eldest daughter. Kira stepped forward, one eye on the supine change-ling. "Kandake Amoye, the Gilead Commission would be interested in knowing who gave Roshonda that boost of Shadow magic. I would like to take her in for questioning."

"Do what you will, Shadowchaser," the kandake said as she took her seat. "I know nothing of her move-ments before she challenged me. I'm done with her."

Kira made a mental note to never cross the were-hyena matriarch. "C'mon, Roshonda. We're going to take a trip downtown."

The young bultungin whimpered, scrabbling in the red dirt where the matriarch had left her. The air around her vibrated as she tried to shift forms but failed.

"I'm not going to kill you," Kira said irritably. "But I *am* going to make sure you don't cause me any trouble."

Khefar strode over to the bultungin and dropped the hilt of his khopesh against the base of Roshonda's skull with more enthusiasm than needed. Several of the were-hyenas darted closer, their eyes glowing as they looked at their defeated former kin.

"We need to get out of here," Khefar urged. "I gotta figure this girl has some accomplices here, and one fight always begets another."

"True, that. Grab her, and I'll cover our backs."

They quickly made their way out of the courtyard, back through the apartment, and to the street, several of the were-hyenas following. Khefar dropped the unconscious changeling to the ground, and then pulled out his keys to disarm the car alarm and open the trunk.

Kira pulled off her glove. "I don't want to do this, but I can't have you waking up and throwing a tantrum."

She dug her fingers into the were-hyena's fur, gripping her skull. Green energy flowed from her hand and over the unconscious changeling. Images flowed back, controlled instead of chaotic. A hooded figure extended something to the young bultungin, something that glowed with the fluorescent yellow of Shadow magic. If she could go back a little further, back to figure out how Roshonda had been exposed to the Shadowling . . .

Khefar touched her shoulder. "That's enough, don't you think?"

"What? Oh." She blinked, and then released the shifter. "I wanted to make sure she'd stay out for a while."

"She's drooling," Khefar said. "I think that's sure."

Kira dragged the unconscious shifter to Khefar's car. "Tell me your trunk's reinforced."

"Probably not enough to contain a pissed off were-hyena regaining consciousness," he said.

"Dammit. I was afraid you'd say that." She dug into her jacket pocket for her phone and touched a speed dial number.

"Travel Department."

"I need a pickup."

"First-class, business, or coach?"

Kira looked down at the hyena. "Business, when she wakes up."

"Triangulating position," the voice on the other end of the line said. "We have you. Looks like there's a transport five minutes from your location."

"Make it three, and leave the engine running."

"Understood."

Kira disconnected, then pocketed her phone. "Retrieval team's on the way."

"Are they going to be able to handle her?" Khefar asked.

"Retrievers are a special brew of brave and crazy," Kira explained. "There's usually at least one combat-trained Light Adept on the team, and they handle transport not only for Shadowchasers, but field agents that have the authority to pull in a Shadowling that's a threat to the general population. A were-hyena won't be a problem for them."

A white van with a pizza delivery sign atop it sped into the complex. The back doors swung open and several heavily armed agents swarmed out before the vehicle could roll to a stop. The team leader, a Slavic male in his late twenties, gave her a salute. "Ma'am. What do we have?"

"Female were-hyena, twenty-one human years," Kira said, pulling her glove back on. "Tried to incite the clan against the matriarch and failed. Then she tried to attack me, and also failed."

"Not a good night to be a were-hyena," one of the guards deadpanned.

"Someone boosted her power," Kira said flatly. "I didn't get a good sense of who or how. We gave her an extra tap to make sure she'd stay out, but I can't say for sure how long that will be. Process her and get her into holding as fast as you can."

"Yes, ma'am."

"Tell the section chief I'll be in at oh eight hundred to submit my report," Kira said as the team loaded the unconscious were-hyena into the back of the van. "Hopefully by then our troublemaker will be willing to tell us who boosted her power."

Chapter 14

"Thank you, by the way."

Khefar watched as Kira pulled the damp towel across her braids, refreshing them. They'd spent the past weekend rebraiding each other's hair—the parts of his that still could be braided anyway. Sure, he could have found a local place to take care of his hair but Kira couldn't. It had been one of those simple yet profound moments that he liked giving her. Besides, he enjoyed the noises she made when he ran his fingers through her hair, down her back. Hell, he enjoyed the noises she made when he touched her, period.

"Thank me for what?" she asked, her brows scrunching.

Instead of answering, he padded over to his side of the dresser. Turning his back to her, he took his time pulling open a drawer, removing a pair of dark red pajama pants. He made a show of pulling the loose-fitting pants on, conscious of her eyes on him. Kira still had skin hunger, but Atlanta had decided to acknowledge the arrival of winter with bone-chilling temperatures that the modifications in the converted warehouse couldn't quite stave off. As much as he liked sleeping naked with Kira, he also liked not freezing his balls off when answering nature's call in the middle of the night.

"For protecting me from the bultungin," he finally said. "I appreciate what you did."

She dipped her head, but not before he caught the discomfort arcing across her face. "That was nothing."

"It was something to me," he said, stepping closer to her. "It's not often that I am defended, or need to be defended. For you to stand between me and the entire pack, risking your life for mine, was awesome in every sense of the word."

She looked up at him, the weird golden light in her eyes darkening with solemnity. "After what you told me about your last time with bultungin, there was no way in heaven or hell that I was going to let them take you. I don't care if it would have caused a diplomatic incident. You have my back all the time. Why shouldn't I return the favor?" She dipped her head again and mumbled, "Besides, I need you too much."

Well, well. He tilted her chin up. "What was that?"

Her eyes glinted. "You heard me."

"Maybe I want you looking at me when you make a special declaration like that."

She shoved him away. "I don't know what's so special about it," she grumbled. "You already know I need you. My life's been turned upside down, and right now you're the only sane part of it."

She tossed the towel into a hamper and raked her fingers through her braids. The action tightened her tank top in interesting ways. "Who would have thought that I'd be calling a four-thousand-year-old guy who can get killed but resurrects with the morning sun the sanest part of my life?"

"I'm glad I could provide a little sanity for you." He

hid a grin. She sounded aggravated, but he knew she wasn't angry. They were still adjusting to each other's company but so far, the transition had been smooth. As long as neither one mentioned his vow to her, they could pretend to be normal lovers cohabitating.

Normal. He snorted. What they had, whatever it was, was likely as close to normal as they would get. He was gone on her and he knew he was gone on her. He wasn't sure when it had happened, but it had. What he didn't know, and wouldn't ask, was if she was as gone on him.

Her eyes swept over him and he could almost see the gears turning behind them in her brain. "What are you thinking?" he asked, not sure he wanted the answer.

"I know that your whole duty has been one of atonement so you could rejoin your family," she said, choosing her words carefully.

She seemed to be waiting for a response, so he said, "That's true."

"I also know you can't have been a monk all that time."

He studied her, but couldn't get a hint of her thoughts and feelings. "You know I haven't been."

She nodded. "Yeah. But what I don't know is if you've had ongoing relationships since you were given your charge. Have you?"

He sat on the edge of the bed. "Four thousand years is a long time to be alone."

"Yes, it is," she agreed. "But that's not what I asked."

"I know. I was trying to avoid answering."

She narrowed her eyes at him. "Now is not the time to be evasive in your storytelling, Nubian."

"All right." He leaned forward, dropping his elbows to his knees. "When I lost my family I was consumed with rage. It took a long time for that rage to burn out, longer still to rejoin humanity. And still longer to *want* to be a part of humanity. Even with that it's a hard thing to go without the company and comfort that another human being can offer."

"I understand," she said softly.

"It was several centuries before my heart even thought about awakening," he said, his voice and expression far away. "I was tasked with protecting a young woman and her children, four of them. I didn't want to—it was too similar to what I'd lost—but Isis was insistent. We were married, and I became a father to her children. I remained with the family long enough to see great-grandchildren."

He fell silent, pushing back through layers of memory. "I suppose Isis was teaching me a lesson."

She sat beside him. "What sort of lesson?"

"Teaching me to care about my charges."

"Of course you care!" she exclaimed. "You wouldn't have saved all those people if you didn't."

"You're right," he said, gratified that she would rush to his defense even in this. "Unfortunately, I cared more that I was adding to my total than that I was saving each person. Staying with that family for four generations . . . I learned to care about the people my charges were and would become. To view them as human beings, not goals. Living with them, celebrating and mourning and loving with them . . . that's the lesson I needed to learn, in all its painful glory. It helped me to remember what it is to be human."

She lifted her hand. After a moment's hesitation, she rubbed it down his forearm to clasp his hand. "For what it's worth, I think you're very caring and very human. I . . . appreciate that you're here, and that you care."

A wicked smile bowed her lips. "Shall I show you how much I appreciate you?"

"Hellz yes."

With a delighted laugh, she pushed him down on the bed and proceeded to show him in no uncertain terms how appreciated he was.

Buzzing slid along Kira's arms as she pulled her bike into the underground garage for Light International, the privately held multinational conglomerate that served as the front and funding source for the Gilead Commission. Light International had been a company longer than the United States had been a country, and no one questioned its existence.

She rolled through the security shield and stopped at the mechanical arm at the guard shack. It looked ubiquitous, exactly as it was supposed to, but Kira knew that layers and layers of protection—both magical and mundane—swathed the entry. She'd heard that a Shadow Adept had tried to breach the entrance five years ago, but had been violently repelled. Kira didn't know if it was urban legend or not, but there was a dark, oil-stain-looking blotch on the pavement in front of her, a blotch that resisted all attempts to pressure-wash it clean.

The security guard squeezed out of the small kiosk, handheld scanner aloft. How Rhino managed to fit his bulk into something the size of a guest closet was beyond Kira. He was so big people were afraid to step into an elevator with him, afraid of being stuck between floors or worse yet, being stuck in his massive layers only to suffocate unnoticed. The fears that kept others from riding with Rhino were the reasons Kira did. His presence kept her from accidental contact.

She lifted her visor, not that Rhino needed to see her eyes to make a positive identification. He held the palm-sized scanner in one beefy hand, and she wondered if it could read the Shadow that still tainted her and turn her into an oily stain on the ground. "Hey, Rhino."

"Hey, Kira." People expected the security guard to be slow, yet he was anything but. He came from a family of hybrids sometimes called slag demons because their highest evolved form looked like a giant lava version of the Thing. His voice was an even tenor, and she knew for a fact that he could cut a rug with the best of them. He lowered the scanner without activating it. "Two visits in as many weeks." Kira had stopped by two weeks before to retrieve some new equipment. "I'm going to stop being surprised when you show up around here."

"I'm here because of the were-hyena the SRT brought in last night," she answered, easing her bike forward. "Don't worry, I'll get back to my hermit-like ways pretty soon."

"I hope not. You're the highlight of my day."

"Then we need to get you out of that guard shack more. Are you staying warm?"

Rhino nodded. "I'm managing. The elders have

gone to ground for the winter, except for the clan leader of course. Atlanta is warm most of the time, but it is not Hawai'i. By the way, I have a chipotle turkey chili recipe you have got to try."

"Are you kidding? You have a molten lava core. I don't, and I'm not planning to get one anytime soon. I felt the effects of that curry you gave me for an entire week!"

Rhino laughed. "You're a gutsy lady, you can handle it."

"I'll think about it while I'm inside, and let you know. See you later."

She rode her bike deeper into the underground parking deck, three levels down to a thick gate that required a pass code. She punched in her code, and then rolled forward as the wide steel barrier silently slid open. Tactical response vans not currently in use neatly lined the concrete, noses out, ready to roll. Opposite them was another massive metal door that led to the bowels of Gilead East's headquarters. This was where the Special Response Teams delivered their high-priority packages for containment.

After parking her bike and punching in another pass code, Kira took the lift to Gilead East's containment area. Outwardly, it looked like an indoor storage facility, long corridors with matching gray doors set at equal distances along the hallway. Colored markers outside each door designated the threat level of the occupant. Low-level hybrids sleeping off an intoxicant were flagged green. Shadow Adepts in the grip of chaos madness were flagged yellow. Shadowlings too dangerous to be let loose into the human population and who needed to be transported were flagged red. The Fallen and their Shadow Avatars were the most dangerous, of course, but no Shadowchaser or Light agent would be insane enough to let one live long enough to be brought in, if one could be brought in anyway.

A blond woman in a navy blue suit beneath a white lab coat walked along the far end of the corridor, a tablet computer in her hands. "Chaser Solomon," she said. "I don't know if you remember me, but I'm Dr. Ingrid Rasmussen."

"I do remember you, sort of." The doctor had been part of Kira's rehabilitation after her encounter with the Fallen. "A team brought in a were-hyena last night. Have you cleared her for questioning?"

Rasmussen tapped her screen. "Oh. That detainee hasn't regained consciousness."

"She hasn't?" Kira frowned. "I know the fight with the bultungin matriarch was pretty intense, and we gave her a good rap to the back of the head, but it's been almost eight hours."

Rasmussen stared at her screen. "The subdural hematoma has improved, as to be expected with a shapeshifting hybrid's rapid physiology," she said, her voice cool. "We detected a high concentration of a Shadow-infused drug. The med sweepers were able to remove most of it, but not all. I expected her to regain consciousness a few hours ago. There's no physical explanation for it, so I can only assume it's something metaphysical."

Crap. Kira reviewed her actions from the previous night. She'd touched the changeling specifically to incapacitate her, not to read her. Khefar had intervened because he'd noticed Roshonda's condition deteriorating.

What would have happened if he hadn't? Would she have killed the bultungin so casually?

"Chaser?"

"Hmm. Yes?"

"Is there anything you can recall about the challenge that you can share?"

"No. Nothing about the fight seemed out of the ordinary to me, except that it was over fairly quickly."

"All right." The doctor made notations. "Thank you. The section chief would like to see you."

"Thanks."

Kira took the elevator up to the administrative levels, her mind whirling. Had she somehow incapacitated the were-hyena as a side effect of her blended nature? She wasn't sure, simply because she hadn't taken the time to think through the ramifications of having Light and Shadow inside her.

Most beings fell somewhere in the middle of the Universal Balance, making choices and living their lives without directed intent to good or evil. Because of that, their free will determined whether they would turn to Shadow or to Light, and also made it easy for most to live in balance. People could reform or backslide, their scales constantly shifting. It was the nature of life.

The elevator doors opened with a soft ping. Kira made her way through the administrative wing to Sanchez's office. The section chief had on her usual uniform of a sharp business suit, chocolate this time, her dark hair pulled into a chignon at the back of her neck. A few files littered her desk, but Kira knew most of the reports and decisions were made via the tablet that was never far from Sanchez's hand.

"Nice work with the were-hyena last night," Estrella Sanchez said in place of a greeting.

"The matriarch did most of the work," Kira said honestly. "We took out the trash. The doctor told me that Roshonda is still unconscious."

Sanchez nodded. "More than unconscious. She's nonresponsive to stimuli. And she hasn't regained her human form."

"Really?" That didn't sound right. "I don't think the matriarch cursed her in any sort of way, but Roshonda was tossed out of the clan last night. There might be some sort of metaphysical backlash that got compounded when she was formally evicted."

"The retrievers told me that you touched her before they arrived. How long did you hold on to her?"

"It wasn't long. Khefar knocked her unconscious. I touched her long enough to know that she got some sort of vial of concentrated Shadow magic from someone in a hoodie. Then I called the retrieval team."

"Dr. Rasmussen needs as much information as possible on our detainee. Her medics found some sort of Shadow-infused drug in the bultungin's system, but she doesn't think that's responsible for the detainee's current condition." Sanchez regarded her, her arms folded across the front of her expensive jacket. "Nothing else out of the ordinary happened?"

"Nothing that I can think of. I'll submit an official report before I leave. You can also ask Khefar if you want."

"I don't think that will be necessary." Sanchez moved around her desk. "Make sure it's a detailed report. Somehow I don't think the were-hyenas are going to be open to another Gilead visit soon."

"Probably not." Kira moved farther into the office. "We need to find out why someone would want to meddle with the bultungin's affairs. They tend to stick to their own kind in their own area. I wouldn't consider them power brokers or anything, so why destabilize the clan? It doesn't make sense."

"I'll have a couple of field agents start a case file," Sanchez said, making a note on her handheld. "It may be tied to that incident we had with the SRT Five back in October."

Kira didn't answer. That "incident" resulted in the loss of the Special Response Team, then her kidnapping and imprisonment by Enig, the Shadow Avatar, and being injected with a psychotropic that left her permanently tainted with Shadow. She didn't want field investigators digging into something that could be detrimental to their collective health, but an investigation needed to happen.

She made a mental note to talk to Demoz and Bale, see what information they had. Neither would talk to a Gilead field agent—at least, they wouldn't provide any useful information. Kira never bothered to ask why she was an exception. She'd assumed it was because she was a Shadowchaser and focused on keeping the peace with occasional bouts of kicking butt. Now she wasn't so sure. Did they both already know about her dual nature, and kept it to themselves?

She took a seat in one of the guest chairs. "I want to talk to you about someone."

A hint of softness brightened Sanchez's eyes. "You're finally going to tell me about your new partner?"

"What? No." Why in the world would Sanchez

think Kira would want to talk about Khefar? "D'Aurius Amoye."

"Amoye." Sanchez considered for a moment, as if trying to recall where she'd heard the name. "That's the name of the were-hyena leader."

"Yes. He is her son."

"What about him?"

Kira hesitated. Better to spit it out and get it over with. "He wants to become a Shadowchaser."

"You want to recommend a were-hyena to enter Shadowchaser training," Sanchez said slowly, as if trying the words on for size. "One of a clan to which our newest detainee belonged to."

"It wouldn't be the first time we've had a hybrid fighting for Light," Kira shot back, defensive. "Hybrids fall on both sides of the Universal Balance. If one wants to fight for Light, and has the strength and agility to take on other hybrids, I say let him."

"You think that highly of him?"

"I think he's out of options. I think he wants it badly. More than that, I think he has a healthy respect for female authority. So he's got at least one thing going for him that I didn't."

A ghost of a dimple formed in Sanchez's right cheek. "A healthy respect for authority," she murmured. "I like him already."

Of course you would, Kira thought to herself. Aloud she said, "Will you meet with him? A recommendation from you would go a long way, and he's sure to be grateful you gave him a chance."

Sanchez eyed her, as if waiting for Kira to shout "Gotcha!" Finally she folded her arms across her chest.

"You seem extremely interested in succession planning all of a sudden," the section chief observed. "Any particular reason?"

Kira shifted in her chair. "Let's just say I've become keenly aware of my own mortality over the last couple of months. I'm not in any hurry to go into the Light, but I also want to make sure the city is protected. The hybrid community here is too large not to have a Shadowchaser. Given that I'm not exactly winning friends and influencing people, it probably wouldn't be a bad idea to have a backup in the area, even one in training."

"Have you spoken to the Balm of Gilead about this?"

"No." She didn't want to think about Balm, the days of silence, and what it all meant. "So will you see him?"

Sanchez regarded her in the cool, measuring way the section chief had. Kira could almost see the gears turning, and wondered how many steps ahead Sanchez was in their particular dance.

Finally, Sanchez unfolded her arms. "Give the young man's number to my assistant. I'll meet with him and see what I think."

"I will." Kira rose. "Thanks."

Sanchez stopped her before Kira could pull open the door. "Solomon."

Kira turned. "Yes?"

"Is everything all right with you?" the section chief asked. "You seem a little out of sorts."

"I'll be fine. You know me. I tend to roll with the punches."

"There's rolling with the punches and there's

becoming a human punching bag," Sanchez told her. "You don't have to take all the hits, you know."

Kira stared at the section chief. She thought she was in pretty good shape today. She'd had a full night's dreamless sleep. How messed up did she have to be for Section Chief Sanchez to offer words of comfort? "Thank you for that," Kira said, her gloved fingers digging into the smooth panel of the wood door. "I'll try to keep it in mind."

"I hope you do, Kira Solomon," Sanchez said. "I hope you do."

Chapter 15

After preparing and delivering her report on the Abultungin incident, Kira made her way out of Gilead East's headquarters and back home. Khefar was blessedly nowhere to be seen, so she made her way to the lower level and her private reinforced office. She lit a stick of incense as an offering of thanks to Ma'at and sat behind her desk.

Her gaze roamed over the office. It had grown more cluttered in the weeks since her return from Cairo and London, stuffed with research books and dozens of mementos from Comstock's offices at his home and the antiques shop. A collection of statuettes formed a semicircle on the left side of her desk: Ma'at, Isis, Osiris, Thoth, and Horus. On the right side of her desk she'd placed Bernie's pocket watch, a fruitwood puzzle box, and a photo of them taken during her field exam at university.

She stripped off her gloves, then picked up the watch. Her office walls shimmered, stilled. They were still covered with shelves of old books, except now they were stacked and ordered differently. Not her office at all, but Bernie's.

She sat opposite him in an overstuffed Queen Anne, watching as he poured tea. They had shared the ritual daily during her time at the university and whenever she'd passed through afterward, whether it was tea-time or not.

"You know, no matter what kind of day I was having, this always made it better," she said, using a pair of silver tongs to drop two cubes of sugar into her china cup. "It didn't matter if I was stressing over exams or a Chase. Having tea with you was always the highlight of my day."

"As it was mine," Comstock said, fussing with the tea service. "A visit from you was always a sure way to warm an old man's heart."

"I bet you say that to all the Chasers you handled." Kira looked up from her cup of tea. "Since when do you pour Darjeeling?"

Bernie Comstock settled into the chair behind his ornate solicitor's desk, a pale bone china cup balanced between his fingertips. "You were never a fan of Earl Grey, and since this construct is as much you as it is me, Darjeeling is what we'll have for tea."

He smiled at her over the rim of his cup, his expression even more foxlike. "Unless of course you prefer to have the rooibos, now that you have the Nubian in your life?"

Kira groaned. "I get enough teasing from Wynne. I thought here at least I'd have some peace of mind. It's *my* dream, after all."

She looked about the office. Comstock's antiques shop had been her home away from home when she wasn't at university or trawling the museum. The deeper you ventured into the shop, crammed mostly with first-edition books on the most esoteric subjects, the better the treasure got. At least in Kira's opinion.

The holy of holies was Comstock's office, brimming with stone carvings from Sumer, Mesopotamia, Egypt, and Babylon. Many people believed Bernie when he told them they were museum replicas, but Kira had known better. After Bernie's memorial service, Kira had almost all of Bernie's office packed up and shipped back to Atlanta.

"You're right, it *is* your dream. Do you have peace of mind?"

"I'm trying, but it's hard. Being able to be here like this, and talk to you like this, helps."

"Good." Comstock leaned back. "Then I'm glad a part of me was able to stay behind to help you."

She stared at him. In this dream that wasn't a dream, he looked much as he had when he was alive, a dapper Englishman in his sixties who liked few objects less than fifty years old.

"How did you do this, Bernie? You say you're a construct of yourself, me, and my magic. Your solicitor swears that you didn't barter your soul. That leaves you as being some sort of spirit, but you don't manifest like other ghosts."

"If you want me to manifest like a ghost, I surely can do that," Comstock told her. "Though I don't believe you really want me popping into your house unannounced, do you?"

Her cheeks heated. Since she and Khefar had sexually tested almost every flat surface in her house, except for her altar room, she was even less inclined to have people dropping by, even ghostly ones.

"You can do that?" she asked. "Manifest independently, I mean."

"Yes. Among other things." He concentrated on placing his teacup back in its saucer, a gesture she knew meant he had something he wanted to say, but needed time to find the words to say it.

"What's on your mind, Bernie? I know it's usually me reaching out to you to answer some burning question or to help me feel better, but today I feel like it's the other way around."

"It is. I have a couple of things I want to share with you."

Answers, she hoped, but it didn't seem like it. "Like what?"

"Among my effects is a pair of spectacles. You should keep them with you from now on."

"Why?"

"They will help how others see you."

"Kind of a Superman sort of thing, a secret identity?" She shook her head. "No, thanks, Bernie. If I suddenly start showing up with glasses on, I'll get more questions, not fewer. I don't really give a damn how other people see me anyway. It's not like I'm trying to be Miss Congeniality."

"That's my girl. Prickly as a porcupine." His smile faded, seriousness pushing the mirth from his expression. "The problem is not your personality, Kira, but your eyes. Especially when you channel Shadow magic."

The teacup wobbled in her hands. "You're saying I'm going to keep experiencing it—Shadow magic. I'm not going to be able to get rid of it."

"Do you plan to rid yourself of your arm, or your right eye?" Comstock asked. "Shadow magic is a part of you. Use it as you use your anger and your quest for truth."

"It's wrong," she protested, shocked that Comstock would suggest she actually use Shadow magic. "It's evil."

"It's evil if there's no rhyme or reason, if it is indiscriminately used," Comstock corrected. "You have guns. You have your Lightblade. You've used both. Does that make you evil?"

She didn't want to answer the question because any answer she gave would be wrong.

Comstock sighed. "All right, then, how about this example? A thief with a gun breaks into a person's home. The homeowner also has a gun. Who's evil?"

"The thief, of course."

"Why?"

"Because he's trying to take something that doesn't belong to him, and he'll use the gun to do it," she answered. "The homeowner is defending what is his."

Comstock nodded. "So it's not the weapon that's evil, it's the intent behind its use."

Kira stared at her mentor, finding it hard not to mistrust him. Considering his construct, she'd also be distrusting herself. "I feel like you're trying to trick me, Bernie, and I don't know why."

"Kira." Now he sounded like himself, lecturing and admonishing simultaneously. "I'm not trying to trick you, dear girl. I'm trying to educate and advise you. That is my duty as a mentor, and that is why you come talk to me. Ask yourself honestly, have I ever made you do something that you did not want to do?"

"No."

He leaned forward. "Have I ever given you reason to doubt me?"

"Besides not telling me that you knew about my Shadowchasing, since you were my handler?"

He smiled, sad at the edges. "Besides that."

"No."

He waved his hand about the room. Vision and reality slid across each other before fading back to the confines of her office. "Old men often have regrets. You already know how much I regret not sharing my association with the Gilead Commission with you. There is a reason for that, which is the same reason why I joined the Commission in the first place."

"What reason is that? Access to their extensive database?"

Comstock went glassy-eyed. "The Gilead archives are a wonder to behold, especially for someone who loves knowledge as much as I do. However, there were two things I loved more: my dearest wife, and you."

"You joined Gilead because you loved me. And you kept that knowledge from me for the same reason." Kira snorted. "You realize that doesn't make a lick of sense, right?"

"Whether you believe me or not, I took my role as your handler very seriously. More than that, I felt as if I had become your guardian. As such, your best interests were always my focus, whether that meant making you the best archaeologist, the best Chaser, or the best person you could be. Or all three. Ensuring that you are the best means that you don't get an easy path."

She laughed. "You're right about that. Nothing

about my life has ever been easy. I don't think I'd trust it if it were."

"Of course not," he agreed, his eyes crinkling at the edges. Then he sobered. "Becoming your handler gave me more means to protect you than a lowly professor had at his disposal," Comstock told her. "Joining Gilead gave me access to thousands of years of history, but also, I'd hoped, clues to who your parents were."

Kira stared at Comstock, shocked. "You were looking for my parents?"

He nodded. "I knew that was important to you. I also knew that your own search had yielded limited results. What I didn't know was whether that was by design or if the information simply wasn't there. So I had to use other means to gather the information I sought."

His hands flanked the puzzle box on her desk." Part of the reason that the Dagger of Kheferatum came to me is because I was doing research into who your parents possibly were."

Kira recoiled in her seat. "You are not going to tell me that Khefar is somehow connected to my parents!"

"No, no, I wouldn't have kept that from you. However, before the Dagger of Kheferatum came into my possession, I received another."

His fingers danced atop the lid of a fruitwood box, tapping out a rhythm along the carved pattern, pushing parts of it flat into the surface. The lid opened with an almost inaudible snick. After opening the lid, he turned the box toward her.

A first glance, it was simply a knife, its design obviously influenced by the Indo-Persian fighting blade styles. The longer she looked at it, the more she realized it was anything but a simple weapon. The blade was a dark charcoal gray, almost black, the metal swirling with sheens of silvery-copper etching. Brass studs secured the grip, which looked to be made of some type of bone.

"I know this blade," she said, her voice slow.

"Yes, you do," Bernie said. "Now."

Then it hit her. "I saw this, when I touched my mother's locket. This is the dagger the Shadowling had, the Lightchaser who attacked my mother."

"When it first came into my possession I didn't know its significance, not for sure," Comstock told her. "All I knew was that it had belonged to a Shadowling who was killed while fighting a female Shadowchaser, and had been confiscated by the Gilead team that came to retrieve her. My intention was to bring this one to you, but then the Dagger of Kheferatum fell into my hands and I thought it the more significant discovery."

"More significant. A dagger that can destroy the world, or a blade that destroyed my world." She looked at her mentor. "You went through a lot of trouble getting this. I know Gilead London had some serious security issues, but I can't imagine it was easy for you to get this Lightchaser's dagger out of whatever Gilead storage facility it was in."

"It wasn't. I had help." He didn't elaborate, but he didn't have to. Kira knew the Commission stored a wide variety of artifacts acquired during its long existence. Some were stored in trap vaults on Santa Costa, others in various inaccessible places around the world. The secretive Commissioners were reputedly the only ones who knew the location of all the vaults, or how to get to them.

"How were you able to do all of this?" she asked, which was a much safer question than asking why her mentor wanted her to have a Lightchaser's dagger.

Comstock's expression closed so definitively that it was so hard to remember he was dead. "I told you, I had help."

"You're going to have to give me more than that, Bernie," she pressed. "As I said before, your lawyer told me that you didn't sell your soul, but that's all he told me."

Irritation crossed his features. "My barrister shouldn't have told you that much."

"Considering that I was grieving, pissed, and sitting across from a demon, you should be *glad* he told me that much."

She stretched a hand across the desk to him. "Bernie, please. I really want to be sure that your afterlife is okay. You've done so much for me, alive and dead, but if it cost you your soul—"

"Kira." His fingers hovered over hers. "Put your mind at ease. I didn't sell my soul to anyone."

"Okay." She slumped back into the plush chair. She couldn't help being worried even as she appreciated the help from beyond. "So you didn't do any soul-bartering. You still used some pretty powerful magic. For my own curiosity as much as my peace of mind, I'd like to know how you were able to bring these daggers with you and how you're able to manifest as you do."

"I acquired the assistance of a shaman and his wife," Bernie finally said after a long silence. "They practice Balance Magic."

"Balance Magic. Why does that sound familiar?"

Bernie smiled. "Probably because I found a

reference to it in an old manuscript in Gilead's archives, took it, and left it stacked with some books I'd asked you to catalog for the antiques shop."

"Of course. Seeing as how I've never met a book I didn't like, I naturally flipped through it," Kira said wryly. "I think I also ran across something about it while reading through the massive library on Santa Costa. Something about using a fusion of Light and Shadow magic to power an intent. No one's practiced it for decades, if not centuries, if Gilead's records are anything to go by."

"No one practices Balance Magic openly anymore," Bernie corrected her. "Gilead seems to have a problem with anything or anyone that hints of Shadow."

Kira flinched.

"I'm sorry, Kira, but you know it as well as I do," Bernie insisted. "The Commission distrusts anything that isn't sourced from Light even though they've been around long enough to know that there are a variety of shades of gray. Balm has done what she could to suppress the other half of your nature, all but stamping it out. Yet there are others like you, people who are of both Light and Shadow, people who walk in the gray space between."

"Which explains why Solis exists, I suppose," Kira said, trying to straighten everything out in her head. "So this shaman and his wife are essentially gray witches of some sort?"

"The shaman is of Light and his wife, who is a powerful magician in her own right, is born of Shadow," Bernie explained. "They have also become Adepts in each other's native magic."

A headache began to buzz between her temples,

her third eye struggling to see clearly through what she thought she knew to what she was learning now. "You mean the Shadow-born is a Light Adept. And the Light shaman channels Chaos magic."

Her mentor nodded again. "They combine their innate magic with their Adept skills for more powerful works, creating Balance magic."

"I can see why Gilead would have a problem with people having this sort of power. If these two can fuse parts of your essence to your personal objects, who knows what else they can do."

"Help me find that, for one," Comstock said, gesturing to the Shadowblade.

Kira eyed the dagger warily. She didn't believe it could move independently, but she had good reason to mistrust daggers not her own. "So what do you expect me to do with it?"

"It's yours, Kira. It is yours as surely as your mother's locket and her Lightblade are yours. I suspect that Balm kept your mother's Lightblade for herself, otherwise I would have secured that for you as well."

"Why?"

He came around the desk, gathered her hands in his. "Because you are who you are, Kira. You have to be able to explore that. After learning what you can, you should accept your truth."

"What truth is that?" she asked, though she already knew.

"Your truth is that you are a child of Light *and* a child of Shadow. You are an excellent Shadowchaser. However, I have no doubt that should you choose to be, you'd make an excellent Lightchaser."

"Is that what you think I should do?" she asked, shocked. "Turn my back on everything I know, everything I am, and become Shadow?"

"Everything you know and everything you are isn't Light alone, Kira. You are half of each. You are both. What you decide to do about it is your choice."

He squeezed her hands. "Never forget that. Others may think they control you, others may think they own you. What they seem to forget, however, is that you have Free Will, and in the end, you are the one who will decide what you are to be. Not your parents, not Balm, not Solis, not Myshael, not Ma'at or Set. Not even me. It is, and has always been, up to you."

"So I'm going to have to make a choice. A choice that will set my path and decide my fate, and it will all be up to me, huh?" Figures. When it was time to stand, one usually stood alone.

Comstock cocked his head. "Hasn't that always been your path, Kira? Stubbornly forging your own way, blazing a trail through the underbrush when there's a perfectly good road beside you?"

"I'm not that bad," she retorted. "Okay, maybe I am, but not without good reason."

"No, not without good reason," he agreed. "Reason is one of your greatest gifts, Kira. Your mind and your heart drive your will. You must remember to gather all the facts and consider all of the possibilities. See truth in all its forms."

"See truth in all its forms," she murmured under her breath. "What does that even mean?"

"You'll know, my girl." His body slowly became ethereal. "You'll know."

Kira blinked rapidly as reality reasserted itself. Bit by bit she pulled herself back together, wiping at her eyes with the backs of her hands. Her gaze fell to the knife nestled in the wooden puzzle box, then to the arrangement of gilded deities. If she believed Comstock, she'd have to add an icon of Set to her collection.

Why wouldn't she believe him, with the proof lying before her? The existence of Lightchasers and practitioners of Balance magic shouldn't have surprised her as much as it did. It made sense on a philosophical scale—Universal Balance and all that. The part that was harder to accept was that this Lightchaser's blade belonged to the being who had sired her.

Her eyes fell to the dagger again. She'd seen enough through her mother's eyes to know that she didn't want to wrap her bare hands around any part of the blade. She didn't want to know what a Lightchaser did in service to Shadow.

Are you sure? Another part of her mind wondered. *That's the kind of information the Commission would love to have. Think of what you could do with the knowledge. It would be easier to fight Shadowlings if you knew more about them than war stories gleaned from dusty volumes.*

She looked at the gilded statues again. Despite what Bernie had told her, she needed Ma'at in her life. Ma'at had saved her, had claimed her. Kira couldn't conceive of turning her back on her goddess, no matter how strong her Shadow nature became.

"I could really use some guidance right now, and a healthy dose of intestinal fortitude."

Closing her eyes, she allowed her breath to flow out

and back in. Her concentration focused on the mark at the base of her throat, the feather brand that claimed her as the Hand of Ma'at. The tattoo stung, heated to a burn, a reminder that truth sometimes wasn't an easy thing to bear.

"Ma'at. Lady of Truth and Justice. You chose me to be Your Hand, to be a bearer of Truth and of Order. I know I should have known what that meant, that I would need to be able to bear my own truth, no matter how hard that is. All I ask is that you give me the strength to walk in truth, to stand in justice, stare truth in the face and be worthy of the honor you have given me."

She touched the feather mark at her throat again. She'd gotten a lot of truth in the last few days. She had a feeling she was going to get a lot more.

Kira tented her hands above the dagger, called up her extrasense. Magic and logic slid against each other, fighting for dominance. The air shimmered. Suddenly, as if she'd thrown a switch, everything magical in her office lit up. The gilded deities glowed golden-white. Comstock's watch glittered a deep turquoise. The Light-chaser's blade emitted a deep lemon-citrine light.

Kira focused her energy into her hands. If she concentrated, she might be able to slice away the memories etched into the blade, leaving only the magic behind. She didn't want to know anything about her sperm-donor father that she hadn't already seen.

Patterns swirled around and through the dagger, resolving themselves into two distinct frequencies: one of magic and one of memory. She'd learned through her years of cataloguing and defusing ceremonial objects that magic, whether Light or Shadow based, had its own metaphysical feel and taste, and she used her extrasense to differentiate between the auras that contain impressions of memories and the auras that contain magic.

She had no idea how much time had passed since she'd begun what was essentially magical surgery. All Kira knew when she finally pulled the Veil back over her sight was that her back, eyes, and brain all ached.

She cracked her knuckles, then rubbed at her eyes. Khefar was probably upstairs somewhere, waiting for her to return. She appreciated that he gave her space to work, to attend to her prayers, to have solitude when she needed it. It almost made her feel guilty for keeping things from him.

Before she could change her mind, Kira stretched out her right hand, gripped the bone hilt of the Lightchaser's dagger, picked it up.

Light seemed to explode from the blade, sunshine yellow. Her extrasense burst through in pure self-defense, battering into the Chaos magic like an opposing storm front. Pain wracked her body from her head down, bowing her back, spasming her hands, throwing her back in the chair. Perception bent, stretched. It shattered beneath the onslaught, searing her senses. Her brain, realizing that her body was in danger of overloading, did the only thing it could do: it shut down, sending her headlong into blackness.

Chapter 16

A hard jangle of sound cut through the room. Khefar rolled over Kira, snatched up her phone, and answered before Kira fully awakened. "Yeah?"

"It's Zoo." Barely restrained panic thrummed through the voice on the other end. "They're taking Wynne to the hospital."

Kira sat up. "What? What's wrong?"

"It's Zoo," Khefar said, ignoring her grab for the phone. "What happened?" he asked into the receiver.

"I don't know. She said she was going to take a nap. I came in to wake her up for dinner—it's our date night. She wouldn't wake up, and you know she's not a heavy sleeper." His voice wobbled. "I took her by the shoulders and shook her. I even tried ice water on her face. Nothing. My girl wouldn't wake up."

"Which hospital?"

"Hospital?" Kira leapt out of bed. "Something's wrong with Wynne, isn't it?"

"Memorial," Zoo answered.

"We're on the way." Khefar disconnected. By the time he got out of bed, Kira had already thrown on jeans and a bra. She pulled a black shirt over her head before he could zip his jeans. "Zoo said Wynne wouldn't wake up, no matter what he did. Paramedics are taking her to Memorial Hospital now."

"You don't have to go." Her voice was clipped as she sat on the bed to pull her boots on. She hopped to her feet, stomping to settle her feet in her boots even as she reached for her Lightblade rigging.

"You don't need to drive," he countered, following as she raced out of the bedroom and down the stairs. He forced himself to stay calm for Kira's sake. Something had been off with her ever since he'd entered her office earlier that evening to find her slumped over her desk, an old dagger in her hand. She'd passed it off as fatigue, but he wasn't so sure. Even so, she didn't need to be on her motorcycle after identifying an antique knife and a night patrol. The Marlowes were chosen family, the nearest and dearest she had left, and she wouldn't be able to focus on driving while thinking about Wynne. "They're your family, and they're my friends. I'm going with you."

"Okay." She buckled on yet another dagger gun-slinger style before shoving her arms into her battered overcoat and tugging on her gloves. "Let's hurry." On her way out, she grabbed Bernie's spectacles and settled them on her face.

The drive from Kira's East Atlanta home to the hospital in the center of downtown was blessedly short, a straight shot down Decatur Street to Jesse Hill Drive. It took longer to find an available spot in the Butler Street parking deck and make their way to the Trauma Center entrance.

Tension hung on Kira like armor. Khefar saw the set of her shoulders and knew she blamed herself. It didn't matter that they had no idea what had happened to Wynne Marlowe. All that mattered to Kira was that her friend had fallen ill and she hadn't been there to prevent it.

"Watch your dagger," she said, speaking for the first time since they left the house. "This hospital has a bustling emergency room and the only Level I trauma center within a hundred miles. Not only are there life-and-death struggles going on inside, there are probably plenty of hybrids from both sides in there too."

"I'll control the dagger," he said. He'd pulled on the long trench, enabling him to wear the dagger at his hip. "What about the hybrids?"

"Unless someone's blatantly doing something they shouldn't, leave them alone," she answered, her voice curt. "My only concern right now is Wynne and Zoo."

A cross-section of Atlanta packed the emergency room waiting area, and their needs were as diverse as the patients themselves. Feverish children, old folks wheezing and hacking or sitting ashen and still, people of all ages and races sporting injuries from minor to serious. Kira approached a curved information desk. A Hispanic woman held up a finger as she answered a coworker's question, a phone tucked between her cheek and shoulder. She took her time completing the call and returning the handset to its cradle. "Yes?"

"We're looking for an emergency patient that may have arrived comatose," Kira told her.

"Stroke and Neuroscience," the woman replied without looking up.

Kira's eyes flashed. The woman behind the desk didn't seem to notice it, but Khefar did. He reached up so that he could lay a bare finger against the back of her neck. Being touched was still a novel enough sensation for her that it instantly distracted her.

"We're here for Wynne," he reminded her when she turned to him.

She nodded once, not trusting herself to speak. Finding out what had happened to Wynne was the important thing, not some nurse who needed to come down from her power trip and show some compassion.

Kira and Khefar followed the directions to the Marcus Stroke and Neurosciences Center. It was like stepping into another world, a peaceful, high-tech oasis far removed from the chained chaos of the general emergency area. Surely someone in a place like this would know what had happened to fell a healthy young woman like Wynne Marlowe.

They found Zoo pacing in a brightly lit waiting area. He wore well-worn jeans, a splattered burgundy sweater that had seen better days, and sneakers that probably had been tan at one point. He must have been crafting spells before the accident. He kept rubbing the owl tattoo on the top of his shaved head, as if seeking comfort or inspiration from his personal totem. Worry etched his olive features, making him look older than his twenty-eight years.

"Zoo."

He looked up at their approach, stumbling to a stop. Kira took a step toward him, then halted. The normal thing, the human thing, would be to hug her friend and offer comfort, Khefar realized, but Kira wouldn't do that. She was dressed for winter's cold from head to toe, but still she was careful not to touch anyone else. Instead, she shoved her hands deep into her pockets and nodded her greeting. "How is she?"

"They don't know." Zoo shook his head. "At first they were thinking stroke, but they're saying they couldn't find any evidence of internal bleeding, no hemorrhage in the brain, no stresses to the heart."

His eyes brightened with unshed tears as he clenched his jaw. "So they started asking me about drug use."

"That's part of the normal screening they'd do," Kira said, trying to reassure her friend.

"If they'd asked about anything else, I'd believe you," Zoo retorted. "But they didn't ask about anything other than drugs."

"Wynne doesn't even use painkillers for PMS," Kira said. "She's the healthiest person I know. Do vitamins and herbal teas count as drugs?"

"That's what I told them." Zoo set his jaw. "They didn't believe me. Started asking where we live, what conditions and environments we've been in, and where we've been in the last couple of days. They took a look at me, at how I'm dressed. They find out what kind of business I own, and they decide that we're drugged-out neo-hippies doing something shady."

Anger burned his cheeks. "They kept saying I might as well tell them now, so they can treat her. It would be worse if they found it in her blood, because then they could hold me responsible for hurting her."

"What?" Behind the glasses, Kira's eyes did that dangerous flash to yellow again. Dread formed a fist in Khefar's gut. Kira's emotions were threatening to unbalance her. Somehow, she needed to find a target for her feelings before they got the best of her. "Green hair doesn't make someone a drug user."

"That's what I told them. I demanded they screen her blood, and offered up mine too while they were at it. Then I called the section chief."

Kira stopped short. "You called Sanchez?"

"What else was I supposed to do?" Zoo demanded. "We did physical and psychological evals for them when Balm brought us on board, the whole nine. Gilead's got the most updated records. Besides, Sanchez has pull. Someone from Gilead is coming to deliver Wynne's files, and then the doctors here will know that Wynne doesn't do drugs."

Khefar had an inkling of who would hand-deliver Wynne's records. From the sour expression Kira wore, she had the same person in mind. Section Chief Estrella Sanchez would be extremely interested in any member of her forces being sent to the hospital, especially since Wynne was a tactical officer assigned to Kira. The Shadowchaser's irritating disdain for the system would ensure Sanchez's personal involvement.

"Do you have a problem with Gilead getting involved?" the witch asked.

"Of course not," Kira answered. "It makes sense, and you're part of the organization now. Gilead's records will show that Wynne's perfectly healthy. The hospital staff can stop making wild assumptions and focus on other causes for her condition."

"Maybe they should focus on you."

Khefar looked at the other man, surprised at the vehemence in his tone. "What's that supposed to mean?"

"This is magic-based, and we all know it!"

"You're probably right," Kira said then, her tone soothing. "Has Wynne been around any assault magic? Shadow magic?"

"The only magic she's been around besides mine is yours, and mine isn't Shadow based."

Something in the other man's voice made Khefar want to reach for his blade, an instinctive gesture in the face of imminent threat. Zoo hadn't looked at Kira directly since they'd arrived, and everything about his demeanor from his stance to his tone of voice screamed antagonism. Khefar knew Zoo was upset about his wife, but there was no need to take his frustrations out on Kira.

"Kira doesn't have Shadow magic, Zoo," Khefar said evenly, even as he edged between them. "You know this."

"You know what I'm talking about, don't you, Kira?" Something ugly crossed Zoo's face. "Wynne's perfectly healthy. She doesn't do drugs. So you tell me: what's left?"

"Magic," she said, her voice bare.

Khefar's shock quickly turned to anger. "Are you accusing Kira?" he demanded. "That's as absurd as accusing you!"

Zoo didn't take his eyes from Kira. "My magic requires a delivery mechanism, and leaves trace amounts behind. It's a clear enough signature for someone with the skills to look. Kira's magic doesn't need anything like that, does it?"

Kira's face turned ashen. "No. I touch something."

"Yeah." Something ugly passed across Zoo's face.

"You touch someone and you can drop a person like a hot potato."

Why in the world wasn't Kira defending herself? Zoo's accusations were completely baseless and outrageous, yet she simply stood there as if they were discussing the weather. "We all know about Kira's touch ability. Again, I say that it is not of Shadow."

"I know what I saw." The witch clenched his fists. "I know how you were in the cemetery, Light and Shadow fighting inside you. I know how you were after that Fallen stabbed you with that dagger full of Chaos magic. And I saw how you were after you came back from that other place."

He rubbed a hand over his owl tattoo again. "You're different, Kira. You can't say that you're not."

"Of course she's different!" Khefar exclaimed before Kira could speak. "No human can go through what she did and emerge unscathed!"

"You're right," the other man said. He flicked his eyes at Kira. "No human could. But Kira did. I know what I saw. I know I saw power riding her, Light and Shadow twirling around her like strands of DNA. The power was waiting for her to make a choice. And she chose to keep all of it."

"What is the point of all this, and what does it have to do with Wynne?" Khefar demanded. The witch needed to remember why they were gathered at the hospital in the first place.

"She's the one." Zoo leveled a finger at Kira. There was something in his stance, something foreign and dangerous. Something so unlike the affable witch Khefar was familiar with.

Khefar blocked him. "You need to step back, witch," he warned. "This is not the place."

The other man's breathing quickened as his tension increased. Khefar had seen too many young men on the battlefield do the same thing, before they acted in a way that cost someone their limb, pride, or life. "Stand down, soldier," he ordered. "Think of how Wynne would feel about this if she saw it."

It was the right thing to say. Zoo stepped back, his ears still red with his anger. "She talked to Wynne about her faith, and religion and belief. Kira's the last person Wynne had a serious conversation with, and now she's in a coma."

Kira gave a soft groan, as if she'd been punched in the stomach and was trying not to show how much it hurt. Khefar saw red. "That is enough! This is Kira you accuse! She cares for Wynne as she would her own flesh and blood."

"'Her own flesh and blood,'" Zoo sneered. "You obviously don't know what happened to her sister, otherwise you'd make a different argument."

Kira flinched again. *Enough of this,* Khefar thought. "Don't you see what you're doing to her? She's your friend—"

"And that's my wife!" Zoo stabbed a finger in the direction of the private rooms. "There's no contest!"

Khefar took a step forward. "You understand little—"

"Khefar."

The soft voice sliced through his anger with the quick precision of a laser cutter. He turned to look at Kira, and what he saw etched on her face almost broke his heart.

No anger, no Shadow, animated her features. Instead he saw a deep, crushing sadness that smothered the light in her eyes and wiped all expression from her face.

"It's the right choice," she finally said, referring to Zoo. "We'd do the same thing. We've both done the same thing."

Khefar bit his tongue. He'd done far worse when his wife and children were butchered. He'd laid waste to an entire village, then proceeded to destroy sixty-four thousand lives.

"I'll get to the bottom of this, Zoo." Kira's voice sounded wooden, as if she'd pressed down hard to squeeze every drop of emotion out of her tone. "I'll make it right, I swear."

"How are you going to do that?" Zoo demanded, tears clogging his throat. "The only way you can make this right is by bringing my wife back."

"I said I'll make it right." Kira spat out every word like a broken tooth. "I'll find out what happened and I'll make sure it never happens again."

Zoo didn't appear mollified. "And if you find out you're the cause? What are you going to do then?"

Kira gave her friend a look so devoid of emotion that she might have been someone else. Something else. "If I am the cause, the Medjay will fulfill his promise to me."

"What sort of promise?" Zoo asked, some of the heat leaching out of his voice.

Kira turned to Khefar. "Tell him," she said, her voice whisper-soft. "Tell him what you promised to me."

Khefar folded his arms across his chest. He didn't

want to tell Zoo anything, much less the vow he'd made. If Marlowe didn't believe Kira's innocence based on their friendship, he didn't deserve to know the details of the pact Khefar and made with her.

"Khefar, please."

He bore down on Zoo, fighting to rein in his anger. "Do you know why I'm still here? Do you?"

"It's obvious to anyone with eyes that you're falling in love with her," Zoo said dismissively. "So?"

Khefar gritted his teeth. He didn't know if he was falling in love with Kira or not, but he'd be damned if he'd let the other man treat it as a casual thing. "I have lived four thousand years of penance because I chose revenge for losing my wife and children. Do not think to trivialize my sentiments or what I will do because of them."

"Fine. But you can't expect me to believe that you're hanging around because you like helping Kira with her Shadowchasing."

"I don't care what you believe," Khefar said. "My reasons are my own, and I don't need to share them with you. But since Kira wants you to know, I'll tell you the primary reason why I'm still here. I'm her fail-safe."

Confusion stirred the anger on Zoo's face. "Fail-safe?"

"It means that I am here to protect Kira from herself, to help her fight Shadow and at least stay balanced. If she doesn't, if she slides into Shadow, I will unmake her."

"Unmake her? What is that supposed to mean?"

Khefar glared at the other man, angry at the emotional damage he'd done to Kira, hating that he had to reveal the details of this awful vow. "If Kira becomes the very thing that she hunts, I will free the Dagger of Kheferatum and call its true power. I will unmake her body and her soul."

"You wouldn't do that," the witch said, horror driving the last of his anger away. "You *couldn't* do that."

"You have no idea what I could do," Khefar said, his voice soft. "You have no idea what I have done to ease my burden and save a soul. I have sworn a vow to Kira, to honor her request to ensure that she is never used for Shadow."

Zoo's mouth dropped open. "She asked you to do this—to kill her?"

Kira didn't bat an eye. She stared her friend down. "The Medjay has sworn that if I am too far gone into Shadow, if I become irredeemably Unbalanced, he will call on the true power of the Dagger of Kheferatum, and unmake me."

"Unmake you. You'd actually let him kill you."

"Oh, it's much more permanent than killing." Something lit Kira's expression. Khefar would have thought it humor, except there was nothing funny about their discussion. "Unmaking means Khefar will take my life and erase my soul. No redemption, no rebirth, no afterlife."

"That which you know as Kira Solomon would cease to exist," Khefar added. "No magic, no matter how powerful, would be able to bring her back. Not even the gods could re-create her. It would truly be a fate worse than death."

Kira brushed her hands together, as if wiping them off. "Kira go *poof.*"

Zoo scrubbed a hand over his head again. "Gods."

She threw back her head, her shoulders straight, her gaze hard. "Will this satisfy?"

"What? You're asking me to be okay with you dying?"

"Come on, Zoo," Kira pulled her lips back from her teeth in a semblance of a smile. "You were out for my blood when we arrived. Don't wimp out on me now. If we find out that I'm guilty, Khefar will be my executioner. So answer me, Zeroun Marlowe: will this satisfy?"

The witch seemed to realize that he'd gone too far. Good, Khefar thought. Still it was too late, far too late, to retreat. The simple act of accusing Kira of something so heinous was enough to push her further into Shadow. If one of the people you loved and trusted above all others no longer had your back, what were you left with?

"I—I guess so."

"Good." Kira nodded curtly. "Now, I need something of Wynne's."

Wariness lit his features again. "Like what? What for?"

Kira sighed. "You know how this works, Zoo. If you want me to find out what happened to Wynne, I need to touch something of hers, something she had on at the time. Even better if it's a piece of jewelry—something she's worn a lot. It'll help me get a clearer picture of the situation. A necklace would be good."

"I made a pendant for her, black tourmaline, rose quartz, and obsidian. She wears it all the time. It was supposed to protect her." His face crumpled.

"Mr. Marlowe?" A nurse entered the room. "We've got your wife settled in her private room. You can go to her now. There's also room for you to rest and refresh yourself."

Zoo gathered himself, took a deep breath. "Okay. Th-thank you."

He prepared to follow the nurse, paused. "I'll bring the pendant to you in a little while," he said quietly, not looking at either of them. With that, he turned and followed the nurse.

Chapter 17

Khefar faced her. "Kira—"

"Not now," she interrupted softly, throwing a hand up. She wasn't ready to talk about Zoo and his accusations. She doubted she'd ever be ready, but right then and there certainly wasn't the time. Not with the wound still fresh and hemorrhaging.

Khefar wouldn't let it go. "If he brings back that pendant, it's going to be charged with his emotions as well as Wynne's, right?"

"Probably." Definitely. The necklace from Balm's box had almost knocked her unconscious. She could still feel the aftereffects of it rippling through her like a stone dropped in a pond. The dagger from the puzzle box—she still didn't know what it had done to her, only that something had happened—hadn't been used in more than twenty-five years. Wynne's pendant—a protection amulet—held in Zoo's hand in his current emotional state was sure to leave a mental scar.

"His anger burns fiercely," Khefar said, stating the obvious. "Are you going to be able to handle experiencing it yourself?"

"Probably not." She hunched down in her long overcoat, still stinging from Zoo's reaction. It was one thing to see Zoo's anger; it would be quite another to feel it. She didn't know how bad trying to read Wynne's pendant would be or how she'd feel about it afterward. Added to that was the fact that she needed to uncover what had happened to Wynne to send her into a coma. Experiencing Zoo's fury would be hard; experiencing Wynne's attack would be almost too much.

"I'm not going to try to read Wynne's pendant here," she finally said. "Besides, I really don't want to be hanging around when Sanchez shows up. She's only going to stoke Zoo's anger and make a bad situation worse."

"Ch-chaser?"

The voice was so soft and timid that Kira almost missed it. She spun to the entryway, one hand going for her blade. A dark-skinned male with shiny straight hair the color of his skin stood in the doorway. He wore the same pale blue scrubs that a large part of the hospital staff wore. The security badge pinned to his shirt displayed his image and the name JESSEN.

"Yes?" Kira's hand dropped from her blade as she pasted on a polite expression. The guy was a Shadowling but if he'd wanted to attack, he would have already. Besides, she was sure Khefar had her back.

Khefar moved in front of her. "Who are you, and what do you want with the Chaser?" he demanded.

"I call myself Jessen," the young man replied, glancing at Kira before dropping his eyes to the floor. "It's an honor to meet you, Chaser Solomon. I have this job because of Bale."

Ah-ha. "Hello, Jessen." Kira turned to Khefar. "You met Bale at the fund-raiser, remember? Jessen's introduction lets me know that he's part of Bale's local clan and under his protection. He wouldn't have mentioned the banaranjan otherwise."

Khefar nodded, his expression still dour. "I remember him."

Kira looked at Jessen. "Is there something that I can do for you, Jessen? I'm in the middle of something here."

"Bale sends you his greetings, Chaser Solomon, but also told me I should speak to you. He said that you would need the information."

"What sort of information?"

Jessen gestured them to the far corner of the waiting room. He leaned close to Kira and said, "What has happened to your friend has happened to other humans."

"How many? How do you know this?"

The male banaranjan covered his eyes, bowed low. "I do not mean to anger you, Chaser. I work in this wing of the hospital, and I hear things. We have had eight humans brought here in as many days. All of them are comatose, all of them without any medical basis. Your friend makes nine."

A momentary guilty rush of relief. She couldn't have harmed Wynne and these others. She shook off the thought, then focused on the banaranjan's words. Nine people in comas. "Do you know if there are others? Maybe victims at other hospitals?"

Jessen darted another glance at her. "I've contacted a couple of friends at other area hospitals, but I haven't heard back from them."

She should have guessed that banaranjans would work in hospitals. These Shadowlings fed off adrenaline and usually worked in athletics of some type. The adrenaline spilling into emergency rooms would be enough to feed two or three banaranjans in their prime.

"What else would Bale have me know? You said he wanted to pass on other information?"

Jessen became grave. "Yes, Chaser. He told me to inform you that it is not only humans. Hybrids have also fallen victim to this strange unconsciousness."

"Hybrids?" The news was even more alarming. Humans had few defenses against psychic or magical attacks without extensive mental training. Hybrids, the mutated offspring of humans and Shadowlings, had the best of both lines of DNA, though the mutations manifested in innumerable and immeasurable ways.

"Any particular type of hybrid?" she asked.

Jessen shook his head. "Bale says there is no discernible pattern that he can find. He bids me tell you that he will arrange interviews with family members for you, if you wish to contact him."

"Oh, I definitely wish to contact him." A minor surge of relief hit her bloodstream. Humans and hybrids attacked across the board. Something or someone, perhaps another Fallen, behind the mysterious events. Not her.

"Jessen." She waited until the banaranjan looked at her. "I need the names of every comatose patient brought here in the last eight days. Can you do that for me?"

He dipped his head. "Bale told me that I would need to." He dug into his breast pocket, extracted a folded sheet of paper. "The names of the others we know of are there as well."

"My thanks to you, Jessen," Kira said formally. "You have shown bravery this day."

The young man beamed, straightening his shoulders with pride. "My thanks to you, Chaser Solomon."

A movement of air, and the squick of sneakers against tile announced Zoo's return. He appeared composed, his earlier antagonism gone. A black nylon cord dangled from his bare knuckles. "Will this do?"

Kira looked at the pendant, three stones wrapped with silver wire: black tourmaline, obsidian, and a bit of rose quartz. One stone for dispelling magical attacks, one for banishing negative energy, and the rose quartz symbolizing the soft glow of confident love.

"It should work fine," she told him, wondering how much of his anger she would have to peel back to get to impressions of Wynne. On top of that, she wondered if the witch had added any extra magical surprises to hurt her. She wouldn't have thought Zoo capable of anything so nasty, but that was before Zoo had accused her of deliberately harming her best friend.

Only one way to find out. She held out her left hand, securely gloved and palm up, for Zoo to drop the pendant into. "Thank you, Zoo."

"Okay." He scrubbed a hand over his head again. "Umm, you might want to be careful when you touch it. It packs a nasty punch if it's triggered."

"Now you want to be considerate?" Khefar hadn't let go of his anger. "Did you know that Wynne's not the only one this has happened to, witch? There are others on this floor experiencing the same symptoms. There are even hybrid victims."

Zoo flushed. "I'm sorry—"

"Save it, both of you." Kira turned to Jessen. "I need to do a reading, and I don't have time to go home. Is there someplace private on this floor that I can use for a little while?"

"There's a consultation room down the hall," Jessen said, his eyes wide. Great, just what she needed—the banaranjan reporting back to Bale about the scene he'd witnessed. It wouldn't be long before the entire hybrid community found out.

"Thanks. Zoo, go back to your wife. Hopefully I'll have something worth sharing when Sanchez arrives."

Zoo nodded curtly, then left. The air pressure lightened perceptibly. "Where's the room, Jessen?"

The orderly led them down a short hallway to a tastefully muted room decorated in professional grays and teal yet with a touch of coral for warmth. "Will this work?"

"Yes, Jessen. Thanks to you."

The banaranjan left. Kira sat behind the desk, bracing her elbows against the flat surface. Khefar took the chair opposite. "Can you do this?"

"It's my job. If there's a clue or a replay of how Wynne got dropped, I need to find it. I have to help her and the others. Besides, the thing with Zoo—something like this was bound to happen eventually. I don't mean getting labeled as a suspect by my best friend's husband, but still . . ."

She shook her head. "Maybe I should be alone for this."

"No." He planted his feet then planted his elbows down on the desk, mirroring her position. "You're still tired from cataloguing that Persian knife. I don't know what's going to happen when you start reading that necklace, and neither do you. I'm staying."

She looked up and saw his expression, the one that told her it was useless to disagree. Even if she'd managed to win the argument and convince him to give her privacy, he'd come back as soon as she pushed through the Veil.

"All right."

He blinked in surprise. "You're not going to argue?"

"I know better." She held out her right hand. "Will you do the honors?"

He tugged off her glove, his expression grave. It was the appropriate attitude, seeing as he'd witnessed the death of a friendship.

She held the pendant aloft in her gloved left hand. It swung slightly on its braided cord. She had no idea what sort of hit she'd get from the amulet. Stones had their own properties, and the ones Zoo had chosen—obsidian, black tourmaline, and rose quartz—had their own associated powers. Zoo had combined them into a protection amulet, and though it hadn't protected Wynne from whatever had made her comatose, it was sure to resist Kira's attempts to push through its barrier. She was pretty sure it would also wallop her with the force of Zoo's anger.

It would have to be borne, however. She needed to know what had happened to Wynne, determine who or what was responsible. Maybe it was something physiological, and she could pass word to Jessen to give to Wynne's doctors. If something supernatural proved to be at the root of Wynne's sudden malady, Kira would hunt it down and make it save her friend.

An enemy. She needed an enemy, one that didn't live inside her.

Conscious of Khefar sitting across from her, Kira relaxed her body muscle by muscle, in time to her slow, rhythmic breathing. Her extrasense welled inside her, bubbling up like a magical spring. *Ma'at be with me, Ma'at guide me, Ma'at protect me*, she silently prayed, reaching for the peace that communing with the goddess always gave her.

The calmness rose up through her extrasense like an obelisk, strong, immovable. Only then did she allow her extrasense to seep up through her pores, assume command of her mundane senses, and push back the Veil of reality.

The office shimmered in curtains of blue and gold slipping against each other in slices of green, further proof of Light and Shadow living inside her, Shadow encroaching. She saw Khefar across the desk, a shell of black, completely devoid of magic. Not with the rainbow aura all humans had, but a solid dark mass as if he was permanently locked in his root chakra. She wondered if it was because he required some sort of super-grounding in order to use the dagger, or because he'd died multiple times.

The hospital hummed with the magic of technology, registering to her senses in a deep, life-affirming red. She caught a flash of yellow-green, realized it was outside the room. Probably the banaranjan, hoping to gather more information to pass on to Bale. A little quid pro quo was fair, as long as they didn't interfere with her Chase.

Her gaze swung to the amulet dangling from her

hand. The protective aura was like a mace, a solid ball of black granite. Spikes seemed to be protruding from it, a warning layer of defense. Encircling it, like the corona of the sun visible during an eclipse, was red-orange light.

"Looks like Zoo was really mad," she murmured, her voice sounding far away to her ears. She didn't like to talk much when she pushed beyond the Veil, not wanting anything to pull her back into reality.

"Be careful," Khefar ordered, his voice muffled on the other side of the Veil.

Of course she'd be careful, but she appreciated the sentiment. At least he wasn't trying to convince her not to read the pendant. Shutting out the mundane world, she pulled her extrasense about her like armor, and then wrapped her bare hand around the pendant.

It was like sticking her hand into lava. Rage boiled over her, melting her defenses, sinking into her aura. Images and sounds burned their way into her mind, branding her psyche.

"I'm telling you, she's changed!" Zoo's voice. *"I don't think we can trust her anymore!"*

"She's my friend!" Wynne's voice, catching. *"She needs us!"*

"And we need to protect ourselves. What if she flips out again? If she blasts you like she did me—"

"She wouldn't do that, not on purpose."

"I swear by the Great Lady, if she ever hurts you, I'm going after her."

"Don't say that!"

"I mean it, Wynne! I know she's your friend, but I also know she's dangerous. I'm gonna give you something

for protection. Don't ever take it off. And don't ever turn your back on her."

Red walls of flaming anger scorched her, charred her awareness. *Let it burn,* she thought. *Let it burn out until there's nothing left.*

A black form entered the conflagration, a hand extended to her. "Kira. Pull back for a moment. Take a breather."

She let Khefar pull her back to reality the way a lifeguard tows an incapacitated swimmer to shore. She found herself back in the room, the pendant clutched in her fist. Khefar leaned over her, trying to pry her fingers open. He succeeded, and the amulet fell to the desk's surface.

"What are you doing?" she asked, her voice hoarse. "I'm fine."

"You're shaking," he told her, his voice squeezed bare. "You were making a sound like—a sound I wish never to hear from you again. And there is moisture on your cheeks."

Kira removed the wire rims and wiped her hand across her face. At least he'd had the decency not to accuse her of crying.

"It was a wall of anger," she said after wiping the back of her hand across her mouth. "More anger than I expected. And he thinks I'm a danger to him and Wynne. I don't know how long ago that was, sometime after the cemetery incident, probably after we returned from Egypt, and definitely before we met them for lunch. This pendant is to protect Wynne from me as well as anything else with Shadow magic."

Khefar cursed. "That damn witch."

"Finding out what someone really thinks of you reeks," she said, wishing she had some aspirin for her pounding head. "Sometimes, ignorance truly is bliss."

"Then maybe you shouldn't try to read it further," he suggested. "Surely Gilead has psychics with this ability."

"They do, but not as directed." Already drained, she pushed her braids back over her shoulder. Fighting to keep Zoo's anger from completely shattering her defenses had taken a lot of energy. "It takes years of study to reach the level of being able to sift through memories and along a timeline at will. I don't know if Sanchez has anyone with the experience in Gilead East, and we don't have time to bring someone else in."

"Okay." He returned to his chair. "Find whatever you need to find, and make it quick. I don't want you connected to this thing longer than you need to be."

She picked up the pendant again. This time the protective aura didn't block her. She breathed deep, allowing her extrasense to take control of her mundane senses. The inherent magic of the stones rose in front of her, allowing her to see the protective crystalline matrix. She pushed through the jeweled forest, pushing aside branches until she finally emerged on the other side.

Images blurred by her again like speeding cars on a highway. She tried to find the ones she needed, moving back through the darkness that marked the onset of Wynne's coma. Keeping her emotions firmly locked down, Kira sifted through the pendant's point of view, looking for something, anything, out of the ordinary.

There. Images she had seen before, but not

together. Wynne standing in the Hall of Judgment. Kira's heart pounded with sudden wild fear. Wynne didn't worship the Egyptian pantheon; as far as Kira knew, her friend hadn't made any decision about her faith.

Wynne held up a bright yellow crystal, and Kira realized Wynne was standing in the reproduced scene inside the museum exhibit, not the hallowed hall she and Khefar had encountered. Wynne dropped the citrine heart scarab onto the empty measuring pan opposite the gleaming white Feather of Truth. She watched in anticipation as the scales swung up and down. Heart thumping as the scales stopped; Ma'at's feather was lighter than the jewel.

The Ammit statue lunged out of the darkness, jaws snapping, eyes gleaming bright bloodred. Wynne shrieked, her fright subsiding into a nervous laugh. It wasn't real, after all. It was only a show.

But the gemstone amulet had recognized that the citrine scarab, the traditional Egyptian representation of the soul, was gone, taken by Ammit.

The Ammit figure had somehow taken on the characteristics of its inspiration and devoured the *ba* stone, the magical stone that was placed with the dead as a heart token. If someone didn't know the spells, didn't know the words of protection, their souls were in certain danger.

Angry now, Kira pushed further back along the timeline, looking for the trigger event. Either something along the path through the tomb or something outside the exhibit had caused Wynne to be marked as a target. Kira needed to find it. Only then could she face it.

Wynne entered the main promenade. Outside the exhibit hall she recognized the exhibit coordinator, Hammond. She called to him, introduced herself as Kira's friend. Hammond beamed as they shook hands. He gave Wynne the scarab and told her the trip through the tomb was not to be missed.

A flare of anger, and the vision wobbled. Kira wrestled her emotions back under control and focused on the remainder of the reading. Hammond had given the scarab to Wynne. Wynne had carried it throughout her journey through the exhibit, charging it with her energy. By the time she had tossed the scarab onto the measuring pan, the gemstone had been coated with her essence.

Had the scarab been be-spelled in some way, programmed to be devoured by Ammit? Was that why Wynne was in a coma?

Had someone reanimated the demoness? Ammit didn't put people into comas. She devoured their souls until nothing was left. Did that mean that Wynne—and all the other victims—were still in danger?

Kira tamped down her emotions again, concentrating instead on fighting her way free of the amulet much the way she would break through jungle undergrowth. It took a long time, as she had to be careful not to trigger the amulet's protective magic. Luckily it seemed to realize she wasn't a threat. She made her way back to herself, allowing her extrasense to slowly seep back into her subconscious.

Khefar stared at her from the other side of the desk, his features tight. "You okay?"

She nodded, wishing she'd thought to bring a bottle of water with her. "Better than the last round."

"What did you see?"

"Disturbing things." She pulled her glove back, feeling better immediately. Anger still simmered below the surface, though, waiting for an outlet. "I think I know what happened to Wynne and the others. And they're not out of danger yet."

Chapter 18

Kira pushed to her feet. "Come on. I need to see if Sanchez is here. If not, I'll have to call the Travel Department."

"Ah. 'Travel.' The Retrievers you called for the were-hyena?" Khefar asked.

"Yup." She dropped the pendant into her coat pocket. "'Travel' is what field agents call the Special Retrieval Team. They respond when an agent is down. We also call them when we need to have a suspect brought in for questioning. 'Coach' means a human or a low-level hybrid. 'Business class' means a pretty strong hybrid and a show of force."

"What's 'first class'?"

"Shadow Adepts. If the agent thinks there's a serious threat, they'll call for a Chaser as backup."

"What about the Fallen?"

"That's 'express,' and that means I go in. We don't send SRTs for that. There's no such thing as backup for a Shadowchaser. Not as far as Gilead is concerned, anyway."

They returned to the coma wing's main corridor. Section Chief Estrella Sanchez, Zoo, and two Gilead agents took up most of the space in the hallway. Zoo and the section chief conferred quietly, heads close

together. Kira's gut roiled at the thought of her friend
and Sanchez being so chummy, but squashed it, blank-
ing her expression instead. She and the section chief
were getting along, but Kira knew it wouldn't take
much to get on Sanchez's bad side. Zoo spilling his guts
about the incident in the cemetery or his unfounded
suspicions would be enough to put Kira and Sanchez
at odds again. She had to remember that when they
agreed to Gilead training, the Marlowes had essentially
stopped working with her and begun working for Gilead, and Sanchez.

Telling herself she had done nothing wrong, Kira
steeled herself to approach the Gilead contingent.
Sanchez turned away from Zoo, who looked decidedly guilty. The section chief looked much the way
she usually did, somewhat suspicious that Kira would
somehow soon be making life more difficult or at least
breaking several protocols any minute. After their conversation at the office, Kira figured Sanchez would be
even more suspicious than usual.

"Marlowe tells me that you were going to attempt
to find the assailant through a pendant he gave his wife.
Were you able to recover anything useful?"

"Yes." Kira pulled the pendant out of her pocket,
intending to return it to Zoo. One of the agents took it
instead, slipping it into a small clear-plastic evidence bag.

"We'll have one of our psychometrists corrobo-
rate and create an official record," Sanchez explained.
"What did you find?"

Don't be defensive, Kira silently cautioned herself.
*Corroborating psychic evidence is standard operating
procedure.* "The problem is the exhibit."

"The exhibit?" Sanchez echoed. "You mean the one you organized down at the Congress Center?"

Kira ground her teeth. "If you recall, I'm not the organizer. I coordinated the artifacts for the exhibit. Mr. Hammond—you remember him, don't you? The one you were so chummy with before you gave him that big check? He's the organizer, and it's his part of the production that's the problem."

Even in the muted light of the corridor, Kira could see a flush staining Sanchez's olive cheeks. "How so?"

"At the end, at the Weighing of the Heart ceremony. Wynne tossed one of those heart gemstones onto the measuring plate. It shifted to being unbalanced, which triggered the Ammit statue. Somehow Ammit is siphoning off the victim's consciousness as a prelude to devouring his or her soul."

Khefar looked stunned. "Are you serious?"

"A statue is the problem?" Sanchez asked, dubious.

"Ammit is more than a statue," Khefar explained. "She is the Devourer of Souls, a demoness who prevents people from crossing into the afterlife by eating them."

"And the electronic 'edutainment' representation of her at the museum seems to be doing Ammit's job. We have to find Hammond and discover what the hell's going on," Kira told them. "I mean, think about it: someone or something is using the Book of the Dead exhibit, or more specifically, the Weighing of the Heart interactive ritual, to actually steal souls."

"Not Ammit." Khefar made the sign of the evil eye. "All of the victims are comatose. The Devourer consumes souls. And the divine rules are that she has to be given the souls, fed them by Anubis. She doesn't have the ability to take them herself."

"That we know of," Kira said, pushing her braids back over her shoulder. "What do we really know about Ammit, except that she's a demoness from the left hand of Shadow?"

"That's enough for me, but this isn't how she works," Khefar said. "So I guess we're looking for something or someone masquerading as Ammit and using the exhibit to harvest souls for some unknown purpose. Do you know any hybrids who specialize in soul stealing?"

"Every culture has some sort of story about soul stealers," Kira replied. "Like the old belief that allowing yourself to be photographed meant your soul was stolen. Seeing one's reflection captured the soul. The Qing dynasty of China believed a person's soul resided in their hair; soul stealers were those who went around cutting off queues—the long, braided ponytails the men wore."

"Wait, wait." Sanchez held up a hand. "You said *souls*, plural."

Kira nodded. "Wynne isn't the only victim."

The news was literally a bombshell. Zoo groaned, covering his face with his hands. The agents looked ready to swing into action. Sanchez looked poleaxed.

"I think you'll find other patients in this wing and in hospitals elsewhere went through that exhibit," Kira added, "all brought in comatose like Wynne was."

"The exhibit's been open for a week," Sanchez said. "Hundreds of people have gone through since it opened. How can you be sure the exhibit is responsible?"

"There have been hybrid victims too," Kira answered. "I have a list of names. We can have sweepers cross-check their activities see if any of them visited the Journey Through the Underworld exhibit. Counting up the victims, there seems to have been two a day—one, human, and one hybrid."

"Before I shut down the exhibit and cost the city an assload of money," Sanchez said, "we need to be sure. After all, we have a were-hyena still inexplicably in a coma."

Kira ground her teeth. "There's a possibility I might have held on too long to Roshonda to keep her down, but I can promise you I don't know any of the people in this wing. I didn't hurt these people or Wynne."

"I believe you," Sanchez said.

Kira's mouth dropped open. "Seriously?"

"Yes." Sanchez nodded. "I may have my doubts about your methods or your willingness to follow orders, but even I don't believe you would harm your closest friend."

The unexpected support caused Kira's throat to tighten. "Thank you." Sanchez believed her innocent, but Zoo didn't. Proof positive that her world had turned completely upside down.

"So I suppose you're going to suggest that I bring in Hammond, the organizer?" Sanchez asked. "I need a good reason."

"I've got one," Kira answered. "Wynne met with him, before she went into the tomb reproduction."

"How did she know who he was?"

"She saw a picture of him on my phone," Khefar said. "Pictures from the gala."

"Hammond gave Wynne a citrine scarab and told her to drop it on the scale. The scale swung out of balance and the Ammit statue moved forward to gobble the stone." Kira shivered at the thought of the Devourer being alive, of having to face down the demoness to get her friend's life back. "Hammond is the last person Wynne had any significant interaction with. That's the only suspicious activity I saw when I replayed her day."

Sanchez considered the information. "I thought Hammond was human."

"So did I, but the other night was the first time I'd been around him for more than a few minutes. And in a crowd like that I shield pretty tightly. He could have willingly agreed to become an Avatar for a Fallen, or agreed to become a Shadow Adept, and gained magical power in exchange for providing souls to someone. It's even possible that the agreement happened after he came to Atlanta. Either way, it doesn't mean he's blameless. If he's not behind it, he damn well knows who is."

The section chief pressed her earpiece. "I need an immediate first-class retrieval on one Bruce Hammond, organizer of the Journey Through the Underworld exhibit at the Georgia World Congress Center. He's probably at the hotel closest to the exhibit hall, in the best suite. Keep it clean and quiet, and let me know as soon as you have him in custody."

She disconnected, looked at Kira. "We need to head back to the office. If Hammond warrants first-class retrieval, we'll have to make use of the underground interrogation facility. I'm assuming you want to be present for the interrogation?"

"You bet your ass I do."

Sanchez pursed her lips in disapproval, but Kira didn't care. "If he's unwilling to talk, you'll need me there."

Sanchez nodded briefly. "I know you feel some distress at your friend's condition and I know you want to act quickly to find those responsible. But if you're right—"

"I *am* right."

"—if you're right, we potentially have hundreds more victims waiting to be claimed. At the very least, their consciousnesses could be held hostage. We need to find out what Hammond knows, without alerting anyone that we're on the trail. We go by the book on this one. Understood?"

Kira bit the inside of her cheek. Her muscles ached with the need for some ass-kicking action. "Understood."

"Marlowe, you'll stay here. Send word when there's any change."

"But—"

"Understood?"

Zoo snapped to. "Yes, ma'am. Understood, ma'am."

Sanchez gave them all a smile. "See how easy that is, Solomon?"

Kira gave the section chief a mock salute. "Yes, ma'am. Understood, ma'am."

With a final disapproving look, Sanchez and the two agents made their way to the exit, leaving Kira, Khefar, and Zoo standing in the hallway. Kira glanced at Zoo. "Has there been any change in Wynne's condition?"

"No." The male witch blew out a breath. "Kira?"

She turned to face him, taking care to keep her expression and posture neutral. "Yes?"

Zoo grew uncomfortable. "I wanted to let you know that I—I didn't tell Sanchez about . . . well, you know."

"About what?" Khefar demanded. "Your unfounded accusations?"

The witch flushed. "Are they unfounded? Ask yourself honestly, and I think you'll understand why I thought the way I did."

"I have asked myself, and I have yet to understand how someone could think so ill of someone they claim as a friend," Khefar said, his words like acid. "It is a shame that the value of friendship is meaningless in this day and age."

"Zoo, I think you need to get back to Wynne," Kira cut in, amazed at how calm she sounded. "And we're going to head to Gilead."

"Wait. What did you see?"

"You already know what I saw," she told him. "Hammond gave the stone to Wynne."

"But that's not all that you saw, is it?" Zoo asked. "Then, tell me what else came through."

Kira looked at Zoo for a long moment. She hoped to see something on his face that would erase the last hour and take them back to a place where they weren't at odds with each other. Nothing presented itself.

"Your wife is worried about you," she finally said. "Wynne wanted to talk to me about your faith and mine, to gain a better understanding of what we believe and how it affects us. So if you want to blame me for what happened to Wynne, go ahead. I told her about my experience with Ma'at, and that's why she went down to the exhibit. But know this: you may think that I've changed and become more dangerous, but your wife thinks you have too. I suggest you take some time off and talk with her when she wakes up."

Zoo started to say something, probably an attempt to deny her words. Instead, she let him read her face— allowed all of the anger, hurt, and resentment to rise to the surface, unfettered. Zoo's eyes widened, and he took a step back, dropping his gaze.

Serves you right, Kira thought to herself, biting her lip to keep further words from erupting. It would be easy, all too easy, to hurt Zoo as he'd hurt her. Only the thought of Wynne's worried face and the need to find her attacker kept Kira from doing so.

"Let's go," she finally said to Khefar, turning her back on the witch.

They left the stroke center, heading for the main entrance. "A warrior never gives his enemy ammunition."

"So says the guy who blew his top twice in one night." Kira snorted. "Besides, I don't really consider Sanchez my enemy. Or Zoo, for that matter."

"Yeah." Khefar's turn to snort. "With friends like that, who needs enemies?"

True enough. "Thanks, by the way," she said off-handedly, though she certainly didn't feel casual about it. "For defending me back there, I mean."

"I did what was right," Khefar told her, the danger back in his voice. "And what was right was also the truth."

"Yeah." She suppressed a twinge of guilt. Khefar's

steadfast faith in her was reassuring even as she wondered if it was misplaced.

Her shoulders slumped. "Looks like I'm going to have to be careful around them, if I ever get the chance to be around them again. Zoo's Gilead now, for better or worse. I mean, I figured that something like this was bound to happen. Didn't think it would happen so soon, though."

"What are you going to do about it?" he asked as they pushed out into the chill night.

"Save Wynne's life, and everyone else's," she answered. "After that, I don't know. See if Zoo will accept a transfer enabling them to become field agents reporting up the chain to Sanchez."

"What if Wynne doesn't want to do that? There's no way she can blame you for this!"

"She won't, but it doesn't matter. Knowing how Zoo feels, there's no way I can trust him to have my back now."

"You sure you want to throw that friendship away?"

She stopped in her tracks. "You were ready to bash Zoo's head in, and now you want to defend him?"

"I still want to bash his head in," Khefar said easily. "If only because it may knock some sense into him. I want you to be sure of your decision. It's a bridge-burning moment."

She tilted her face skyward, allowing the cool winter night to seep into her. "I was sure before Cairo. I tried to push them away then. They went to Gilead and joined up. It was their idea to be my backup on the mission to return the Vessel of Nun," she said, scanning the sidewalk. "I shouldn't have brought them into my world to start with. But Zoo knew about Light and Shadow, since he worships an incarnation of the Great Lady, and Wynne . . . was Wynne."

Kira sighed. Wynne had seemed like someone she could trust with her life. But she wasn't sure why. Then again, when she'd first met her, Kira hadn't valued her own life all that highly. Life was lonely and risky. Wynne and Zoo somehow made it less so.

"After I first met them," she continued, "I had them tagged after the scrying mirror incident so that Gilead would keep an eye on them in case they were trafficking in magically enhanced artifacts instead of just accidentally receiving one."

"You reported them to Gilead?" Khefar asked, surprise ringing in his voice. "Did they know?"

"I never told them," she admitted. "I kept seeing them around Little Five Points after I cleansed the mirror. I could have had one of Gilead's psychics put a mental block on them, but I really don't like to do that unless it's absolutely necessary. Besides, they've done a good job of keeping Zoo's bloodline from being public knowledge. I figured they could keep my secret too. The Shadowchaser secret anyway."

"What do you mean, Zoo's bloodline?"

"Zoo's a natural-born witch," Kira explained as they headed for the parking deck. "He's got hybrid blood from his Romanian ancestry. He does Wiccan charms and spells as a cover for the fact that he really can do magic. With them keeping that kind of secret even from the U.S. military, I figured they'd have no problem keeping my secrets. Anyway, they're Gilead agents now, and cozy with Sanchez. Reason enough for some distance, especially considering my parentage."

She pulled her coat tighter about herself. "I need to get my energy back. Tell me we still have some protein bars in the car."

"We do, and bottles of water. But there's an all-night burger place next to the parking deck. Would you rather go there?"

"No." She shuddered. "I don't know if I have enough reserves right now to blast my food clean and keep my shielding in place. This time of night, I don't know who or what will be in there."

He studied her. "Maybe we should swing back by the house, let you regroup."

She shook her head. "There's no time. Besides, Shadowchasers train for this. When the Chase is on, there's no stopping. I'll be fine with the bars and some water. I don't want to give Hammond any more time than we already have."

At the car, she quickly downed a couple of bars and a liter of water kept cool by the early morning temperature. "You know . . . we're not all that far from the Congress Center."

Khefar studied her. "You want to go after Hammond yourself."

"Damn right I do. He deliberately gave Wynne that heart scarab. He knew what he was doing. He called me out. The least I can do is answer."

"I don't think that's a good idea."

His hesitation surprised her. "Why the hell not?"

"In case you haven't noticed, we're down a

demigod, a witch, and a firearms expert. You're fatigued. The odds aren't in our favor."

"When have they ever been?" Khefar was right. Dammit. Hammond had a time advantage over them. He'd set things in motion on his own timetable from the moment he gave the scarab to Wynne.

"Let's head over to Gilead," Khefar suggested, adjusting the car's thermostat to a warmer temperature.

"Why?" Kira demanded, irritated. "So I can sit around with my thumb up my butt, waiting on the retrieval team to bring in my target?"

She crumpled the empty water bottle in her fist. "That supercilious son of a bitch! I completely bought that overeager, bumbling, barely-this-side-of-competent act!"

Khefar's lips quirked as he started the car. "Tell me how you really feel."

"I'm angry. I'm angry because I'm supposed to be better than this. I'm supposed to know if something supernatural's going on in my town."

"You can't know everything," Khefar pointed out. "Even Gilead's sweepers didn't pick up on this."

His mild tone did nothing to soothe her anger. "I should have known about this," she argued. "Putting this exhibit together took months—on and off—of careful planning, paperwork, insurance, gathering permits, crating, transporting, and uncrating. I had to inspect each artifact brought in, making sure none of them had any nasty metaphysical surprises. I did everything I knew to do to make sure that the artifacts were safe for the public."

She turned to him. "I worked with Hammond

quite a bit over the last couple of months. Granted, none of it was in person until we started the installation and even then our encounters were brief. In retrospect, that may have been intentional on his part. Still, I should have realized something. I've let these friggin' distractions get to me."

"You have to admit, as far as distractions go, yours have been pretty huge."

"You think? I'm ready for them to be over and done with so I can go back to doing my job." She tapped her bottom lip. "I do have to wonder, though, what's going on. Neither Ma'at nor Isis gave us any indication that this soul-snatching thing was happening."

"Careful," Khefar warned. "I strongly believe that our patronesses trust in our ability to figure things out for ourselves. Besides, if this comes from the mind of the Lord of the Desert, Isis would have good reason to steer clear."

"Or work harder against him." Kira wouldn't admit it, not even to Khefar, but the silence from Ma'at worried her. No, she didn't need hand-holding, but wasn't it natural to want reassurance from above? "Balm's still silent, and I get visited by the Ladies of Shadow and Between like it's Christmas Eve and I've been a stingy bastard. Something's up."

"Something like what?"

"Think about it. Nansee decides to go visit his wife, something you say he hasn't done in a couple of decades. Balm has that chest delivered, then goes all incommunicado on me. And neither Isis nor Ma'at warned us about this exhibit stealing souls. Why didn't we get a heads-up? Why are they not giving us any guidance—especially since we had help up to our ears with the Vessel of Nun?" Kira shook her head. "Something reeks, and I don't like it."

"We've been on our own before." Khefar exited the parking deck, made his way over to Peachtree Street, and then headed north for Midtown. "Maybe this means that we're supposed to figure this out on our own."

Kira remained silent. Now would be the perfect time to tell Khefar about being driven toward a choice by the Ladies of Light and Shadow, about having her Shadowling sire's Shadowblade in her spare sheath. She had no idea why she'd impulsively strapped the blade on, especially given her initial revulsion to it. Khefar would argue against her carrying it. Then again, he would argue against her confronting Hammond, and she really wanted to confront Hammond.

"Great. And what if we make the wrong choice?"

"Then we fix it."

Kira's mobile chimed. "Crap. That's Sanchez." She touched her earpiece to answer the phone. "Solomon here."

"The SRT was unsuccessful in retrieving Hammond," the section chief said, her tone clipped.

"Dammit!"

"What is it?" Khefar asked as he slowed the car down.

"They didn't find Hammond," she mouthed before turning her attention back to the phone. "Chief, do you mean that they couldn't locate him or he was already gone when they got there?"

"One of the sweepers managed to tag him. He's

renting one of the condos across from Olympic Park instead of staying in a hotel. By the time Spec Team One got there, he was gone. Looked like he left in a hurry, judging by the looks of the place. I'm en route to HQ. I want you and the Nubian to meet the SRT at Olympic Park Towers. See if you can get any hits off the place."

"Ma'am, I really think we should go on to the Congress Center," Kira said, keeping in mind Khefar's suggestion of having more boots on the ground. "Hammond may be heading there."

"If he is, we need to have a better idea of what we're facing, Chaser Solomon," Sanchez replied, her voice stern. "I'm not risking you or any of the response teams because we didn't take the time to gather more information. The exhibit is closed for now. We have eyes on the scene, and there has been no activity since we left the hospital. Take the time to do this right, Solomon, so we can minimize the collateral damage."

Kira ground her teeth in frustration. She knew the section chief was right. Going off half-cocked would only get them in a whole world of trouble. The last thing she wanted to do was lose any more people. "Yes, ma'am."

"All right." Sanchez seemed surprised that Kira hadn't argued further. Kira was a little surprised herself. "Report back to HQ the minute you have information."

"Of course. Solomon out." She disconnected.

Khefar sped the car back up. "Did you just agree to follow one of Sanchez's orders?"

"Yeah, don't rub it in. They came up empty at the

condo Hammond is renting. Sanchez wants me over there to see what sort of lead I can pick up. The SRT is already waiting on us there."

"How are we going to find him?" Khefar asked. "Do you think he found out that we were onto him?"

"He knew from the moment he gave Wynne that scarab that I would be coming after him," Kira said, curling her hands into fists. She jammed her knuckles into her knees. "He's probably at the exhibit now, waiting for us. Daring us to come after him, that supercilious son of a bitch!"

"All the more reason to go in with a team, fully prepared for whatever he decides to throw at us." Khefar paused. "Are you going to tell Sanchez about your dream?"

"About Set wanting me to join him or die?" Kira shook her head. "Me and Sanchez seem to be on good terms right now. I'm pretty sure that knowing that an Egyptian god of chaos thinks I'm part of his family at the same time that an exhibit on the Egyptian afterlife is stealing souls would strain my credibility with the section chief."

"You're probably right. Where to?"

"Olympic Park. We're meeting the SRT at the Olympic Towers. Hammond rented a condo there for the duration of the exhibit."

Khefar darted a look at her before looking for a way to backtrack from Midtown to Olympic Park. "You know it might come out when we get to the exhibit. If Set is going to make an appearance anywhere, it will be there."

"I know." She stared at the window as downtown

Atlanta swept by. "I'll have to cross that bridge when I come to it."

"But—"

"But nothing. I'm not giving up my Lightblade without a fight. Trust me, if the god of storms and chaos is wanting me on his side, I'm going to fight with everything I've got to ruin his plans."

Chapter 19

Kira's cell rang again. She touched her headset. "Solomon here."

"Kira, darling," Bale's smooth voice purred in her ear. "How much do you love me?"

"Jessen didn't waste any time contacting you, I see," she said, torn between admiration and irritation. "Can you make this quick? While I appreciate the information you gave me, I'm kind of in the middle of something here."

"You didn't answer my question," he chided her.

"Fine. I love you when you're useful," she retorted, ignoring Khefar's jerk of the steering wheel in reaction. "Now, do you have something for me?"

"I do indeed, my dear Shadowchaser." Laughter lined the banaranjan's voice. "Unlike your Special Response Team, my people had a most successful hunt."

She motioned for Khefar to stop the car. "Bale, what did you do?" The banaranjan laughed again, and Kira realized he was on an adrenaline high. "Bale. Are you saying that you found Hammond?"

"Found him and am on the way to delivering him."

Dread filled Kira's stomach. "Delivering him where?"

"To Gilead, of course."

"Dammit, Bale! Don't you realize that if you show up with Hammond at Gilead, security will shoot first and ask questions later?"

"Hammond hurt my people," Bale said, completely unfazed by Kira's warning. "You are lucky you're getting him at all. It is only because of the regard I have for you and the continued goodwill of the human community that you are getting such excellent prey."

"Khefar, we need to get to Gilead, now."

The car leapt forward as Khefar depressed the pedal. "Are you flying or driving, Bale?"

"Which do you think?"

"Bale. Snap the hell out of your adrenaline high and give me some details here. I'm trying to keep you from getting killed in your absolutely fucking stupidity!"

Bale sighed. "You sure know how to be a buzz kill, Kira, my dear. It is hardly my fault that your Mr. Hammond is so adrenaline rich. His taste is . . . delicious."

"You scared him, didn't you? Did you at least get some information out of him?"

"Probably nothing you can use," the banaranjan replied. "We will meet you atop the gilded towers of Gilead."

Kira pressed the heel of her hand to her temple, which did nothing to relieve her headache. "Taking him to Gilead means you may all get your damn fool heads shot off, Bale!"

"Then I trust that you'll send word of our arrival. I would hate for our party favor to be damaged because we're not on the invite list."

"Bale? Bale!" He'd disconnected. "Son of a bitch!"

"What is it?" Khefar asked, pausing at a traffic light.

"Get us to Gilead pronto." Kira dialed Sanchez on her phone. "Section Chief, we've got trouble."

"What sort of trouble, Solomon? Have you rendez-voused with the Special Response Team yet?"

"No, there's no need to do that now. I just got a call from the leader of the banaranjan community. They've apprehended our suspect and are bringing him into custody. They're going to drop him off—and I mean that in every literal sense—on the roof of Gilead East."

"Dammit, Solomon! How did *that* happen?"

"Apparently the informant who gave me informa-tion on the other victims gave the banaranjans infor-mation about our prime suspect," Kira said, making a mental note to twist wings and take names later. "We're a minute out. I don't know how long before Bale and his people get there, but it will be minutes, since they're flying. Send a team up, but for the love of Light, don't allow them to engage. Banaranjans feed off adrenaline, and the easiest way to get it on a roof is by throwing people off of it."

Sanchez paused. "If they attack my people—"

"I'm not going to let that happen," Kira assured the section chief. "Tell them to stand down and not engage. If any of them can't keep their emotions under control, they don't need to go out on the roof."

Another choice expletive spilled through Kira's earpiece. "I'm sending multiple strike teams to the roof as well as SRTs Two and Four. Get your ass over here now." The section chief disconnected.

"Two hangups in a row," Kira said, ripping her

earpiece off to satisfy her need to do something. "If we don't get to Gilead East in the next thirty seconds, all kinds of hell are going to break loose."

"They need to be careful," Khefar warned. "Banaranjans are dangerous even when they aren't on an adrenaline high."

Kira cut a glance at him. "You said something to Bale about them at the fund-raiser. I guess you've had experience with them?"

"Not the way you have. My experience was mostly battle related—like I told you before, I was there when Mehmed the Conqueror ruled the Ottoman Empire. The banaranjans served several sultans as their personal guards. From what I understand, they learn to be vicious and quick from the crèche."

"The strong eat and the weak get eaten," Kira murmured.

"Exactly. Their love of combat and inner dominance squabbles kept the population low. At some point, however, one of the viziers convinced the sultan that the banaranjans had outlived their usefulness."

"I bet that went over well."

"Like the proverbial lead balloon," Khefar answered. "After all, banaranjans only have loyalty to themselves and whichever one is strong enough to lead. They . . . withdrew their support of the sultanate in a dramatic fashion. A lot of them died. The remaining banaranjans retreated to the mountains and the Empire continued its long march to dissolution."

"They've adapted like every other race has adapted," Kira said, watching the city whiz by her window. "Those who left Turkey seemed to adapt from participating in wars for harvesting adrenaline to using sporting events instead. Almost all of the banaranjans here in town seem more than capable of suppressing the more violent tendencies of their nature. Bale has a lot to do with that."

"Yet he's the one inciting a firefight by bringing a high-profile suspect of unknown power to Gilead's doorstep," Khefar pointed out. "Sometimes nature wins out."

Kira fell silent. Unfortunately, when it came to fighting her inner demons, she had no idea which side of her nature would win.

What was fortunate was that Peachtree Street was nearly deserted, giving them a straight shot into Midtown and the glass and steel fortification of Gilead East's headquarters. As Khefar pulled onto the ramp for the underground parking garage, Kira belatedly remembered the Shadowblade tucked in a second sheath under her left arm. "Crappity crap."

"What now?" Khefar asked.

Rhino stood beside the security kiosk, the detaining arm already raised. He waved as he recognized Kira, and she relaxed. "I was worried about the layers of security that would trip with the presence of the dagger. Since Rhino's waving us in, I guess they temporarily lowered the security level."

She could feel his eyes on her, as if he knew it wasn't a complete answer. It was the truth, though; she just wanted him to believe she meant the Dagger of Kheferatum and not the new blade she'd acquired.

She had no idea why she had brought it with her. It seemed important that she have the blade on hand.

Besides, she always had at least two other blades on her person in addition to her Lightblade. Now she had an extra one that was forged with Shadow magic.

Khefar braked to a stop, rolling down the window as Rhino gestured to them. "Security's already waiting for you at the elevator, Kira," he told her. "The last lift at the end of the bay will express you up. The chief's waiting too."

"Thanks, Rhino."

At Kira's direction, Khefar made a couple of quick turns lower into the parking deck, passing through another barrier waiting open for them. He parked the Charger between two black SUVs. Kira had her door open before he killed the engine, moving quickly to the waiting freight elevator and the pair of officers in black tactical gear.

"Chaser Solomon," the male said with a nod as the female keyed a code into the data panel on the left side of the elevator doors. "I suggest feet shoulder-width apart but not locking your knees. This is going to be a fast ride."

She complied, noted that Khefar did the same. The female officer placed her palm against the panel. It flashed blue as it scanned her hand. As it flashed white, the elevator lifted off smoothly, but Kira could feel the tingle along her arms as it magically gathered speed. Pressure increased with the speed of her ascent, pushing her down and making her want to lock her knees. She was grateful the energy bars were the only things in her stomach as her equilibrium went haywire.

Gilead East was typical of the buildings in Midtown: tall, glass, modern. Gilead's building encompassed more than twenty-five floors aboveground and at least five below. It would normally take several minutes to traverse the elevator's route even without stopping on every floor. They were traveling fast—faster than Kira's brain wanted to account for—causing her to shut her eyes and grit her teeth as magic and physics fought, scratched, and crawled to a draw.

Her stomach leapt to her throat as the elevator car abruptly slowed before stopping. The male guard murmured something into his earpiece, and nodded to the other guard. She tapped a code into the panel. The doors slid open onto a long utilitarian corridor painted discount gray and lit by a row of fluorescent light bars running down the center of the ceiling.

"I never want to do that again," Khefar finally said, slowly stepping out of the elevator.

"Most people don't," the male guard said. He pointed down the corridor. "The way is safe now. Follow that to the end. There's a short flight of stairs leading up to the roof access. Rigger will be waiting to guide you the rest of the way."

"Thanks." They made their way down the hall, their heavy boots loud on the polished concrete floor.

"Should I even ask what he meant by that whole 'the way is safe' thing?" Khefar asked.

"I've only been up here once or twice. I know there are usually lasers on when no one's up here. Maybe they've installed something nastier that would activate if we don't make it off the roof or if Gilead East is ever attacked from above. Hopefully Bale and his people won't give us cause to find out."

The corridor made a sharp ninety-degree turn

before abruptly stopping at a reinforced door of heavy steel. Another guard in full black combat gear waited there, assault rifle pointed at the floor. "Ma'am, sir," he said, "if you would please step on the mat."

Khefar raised an eyebrow, but complied. Kira stepped onto the mat beside him. The guard punched a string of code into the data panel beside the door. A swoosh of powerful energy swept through Kira, prickling her extrasense like a cotton sock fresh from the dryer. She could sense the defense grid filling the corridor with a fine mesh. Since the guard had them stand on the mat, it obviously didn't matter whether someone from Light or Shadow stepped into the corridor. If anything dared walk down the hallway, that pattern of energy would rip them to ribbons.

The guard pushed the door outward and raised his gun. "Please follow me."

Frigid air rushed down at them as they climbed the steep concrete steps up to the rooftop proper. Kira had a feeling the below-freezing temperature would be the least of her problems.

She strode to the center of the helicopter pad, hand on the hilt of her Lightblade to keep her anger from boiling over. The banaranjans usually kept their night flying to the upper atmosphere or heavily storming or cloudy nights. This frigid early-December morning was neither. Sanchez wasn't happy about the banaranjans intercepting their suspect, and Kira completely understood. Gilead didn't have to follow mundane protocols when it came to their investigations, but they did have rules. If Bale and his clan ruined their chances to get useful information out of Hammond . . .

She huddled in her battered trench coat, shoulders tightened against the cold and the tension. Twenty-five stories up in the wind tunnel of the Midtown Atlanta corridor was not the way she wanted to spend a night. Then again, being called to the hospital wasn't a stroll in the park either.

She surveyed the rooftop again. Sanchez stood to her left, Khefar to her right, slightly ahead and a little apart so they could both draw their weapons if the need arose.

The section chief's demeanor, cool, authoritative, and composed, spread out from her—an invisible mist blanketing the support personnel arranged around them. The subtle and overt energies of command were magical in their own way as Sanchez held her subordinates steady and in place by the sheer force of her will. It made Kira wonder how far the section chief's military career would have gone if her niece hadn't been killed by a Shadowling during summer camp.

A heavily armed security team, some thirty in all, formed a half-moon behind them, weapons ready but lowered. Sharpshooters had stationed themselves behind the HVAC units to provide cover fire if need be. Kira couldn't see them now, but she'd noticed a pair of snipers in night-vision goggles and anti-detection gear settle into place, their surface-to-air weapons trained on the frigid night sky. For an emergency deployment, Sanchez had assembled an oppressive force.

Kira hoped the section chief wouldn't have cause to open fire. For banaranjans, adrenaline was like catnip. Fear, excitement—any emotion that caused a surge of human adrenaline—would be exploited and metabolized into an intoxicant. The last thing they needed was the murders of stoned banaranjans landing on the roof.

There was an ace in the hole, Kira realized. With the helicopter pad empty, she could clearly see the steel graphic swirled into the concrete roof: one large circle outlined by stone pillars that stood over three feet high. They weren't ordinary pillars, though: instead of reinforced concrete, rock crystal, quartz, and salts composed the cylindrical structures. The minerals were good power conductors, and being exposed to the constant barrage of the elements, charging up on sunshine and moonlight, they would make excellent boosters for someone looking to enhance their magical strength.

Kira had no doubt the power generated by the mineral pillars would be incredible. It also made her wonder who Gilead East had at their disposal who was capable of harnessing that much energy with any sort of cohesive direction. It would take a highly trained Light Adept to be able to survive channeling that much raw power through their magical filters, let alone manipulate it.

A tingle of awareness along the outer reaches of her extrasense alerted Kira. "We've got incoming," she murmured to Sanchez.

Tension ramped higher as heads swiveled to catch a glimpse of the descending banaranjans. The security teams had their work cut out for them. Despite their size—banaranjans were slightly larger than humans in their native form—and their penchant for flying in raging storms, banaranjans were stealth flyers. In full flight and high on human adrenaline, they had a knack for tricking the eye.

"How many?" Sanchez asked, scanning the darkness above them. A few clouds hung in the chilly night sky, the only thing keeping the temperature bearable. Yet even with the thin cloud cover and a sliver of moon high in the sky, the winged hybrids couldn't be seen.

"Three."

Sanchez relaxed. Kira didn't. Neither, she noticed, did Khefar. The section chief might believe outnumbering the hybrids ten to one gave her an advantage, but Kira knew better. At least tonight, they had a common enemy. Because of that, the power plays and displays would be nonexistent or at least kept to a minimum.

The heavy thump of wing beats cut through the wind whistling over the rooftop. Several of the team members stirred. Kira groaned. It looked like there was going to be some posturing going on after all.

"Solomon." Sanchez's voice frosted the night air. "You better do your damndest to keep your friends in line. They have blatantly interfered with an ongoing Gilead investigation. I am not happy."

Kira grit her teeth. When the section chief was unhappy, that crap rolled downhill real fast. She and the chief had been getting along as well as any bureaucrat and someone who acted first and apologized later could; Kira didn't want back on her shit list.

"It will be okay," Kira said as the sound of beating wings grew louder and closer, as if coming from right above them. "Think of this as a Special Response Team making a delivery. A very special team making a very special delivery."

She lifted her face skyward and raised her voice.

"Cut it out, Bale, and get this over with! Some of us actually prefer to be inside where it's warm."

The overwhelming sound abruptly ceased. Another wave of unease swept through the team before it subsided. They trained for situations like this—this and the hope-it-never-happens, all-out war between Light and Shadow. Sanchez had obviously picked the elite of her Special Response Teams to handle the exchange.

A shout went up from the far side of the semi-circle. Three large forms dropped out of the night sky, descending feetfirst. Two of the banaranjans carried a large canvas bag, something that looked suspiciously like an army-issue gear bag.

Banaranjans were experts at glamour, yet there was nothing glamorous about their true form. Shedding their human guise, banaranjans looked like something out of a prehistoric nightmare, as if a pterodactyl and a Neanderthal had come across each other and decided to propagate. The night flyers weren't giant bats or dragons, but it was easy to see how they inspired such tales.

The hybrids in their natural forms were impressive, standing a little over seven feet tall from the crest on their heads to the claws of their feet. Their hides were a ruddy gray brown, thick enough to protect them from the elements. Just as they could make themselves appear human, banaranjans could alter the color and texture of their skin to blend into their surroundings. Their faces were more fox-like than reptilian, with elongated snouts displaying a fear-inspiring array of sharp pointed teeth. Their long-fingered hands were more human than not, but their feet were clawed and splayed to grip. They had a single claw at the tips of their wings like most bats. Lean, muscular, and wiry, banaranjans were lethal fighting machines.

The tallest of the trio, the one not carrying the duffel bag, stepped forward. "Shadowchaser Solomon, I present a gift to you from the hybrid community."

The voice was Bale's smooth tone, surprising coming from the banaranjan's fierce visage. Kira could feel Sanchez's eyes on her as she stepped forward. "You didn't bring me a gift, Bale," she corrected him, fighting to keep anger and irritation out of her voice and failing miserably. She had to look carefully to see anything of Bale's human face in the hybrid's features. "You brought me a material witness in an ongoing Gilead investigation, a witness who was in the process of being retrieved by Gilead agents."

She looked at the bag. "What in the name of Light did you do to him?"

"Nothing in the name of Light," the banaranjan told her. It bared its teeth in what was probably supposed to be a smile but looked like a snarl instead. "We thought Hammond might be more agreeable if we relaxed his tongue a bit."

Kira put her hands on her hips. "Exactly how did you relax his tongue?"

"We took him to the old quarry for a game of catch." Bale's eyes closed to slits. "Ah, the Bellwood quarry. It brings back such happy memories."

Crap. The banaranjan version of catch involved tossing a hapless victim around thirty or forty feet in the air. Kira had seen killer whales do something similar with a seal in the ocean. Fear was a powerful adrenaline inducer, and Kira didn't know anyone who thought of falling the equivalent of several stories to their deaths as a fun time. Hammond didn't stand a chance with banaranjans on adrenaline highs, no matter how far into Shadow he was.

"Bale, you can't do that with a Gilead witness!" Kira exclaimed. "You should have let us bring him in!"

The banaranjan shrugged, his folded wings rising and falling with the movement. "We wanted to make sure your quarry didn't escape your grasp. We knew you would move once you had human victims, but your pace is not a banaranjan's pace."

"We have to investigate. We have to gather facts and assess information," Kira protested. "We can't rush into places unprepared—"

"And we cannot allow another hybrid to fall victim to this man and his exhibit while Gilead takes its time."

Kira settled her hands on her hips. She didn't know if Bale was posturing for the two hybrids behind him or if he really meant his criticism of Gilead's—and her—actions. Maybe he was still high on adrenaline from the thrill of the hunt. He was still her friend, and a stabilizing force in the hybrid community. She needed both of those.

She tried for reason. "You've had him in your custody for long enough. Did you acquire any proof that Hammond is responsible? Did you discover how to awaken the people who are comatose?"

The other two banaranjans shifted uneasily, and Kira had her answer before Bale spoke. "If we did, our people would already be awake," he told her. "Hammond has proven to be . . . unresponsive to our methods of persuasion. Perhaps Gilead will have success questioning him. When you have the answers, we will join you in your final assault."

Sanchez's response was immediate and unequivocal. "Absolutely not."

The banaranjans' wings rustled, an ominous sign. A metallic sound behind Kira alerted her to the fact that someone had shifted a rifle. Bale swung his sharp-eyed gaze from Sanchez to the guard, eyes glowing green.

"Stop!" Kira barked, before things could go to hell. "Everybody stop for a damn minute."

She turned to Sanchez. "Section Chief, a word, please?"

She took a couple of steps away from the guards and the banaranjans. Sanchez followed, her steps reluctant. "Say whatever you want to say, Solomon, I'm still going to disagree."

Kira felt a headache start at the back of her skull. Reading Wynne's necklace had taken more out of her than she wanted to admit. She wanted ten minutes of quiet and a dark place to sit. Correction—a dark, *warm* place to sit. "Don't you want to know why I think we should agree to Bale's request?"

"I don't care what the reason is." The section chief's face hardened into implacable lines. "I'm not trusting my people to those creatures."

"'Those creatures' are law-abiding members of our community," Kira pointed out, too cold, and tired, and mentally ragged to watch her tone. "Bale is a respected leader in that community and does a lot of heavy lifting in keeping the peace between hybrids and humans. According to Khefar, banaranjans are serous fighters.

It wouldn't be a bad idea to have a couple of them on our side when we head to the Congress Center. Besides, they brought us Hammond. It wouldn't take much for them to take off with him again."

"I would consider that a reason to open fire."

"And risk hitting Hammond, our lone witness?" Kira shook her head. "I know you've got issues with hybrids. I get it, considering what happened with your niece and all. But they aren't our enemies. Even if they were, the old saying holds true: the enemy of my enemy is my friend."

She could see Sanchez struggle with it, struggle to set aside her emotional response. It made the section chief appcar more human to Kira—which was ironic, considering the situation. She decided to press a little more.

"Chief, you're the most practical strategist I know, and that's saying something. I know you don't like to move without having as many facts as possible. I also know you don't like going into a situation out-manned or underpowered. We could use some metaphysical muscle on our side. The banaranjans are offering to help Gilead. Think of how that will play in the hybrid community when word gets out. It will be good P.R. for you."

The section chief blew out a breath. "Who would have thought that you would be the practical one here?" Sanchez said wryly. She smoothed a gloved hand over her dark bun. "Fine. They can join us in the field. But if anything happens, I'm holding you person- ally responsible. Understood?"

"Loud and clear." Kira refrained from offering a

mock salute, but it was a near thing. She didn't need to push her luck with the section chief, especially since she had to use that luck and goodwill for a while longer.

They returned to their places, and Kira turned to the banaranjans. "Section Chief Sanchez appreciates the assistance of the hybrid community in apprehending a common enemy. We welcome your presence when we begin the next offensive."

"When will that be, Shadowchaser Solomon?"

"Hand over Hammond so we can interview him," Kira replied. "We have to know what we're facing, where, and how dangerous it is. Once we know that, we can make a plan."

"Tonight?"

Kira nodded. "I can call you when we begin strategizing, and conference you in. Is this acceptable?"

"We accept." Bale gestured to one of the banaranjans. The hybrid dragged the oversized duffel forward, unceremoniously releasing it.

"Is he still alive?" Sanchez asked, eyeing the bag.

"He is," Bale said, eyes still brilliant green. "Most find night flying with banaranjans to be somewhat stressful, so I had to calm him down a bit." All of the flyers grinned, a display of teeth that could have set the guards off again if the hybrids hadn't stepped back.

Bale turned to Kira, inclined his head. "I look forward to your call, Kira Solomon. Until then."

All three snapped their wings open—a sound like a minor clap of thunder. Each turned toward the side of the building unpopulated by guards. As they turned, they shimmered and disappeared. No, Kira realized, *disappeared* was the wrong word. She could hear the flap of their wings as each one launched into the air. It was more like they simply blended into their surroundings, a kind of metaphysical camouflage the military would kill to acquire.

"Are they gone?" Sanchez asked, seemingly to no one in particular.

Kira nodded. One team member with an infrared scanner gave a thumbs-up. Sanchez gestured, and two of her guards cautiously approached the canvas bag. One knelt to unzip it while the other watched, assault rifle ready.

"He's alive, ma'am," the guard reported, "Duct taped and trussed up like a Christmas turkey."

Sanchez turned to her aide. "Contact Rasmussen and tell her we're good to go. She and her team are set up in Interrogation Room Five. Escort our witness there. I don't care what it takes, I want Hammond up and talking in fifteen."

Chapter 20

Interrogation Room Five was part of a collection of staging areas that made up the high-security section of Gilead East's underground detainment facility. Any Adepts or hybrids needing to be held for their own good or the public's safety—whether for being under the influence of magic or more mundane substances—were housed on the upper levels in rooms that looked more like they belonged in mid-grade hotels. The higher the threat risk, however, the lower the level and the more utilitarian the room became, until they were no more than cinder block and steel cells reinforced with magic and titanium.

It took Dr. Rasmussen and her team twenty minutes to get Hammond warmed, dressed, and functioning but he still looked worse for wear with duct tape residue framing his loose-lipped mouth, his disheveled hair tinged red beneath the overhead ultraviolet lights. Thanks to his time with the banaranjans, he now barely resembled the suave salesman from the fund-raiser.

Banaranjans didn't have a word for *gentle* in their native tongue, but they had more than a dozen for *survive*. So while Bale and his compatriots hadn't been gentle in their handling of the man, they had made sure that he'd survive. Even enduring a banaranjan's flight was no mean feat. Kira had flown with Bale once, partly on a dare and partly to satisfy her curiosity. She never wanted to suffer the experience again.

A two-way mirror separated the interrogation chamber from the observation room. Kira waited with Khefar, Sanchez and her aide, Amanda Duncan, field agent Dustin Nguyen, and the heads of two Special Response Teams, Commander Charlie Jenkins and Commander Siri Sonoranvan.

Nguyen was an affable guy, Kira recalled, with strong ties to the local Vietnamese community north of Atlanta. He also served as a liaison of sorts between the human, hybrid, and Gilead communities. In other words, Special Agent Nguyen had the worst job in the city. How he was able to do his job and still maintain a cheerful disposition was beyond Kira. Better living through chemistry, maybe.

She had a passing acquaintance with the commanders, having backed them up on several missions. Jenkins looked as if he'd be better suited to a career on the pro wrestling circuit than private security. Tall, bald, and broad-shouldered, with skin a couple of shades lighter than his black fatigues, Commander Jenkins exuded power and command. Kira knew his intimidating looks concealed a kind soul, though. He'd once stopped a convoy to hustle a flock of geese and goslings across the busy highway.

The top of Siri Sonoranvan's head came up only to Jenkins's name tag, but her small frame was all muscle. *Delicate* wasn't a word used to describe the commander—or if someone did use it in her hearing, it was the last time. Siri specialized in hand-to-hand combat.

On the other side of the glass, Hammond lay strapped down to a chair that resembled something out of a dentist's office. Several guards took up strategic positions around the perimeter of the room. Behind Hammond's chair sat a large man with naturally red hair, but the color was so intense you'd think it had come out of a bottle. With his arms folded across his chest and his expression completely neutral, he could have given the bouncers at Demoz's club a run for their money. Kira had seen him before at headquarters—you didn't forget hair like that—and recalled his name was Donohue, but had no idea of his role with Gilead.

On Hammond's left was a highly nondescript man who looked to be in his mid- to late thirties. Mousy hair, average height and weight, eyes hidden behind wire-rimmed glasses—all contributed to his unremarkable looks. Unlike others in the room, he dressed very casually in dark loafers, olive-colored khaki trousers, and a dark brown sweater.

"Who's that guy?" Kira asked, jerking her head toward the glass.

"That's a Light Adept named Warren," Amanda said, her hair still managing to shine golden in the low light. "He's a Suppressor."

Khefar quietly asked, "What does he . . . suppress?"

"A variety of things," Kira replied. "Violent tendencies, frenetic behavior, insomnia."

"Warren suppresses damn near everything," the aide added.

"Since we don't know Hammond's status yet,

Warren is a good soporific," Sanchez said, looking up from her tablet. "He'll make sure Hammond isn't able to harm anyone in there. Or in here, for that matter."

The section chief nodded at the window. "Donohue will act as a veracity meter and record the proceedings. Monica Couchman will conduct the interview."

Couchman, a dark-skinned woman with close-cropped salt-and-pepper hair, took her place in the chair on Hammond's left. After receiving nods of assent from her two colleagues, she turned to the two-way glass. "We're ready to begin."

Sanchez touched a button beside the glass. "Proceed."

"Warren, bring him around," Couchman said.

The Suppressor nodded, focusing intently on the semi-supine Hammond. He seemed lifeless and innocuous. Then he opened his eyes.

Hammond's eyes burned with awareness, with fanatical determination, and fury. "Where is she?" he asked, his voice like gravel crunching underfoot. Kira wondered if he'd screamed a lot while with the banaranjans. Probably.

The interrogator leaned forward, snagging Hammond's attention. "Dr. Peter Hammond," Couchman began, "you are a material witness in a Gilead Commission investigation."

"What is a Gilead Commission?"

Donohue's hair bled from bright red to pale blond. *So he's a human lie detector,* Kira thought. *Good to know.*

Couchman glanced at Donohue before turning her attention back to Hammond. "You should know that we have protocols in place to monitor you physically and psychically during your interrogation," the older woman said. "Any attempt to evade the truth, to lie, will be noted. Any refusal to be forthcoming will also be noted. Do you understand?"

"More than you can imagine," Hammond answered. "More than you can begin to comprehend!"

"Do you know why you're here?"

"Of course."

"Why are you here?"

"Because my mistress wishes me to be," he said, as if it were obvious. "I live to serve her wishes."

Couchman made a notation on her tablet. "Who is your mistress?"

Hammond's eyes burned with a zealot's conviction. "Myshael, Lady of Shadows. Mother of Darkness, Bringer of Chaos. Mother of the ultimate sleeper agent." He strained against his bonds. "Where is Kira Solomon?" he demanded again. "Mummy and Daddy want to say hello."

It took effort for Kira to keep her features neutral, to stay impassive even with butterflies dropkicking her in the stomach. It didn't help that she could feel everyone in the room staring at her. She folded her arms across her chest, and then forced herself to speak. "Well. I guess we now know he's not an innocent party in all of this."

"Who is he talking about?" Sanchez asked. "These 'Mummy and Daddy' people. Who are they?"

Kira kept her eyes on the window. "He's talking about Balm's counterpart. The Lady of Shadows, mother of Shadowlings and the darker hybrids."

Silence, thick and total, filled the room like a fog. These people worked for the Gilead Commission, which meant they worked for Balm. A few of them might have seen the Lady of Light when she'd been in town a couple of months back, but they all had heard of what had happened in Gilead London. They knew the kind of power Balm had, which meant they had a pretty good idea of what sort of power her counterpart could wield.

"So there's someone out there like the Balm of Gilead, someone who leads Shadowlings?" Duncan asked, surprise filling her voice.

So Gilead East hadn't thought through the idea of there being something out there to Balance Balm either. Kira felt less ignorant. "They're not as organized as we are. Thank the Light for that."

"If she's the mother of Shadowlings," Duncan said slowly, her voice wavering, "and he says she's your mother, then that means—"

"It means nothing," Kira cut in, her voice like a whip.

"But Donohue's hair . . ." Duncan faltered as Kira turned to face her. Sanchez merely watched, her expression impassive. The Gilead agents looked to the section chief, poised to act on her orders.

Out of all the Gilead agents in the room, only Nguyen seemed to be rationally using his brain. "Since Hammond serves the Lady of Shadows, he would believe anything she tells him, right?" Nguyen said. "I mean, he calls her 'mistress.' That sounds pretty devoted to me." He gestured at Kira. "Kira has a Lightblade. Very few people can even pick one of those up, much less use it. Certainly no one with the Lady of Shadows as a parent could."

"Hammond believes what his mistress tells him to believe," Kira said, with a nod of thanks to Nguyen. "As much as he believes it, that doesn't make it true. My mother was a Shadowchaser who died shortly after giving birth to me. I was raised and trained by the Balm of Gilead herself. Hammond is saying all of this to get to me. Don't let him get to you in the process."

"Kira, Kira," Hammond crooned, "come out, come out, wherever you are."

"The bigger question is, is he still sane?" Nguyen asked with concern. "If he's not competent enough to give testimony, can we even use anything he says?"

"He's sane," Kira asserted, her eyes never leaving the sight on the other side of the glass. "He may be Shadow-struck, but he's still sane. Besides, we already know who and what. We need to find out why and how to reverse it."

"Why don't you tell me about the exhibit, Dr. Hammond?" Couchman asked as if she'd heard their discussion. Her voice brushed against the glass, calm, beguiling. "We know that something in your exhibit is causing innocent people to fall into comas. What we don't know is why only a few people are comatose out of the hundreds who have visited the exhibit since it opened. Can you tell me that?"

"No."

Donohue's hair faded again.

"Dr. Hammond—"

"I probably should have said that I certainly can." He smiled. "But I won't."

"We know that you gave the Shadowchaser's friend a carved stone," Couchman said, continuing with her questioning. "Is that how you were able to steal all those people's souls? Something in the stone acted as a trigger?"

"It's the Egyptian journey through the underworld," Hammond retorted, his haughty demeanor returning. "How do you think their souls were taken?"

Couchman appeared unflappable. Kira, on the other hand, wanted to punch something, starting with Hammond's snobby face. The older woman made another notation on her tablet. "Do you mean to say that Ammit the Devourer is alive?"

Hammond laughed. "That's for me to know and you to find out."

Couchman handed her pen and notepad to Donohue, who then pushed his chair back a couple of feet. "I will find out, Doctor," the woman said, her voice still smooth, still unruffled. "Of course, my superiors would prefer you be forthcoming with the information that they require. I, on the other hand, don't have a preference for how I get the information. All that matters is that I get it."

"You can't do anything to me. I know my rights."

Couchman reached up, removing her glasses with precise movements before tucking them into her jacket pocket. "I am required to inform you that the Geneva Conventions do not apply to you. You have admitted to being aligned with Shadow. That makes you an enemy combatant, a hostile witness, a reluctant partner in helping us save some innocent people's lives. That also means that I do not have to be as gentle with you as the banaranjans were."

Kira swiveled to look at Sanchez. "What's she talking about? The banaranjans turned Hammond into a human volleyball."

"Couchman has been authorized to use any means necessary to get the information that we need," Sanchez said. "She is very good at what she does, although it's been a while since she's had to get persuasive."

"Do we have to worry about what her method of persuasion is?" Khefar asked, speaking for the first time.

"Don't worry." Sanchez turned back to the glass. "There won't be any blood. At least, not from Hammond."

Hammond laughed, sounding unhinged to Kira's ears. "You can torture me all you want," he taunted. "I'm not going to tell you anything."

"I'm sorry, Dr. Hammond, but you're wrong on both counts," Couchman said, her voice full of reproach. "The Gilead Commission doesn't condone torture. We do, however, believe that confession is good for the soul. Do you have anything you would like to confess?"

The interviewer's easygoing demeanor finally penetrated whatever haze Hammond was in. He glanced at her, suspicion shoving away haughtiness. "Nothing to confess to you," he sneered. "And who are you that I should seek absolution from you?"

Couchman leaned over him, splaying her hands on either side of his temples. "I am the Light that illuminates the Shadows in your soul," she intoned. "I am the mirror that allows you to see yourself clearly."

Hammond laughed, a sound that quickly devolved

into choking. He jerked, then went rigid as his eyes widened. "No, no, no!" he shouted, the last word a high-pitched scream.

Power erupted in the room. Kira instinctively threw up her hand, her extrasense igniting blue-green in a protective shield as magical pressure built to a breaking point. On the other side of the glass, Donohue's hair flared orange-red.

"Get them out of there!" Kira shouted.

"Wait," Sanchez said, her voice unruffled. "Warren's got it under control."

Kira turned back to the window. Warren lifted his hands above his head, palms cupped toward the ceiling. With her extrasense activated, Kira could see and feel Warren's magic flow out from his hands in a muddy, brownish-black wave. It spread like a mudslide over Hammond's chaotic Shadow magic.

The Suppressor then lowered his hands. As he did, the level and intensity of power in the room decreased. By the time Warren's hands returned to his knees, the power was all but extinguished.

"See what you have done," Couchman said to Hammond, as if magic hadn't reached explosive levels moments before. "See the lives you have taken, the souls you have destroyed. Hear their cries, the wailing of their loved ones."

Hammond's entire body twitched. A mewling sound slipped from his slacked mouth. He arched against the restraints, struggling to free himself from the ties and Couchman's all-seeing gaze. His efforts were futile, Kira now knew. Couchman was an Illuminator. She hadn't met an Adept yet capable of withstanding one. *When in the world had Sanchez brought an Illuminator on board?*

"What is she doing to him?" Khefar asked, his tone hushed. He sounded horrified, and Kira didn't blame him. Her gut tightened as Hammond cried out again.

"She's an Illuminator," Kira said, locking her emotions down. "Couchman finds all the evil in Hammond's life, every bad thing that he's done, and lights it up, making him live through it from the victim's perspective. They call it Confession."

Kira would never have thought Sanchez would use an Illuminator. A lie detector like Donohue or a Suppressor like Warren was almost benign magic, and commonly used in Gilead interrogations. No serious or lingering harm had ever been caused by anyone exercising those talents.

An Illuminator was something else entirely. They were usually marked by the fact that they always wore dark sunglasses inside or out, so their eyes were completely concealed—a necessary measure to protect the public from inadvertently having their every dark deed brought to the surface. It took a while, Kira knew—four, five seconds—before an Illuminator's power overwhelmed their target.

Illuminators answered only to the Commissioners, the little-seen governing body of the Gilead Commission. Kira had met a pair of them when she lived on Santa Costa—they were brought in whenever a Shadowchaser needed to undergo refinement. The few Chasers she knew didn't fear the Fallen—who made Shadow Adepts look like second-rate magicians—but they all feared the Illuminators.

"How long has she been in town?" Kira asked, her voice strained thin to her ears. Her extrasense was still dialed up to a protective shield, her gaze glued to the people on the other side of the window. Now that she knew what Couchman was, her sense of self-preservation wouldn't drop until she left the building.

"Ms. Couchman has been with us since you left for London to take care of your handler's affairs," Sanchez said, her tone sounding as if they were discussing general personnel movements and the paperwork it generated. As if she hadn't just dropped a bomb on Kira. "She's been helping our field agents find the Shadowlings who helped that Fallen who came to town."

Kira didn't bother asking the next obvious question. The Illuminator had been in town for two months, and no one at Gilead East had bothered to tell her. She knew other Shadowchasers had blown through town, and no one had bothered to tell her that either. *I'm not paranoid, but this crap don't smell right,* she thought. *If it walks like a duck and talks like a duck, chances are it's a velociraptor with a machine gun.*

"Mother of Darkness," Hammond crooned, his eyes glazed. "She comes for you, she waits for you."

"Who is he talking about?" someone asked.

As if in answer, Hammond turned his face to the window, his entire body straining to point. "He comes for you. The Lord of Storms comes to claim you."

Fear skittered along Kira's nerve endings. *The Lord of Storms. Another name for Set. Sweet Lady of Truth, please don't tell me Set has finally awakened.*

"Tell me how to reclaim the souls you've stolen,"

Couchman said in her soothing tone of voice. "How do we save those people?"

Hammond's eyes rolled up to the whites. "You can claim nothing. Only she can decide. She will stand before the Throne of Set, she will face the Devourer of Souls. She will give her soul to the Chaos and decide the fate of the sleeping."

Mother of Truth, Kira breathed, fear making it difficult to think clearly. *Is that what you want me to do? Is this what the last few months have been leading me to?*

"No." Khefar's voice cut like a whip through her thoughts. "That's not going to happen. I'm not going to let that happen."

"She will come," Hammond said in his high, thin voice that sawed through Kira's senses like a dull, rusty knife. "She will come and be judged, or the sleeping will die. The Devourer will be unchained by Set's hand, and more souls will enter the great nothingness. Chaos will reign."

He laughed, the sound degenerating into an insane cackle. "Go then, Kira Solomon. Go then to your destiny. The Lady of Shadows waits to take you into her embrace."

Kira's stomach began to roil. "I think . . . I need to get some air."

She pushed her way out of the room and down the hall, searching for a ladies' room. She found a unisex toilet and pushed her way in, standing over the bowl as her breath came fast and hard. The energy bars sat like a stone in her stomach, a boulder being tossed around by the earthquake of her emotions. "I don't want to do this. I can't do this. I can't."

Shadowlings she could handle. Seeker demons you fought or got killed. One of the Fallen you faced with everything you had, leaving no room for fear. But facing the Chaos god of your pantheon? Confronting Ammit, the Devourer of Souls? Knowing that they were acting as agents of the Lady of Shadows? She couldn't do it.

Hammond's voice pressed in on her brain, as insistent as a woodpecker digging for insects. She clamped her hands to her ears, spinning away from the commode. At the sink, she put her back against the wall then slid down it, her coat fanning out around her. Drawing her knees up, she locked her arms around them and rocked back and forth like a child fresh from a nightmare.

Except this wasn't a dream. If Hammond were to be believed, both Set and the Lady of Shadows would be waiting for her in the exhibit. She had no reason to doubt him, especially when she considered the fact that he'd disclosed the information while being questioned by an Illuminator.

The Lady of Shadows had played everything perfectly. The Fallen sacrificed for a Shadowling's errand, in order to inject her with Chaos to awaken her own Shadow magic. Her parents. The Shadowblade coming into her possession. Balm's absence. The dreams of Set demanding that she join him.

Kira had believed she was safe, despite the nightmares. That, somehow, the dreams could be ignored or conquered. Now, knowing everything the Lady of Shadows had done to bring her to this moment, terror gripped her and wouldn't let go. The idea of the dreams coming true, of having to actually face the Egyptian god of storms and chaos, of giving in to him, was almost too much. If she refused, they would destroy the souls they held. They would then kill her, and she'd become Shadow anyway.

A soft knock at the door almost had her reaching for her blades. She swallowed down the yelp, and cleared her throat. "Yeah?"

"It's Khefar. I'm coming in."

"You could at least ask," she said as he pushed the door open.

"Would you have invited me in?"

"Probably not."

"There you go, then." He sat down beside her on the gray tiled floor, his booted feet stretching the length of the room. "That was pretty intense."

"You think?" She loosened her grip on her knees.

"You were right about the scarabs being the key to saving those people. They can be purified with Light magic and the recitation of one of the prayers from the Book of the Dead. Sanchez has someone working up a translation right now."

"The Illuminator really got Hammond talking, didn't she?"

"Singing like the proverbial canary." He grimaced. "An off-key, mentally unstable canary. Let me state for the record that I never want to be on the receiving end of that particular brand of confession."

"You and me both." She shifted, a move that put her slightly closer to him, their sleeves almost touching. Selfishly she wished that they could have had one more night together, but trouble never waited.

He reached over, taking hold of her hand, squeezing her fingers. She wanted to remove her glove, feel the warmth of his skin against hers, but she didn't dare risk it. She needed to save her energy for whatever she needed to do next.

Khefar, attuned to her as always, gave her fingers another squeeze. "I guess this means your dreams weren't random dreams."

"No, they weren't." *Set's waiting for me. Freakin' Set. He's gonna ask me to join him, I'm going to refuse, and he's going to kill me with a* was *scepter.*

He pulled her hand into his lap. "You didn't ask my opinion, but I'm going to give it anyway. It's a trap. They know we know it's a trap, and they don't care. That means they think they've got the upper hand."

She gave a weak laugh. "I think they do too. Facing the Lady of Shadows, Set, and Ammit the Devourer in the Hall of Judgment is scary. It was bad enough the last time, when Ma'at elevated me. I don't think I can go back there."

"All right."

"All right?" she echoed. "Just like that, you're okay with me not going in there?"

"My vow is to protect your soul," Khefar reminded her. "Doing as Hammond says is a sure way of endangering your life. We'll find some other way."

"The only other way that wouldn't endanger those souls is to bomb the place," Kira said. "We can't destroy those artifacts, and we definitely can't sacrifice those souls because I have cold feet."

She leaned forward, catching his expression. "What aren't you telling me?"

"Sanchez is going to attack with or without you," he said, his expression bleak. "Hammond told us that everyone who went through the Hall of Judgment—men, women, children—all of them are in danger of losing their souls and falling into comas."

A chill crept along Kira's nerves. "That could be hundreds of people. Maybe thousands."

"I know." Khefar nodded. "Sanchez realizes it too. Hundreds of people abruptly falling into comas for no apparent reason will incite a citywide panic."

"One way or another, the reason behind the spontaneous unconsciousness would get out," Kira said. "Gilead can't risk that type of exposure. I can't even begin to imagine what sort of containment that would require."

"Which is why Sanchez is assembling a volunteer strike force to launch a Level One assault on the Congress Center."

"Mother of Light," Kira breathed. "If she does that, the Lady of Shadows could start destroying scarabs. People would think there's some sort of pandemic. Chaos would erupt."

"Giving them exactly what they want." Khefar cursed. "Either way, they win."

"The only way we have a chance is if I go in. I can at least buy some time for you and the SRT to find the scarabs and get them to someone who can purify them. I can call the DMZ, see if Yessara will help us."

"Good idea." Khefar climbed to his feet, extending a hand to help her up. "I'm not happy about you being the sacrificial lamb in all of this."

"Me either, but is there really another choice? I

can't walk away. I don't want any more deaths on my hands. Not when I know there's something I can do to prevent it."

"I know." He brushed the back of his hand down her cheek, his gaze lingering on her eyes. "You ready to go back?"

"Yeah." She scrubbed her gloved hands over her face, the smell of the synthetic material comforting. "You knew I'd decide to face Set, didn't you?"

"I know that you haven't run from a challenge since I've known you, and you've faced some pretty intense challenges," he said. "I also figured that at the very least you'd want to face the Lady of Shadows so you can tell her to screw off to her face."

Kira grinned. "That does have a certain allure."

"I didn't exactly think you were paranoid before, but now I'm beginning to wonder."

"Wonder about me being paranoid?"

"No. I can't reach Anansi and you can't reach Balm. To say those two are interested in what we do is a gross understatement."

"So you're finally on board with my paranoia, huh?"

"It's not paranoia when there's someone actually after you."

That brought her up short. "You think someone's after me?"

He nodded. "I've tried reaching out to Anansi since we went to the hospital. Granted, when he's visiting his wife he tends to get distracted, but he told me to contact him if there's a need."

"I say this qualifies." Kira settled her coat into

place. "I still can't reach Balm, I haven't had any direct responses from Ma'at, there's an Illuminator in town, and we're about to walk into a trap set by the Lady of Shadows herself. And everybody seems to be fine with it. Why?"

Khefar's expression grew grim. "Maybe you shouldn't go."

"You know I have to. There are literally souls at stake. I don't know why everyone has bailed on us, but if they want us to handle this on our own, fine."

"Whatever this is," Khefar said darkly.

"We won't know until we get there."

"True." Khefar settled his gear.

"Let's go find Sanchez."

"Wait."

She turned to him. "What now?"

"This." He pulled her close, kissed her. She hesitated for a moment. Then her eyes slid shut as she wrapped her arms around his waist, kissing him back with equal intensity.

"You need to make it through too," he told her. "Don't go dying on me in there."

"I'm going to try not to," she promised. "Have I told you how much I appreciate you?"

"No."

She smiled, pushed open the door. "Remind me to get around to it sometime."

Chapter 21

They returned to the viewing room. To Kira's relief, the interrogation side was empty, Hammond and the Illuminator nowhere to be seen. "What happened to him?"

"Dr. Rasmussen has taken him into her care," Duncan answered, her professionalism firmly back in place. "It's doubtful that he'll be a functioning member of society again—not without a lot of work."

Which meant that people at the Carlos Museum and elsewhere in the museum exhibition and academic world—people who knew and worked with Kira as an antiquities expert—would wonder about their colleague's disappearance. "He can't disappear without a reasonable explanation. I need to be able to tell people something when they ask. And they will ask."

"I'm sure we'll be able to provide a plausible cover story for you to disseminate," Sanchez said. "The Nubian bring you up to speed?"

"Yeah."

"And?" Sanchez prompted.

"And it sounds like there's going to be a heckuva party at the Congress Center." Kira tried for a careless shrug. "Since I'm on the guest list, I'd better show up."

Sanchez continued her basilisk-like gaze. "Seems

to me that you're the guest of honor." She nodded toward the two-way window. "Know what he was talking about?"

Kira hesitated. "Which part?"

"The part about the Lady of Shadows waiting for you."

"Oh, that."

Sanchez cocked an eyebrow. "Well?"

"I've sent a lot of her children back to Shadow," Kira said with a shrug. "Makes sense that she'd hold it against me."

The section chief gave Kira a stare that rivaled the most intense of Balm's formidable glares. "So we're potentially confronting the Mother of Shadow, and this creature called Ammit the Devourer who is somehow holding people's souls hostage."

"Yeah. We're not going to have an easy time getting those souls back."

"Tell me something I don't know." Sanchez actually looked . . . discomfited. "This is a trap. It's almost certain suicide for anyone who goes into the exhibit—that is, if the whole Center isn't booby-trapped."

"I know." The thought of more Gilead agents—or anyone else for that matter—dying on her watch made Kira feel more than a little ill herself. "Maybe we should leave your men out of this."

"Like hell."

The retort came to her in stereo. She looked between Khefar and Sanchez. Both wore equal expressions of stubborn determination. "Fine," Kira said, holding up her hands in surrender. "I was mostly joking anyway."

"Uh-huh." Sanchez didn't look or sound convinced. "Let's head to Control. You can give us a full debrief there."

Gilead East's Control Room was the equivalent of Mission Control at NASA. TacRoom One was the largest in Gilead East, boasting one wall of monitors cued to various locations around Atlanta, and another containing an interactive electronic map. More than a dozen analysts were bent over keyboards and headsets at tiered workstations placed in pods of four about the cavernous room. A stream of runners continuously made their way to the analysts via a set of double doors. Those doors, Kira knew, led to a set of windowless rooms holding the ergonomic loungers for the cadre of psychics Gilead called "sweepers." The sweepers detected every minuscule flare of Shadow magic in the Greater Metropolitan Atlanta area while the analyst crunched the data to detect potential threats.

Sanchez took her place on a bridge of sorts looking down onto the bustling activity below. Beside Sanchez stood the two commanders from the interrogation room. Rows of black-clad guards stood in formation, waiting expectantly. Several of them had been on standby when Kira and Khefar had taken the fake Dagger of Kheferatum into Demoz's club. Kira knew they'd leap at the chance to avenge their comrades lost at Enig's hands.

Sanchez took an earbud and a handheld from her assistant, her version of battle gear. "Chaser Solomon, you already met Commander Charlie Jenkins and

Commander Siri Sonoranvan. They'll lead the Gilead strike teams."

Kira nodded, not bothering to extend her hand. The commanders didn't either. Gilead associates had learned early on not to touch her.

Sonoranvan nodded at Khefar. "I saw him in the interrogation room. Who's he? Another Chaser or a civilian?"

"Neither." Kira turned to Khefar. "Khefar backs me up. Once we engage in the field, he's second to me."

That surprised both captains. They knew to take orders from a Shadowchaser when hunting Shadow Adepts or Avatars, but if Khefar wasn't a Chaser . . . "Ma'am?"

"You both have been through Gilead tactical training so you know your military history," Sanchez said, barely glancing up from her handheld. "You remember Hannibal of Carthage?"

"Yes."

"Well, then, meet the man who suggested the elephant as a war animal."

Both agents gave Khefar a second measured glance. Kira bit the inside of her jaw to keep from smiling. She didn't know if the story was true or not, and neither did Sanchez. But the section chief liked to keep everyone on their toes.

Sonoranvan gave Khefar another assessing look. "Excuse me for saying so, but he doesn't look a day over thirty."

"Multiply that by one hundred fifty," Khefar suggested, "give or take a decade."

"Let's just say he's got several lifetimes of military

experience," Kira said. She turned to Sanchez. "Are we ready for the debrief?"

The section chief nodded. "Tell us seriously what we're facing."

"From what we saw with the Illuminator, Hammond is an ardent follower of Shadow. He used the Journey Through the Underworld exhibit as a ruse to collect souls for Shadow using a construct that mimics the aspects of Ammit, an ancient Egyptian demoness. When the deceased reached the Hall of Judgment, his or her heart—considered the center of thought, memory, and emotion—was placed on a large scale. Ammit devoured those whose souls weren't in balance with Ma'at's feather of Truth and Justice."

"So you don't think this is the real Ammit?"

"No," Khefar answered. "The real Ammit doesn't put people into comas. She eats your soul. While some traditions say the soul is doomed to a restless existence, most believed that for the soul to be devoured by Ammit meant that you were forever destroyed. No passing 'Go,' no collecting two hundred dollars."

"I'm not at all one hundred percent sure on the rules, but I don't think the Lady of Shadows can enter this plane of existence as long as Balm is here. That won't slow her down, though, since she controls Fallen and Shadow Adepts," Kira explained. "She has someone acting on her behalf, a Lightchaser or a Shadow Avatar. It may even be the same person we encountered in London and Cairo." Kira hoped it was. She still had a score to settle with Marit.

"Whoever it is can pick and choose which people

to put into a coma. I'm not sure why the other humans and hybrids were picked as victims, but Wynne Marlowe was specially selected. These souls are being used as leverage to get us—me in particular—to come to the exhibit for some sort of showdown."

Kira clenched her hands, anger and worry melding like alloy in her gut. "They didn't have to go through all this trouble. Harming all these people, holding their souls as hostage."

"They wanted you there on their terms, not ours," Sanchez said. "Makes them think they have us at a disadvantage. I say let them keep thinking that way. People who are overconfident tend to make mistakes, and when they do, we turn it to our advantage."

Good information to know, Kira thought. Good thing she wasn't feeling all that confident. "That's the *Reader's Digest* version. What's the plan?"

"We've got the blueprints of the Congress Center, as well as the exhibit layout and the delivery area," Sanchez said. She tapped her tablet computer, and the display wall showed the sprawling layout for the Georgia World Congress Center. "You will have the first two strike teams with you, making entry here and here. The sweepers will work from here to set up a net around the Center. We will have Special Response Teams Three and Four on standby, and the convention center's police force and security have already been ordered to make themselves scarce."

Kira nodded. "That will work. We don't know what or how many we're facing. But I'm betting that our answer lies at the end of the exhibit, in the Weighing of the Heart ceremony. That's where people were getting their souls taken, so it's more than likely where the showdown will take place."

"Since they are using the Weighing of the Heart ceremony as a basis for their thievery, it might be wise to take a copy of the spells with us," Khefar suggested.

"Good idea. If they're using the Weighing of the Heart ceremony to take the souls, they've basically agreed by default to go by the rules of Egyptian funerary practices and religion. That means we should be able to use the spells from the book to counteract it."

"Which spell, though?" Khefar wondered. "The Negative Confessions?"

"We'll probably need that one for us." Kira rubbed her forehead. "It's been a long time since I've looked through the book of spells. Aren't there references to prevent the soul from being stolen?"

"If you're unsure, we'll need to rely on the analysts," Sanchez said. "Data is their specialty. It's what we pay them for."

Sanchez was right. The analysts would be a faster and more reliable resource than her memory of Egyptian funerary text. "They'll need to work quickly," she said. "We'll probably need answers almost instantaneously."

Sanchez gestured to an aide, who immediately approached with a tray of tiny communication devices. "Everyone will have communicators and will be in constant contact. We'll be able to monitor what you're hearing and seeing." Sanchez turned to Kira. "Do you have a plan for returning the souls to their rightful owners?"

Kira nodded. "Kill the Ammit construct, recover

the heart scarabs that were used as tokens, and, if necessary, purify them with my Lightblade, though it may be better to have a Light Healer on hand for that. If I recall correctly, there are a number of spells that protect the soul and return the heart to the deceased."

"Good. I'll have several analysts working the various copies of the funerary texts. Any clue you can give us as to which one we should rely on could be vital."

"Agreed." Kira balanced the communicator in the palm of one gloved hand and used her teeth to pull off the other glove. She held her bare fingers over the earpiece, concentrating a focused brush of power over the device. Sure, they were spares and probably not used recently, but she didn't need to get an accidental earful of someone else's psychic communications.

"Are you going into combat like that?" Sanchez asked.

Kira looked down at her jeans and overcoat. "Somehow I don't think the Lady of Shadows is going to care how I'm dressed," she said. "However, Khefar and I have extra gear in the car. We'll gear up in the parking deck, then head out."

"See that you do. I won't have the Balm of Gilead riding my ass because I sent you out ill-prepared." Sanchez turned to the guards assembled below. "We are facing a Level One incursion," she told them. "Our enemy knows we're coming, and in fact has done everything to ensure that we come by taking the souls of innocents on both sides of the Balance. With that sort of invitation, it would be rude of us not to show up."

Several of the guards laughed. The room quickly sobered. "We are going to get those souls back. We're going to save lives tonight. Given what we encountered with that Level Two event two months ago, it's entirely possible that winning those souls back is going to cost some lives on our side. The commanders and the Shadowchaser are going to do everything they can to make sure that doesn't happen, but make no mistake: this is an extremely dangerous situation. This mission is strictly volunteer only. No one is ordered to go. No one will be rebuked if they choose to stay behind. If you prefer not to go, now's the time to speak up."

No one moved. No one made a sound. Everyone waited, ready.

Sanchez nodded. "All right, then. May the Light shine on you all. Commanders, you're a go."

Chapter 22

Less than five minutes later, Khefar's Charger rendezvoused with two armored vans for the short trek to the convention center's B Building loading docks. Train tracks ran beside the yard, beneath the convention center, and close to the loading docks. It was the perfect place for the Gilead vehicles to sit, and an even better vantage point from which the Special Response Teams could breach the convention center complex.

Khefar popped the Charger's trunk and followed Kira out of the car. Luckily they hadn't switched out gear since their altercation with the bultungin. Kira quickly stripped off her coat. She tossed it into the trunk and pulled out her tactical vest. Anticipation and fear coiled inside her, tightening her muscles for action. When it came down to it, she preferred fighting over thinking. Thinking always led to trouble of one sort or another. She couldn't think about what lay ahead of her in the exhibit hall. She couldn't think about Hammond's high-pitched hysterical ramblings. She couldn't think about what could happen once she reached the Hall of Two Truths. She certainly couldn't think about whether or not she'd leave the building alive.

After fastening her vest, she handed a second one

to Khefar, then checked the clips on several guns before holstering each in its assigned spot. Like Khefar, she preferred her blades over other weapons, but without knowing her target, she'd take all the weapons she could carry while still being able to handle herself in hand-to-hand combat.

Khefar tried the second vest on but immediately shrugged out of it. "No, thanks," he said, handing it back to her. "I'd rather move freely."

"Humor me." Kira thrust the jacket back at him, turning to reach for ammunition. "It's hours before sunrise, we don't know what we're walking into, and while we're going to have the banaranjans and a couple of strike teams as backup, it's really going to come down to you and me. I need you to make it through."

"Since you ask so diplomatically . . ." Khefar took the tactical vest, slid it on. The Gilead-issued vests had lightweight body armor plates augmented with anti-assault spells that could deflect most attacks and multiple calibers of bullets. The magical enhancements wouldn't protect against someone trying to dispatch the wearer up close, but, Kira thought, if you let the person get that close to you, you probably were beyond the need for the protective spells anyway.

"You're going to take that artifact into battle?" Khefar asked, gesturing to the blade strapped to her left thigh.

Kira dropped her hand to the dagger, but didn't touch it. She hadn't told him about the Shadowblade yet. He'd just demand that she take it off, and he'd worry and wonder when she refused. He'd wonder why she had been carrying a Lightchaser's dagger and the only explanation she could give him was that it had seemed like a good idea at the time. Of course, if she tried to wield it in his presence and attempted to charge it with the Shadow portion of her extrasense, his Dagger of Kheferatum would react, thinking her a threat.

"Yeah," she finally said, switching out her gloves for a fingerless pair. "I can't just leave it lying around and blades channel my magic better than bullets. Don't have to worry about the mechanics getting mucked up. Do you mind if I take the khopesh too? It's got a longer reach than my Lightblade. I should be able to channel my extrasense through it with no problem."

Khefar gave her a suspicious look before pulling the weapon out of the trunk. She'd told him the truth, but if his expression was anything to go by he knew she hadn't told him the whole truth. His ability to read her was beginning to be an inconvenience. Luckily he had other benefits in his favor. Still, she didn't like keeping things from him. With Comstock gone and Balm out of reach, Khefar was now the only one who didn't judge her. It made her want to confess all to him. And she would. She'd explain everything to him once they were on the back side of this confrontation.

He handed her the scabbard without a word. She slung it over her head so that it rested diagonally across her back, enabling her to pull the blade free with her right hand. While she hoped to be able to charge the blade with her extrasense, she certainly couldn't tell Khefar that she was half-afraid her Lightblade would fail her when she needed it most, afraid that the Shadow half of her would try to assert itself when in the presence of the Lady of Shadows and the Lord of

Chaos. If she told him that, he would try to stop her from entering the exhibit, and more people would die.

A tingle of motion buzzed along her subconscious. "Bale's incoming," she said, pointing up. She'd notified him, as promised, of the impending confrontation on the way to the Center.

Bale and three other banaranjans glided down from the semidarkness of the parking deck as Kira and Khefar headed toward the loading dock. They shimmered into human shape. She didn't see any weapons on them, but when your other form was something that looked like a pterodactyl, she supposed guns were unnecessary.

"All has been quiet since we got here," Bale said after he'd fully assumed his human form. He and the others were clothed in what looked to Kira to be some sort of ninja gear. "Other than security disappearing, there hasn't been any activity."

"So that's either good news or very bad news."

"Whichever one it is, we'll handle it."

They joined the strike teams up on one of the loading docks. It took no time at all for the Special Response Teams to breach the loading dock entrance to the center building. They quickly fanned out, moving silently through the receiving area to the exhibition space. Kira hadn't expected they would encounter any resistance, but the lack of challenge scraped her already bare nerves.

Would they be given passage through the display section of the exhibit, coming into conflict only when they approached the mock tomb? Or were their opponents wanting to spread them out in order to better pick them off one by one?

With no nighttime events scheduled in any of the exhibit halls, an energy-saving light scheme illuminated only the public-facing areas of the convention center. In semidarkness, they made their way down the back corridors to the cavernous hall that housed the Egyptian exhibit. They paused outside the large doors leading to the main exhibit floor, the guards fanned out protectively around them, assault rifles at the ready.

One team member extended a thin rod with a tiny mirror attached to its end and slipped it beneath the door. He shook his head and drew the mirror back. Nothing to see on the other side, or no visibility to see what awaited them.

The banaranjans shifted, restless. Kira couldn't blame them. She was more of a charge-in-and-start-hurting-people type of person herself. The precautions were necessary: the Gilead team didn't have innate magic, but they were doing their jobs because they were dedicated. She could swallow down her impatience knowing the Gilead teams were willingly putting their lives on the line to rescue the souls of people they didn't know.

There was a secondary reason for caution as well.

"We need to be careful in this area," Kira whispered. "There are irreplaceable artifacts on the other side of those doors." They might be insured for millions, but they were, in truth, priceless.

Sonoranvan gave a curt nod, then signaled to Commander Jenkins, communicating the placement of their teams for the incursion. Jenkins acknowledged and gestured to his team. The black-clad men and women shifted into position. Kira caught Bale's attention, pointing up. The banaranjans would take to the air.

Jenkins held up a hand, counted down to one. Two of the squad pushed open the double doors, and the banaranjans entered in a blur of wind and speed.

The already minimal night lighting went out. Team members quickly switched to night-vision, sweeping the large room for any potential threats. Several tense moments passed before the all clear was called.

Kira breathed a sigh of relief even as tension coiled in her stomach. She drew her Lightblade, and called her extrasense. Blue-green light flickered along the silvery metal of the dagger. She swallowed a curse, then concentrated, willing the power back to cobalt blue.

A glowing trail of Chaos magic led from the replica of the Book of the Dead papyrus to the entrance of the pseudo-tomb.

"Either one of you know what's on the other side of that door?" Jenkins asked. "Other than a trap, I mean."

"What's supposed to be on the other side of the door is a long corridor with funeral texts and spells emblazoned on the walls. It leads to a chamber where they have the Weighing of the Heart Ceremony exhibit set up. There's a burial chamber off to the west side, but you exit from the main room," Kira explained. "What we'll actually find is anyone's guess."

"That's all right. Jenkins here loves surprises," Sonoranvan said, settling her assault rifle.

"Not the kind that get you killed, though," Jenkins said.

Both the commanders looked far too eager for Kira's tastes. They were about to face something that could very well kill them in creative and excruciating ways. Maybe they and their teams all had a bit of berserker in them.

As a unit they moved through the opening to the exhibition tomb. It was as Kira had described. A long narrow corridor, barely wide enough to fit three people abreast, stretched some twenty yards before widening into what she assumed was the antechamber beneath the crux of the pyramid. A golden light spilled out into the end of the passageway, faintly illuminating the last few feet.

"We need to get down this passageway as quickly as possible," Kira said, drawing the khopesh. There was barely enough room to maneuver the two-foot-long weapon, adding to her anxiety. If the intent was supposed to creep out visitors as they embarked on an otherworldly journey, Hammond's setup certainly did the trick.

"Do you hear that?" someone asked behind them.

A scrabbling noise filled the corridor. "It could be anything," Kira said, keeping her voice even. Egypt had a wide variety of fantastical creatures in its ancient mythology. "Maybe a bunch of scorpions, or . . . beetles."

She looked up and saw a seething, shifting dark mass take up the majority of the left wall and the ceiling. Beetles were better than scorpions, but knowing the gods of Shadow, these critters probably packed a hell of a supernatural wallop.

"That's a helluva lot of beetles," Jenkins said. "And we're fresh out of bug spray."

Kira tapped her earpiece. "Control, I need a prayer or spell from the book that references beetles."

"Searching."

The beetles swarmed overhead. As several of the squad began firing up at them, shattering the hard carapaces with bullets, fluid bubbled through the shattered exoskeletons. Someone swore, then repeatedly stomped their feet. "Their guts are eating the floor away like acid!"

The team's boots and protective gear were sturdy and charged with enough magic to temporarily avoid the corrosive effects of small amounts of the substance, but Kira assumed that unprotected flesh was immediately endangered—and prolonged exposure or a larger quantity of the stuff would be deadly. And no telling what a bite from the beasties could do . . . "Control, you need to search faster."

"Move deeper in!" Sonoranvan called. "But hold your fire. Try to avoid cracking the shells and releasing the acid . . . I fucking hate bugs!"

"Got it!" Kira's earpiece crackled. "Spell thirty-six. It's pretty short and it doesn't really say all that much—"

Someone screamed as a mass of the black bugs swarmed over him. "Give it to me anyway!"

"Here goes: Begone from me, O crooked-lips! I am Khnum, Lord of Peshnu, who dispatches the words of the gods to Re."

Kira repeated the spell at the top of her lungs. A collective shiver ran through the plague-worthy mass of insects. They fell like a deadly black rain. The swamped guard swayed, and then pitched forward noiselessly. His teammate knelt beside him. "His exposed skin is covered in welts, ma'am," she said to Sonoranvan. "And his breathing's really shallow."

"You." Sonoranvan pointed to another guard. "Help Patterson get Matthews to safety. The medical team should already be on standby at the inception point."

"But—"

"Did I stutter, Burkholtz?"

"No, ma'am. Right away, ma'am." The two guards lifted the unconscious man to his feet. Balancing his weight between them, they quickly made their way back to the entrance.

"At least we know the spells work," Khefar said.

"Yeah, but we need to get them cued up faster." Kira tapped her earpiece for emphasis.

"We'll do our best, ma'am," a voice on the other end said meekly.

"All right, let's keep moving," Jenkins called. "I don't want to stay in this slaughter tube longer than necessary."

Tension pressed down on Kira's shoulders as they quickly made their way down the long corridor. She hoped the Gilead agent would be okay; she knew nothing about beetle toxin, but could guess that ones sent by Shadow had to possess some nasty poison. *One more thing to thank the Lady of Shadows for.*

"What's that scrabbling noise?" someone asked.

An eerie, skittering noise filled the corridor. Kira holstered her gun, her skin crawling with wariness. "That doesn't sound good."

"What now?"

"Seeker demons!" Khefar yelled.

Plural? Kira peered down the stone walkway. Sure enough, five seeker demons scrambled down the corridor toward them, one running along the ceiling.

One seeker demon was bad enough. Five were impossible odds. "Bale, if your guys are looking for a fight, now's a good time to join in!"

"Finally, some excitement." Bale shed his human form. "Tell your humans to stay back unless these creatures get by us."

The banaranjans pushed to the forefront, each making a beeline for a seeker demon. Unfortunately that meant the humans had to face one too.

Shots rang out in rapid-fire succession as the squad lay down a barrage of bullets while the team tracked the fifth demon, dust and debris falling down around them. Regular bullets wouldn't kill a seeker demon, but a few well-placed headshots could at least slow them down slightly.

Problem was, seeker demons didn't like to sit still long enough for a shooter to take aim. On top of that, in the tight confines of the narrow corridor with only night-vision goggles to see by, the possibilities of being struck by friendly fire increased a thousandfold. The banaranjans surged ahead, moving quickly despite not being able to take flight. Yet even their fighting ferocity could barely stand against the single-minded malevolence of seeker demons.

"Commanders, get your people back!" Kira shouted. She didn't want them to die needlessly, but if the seeker managed to get by her and Khefar, they were dead anyway.

"Back up, back up!" one of the commanders yelled. "We're gonna get slaughtered if we stay here!"

Kira and Khefar took the front line, bracing themselves for the seeker demon's attack. "You take right,

I'll take left," Khefar said. Kira nodded, charging the khopesh with her extrasense. Power flared bluish-green along the blade. She didn't have time to worry about it as the seeker demon closed the distance between them with a leap, claws extended, jaws wide.

Kira spun right, swinging the khopesh so that the hooked end caught the deadly beast about its neck. The Dagger of Kheferatum blazed with power, severing one of the creature's arms. The limb disintegrated with a caustic cloud of dust, glowing green in the night-vision glasses.

Grimly holding on to the khopesh, Kira gripped the demon's free arm with her left hand. Straining to hold the creature, she put a boot in its back. "Now, Khefar!"

The Nubian swung his dagger up again, jamming the blade deep into the seeker's skull. A piercing howl rent the close confines as the seeker shuddered violently, then disintegrated.

The banaranjans had already made short work of their targets. "Are any of your guys hurt?" Kira asked.

Bale grinned. He'd obviously fed well on the adrenaline Kira and the others had pumped out. "These pitiful Shadowlings are no match for banaranjans in their prime. Only a weak banring fresh from the crèche would fall to a seeker demon."

"You all right, Nubian?" He'd faced the worst of the seeker's wrath.

Khefar sucked in a breath. "The vest took the hit. Thanks for making me wear it."

Commander Jenkins thumped Khefar on the shoulder. "Y'all are making this look too easy."

"You think that was easy?"

"It was easy only because we've had experience—
that's the third one we've faced in as many months,"
Kira said. "I gotta wonder, though: if we're getting seek-
ers now, what's waiting for us at the end of this?"

"Only one way to find out."

They made their way down the corridor to the
chamber containing the Weighing of the Heart exhibit.

Except for the two dozen people and Halflings who
had entered, the room was empty.

No seated Osiris. No gleaming giant scales. No
Ammit the Devourer. The only light was a faint glow
emanating from the entryway to the burial chamber on
the west wall.

What the—?

"Check the burial chamber," Kira called.

One of the banaranjans poked his head in. "There's
a big granite box that's glowing, and something that
looks like a doorway but isn't."

Glowing? "Everybody, stay back. I'll check it out."
Kira stepped into the burial chamber, pulling off
her night-vision goggles. The sarcophagus, made to
look like real granite, emitted a subtle golden glow.
Beyond it, set into the wall, was a re-creation of the
false door that—in real Egyptian tombs—was typi-
cally used by the deceased to pass from the land of
the dead to the land of the living. Kira's eyes widened
as she translated the hieroglyphs carved into the side
panels of the door's design. The inscriptions were
praises, but not honoring the deceased as one would
expect. Instead, each seemed to be a prayer or exul-
tation to Set. She read the words aloud. "The lord of

the desert, the hand of Chaos, the subduer of Apep. He who is, he who will come again. The great lord Set."

Loud slithering sounds filled the antechamber. *Gods, no.* Apep. There was a reason why astronomers had taken its Greek name, Apophis, and named a comet after it. Apep was destruction personified.

"Do we even want to know what that noise is?" Sanchez asked Kira over the communicator.

"Chances are, Commander, it's a giant snake." Kira replied, the glibness doing nothing to ease her sudden worry.

"I fucking hate snakes," Sanchez said under her breath.

Kira saw Khefar reach for his earpiece. "There's a spell to use against Apep. Find it and send it to us now. Kira, get out of there."

Kira scooted back around the sarcophagus, intending to rejoin Khefar and the SRT to figure out their next step. But when she attempted to exit the door she'd entered through, she bounced off a hard plane of air. She was alone, trapped in the burial chamber.

Her pulse kicked up, sending blood racing hard through her veins. Kira pounded against the invisible barrier, shouting at Khefar, at Bale, at the commanders.

"We can't hear you, Kira!" Khefar growled. "And it is obvious something is keeping you in there."

How could she hear them but they couldn't hear her? She reached to activate her earpiece, intending to call them, but it was missing. Dammit!

Rage poured from her into the khopesh. She hammered at the invisible shield with the blade but not even her power dented it. What sort of magic was this thing made of?

The slithering sound increased. She could hear hissing now, the combined sounds unnerving as they echoed off the walls. Out of the shadows of the chamber's dimly lit southwest corner she saw glittering light fracturing off scales.

Gods. Kira tapped into her fear and rage, channeling the energy through her extrasense. She didn't know if it would be enough to withstand the snake's strike, but hopefully it would give her enough time to wrack her brain for spells to use against Apep.

You can defeat it, a voice echoed inside her head, familiar yet foreign. *You have but to call on me, and I will give you the strength of my arm to stand against Apep.*

Bile filled Kira's gut, acid and ice coiling together as her vision wavered. Set speaking to her, the Lord of Chaos inside her head—inside her head!—almost unhinged her knees.

"No!" Kira put the sarcophagus between her and the snake. Not that it would do much good. She darted a look at the entryway, hoping that Khefar would find a way inside, and soon.

Join me. Embrace me, and my power will be yours. None will stand against you, Apep will hold no threat to you.

"No, no, no! I will never join you. Never! Stay out of my head!"

Then, face Apep and die.

Khefar readied the Dagger of Kheferatum. "I'm going in. Draw back to a safe distance. I don't want any of you to get hit with the Dagger."

"I think we can survive an accidental cut, sir, as long as you miss vital organs," Jenkins said.

"I can knick you with this and that would be the end of it," Khefar retorted. "You disintegrate. It's not dying, so it won't be painful. You'll simply cease to exist."

The commander went pale beneath his tactical helmet. "Understood. We'll give you a wide berth, sir."

"Kira!" Khefar shouted from the door opening to the burial chamber.

Kira nodded to acknowledge, but kept her focus on the corner. She looked composed, but he'd seen her scream wordlessly, saw the sweat beading on her forehead.

He had to get her out of there.

"I'm using the Dagger, Kira. I don't know the effect it will have on the force field. Retreat as far back as you can."

Kira moved to the northwest corner, her eyes glowing with power and rounded with fear. Sand sprinkled down from the ceiling, clogging the air.

Khefar lifted his dagger. "I call upon Atum, creator and destroyer. Give me your power!"

He slammed the ancient blade into the invisible barrier with all his might. The shield shattered with a shock wave preceding an explosion of boiling red light, a rush of pressure that nearly felled him. Sand began to fall like heavy rain, quickly covering the chamber floor.

Blinking to clear his vision, Khefar stepped into the chamber, blade ready as he recited the spell. "O you waxen one who takes by robbery and who lives on the inert ones, I will not be inert for you, I will not be weak for you."

Kira slipped through the sand to his side as the serpent slithered out of the darkness, forked tongue testing the air. It was smaller than he'd expected, but that was like saying an elephant was small compared to a mastodon. The snake was still huge—its girth equal to a man's. Khefar had no idea how long it actually was, but from the thrashing and slithering sounds it made, there were plenty of coils to cause him trouble.

He thrust Kira behind him. "Give me room to fight, woman!"

She clambered atop the sarcophagus, brandishing the khopesh. The others crowded the door but didn't come inside, for which Khefar was grateful. The burial chamber simply wasn't big enough for all of them to fight in.

Apep lifted its triangular head, yellow eyes glowing as it tried to determine which of them was the greater threat. Khefar raised his blade. "Your poison shall not enter into my members, for my members are the members of Atum. If I am not weak for you, suffering from you shall not enter into these members of mine."

The serpent hissed, the only warning Khefar had. It struck lightning fast. Khefar dodged left, spinning to leap onto the giant snake behind the massive head and dripping fangs. It reacted immediately, coils slithering as it slammed him into the floor.

He grimly held on, fighting blows that threatened to leave him dazed. For all that it was a snake, it was a magical one, a serpent that had threatened the Lord of the Gods. Kira screamed in wordless rage, a sound that drove him back to his feet. He saw her swing the khopesh at Apep, the blade failing to mar the glittering hide. But her wild swings served to distract the reptile, allowing Khefar to hang on as the serpent tried to free itself enough to turn its head to bite him.

"Khefar, watch out!"

It was time to end this. Khefar plunged the dagger into the back of the writhing snake's head. "Earth, devour that which has come forth from thee. Monster, lie down, glide away!"

The giant serpent thrashed, throwing up clouds of sand. It froze and seemed to fold in on itself, collapsing down to nothingness.

Khefar sucked in a sandy breath, wincing as his ribs protested. Being slammed to the ground by a magical serpent had probably given him a couple of cracked ribs. The pain was worth it, though, to get Kira back.

"Kira? You okay?"

No answer.

Alarmed, Khefar climbed to his feet, wiping sand from his eyes. The sarcophagus no longer glowed. Instead, the false door set into the western wall emitted a soft golden light that faded as he watched.

Kira was gone.

Chapter 23

Kira shouted in triumph as Khefar thrust the Dagger of Kheferatum into Apep's head, chanting the last of the spell.

Time slowed. The sarcophagus's glow winked out. Light brightened behind her. She turned and saw that golden light emanated from the false door. The door between the worlds of the living and the dead. The door bearing praises to Set.

Oh, hell no. Sand poured from a fissure in the ceiling above her like an hourglass filling. It rained down around her, pooling atop the sarcophagus and reducing hearing and visibility to zero. Kira closed her eyes to slits but that did little to prevent sand granules from stinging her eyes. She threw up her forearm to block the brunt of the sand, trying to feel her way forward.

A thick disintegrating coil whipped at her, throwing her backward. She flailed out, the shifting sand upsetting her balance. She tried to call out to Khefar, but sand clogged her throat.

Coughing, spluttering, she fell back, passing through the glowing doorway. A roaring sound filled her ears, as if she'd stepped into a wind tunnel. She tried to orient herself, find the other side of the doorway so that she could return to Khefar. Fighting the vortex of chaotic power proved futile, making her gag as it pushed wrongly along her nerve endings. Finally she broke through.

And realized she wasn't in Atlanta anymore.

The absence of sound was almost as loud as the sound itself.

Unfortunately the effects of the sand-filled maelstrom muffled the sound of her assailant approaching until it was almost too late. She dodged too slowly to completely miss the blow, absorbing the impact with her collarbone instead of the back of her skull. The second hit to the back of her knees dropped her like a sack of potatoes. She fell hard to the ground but rolled with it, grimacing against the pain. Stupid, to get caught so easily!

"Hiya, Kira." Marit kicked her once more. "So nice to see you again. I would ask you how you're doing, but I think I can guess."

"Gods damn it! Can I not get rid of you?"

"Funny." Marit bared her teeth. "I asked myself the same thing about you."

"Children, play nice."

Kira looked up. She was in the Hall of Judgment, but it wasn't like any previous version she had experienced before. Instead of Osiris, Set sat upon the gilded throne, the *was* scepter gripped in his hand. Neither Isis or Nepthys, his wife, stood behind him. A young woman with glowing gold eyes stood next to the throne instead, one hand upon the shoulder of the Egyptian god of chaos and storms.

"Welcome, child of mine."

Fear coated Kira's stomach with bile as Set's multi-faceted voice rumbled over her. "I am not your child. I belong to the Lady of Truth."

"You have been shown the truth, that you are a child of Shadow. Since you claim to be a sworn follower of Truth, it is foolish to deny that which stares you in the face."

"No."

"Come now, child," the Lady of Shadows said after clucking her tongue. "Is that any way to talk to your grandfather?"

While Set's presence scared her and tied her tongue, Myshael, looking so much like a younger version of Balm, only angered her. Spitting out a mouthful of blood, she rolled to a sitting position, the khopesh still in her hand. "You're confusing yourself with your sister, Lady of Shadows. I am not your child. Now, tell me how to release those souls."

Myshael sighed. "You really are hardheaded and foolish, aren't you?" the Lady of Shadows said. "You already know what you have to do to save those people."

"I'm not giving in to you," Kira declared, clenching her teeth against pain as she regained her feet. "I'd rather die than give myself to Shadow!"

"Of course you would. That would be the easy way out. But you don't get easy. There's no fun in easy. You will submit, willingly. Even if I have to beat submission into you. Consider it tough love."

She wouldn't get a better chance. Kira charged the throne. Set held up his free hand. The air in front of him flashed with yellow-gold power. Kira careened off another invisible shield, stumbling back several paces.

"You think to defeat me? Me? A god?"

Kira's knees unhinged as the god rose to his feet, the *was* scepter glowing as he lifted it. The Lady of Shadows she didn't fear, but Set, the bad boy of her pantheon, caused her knees to give way in pure, abject terror.

"You are of my line," the Egyptian god of storms said, his voice a rumble of thunder. His eyes blazed lightning-yellow. "Your mother and your father descended through me."

Shock raced through Kira's system. She'd expected something like that, but still, to hear it was almost too much. Her mother's family had turned their back on their heritage. Did it happen when worshipping Set was no longer a good idea?

"You will learn what you need to learn to accept your fate, Hand of Ma'at. You will feel the power that is the Hand of Set, and you will know."

Marit stepped forward, accepting the power rod from Set with more decorum than Kira had seen the woman display before. When she turned to face Kira, Kira could clearly sense Set's power transferring to the Shadow Adept. Marit spun the staff, her movements indicating that she had more than a passing familiarity with using the *was* scepter. "Hey, sis, I think you owe me a hand. Wonder if Lord Set will give you another hand like he did me."

Crap. Marit spun the *was* scepter, her face alive with chaotic delight. The power rod was twice as long as the khopesh Kira held, and glowed with Shadow magic. Still, the hooked blade of the khopesh was a formidable weapon in its own right, provided one knew how to use it. Thanks to Khefar and their daily training sessions, Kira did.

Marit swung the staff overhead. Kira blocked it easily with the flat of the khopesh, feeling the blow reverberate up her arms. The opposing powers flared, casting a shower of sparks.

The Shadow Adept thrust forward with the twin tines of the power rod aiming for the center of Kira's chest. Kira rotated her wrist, hooking the curved end of the khopesh around the staff. Again power sparked incandescent green. Marit whipped the other end of the staff around, landing a blow to Kira's already abused side.

"What's the matter, Shadowchaser?" Marit taunted. "Why don't you pull that fancy blade of yours? What are you scared of?"

Kira gritted her teeth against the anger that spiked deep inside her. Marit couldn't know about her fears concerning her Lightblade, or her father's dagger. A knowing glint in the Shadow Adept's eyes, though, made her wonder. Set and the Lady of Shadows had returned to their places on the raised dais, looking on in amusement as she and Marit fought. Dammit, she wouldn't be a pawn for their pleasure!

Kira swung the khopesh like a sickle, her ribs protesting the movements she demanded of her body. Marit faked a jab with the end of the staff, the twin points aiming for Kira's torso. Kira bent backward to avoid the swing of the scepter, her beaten torso protesting the quick movement. She spun, thrusting with the hooked blade, rewarded with a grunt of pain from the Shadow Adept. Kira then stumbled backward, putting some distance between her and Marit, trying to catch her breath and banish the stars dancing before her eyes.

"You've wanted the truth," Marit sneered. "All your life, or so you claim. I'm here, telling you the truth, and you don't want to believe it." The dark-haired woman laughed. "That's irony for you."

"If you think I'm going to believe someone who's been trying to kill me, you're out of your ever-lovin' mind," Kira said, balancing the khopesh with both hands. The longer Marit talked, the longer Kira had to catch her breath.

Marit laughed. "You may be right. I may be crazy. But I'm keeping it real, all in the family, so to speak."

"What are you talking about?"

"There's nothing more brutally honest than someone trying to kill you. Really, though, I haven't been trying all that hard."

Kira glanced down at the blood staining her hands. "What do you call this, then?"

"Getting your attention. Mommy and Daddy tend to be rather harsh when it comes to disciplining their wayward children."

"Trying to understand someone as psychotic as you is tiring. Can we get back to beating each other's brains out while I still have some energy?"

Marit stomped her foot. "You're always spoiling my fun. Really, I have no idea why Mom and Dad want to claim you."

"That's something we can both agree on," Kira panted. "So why don't we stop and you help me free those souls and we call it a day?"

Marit laughed. "Sure, and afterward we can go out

shopping and have tea. Make it a supernatural Girl's Night Out." The Shadow Adept shook her head. "Unlike you, I'm obedient to the Lady who saved me. I do what she wants me to do."

"And what, exactly, is it that she wants you to do?"

"This."

Marit moved faster than Kira had expected, sweeping the *was* scepter at Kira's knees. Kira attempted to jump over the swinging staff, but her feet got tangled. She fell, hard, the impact stealing her breath. The *was* scepter burned with power as Marit sent the khopesh flying. Before Kira could reach for her Lightblade, Marit jammed the *was* scepter into her shoulder. The protective shielding of the tactical vest fizzled out like an electrical short, blown away by the surge of Shadow magic. Then the tines of the staff of power pierced her flesh.

She screamed. Pain. Agonizing, unrelenting pain, pain so excruciating she couldn't think, couldn't breathe, couldn't do anything other than pray for death so the pain could stop. It pushed with every heartbeat, as if her skin were peeling off inch by rending inch.

Brilliant lemon-yellow light crashed into brilliant lapis blue power, swirling emerald green, changing to spring green. Still the pain continued, boiling through her system.

The Lady of Shadows leaned over her, Myshael's young face stretched by a gleeful grin. "Unfortunately for you, Kira Solomon, this won't kill you. It will, however, make you wish you were dead."

Kira's hands flailed impotently. "Go to hell, bitch."

Myshael laughed. "Ooh, was that supposed to scare

me? You know I created it, right? With a lot of help from fearful believers in the Dark Ages. Ah, the Dark Ages. Now, that was a party."

She nodded to Marit, who leaned on the scepter. Kira shrieked in agony.

The Lady of Shadows leaned closer. "Let me tell you something about Set's staff of power. It doesn't like Light magic. No, it doesn't. In fact, it tends to increase the pain of anyone who carries Light magic. What that means, my darling, stubborn child, is that you will continue to suffer as long as you continue to fight."

Myshael feigned a sympathetic expression. "Why do this to yourself? You can stop this, you know. You have the power. All you have to do is let go of Light and claim the Shadow part of your soul. Grip your father's Shadowblade and call on its power. The *was* scepter will sense your Shadow magic. Only then will the torment stop. Only then will you be able to face Ammit and retrieve the souls you seem so intent on rescuing."

"N-never!"

Myshael sighed. "Never is a mighty long time, dear girl. I can afford to wait. Somehow I don't think *you* can."

"I won't," Kira gasped. "I won't turn my back on the Light!"

"Why not? Surely you can tell that it's turned its back on you?"

Myshael took on the voice and appearance of a girl of seven, flitting about as she chanted in a singsong voice. "Where is Balm, the Lady of Light? Where is Ma'at, the Lady of Truth? Where are all those you call your friends? Oh that's right, they all left you. Left you alone in your time of need. Some friends they turned out to be."

Emotional pain swamped the physical agony, bringing tears to Kira's eyes. She didn't need Myshael's reminder. Comstock was dead. Balm had been unreachable, ever since she'd had Lysander deliver the box of Ana's mementos. Anansi, who'd helped Khefar and her repeatedly, had abruptly returned home, wherever that was. Wynne and Zoo were no longer her friends, Khefar had been separated from her, and Ma'at . . .

No. She refused to believe the goddess of Truth and Order would elevate her only to abandon her. This was a test, a very painful lesson that she had to learn. If she was truly to be a devotee of the goddess of Truth, she had to own up to her own truth. On her own terms.

She forced her eyes open. "I am the Hand of Ma'at," she declared, wrapping her blood-slick hands around the scepter. Power and pain crashed inside her, bowing her back. Instead of fighting it, she inhaled it, letting it into her pores, her lungs, her being. "By Her grace am I here, and by Her grace will I remain. She is Truth. Truth is neither good nor bad, Light nor Shadow. Truth simply is."

Confusion crossed Marit's face. "She's grinning. What in the name of Shadow is going on here?"

She put a boot to Kira's shoulder, yanking the scepter free. Kira's vision grayed, but she bit her tongue and held on. Too much depended on her making it through.

She called her power, the burning desire to know the truth. Everything else could wait. What she was, where her life was supposed to go, whom she'd have with her—all of that could wait. Nothing mattered more than uncovering this particular truth.

Her extrasense sparked inside her, blowing away all doubts and uncertainty. She reached out to the raw power still flowing from the *was* scepter. The magics connected, flowing back into her body, infusing her. Changing her.

Her right hand moved, sliding across her body to grip the handle of her Lightblade. Magic flared, blue-white, but sputtered against the overwhelming flow of Chaos pumping into her. Still, the Light was enough to afford her some distance from the pain, enough distance for her mind to think.

Move, she willed her left hand. It flopped against her chest, slick with blood and burnt with Shadow magic. *You've got to reach the other blade.*

Kira. A voice whispered in her head, a voice that sounded suspiciously like Khefar's. *If Light and Darkness live inside you, own them. Claim them. Use them to kick some ass. Say the spell and show them all.*

She had no idea what he was talking about, if it was actually Khefar who spoke to her. What spell was there that combined Light and Darkness?

Suddenly, in her mind's eye, she saw a papyrus scroll unfurl, saw the gilded inscriptions of the Book of the Dead. Strange, that out of the hundreds of spells in the scroll, the words of this one would come to her, clearly and easily.

Her fingers wrapped around the Shadowblade. With both daggers in her hands, she sucked in the power flooding through her. Using that power to charge both her blades and her will, she began to chant the spell for Giving Light and Darkness.

"I am she who donned the white-bright fringed cloak of Nun, which gives light in darkness, which unites the two companion goddesses who are in my body by means of the great magic which is on my mouth."

Thunder rumbled; Set was angry. He rose to his feet, gesturing toward her as he issued a command. Kira didn't understand the words, but she definitely understood his intent. He wanted her stopped.

She made it to her knees. Marit shrieked in anger as she swung the staff at Kira. Kira caught it between the crossed blades of her daggers. Magic broke like lightning through the room, slamming into the ground, the walls, everything. Marit shrieked as the power struck her, her entire body stiffening before falling to the ground.

Kira grinned through her pain, then continued the spell, the words ringing from her in a voice not her own. "My fallen enemy who was with me in the valley of Abydos will not be raised up, and I am content."

She used her foot to knock the *was* scepter away from Marit's still body, then picked it up, juggling blades and staff. She lifted it up as high overhead as she could, then shoved it down, burying the forked end into the stone floor. The entire chamber rocked and rumbled as a ball of bright-green power, her power, welled up like a mushroom cloud. "I have brought darkness by means of my power. I have separated Set from the houses of the Above. I am the Woman Who Lightens Darkness, I have come to lighten the darkness and it is bright."

Kira held on to the staff for support and the ball of power filled the room, blinding her. Slowly the light faded, showing that the false Hall of Judgment was empty. No Marit, no Set, no Lady of Shadows.

The *was* scepter stood rooted in the center of the room, now a blackened, charcoal-crusted stick. Her khopesh lay on the ground halfway between the empty throne and the Scales of Truth. Had they always been there?

She tottered over to the khopesh and fell to her knees beside it. She still had to find Ammit, find the heart scarabs, before her strength gave out. If she couldn't restore the people who were in comas, giving in to Shadow would be for nothing.

With her extrasense glowing a steady fern green, Kira sheathed both blades and picked up the khopesh. The sickle-sword immediately suffused with her magic, making her light-headed. Or maybe that was the blood loss.

She tried to stand, but seemed to have difficulty making her legs obey. She couldn't feel her left arm at all anymore; it was a miracle that she'd been able to sheath the Shadowblade. If the real Ammit was around somewhere, she'd be in serious trouble. Hell, she was in serious trouble anyway, taking so much raw Shadow magic into her system.

The very thing she'd feared, she'd become. It wasn't a question of how far she'd Fallen. The true question was: would she be able to fight off the Shadow part of her nature long enough to face the Ammit construct and save the innocents?

Magic and anger burned through her. Marit was a

sadistic bitch, but it was her own fault for allowing the Shadow Adept to jump her. She could only hope that she lived long enough to have a proper showdown.

She half-crawled, half-dragged herself back over to the scepter. She didn't want to touch it again, but she preferred to die on her feet than flat on her back. It seemed to take ages, yet she managed to use the *was* scepter and the khopesh as lopsided makeshift crutches to gain her feet.

Breathing hard, she stared up at the ceiling, trying to marshal the strength to move, to do the last bit that needed to be done. "Okay, so I know I had to come through that part alone. I get it, I really do. But I could use some help. So if you guys are listening, I think now would be a good time to send the cavalry."

Chapter 24

Khefar ran around the sarcophagus and through the doorway, his heart in his throat. The Dagger of Kheferatum reacted violently. He looked around for another threat, only to realize it emanated from the other side of the door.

Before the squad stuck a C-4 charge on the fake stone lintel, the frame glowed bright emerald green and dissolved. Khefar leapt through the doorway, the Special Response Team following.

They were in the Hall of Judgment, but not the one he'd seen in his vision when he'd died. This one looked as if it had been turned into a war zone. Scorch marks marred the walls and area before the raised throne. Dark splotches like brushstrokes dotted the floor, splotches Khefar realized were blood. Kira stood in the center of the room, the khopesh hanging limply in her right hand. She held on to a blackened *was* scepter with her left, slumped against it as if it was the only thing keeping her upright. The sleeves of her shirt were gone, and her left hand looked as charred as the staff.

Mother of All. "Kira!"

He started to run to her, but his dagger throbbed with warning. "Kira, look at me."

She lifted her head. Dread knotted his gut. Through

the blood, sweat, and dirt that smudged her face, her eyes glowed a fierce, bright yellow. "Khefar." Her voice dragged from her in chunks. "How did you get here?"

"Don't worry about that." He waved the others back, took another step toward her, forcing himself to stay calm. "I need you to let go of that staff."

She looked at the scepter as if surprised to find herself holding it. "I can't. If I do, I'll fall."

"I'll catch you."

"Promise?"

He sheathed his blade, held his arms out. "I promise."

"Okay." Grimacing with effort, she pushed herself away from the blackened staff.

He caught her before she collapsed, lowering her carefully to the floor. Blood ran from a wound beneath her left collarbone, running down her bare arm and burned hand to stain the floor beneath her. "Where does it hurt?"

"Everywhere."

Fury burned inside him as he quickly checked her for other injuries. "He did it, didn't he? Set stabbed you with that *was* scepter."

She blinked, her eyes now a brilliant hazel green and tarnished with pain. "No. Marit did, while Set and Myshael watched."

She'd faced all three of them alone? He dug into a pocket of the tactical vest and found several gauze bandages and tape. He unzipped her vest enough to quickly dress the wound and wrap her left hand. "Can you stand? We need to get you out of here!"

"No." She gripped his vest with her good hand.

"Haven't found the scarabs yet. Need to find them, or it was for nothing."

"What was?" he asked, trying to keep her talking. She sounded irrational, and that worried him. They probably needed her extrasense to fix the heart scarabs and save each exhibit visitor, but she couldn't last much longer without real medical attention.

"It happened like my dreams. 'Cept this time I won." Her breath shuddered. "And lost."

Her head rolled, her gaze going to the scepter still embedded in the floor. "Need to destroy it," she whispered. "Will you do it?"

"With pleasure." He rose, unsheathing the Dagger of Kheferatum.

"Sir." Commander Jenkins stepped up to him. "We should take the artifact back to Gilead."

"No, we shouldn't."

"It's obviously a powerful weapon. Protocol states that any weapons recovered from hybrids are to be confiscated immediately."

Khefar grit his teeth. "I don't work for Gilead, so to hell with your protocol! Kira says destroy it, so that's what I'm going to do."

Bale stepped forward. "The Eternal Man wants to destroy the weapon that harmed his woman. I don't see a problem with that, do you?"

Jenkins looked from one to the other. A soft curse fell from his lips as he looked at Kira. "No, don't see any problems here. We'll go do a security sweep."

"Good." Khefar swung his blade at the charred staff. It was like striking an iron bar. The impact reverberated up his arm, numbing it. He tightened his grip, holding the blade against the staff. The burnt surface glowed yellow white. A sudden whoosh of air and the staff disintegrated into a shower of golden sparks.

Khefar quickly sheathed his blade, returning to Kira. "It's gone."

"Thanks. I'm ready now."

He got his arms beneath her, cursing softly when she gasped. "This is gonna hurt."

"Better make it quick, then."

He was a gentle as he could be, but Kira still let out a short, sharp shriek as he pulled her upright. "I'm sorry, I'm sorry," he muttered into her hair, holding her close. "Sorry I wasn't here to help you."

"You're here now. And you will help me."

"Chaser Solomon?"

They turned as one of the squad members approached. Kira stepped back from him, trying to project that she wasn't using the khopesh as a cane to keep her upright. "Yeah?"

"The commanders say they've found an Ammit statue, and it's got a jar of scarabs at its feet," she said.

"Great. Make sure no one touches it. It's bound to have some sort of protective spell on it. We're right behind you."

The guard hesitated. "Can I help?"

Kira grimaced. "No, you can't, but thank you for the offer."

Khefar thrust his shoulder beneath Kira's right arm, wrapping his arm securely around her waist. He would have rather carried her, but she'd retaliate by shooting him when she recuperated. As soon as she finished with the scarabs, though, he'd carry her out.

She could kick and scream until she passed out from the pain.

The rest of the squad and the banaranjans were crowded into the far corner of the room, on the other side of the massive set of scales. They shuffled aside to reveal the closest he ever wanted to come to Ammit the Devourer: a four-foot-tall statue of the demoness.

The statue looked as if someone had caught the Devourer in suspended animation, eyes glinting citrine yellow, jaws open in preparation to rend, to tear, to destroy. "Thank the gods it's only a statue."

"It is, but it isn't," Kira said, her breathing harder than necessary. Sweat beaded her brow, and fresh blood seeped from beneath the bandage. "There's some sort of spirit trapped inside it. To get to it, I'll have to breach the Shadow magic. Then I need to say a spell to break the spell on the heart scarabs."

He turned his head, trying to see her expression. Not that he needed to. He'd seen her eyes, noticed the change in color. She may have faced—and defeated— the Lady of Shadows and the Lord of Chaos, but the confrontation had left her with more Shadow than she'd started with.

"Are you sure about this?" he asked, his voice low. "Haven't you taken on enough already?"

"Who else is gonna do it?" she asked, her words slurring.

He swallowed a growl of frustration. Kira needed to be in a hospital, not facing another danger. "We could call Yessara. Doesn't she do that siphoning thing?"

"Emotions. She works with negative emotions."

Kira rested heavily against him. "Not the same thing. Not enough time. They set it up for me to do. I have to be the one."

She was right, he knew. It didn't mean he had to like it. "All right. What do you need me to do?"

She quirked a smile. "Hold me up."

"Of course. Everybody, give her some space."

The banaranjans backed up with humans ranged behind them, leaving Kira and Khefar in front of the statue. Kira lifted the khopesh in her right hand. *Why isn't she using her Lightblade?*

The Dagger of Kheferatum thrummed at his hip; Kira must have called her power. Yes. Her eyes fairly glowed a brilliant new-spring green. Khefar was suddenly glad the banaranjans were between them and the human squad. He was certain Kira wouldn't want news of her new eye color to get back to Sanchez.

Gritting her teeth, Kira thrust the hooked blade of the khopesh into the statue's mouth. Even with his insensitivity to magic, he could make out the flare of power that surrounded her, the golden nimbus that surrounded the Ammit statue.

Kira groaned, clenching her teeth before speaking. "My heart . . . my heart. May my heart be with me, and may it rest in me. May my mouth be given unto me that I may speak with it, and my two feet to it walk withal, and my two hands and arms to overthrow my foe."

She sagged, the khopesh dropping slightly as her power faded. "I can't . . . it's too much."

"Yes you can."

"Can't you help her?" Bale asked angrily. "You took out that damned snake with no problem!"

"No." Khefar grit his teeth. He'd cracked a couple of ribs taking out that damned snake. Like hell it was no problem. "It's keyed to her magic. She's the only one who can do it."

He kept his left arm around her waist and reached up with his right hand to steady her grip. "You can do this, Kira. You have the power and the will."

"Lady of Justice, be with me," she whispered. "Mother of All, give me strength."

He repeated the prayer with her, helping her shove the hooked blade all the way through the statue's yawning maw. Together they faced the swirling golden light, the darkness of the disorder that was Chaos that emanated from the Ammit construct. "Turn thou back, O messenger of all the gods. Is it that thou art come to carry away this my heart which liveth? My heart which liveth shall not be given unto thee. I advance, the gods give ear unto my supplications, and they fall down upon their faces wheresoever they be."

Summoning the last vestiges of her strength, she thrust down with the khopesh, glowing emerald green with the combined power. The magic surrounding the statue combusted, blowing them back a foot or two. Kira staggered but he managed to steady her. The khopesh clattered to the floor. "The spirit's been sent back to Shadow," she said, the words dragging out of her. "Now I need to purify the gemstones if I can. Help me get closer to the scarabs, please."

He shuffled her forward. She thrust her hands into the oversized bowl that was closer to being a barrel. A low moan slipped from her. "Heart . . . must be able to go out . . ."

"Control, are there any rituals or spells referring to the heart?" he demanded.

"I'm sorry, sir, but most of the spells in the book mention the heart in some way," the analyst said in his ear. "There are hundreds."

"I know," Kira said, her voice thready. "Know the words. Give me a moment to catch my breath."

There wasn't a lot of time, Khefar knew. He had to get Kira to safety, to someone who could quickly patch her up. "Kira, say the damn spell and save your heart!"

Once again she called her power, channeling it into the collection of carved scarabs. "I—I know my heart. I have gotten the mastery over my heart. I have gotten the mastery over my two hands and arms. I have gotten the mastery over my feet, and I have gained the power to do whatsoever my *ka* pleaseth."

Khefar's heart ached as he watched Kira sway with the effort to remain strong, to focus her magic and her will to finish speaking the ritual words that would break the Shadow spell and free the souls held hostage.

Bleeding, shivering, power tripping through her and around her, she threw her head back, power flowing out of her and into the trove of gemstone scarabs. Her voice deepened, coming from a place deep inside of her. "My soul shall not be shut off from my body at the gates of the underworld; but I shall enter in peace, and I shall come forth in peace."

A howl of denial, rage at being denied, blew through the air with a sonic boom, causing everyone to duck and seek out an imminent threat. Kira turned to face Khefar, a crooked smile on her face. *"I have thwarted the chance of Set, the mighty one of strength."*

She lifted her head. "Do you hear that, Grandpa? Today's not your day. Tomorrow won't be either!"

She fell back into his arms. "Need your help," she murmured. "But I think I . . . I think I need to close my eyes for a little bit first."

"Kira? Kira!"

He scooped her up into his arms. "Someone make me a door. Now."

The group quickly made their way back to the loading dock. Sanchez and the support teams were already there, ready to handle the rest of the wounded. The Special Response Teams had only lost one member. Bale and his banaranjans appeared to have come through their conflict without a scratch.

An EMT rushed over to Khefar with a gurney and a blanket. "We can take the Shadowchaser, sir," he said.

Khefar tightened his grip on Kira. "Like hell you will."

The technician froze, surprised. "Sir. We were told that the Chaser was seriously injured. That she lost a lot of blood."

"She did. She was pierced below her collarbone by a *was* scepter."

"A what?"

Khefar shook his head. "It doesn't matter. You're not touching her."

"But—"

"But nothing." He wasn't letting Kira go. He certainly wasn't going to turn her over to Gilead medics. Let them think he was irrational—he didn't really give a damn. Despite his inclination, something told him that Kira wouldn't want to go to Gilead for treatment, no matter how busted up she was.

"I need you to step the hell back. I don't care that you're wearing gloves and a mask and a jacket. I don't know where that gurney or that blanket have been or what's still attached to it. Kira has been put through a metaphysical wringer. She's not going to be able to control her extrasense right now, so I really don't need you poking and prodding at her."

"Sir, we take every precaution. Our equipment is sterilized—"

"Surely you've been given instruction on how to deal with the Shadowchaser in emergency medical situations?"

The young man flushed. "Yes, sir, but she's hurt—"

"But nothing. Those protocols are in place for a reason."

"Sir. She needs medical attention."

Bale and the other banaranjans joined them, flanking Khefar. "So will you if you don't back the hell up," Bale said, his smile less than human.

"Medic, stand down." Sanchez's voice cut through the EMT's response. She walked up to him as if she weren't surrounded by emergency crews. "Khefar, a moment, please."

"Yes, ma'am." The medic backed away.

The section chief turned back to Khefar. "You do realize that she has a hole in her shoulder, yes?"

"You do realize that asking stupid questions is delaying me from giving her the medical attention she needs?"

Sanchez pursed her lips, not even looking at the

banaranjans ranged around them. "She's a member of Gilead. We take care of our own."

Kira stirred, blinked her eyes open. "The injured woman wants to go home. Now."

Khefar smiled. "Of course." He turned to Sanchez. "You heard her. She wants to go home."

"Fine. But my report will clearly state that I disagreed."

"Thanks, Section Chief." Kira subsided again.

Sanchez put her hands on her hips. "Kira Solomon, thanking me? Now I know she isn't all right."

"Just glad to be alive."

"No doubt. I don't know anyone else brave enough—or insane enough—to face down an Egyptian demon and a god of Chaos by herself."

Kira hunched her shoulders, wincing with pain. "They separated us. I didn't have much of a choice. I wanted to be sure your team would be safe."

"If that's the reason you want to give, fine. Your bravery, foolish though it may have been, saved a lot of lives tonight. Well done."

"I . . . appreciate the vote of confidence, Chief," Kira said, her voice muffled against Khefar's coat. "I know I haven't been the easiest person to work with since I came to your city. I'm glad we were able to work together today."

"I guess it is the season of miracles," Sanchez said. "I've received word from the hospital. The recent coma patients have begun to wake up."

Kira stirred in Khefar's arms. "What about Wynne? Did she wake up too?"

Sanchez nodded. "I heard from Marlowe myself.

They're going to keep her and the others in observation for at least another twenty-four hours."

"Good."

Sanchez stared at Kira for a long, silent moment. Finally she looked at the Nubian. "Take her home and put her to bed," the section chief ordered. "And make sure she stays there. I expect to be notified of her condition."

"Yes, ma'am."

Kira groaned as soon as Sanchez got out of earshot. "I hurt like hell," she moaned. "We need to get Zoo and Wynne—"

"Kira." His heart squeezed. "They're kinda busy right now."

"Oh." She closed her eyes, her mouth opening in a silent grunt of pain. "I'm having some trouble right now."

"Nubian."

Khefar turned carefully as Bale approached. "Yessara might be of use to Kira. She can meet us at Kira's place."

Khefar looked down at Kira. She'd passed out again. "Kira's place. She's going to hate that."

Bale smiled. "Probably. But she can reset the wards once she's well."

"True. I'm going to take her home. Can you bring Yessara immediately?"

Bale inclined his head. "Of course. It's the least we can do, since she's restored our people to us."

He turned, paused, turned back. "You both are capable fighters. Even the Gilead humans were impressive in their courage. The banaranjans were honored to fight alongside you."

High praise coming from some of the fiercest fighters on the planet. "Today was a good day."

"We accomplish much when we work together," Bale said. "Kira understands that, if her superiors do not. We must make sure she survives, so that we all can."

Chapter 25

Kira swam up through the quicksand of unconsciousness slowly. She was alive and grateful for it, and wanted to linger in the sensations of being connected and present again.

Khefar filled her vision as she opened her eyes. "Hey."

"Hey yourself." He smiled down at her, sitting close beside her on the bed. "Want the highlights?"

"Sure." She sat up carefully, surprised that there was only a small twinge of ache beneath her collarbone. "How did I heal so fast? Or has it been a while?"

"It's only been two days. You're at home and it's about three in the afternoon. Bale called Yessara, who came over and healed you. Said it took her longer than it normally would, because your body has undergone some . . . changes."

Changes. She could guess at what those changes were. "Did we lose anyone?"

"The guard who got covered by the beetles, he's gone. We had several injuries, but the rest are expected to be all right in the next couple of days."

She nodded. One loss was a loss too many, but it was a reality of the job. "The people in comas?"

"All of them, human and hybrid, have recovered." He hesitated. "Wynne's called a couple of times."

Her fingers curled around the blanket. "I don't want to talk to her."

He nodded. "Okay. As long as you realize she probably won't give up for a while."

"She'll give up eventually." Bitterness clogged her throat. "I'm sure Zoo will make sure of that."

He cleared his throat. "There's a message on your phone from Lysander. He said that Balm is able to talk to you now. Or dreamwalk, if you prefer."

"Hmm." Balm able to talk. She could interpret that a bunch of different ways. There were things she wanted to say to her foster mother. Her co-mother? All Kira knew of her birth mother was what she'd gleaned from the locket. Balm had raised her, prepared her for life. Balm was Kira's mother in the ways that counted.

"Khefar."

"Yeah?" He reached out, clasped her hands in his own, his thumbs lightly rubbing across the backs of her hands.

"Thank you for not dying. Thank you for being here now."

He thumbs stopped the gentle caress. "I had the SRT and a pair of banaranjans helping me. You faced Set, Marit, and the Lady of Shadows on your own. I should be the one thanking you for not dying."

"It was close." It was still close. She could feel it, hovering at the edge of her senses. The burden of the choice that she'd made pressed down on her. If she had died, she would have had to stand before Ma'at again, stand in the true Hall of Judgment again. Or maybe the Shadow inside her would preclude her from that.

He stared at her, and she wondered what he saw,

and what he'd seen while she'd been recovering. She couldn't remember any dreams, walking or otherwise, but that didn't mean she hadn't reenacted the events of the past few days.

"Are you all right?"

"I don't know," she answered honestly. "There's still a lot to process, to talk out."

"How about some quality time in the bathroom? Then we can get something to eat. It won't be up to Anansi's celebratory breakfast standards, but I can make a mean omelet."

"Sounds good."

He helped her in the bathroom, much to her embarrassment. Despite Yessara's expert touch, the peace angel wasn't a miracle worker, at least not when it came to wounds from Shadow-infused ritual objects. Kira still experienced flashes of pain whenever she raised her left arm, but her ribs felt almost normal. A few more days, she was sure, and she'd be in fighting form again.

If she had a few more days. She checked her reflection in the bathroom mirror. Haunted. That's how she looked. Her eyes were overlarge and sporting a new greenish-hazel color. Her hands had a slight tremble to them that even a steaming hot shower couldn't ease.

The Shadow magic had become part of her. She'd known that it would, she just hadn't known how much.

She turned her back on her reflection, then left the bathroom, making a beeline for the closet. "Thanks for not taking me to Gilead East for treatment," she said, choosing a comfortable ankle-length knit dress of pale blue.

"No problem. I kinda figured you wouldn't want to go, though I can't figure out why."

She smoothed the soft material down her arms. "I don't trust Sanchez."

"But you guys were so civil to each other before and after storming the Congress Center," Khefar pointed out. "I thought you guys were cool."

"Something's up. I don't know what it is, but my instincts are telling me it's not good. Shadowchasers passing through town. An Illuminator inside Gilead East. Balm's silence. It didn't feel right. It still doesn't."

She gestured to her side of the dresser. Both of her blades had been placed on the polished surface. Khefar, as usual, had the Dagger of Kheferatum strapped to his side. "Besides, I don't know how I or that blade"—she gestured at the Shadow blade—"would have fared going back in there after the confrontation with the Lady of Shadow."

Khefar looked at the weapons and back to her. "That blade . . . it's a Shadowblade, isn't it?"

She nodded. "Comstock had it hidden among his possessions."

That surprised him. "Your mentor Comstock? He intended to give you this? Why?"

"Because it belonged to my father."

"Your father." She could almost hear his thoughts come into being. "Comstock tracked down your father's dagger. He knew? He knew your father was a Shadowling, a Lightchaser?"

She gave him a weak smile. "Seems like it."

Khefar studied her, trying to come to grips with the stunning revelation. She'd obviously had some time to reconcile herself to what Comstock had known, what he'd done. "How long ago did you find out?"

"The night before Wynne went into the hospital. "

"I see. When were you going to tell me?"

"There wasn't time before," she said, her voice calm. "I'm telling you now."

"What are you going to do with it?"

"Keep it."

"Keep it? Are you out of your mind? Why would you want to keep a Lightchaser's blade?"

Instead of answering, she sat on the edge of the bed, patting the space beside her. Anger pricked his pride. He wanted to refuse—why hadn't she trusted him?—but the look in her eyes, a silent pleading, made him relent.

He crossed to her, sitting on the bed but turning so that he faced her. "Why do you want to keep that blade?"

"It belonged to my father—"

"And you know what he did to your mother," he retorted. "He was a Shadow Adept, a Lightchaser, and he hunted people like your mother, like you, at Myshael's behest."

"I know. But that dagger saved my life while I was fighting Marit. It took some of the Shadow magic that poured into me from Set's staff. Its former owner gave me half of my DNA, for better or worse. And Comstock went to a lot of trouble to get it to me. It's obviously important that I have it. I'm keeping it."

"I think you're playing a dangerous game," he finally said. "I don't have to like it, but it's your call."

She gave him another smile, this one tinged with sadness. "Take out your dagger."

"What?"

"Please. The Dagger of Kheferatum, take it out."

Without taking his eyes off her, he reached for the plain leather sheath at his right hip. He unsheathed the dagger with a reverse grip, the blade nestled along his forearm. "What now?"

She shifted carefully on the bed, folding her legs beneath her. "Is it saying anything to you?"

He held the dagger securely, waiting for it to speak to him. Obviously Kira wanted to prove something to him, show him something. He didn't know what it was, but if she thought today would be the day that she'd die, after saving all those people, she was sadly mistaken.

Sometimes he cursed his inability to sense and generate magic, especially since his entire existence since his first death resided among magical beings. Yet it was his insensitivity to magic and its influences that made him able to wield and control the Dagger of Kheferatum. The dagger could speak to him, but it could not make him do anything he did not wish to do.

"The dagger is silent," he finally said. "Probably because it was well-sated during the battle through the underworld."

"Probably." She smiled, a small sad smile. Then her eyes flashed green. "How about now?"

He didn't answer her. The Dagger of Kheferatum throbbed in his hand. He tightened his grip on it. The cool half-sentience of the dagger stirred, sensing the power that had erupted inside Kira.

Kira wrapped her good hand around his. "It's never going away," she told him, a tear sliding down her cheek. "The Eternal Ladies saw to that. Set called to me because

I'm part of his line, through my father *and* my mother. Balm and Myshael did their parts to ensure that a child of both Light and Shadow would come into the world."

She lifted their hands, lifted the dagger between them, until the tip pointed at her chest, centered on her heart. "I didn't win, Khefar. I didn't beat Shadow. I deliberately chose Chaos magic, and used the Shadowblade. My father's blade. I did exactly what Myshael wanted me to do."

"You saved a lot of people's lives," he reminded her, pulling the dagger back. "Did she want you to do that?"

"She didn't care about those souls. She didn't care about Ammit, or Marit. I don't even know if she cared about Set. What she cared about was me acknowledging the other side of my nature. She wanted me to use Shadow magic. I did. And it felt . . . it felt good."

"Why do you tell me this?" He thought he knew, but he wanted her to say it.

She licked her lips, more tears brightening her eyes. "Because if ever there's a time for you to keep your vow to me, now is that time. We got the right outcome at the convention center, but it was close. So close. I don't know how long I can keep holding on, keep fighting. Please, Khefar. I'm tired and injured and scared. I'm too weak to fight you. Please do this."

He tightened his grip on the dagger of creation and destruction, making and unmaking. The tip touched her flesh, at the swell of her breast. If it pricked her, if he drew blood, the dagger would fully awaken, clamor for her blood despite having drank its fill two days ago. Kira stared at him, her eyes overly large, overly trusting. Believing that he'd do the right thing.

"No."

Pain filled her eyes. "No because you can't?' she asked, her voice anguished. "Or because you won't?"

"Won't. Not until you do something for me first."

"Do what?"

He climbed off the bed and headed to the dresser, taking the dagger with him. No one knew the spells of making and unmaking except for him, and he intended to keep it that way. That didn't mean that the dagger wasn't a threat in Kira's hands.

He sheathed the dagger, quieting it down. Then he reached into the topmost drawer and pulled out a faux leather box. "I want you to put on Amanirenas's cuff," he said, returning to the bed. "I want you to wear it and experience it. Then, if you are still determined that today is the day that I fulfill my vow, I will do so."

She looked at him for a long moment. Without a word she held up her right hand. He wasted no time, joining her on the bed, twining her fingers with his own. Then, without a word, he pushed the cuff onto her wrist.

Her eyes went from hazel to peridot green as her innate magic welled up in response to the ancient golden circlet. He maintained his grip on her hand as she fell back against the pillows, hoping to ameliorate some of the shock of reading the centuries of history the cuff contained. Her eyes, mere slits now, flickered as she received impressions embedded in the bracelet. It was as if she were having a seizure without the violent convulsions.

He knew what Amanirenas's gift would show her. She would see a proud and noble queen faced with loss and overwhelming odds, marshalling her courage and her army to protect those she loved. She would see what it was like to face a supposedly all-powerful foe, to be on the brink of complete defeat, only to rally and wrestle victory away from the enemy.

She would see him taking the queen's cherished gift, all the while believing he would never be able to do what the kandake wanted, would never be able to find someone in his future that he would want to give this treasure to. Until he'd met Kira.

He held her hand, hoping to keep her connected, hoping to keep her here. Dammit, he did *not* want to kill Kira.

He had no idea how much time had passed. Moments, minutes, as she absorbed two thousand years of memories. Then she gasped, her eyes flying open. She immediately closed them again, covering her eyes with a trembling hand, deep shudders wracking her body.

She drew in a steadying breath, wiping the moisture from her cheeks. "There's more of you on this cuff than I think you realize," she said, her voice shaky. She pulled the cuff off. "You probably shouldn't have given it to me."

"Do you know why I did?"

"Yes." She licked her lips before speaking again. "The Kandake Amanirenas—gods, she was something—gave this to you to give to someone special."

"Which I did."

"Someone you love."

He smiled. "I do."

"You mean me?"

His grin widened. "Is there someone else here?"

"No." She still looked shell-shocked. "But me? Really?"

"Why are you surprised?"

"I—I don't know. I guess I stupidly assumed that I stood in the way of you joining your family. I mean, four thousand years is a long time to be single-mindedly focused on one thing. That's always been your goal, you said. You said you wanted to be with them."

He took her hand. "I *do* want to be with them. Eventually. They don't need me where they are. Not like you do."

She lowered her head. "So the only reason you're hanging around is because you think I can't make it without you?"

"Oh, you can make it. I don't doubt that for a minute. The fact that you faced down Set and the Lady of Shadows after being stabbed with a *was* scepter full of Shadow magic tells me that."

"But I failed."

"You didn't fail. I doubt you'll find anyone who would call this outcome a failure."

He wrapped his fingers around her wrist. "You know I'm not good at words. I fight. I fight for people, I fight for a cause. I have never fought for a bigger cause than you. Seeing you smiling, seeing you forget your burdens for a while—that is worth fighting for. That is worth staying here for. So I will."

"Thank you for that."

He hesitated. "Kira."

"Yes?"

"Is the only reason you want me around is because I'm your fail-safe? Nothing else?"

Her chin rose, until she met his gaze. "I need you. Not because you're my fail-safe. Not because you can touch me. I need you because you understand. Because you've seen my worst and stick around anyway. Because you know when to kick my ass. Mostly because when I'm with you, here, I get to be Kira. Not a Shadowchaser. Not the Hand of Ma'at. Not a wielder of a Shadowblade and a Lightblade. Simply a woman, simply Kira. And I crave that. I love that." She paused. "I love you."

He relaxed. "Good."

"Does this mean that you're not going to kill me?"

"You've been waiting to die for a long time," Khefar said, his voice light. He took the cuff from her, then slipped it back onto her wrist. "Maybe it's time to try living for a while."

"Try living. I like the sound of that."

Chapter 26

Sometime later, Kira awakened to find herself lying on a pale blanket cushioned by a thick padding of grass. Fluffy clouds skipped through the brilliant robin's-egg-blue sky overhead, pushed by a warm wind laden with the pungent smell of the sea.

Santa Costa.

"This was a favorite spot of your mother's," Balm said. She sat beside Kira with her knees drawn up to her chin, dressed in a flowing ivory robe with her bare toes peeking from beneath the hem. "And it became a favorite place of mine too."

"Balm! Where have you been? What happened to you? Why did you shut me out?"

"I know you have questions, daughter. I'm here to answer as many of them as I can." She dug her toes into the grass. "As for what happened, my dear sister of Shadow gave me a nasty surprise that incapacitated me. I had to go the Southern Hemisphere, to southern Chile. There's a large dryad community there, and they helped me recover. Not soon enough to help you, for which I'm sorry."

Kira looked at the other woman. With her dark hair unbound and flowing to her waist, she looked younger than Kira did. "You and my mother were lovers."

"It's such a small word to describe what Ana was to me, what I felt for her," Balm said, staring out toward the sea. "I was young, not more than a child, when I was elevated to Balm. So the ideas of love and desire in a human way were completely foreign to me. I knew intellectually what they were, of course, but experiencing them myself?" Balm shook her head. "I didn't know them, so I didn't miss them. Then I met your mother."

"She came here to be a Shadowchaser."

"No. She came to Santa Costa because after two hundred years of breeding with and assimilating into human culture, her family birthed a hybrid with the power to manipulate lightning and call up storms. Ana came here to learn to control her powers, and one day become an analyst or a handler. She stayed because of me. She left for the same reason."

"Because you needed Shadowchasers."

Balm settled her chin on her knees. "We lost so many during the first half of the twentieth century, and had a difficult time finding candidates who could handle the training. Your mother could—she was a lot stronger than she gave herself credit for. She knew how short-handed we were. So even though she'd already passed the trials to become a handler, she became a Shadowchaser instead, and was sent out into the world."

"You have her blade."

"I do." Balm's voice wobbled. "It's all I have left. I gave you her locket because I felt it was important for you to have it, to touch it and learn what your mother was like, how very special she was."

"I think you should have the locket back," Kira

said. "You've worn it for nearly three decades now. It's as much yours as it was hers. It doesn't feel right for me to keep it."

"Are you sure?"

The hope in Balm's eyes was almost painful to see, making Kira glad she could do this for her foster mother. "I'm sure."

"Would you like your mother's Lightblade?"

Kira lowered her gaze. "No, I think I've got all the blades I can handle."

"Yes. A Lightblade and a Shadowblade. It's fitting, though I would have preferred a different Shadowblade for you."

"You knew? And you didn't you tell me about any of this? Why not?"

"I wanted to, Kira, please believe that. But believe it or not, the Ladies of Light, Shadow, and Balance all have rules that we must work within in order to keep the fabric of our universe intact. Not even Myshael wants to completely destroy existence, she just wants her particular brand of Chaos to rule."

"And you want Order, and Solis wants us all to get along and play nice."

"Something like that." Balm's brief smile disappeared. "You walk the path of Balance now, Kira, and it suits you. It suits your nature."

"Both sides of my nature."

Balm nodded. "And both your magics. Light and Shadow live inside you, Kira. They always have. Your mother and I, we did what we could before you were born to sublimate the Shadow half of your soul, and perhaps that was a mistake. What that Fallen named

Enig did to you was at Myshael's direction, to awaken what was already there, and maybe push you further to the side of Shadow. But there is enough Light in you, enough of your mother's goodness in you, that you wouldn't let yourself be consumed by it."

"It's not only Light," Kira said. "It's knowing the difference between right and wrong. It's gathering all the facts, all sides of the story, before committing to a course of action. You taught me that. So whatever my nature would have been, you nurtured me and guided me. And trained me and at times made my life hell—but there's no doubt in my mind that nurture won out over nature."

Balm's eyes shone and a smile curved her lips. "Thank you for that."

"No. Thank *you*." Kira sat back. "Without your training, I certainly don't think I would have been able to survive as long as I have."

"You're welcome, daughter. Though I think, if you wish to learn more about Balance magic, you need to talk to Solis."

Kira perked up. "Solis?"

A rueful expression crossed Balm's features. "I have no doubt that Solis has meddled as much as Myshael meddled," she said. "In fact, I would daresay that your Mr. Comstock acted at Solis's behest as much as if not more than he did at mine."

Balm's supposition made sense. Comstock had told her that he'd used the assistance of a Balance witch to acquire the Shadowblade. He hadn't thought that embracing her Shadow half would be that big of a deal.

Balm seemed to read her thoughts, and understand.

The Lady of Light reached over, clasped Kira's hand. "Don't be angry at Comstock. Or Solis, for that matter."

"Why not? I'm really good at angry."

"An expert, even." Balm's smile was soft with remembrance. "However, from the moment of your birth you were headed to a moment like this. A moment when you would be forced to make a choice, to decide which half of your nature would dominate. With Solis's well-executed interference, you were able to embrace both halves, and in so doing, you've survived." Balm squeezed her hand. "Believe me when I say that I'd rather you be under Solis's Balanced eye than under Myshael's Chaotic regard."

"You and me both." Kira suppressed a shudder.

"Solis can be . . . difficult at times, but she is a good teacher," Balm continued. "You will wrestle with your nature, and it will be difficult for you to stay in Balance. There may even be times when your Light side and your Shadow side will turn on each other. My sister of Shadow will continue to push you toward her path. She's stubborn that way."

"Really? I wouldn't have guessed."

"I'm serious, Kira. You pushed her back once, but once is never enough with Myshael. She will come at you again. You must be ready when that happens."

"So I'm supposed to hole up behind the Veil with Solis while waiting for the Lady of Shadows to pounce?" Kira shook her head. "I can't do that."

"I don't think anyone expects you to. Least of all me." Balm rose. "Live your life. Keep helping those who need it, regardless of where they are in the Universal Balance. Enjoy your time with the Nubian."

Kira climbed to her feet. "You're giving me your blessing?"

Balm snorted. "Like you'd stop seeing him if I didn't. Khefar is good for you, and you're good for him. Enjoy your time with him."

Cold seeped into Kira's stomach. "You make it sound like I'm not going to have a lot of time with him."

"I don't know how long you and the Nubian have together, daughter. I didn't know how much time I'd have with Ana. I didn't know when I sent her out that she would come back to me to die."

She hugged Kira, pressing a kiss to her forehead. When she stepped back, serenity filled her expression once more. "What I am saying is live each moment fully. Live to the best of your ability. And jealously guard what you hold most dear. Myshael is an expert at striking at her opponent's weaknesses."

"I don't have to worry about Khefar. He's immortal. No matter what happens, he always comes back."

"Of course he does." Balm kissed her cheek. "Give Khefar my regards. And do reach out to Solis as soon as you can. At this point in your life, she will be a much better teacher than I."

Kira looked at the woman who had left an indelible mark on her life. An eternal woman who she'd thought had hated her all those years ago. "Is this good-bye forever?"

"Forever is a long time, Kira," Balm said. "I'm sure our paths will cross again." She smoothed her skirts. "You should be getting back. He's waiting for you."

"Good-bye, Balm."

"Good-bye, Kira. May the Light always shine on you."

Kira opened her eyes to find herself back in her bedroom, alone. Her heart skipped in her chest. Balm's words had an undercurrent to them, a warning she'd be foolish to ignore.

"Hey, Kira, are you coming down?" Khefar called. "A cold omelet is a bad omelet."

"I'm coming." She scrubbed at her eyes, then quickly headed for the stairs. Khefar was hers and she was his. Let them try taking him away from her. Hell or high water, Light or Shadow, she would make them pay.

CPSIA information can be obtained
at www.ICGtesting.com
Printed in the USA
LVOW11s0010260717
542602LV00001BA/24/P